ALSO BY SUE-ELLEN WELFONDER

Devil in A Kilt
Knight in My Bed
Bride of the Beast
Master of the Highlands

Wedding for a Knight

SUE-ELLEN WELFONDER

WARNER FOREVER

NEW YORK   BOSTON

Cover design by Diane Luger
Cover art by John Ennis
Hand lettering by David Gatti
Book design by Giorgetta Bell McRee

Warner Books

Time Warner Book Group
1271 Avenue of the Americas
New York, NY 10020
Visit our Web site at www.twbookmark.com

Printed in the United States of America

First Paperback Printing: September 2004

10 9 8 7 6 5 4 3 2 1

In loving memory of my father, Earl MacDuffie, my first and forever hero. Tall, red-haired, and dashingly handsome, his life-long good looks reflected his Scottish ancestry, but it was his big heart and generous spirit that set him apart and made him so beloved by all who knew him. Soft-spoken, unassuming and dear, his friends called him a gentle giant, praising him as a man who had a good word and a smile for everyone, including God's littlest creatures. Yes, he loved dogs. And if I should live a thousand lifetimes, I will never stop missing him.

Acknowledgments

❧

$\mathscr{S}$cotland is the wellspring of my inspiration and I write Scottish-set books because Scotland takes my breath away. The land, the people, and the history make my heart pound, fuel my imagination, and are the substance of my every dream. The wild beauty of Strathnaver in Scotland's far north is legend. A vast expanse of moorland, lochs, and mountains, to walk there is to lose your heart. To feel at one with the past and appreciate how such a magical place can influence those who live there.

One such soul was Rob Donn, a great Gaelic bard of the 1700s whose golden voice (and love of dogs) is well-remembered to this day in his beloved Strathnaver and elsewhere in the Highlands. It was while exploring places he held dear that I met the dog who became 'Boiny' in this book. My four-legged companion for an afternoon reminded me of a dog named Boiny in one of Rob Donn's verses—a lovely passage about an endearing old mongrel who attaches himself to the bard and won't leave his side. Both the bard and Boiny have a special place in my affections and I will never visit Strathnaver without feeling them beside me.

A wink and a nod, too, to the German translator of my books, Ulrike Moreno, friend and fellow animal lover, and her own 'Boiny,' her beloved rescue dog, Mustafa, who lives on in her heart and memory.

Special appreciation, too, to my editor, Karen Kosztolnyik, for her sensitivity, insight, and guidance, and because she understands not only my passion for Scotland and my great love of dogs but also my absolute belief in soul mates.

And as ever, deepest thanks to my handsome husband, Manfred, my real-life knight, for continuing to keep my dragons at bay and all would-be besiegers far from my garret door. And, of course, the whole of my heart to wee Em, my own four-legged champion whose furry-warm snuggles have the power to make all my cares fade away.

Prologue

❖

DUPPLIN MOOR
AUGUST 1332

AT SUNRISE ON A HOT SUMMER'S DAY, on the banks of the River Earn near Perth, Scotland's new Guardian, Donald, Earl of Mar, and a large army of the realm's finest men engaged in a fierce and bloody battle that would last but a few short hours.

By noon, the whistling cloth-yards of the English enemy had decimated the proud Scottish *schiltrons*. . . . the bristling spear rings proving no match for the expert aim of English archers and their constant rain of deadly arrows.

The Guardian, two Scottish earls, a handful of nobles, sixty knights, and several thousand brave spearmen lay dead upon the field. The English aggressors and the Scottish turn-coats fighting with them, and known as the Disinheriteds, lost but thirty men.

Those few Scots who were wounded, or simply pinned beneath the towering pile of their fallen countrymen, wished they, too, had died.

Of a certainty, they did not consider themselves fortunate.

And along with the endless rivers of blood soaking the ground that ill-fated day, each and every Scotsman to walk away from Dupplin Moor left his heart behind as well.

Magnus MacKinnon was amongst the survivors.

But he left more behind than most.

For along with his heart, he lost the fortune he'd worked three long years to amass. Monies he'd won in tourneys and hoped to use to restore his clan's destroyed fleet of galleys.

And mayhap a bit of his family's pride.

But even losing such riches wasn't the worst to befall him.

Nay, the most bitter blow of all was the crushing of his soul.

Chapter One

✦

BALDOON CASTLE
THE ISLE OF DOON, ONE MONTH LATER

"A PROXY WEDDING?"

Amicia MacLean shot from her seat at the dais table, her fine good humor of moments before, forgotten. The pleasure she'd taken at having both her brothers beneath the same roof again for the first time in well over a year, soundly replaced by wave after wave of stunned disbelief.

"To Magnus MacKinnon?" Her heart so firmly lodged in her throat she could scarce push words past it, she stared at her brother, Donall the Bold, proud laird of Clan MacLean and bearer of the most startling news she'd heard in longer than she could remember.

Wondrous news.

And joyous beyond belief . . . not that she was about to voice any such admission.

Too great were the disappointments of past assurances of a suitable match, too numerous the empty promises and hopes of e'er having a family—a home—of her own.

A husband to love her.

"You needn't speak his name as if he's unworthy, lass." Clearly mistaking the reason for her wide-eyed astonishment, Donall MacLean raised his hand for quiet when others in the smoke-hazed great hall sought to voice their opinions. "The MacKinnons may be in sore need of your dowry, but Magnus is a valiant and influential knight. You could do worse."

She could do no better, Amicia's heart sang, long-cherished images of the bonny Magnus racing past her mind's eye, each fleeting memory dazzling her with its sweetness.

Just recalling his dimpled smile and twinkling eyes weakened her knees.

And he'd been but a strapping young lad when she'd last seen him, years before at a game of champions held on the neighboring Isle of Islay. He'd won every archery competition, each trial of strength, and turned the heads of all the lasses with his easy charm and fine, quick wit.

Magnus *the man* would no doubt steal her breath.

Of that, she was certain.

"'Tis said he is of arresting looks, ardent, and a warrior of great renown," Donall's wife, the lady Isolde, chimed in from the head of the high table, her words only confirming what Amicia already suspected.

Her pulse thundering ever louder in her ears, Amicia scanned the faces of her kinfolk, stood silent for a few agonizingly long moments, using each precious one to steel her backbone and make certain naught but cool aloofness touched her brow.

Could it be true?

Dear saints, dared she hope?

If this offer, too, proved fruitless, she would die.

Wither away inside and plead the saints to have done with her and make her demise swift and painless.

She narrowed her eyes at Donall, moistened annoyingly dry lips. "Be this a true offer?" she asked, hugging herself against an answer she'd rather not hear. "Has Magnus MacKinnon declared himself, or is this another of your well-meant but doomed-to-failure attempts to see me wed?"

Her other brother, Iain, set down his ale cup and swiped the back of his hand over his mouth. "Sakes, lass, think you Donall or I can do aught about the troubles plaguing our land in recent years? You ken why it's been difficult to court viable suitors for you."

Amicia squared her shoulders. "I am well aware of the myriad reasons we've been given for each broken offer," she said, her gaze fixed on the inky shadows of a deep window embrasure across the hall. "What I wish to hear is whether Magnus MacKinnon himself seeks this union?"

The words *proxy wedding* and *sore need of her dowry* jellied her knees.

The glaring silence spreading across the dais end of the cavernous great hall answered her question. Her belly clenching, she glanced up at the high, vaulted ceiling, blew out a nervous breath.

Faith, the quiet loomed so deafening she could hear every hiss and crackle of the pitch-pine torches lighting the hall, the low-rumbling snores of Donall's hounds sleeping near the hearth fire, and even the wash of the night sea against the rocks far below Baldoon's massive curtain walls.

Almost imperceptibly, she shook her head and looked

back at her brothers, not surprised to detect faint flickers of guilt flitting across both their handsome faces.

"I mislike being cozened," she said with all the serene dignity she could muster. Taking her seat, she helped herself to a blessedly welcome sip of finest Gascon wine. "Nor will I allow it. Not so long as I have a single breath in my body."

"God's mercy, lass, it ill becomes you to play so stubborn." Donall eyed her from his laird's chair, a great oaken monstrosity, its back and arms carved with mythical sea beasts. He raked a hand through his raven hair, the same blue-black shade as Amicia's own.

"Nay, Magnus knows naught of the union," he admitted, holding her gaze. "But he will hear of it upon his arrival on MacKinnons' Isle. He's been gone some years, competing in tourneys, as you likely ken, but he is expected home within a fortnight and his father is certain he will welcome the match."

Amicia stifled a most unladylike snort.

She *did* rake her brothers and everyone else at the table with a challenging stare. "Old Laird MacKinnon will be desirous of the filled coffers you'll send along as my dowry. All ken he burns to rebuild the galley fleet they lost to a storm a year or so ago."

"That is as may be, but he also loves his son and would see him well-matched and at peace," Donall countered. "And I would be glad of the marriage, too. Our late father and old MacKinnon were once good friends. Wedding you to Magnus would seal our truce with the MacKinnons once and for all time."

Amicia's heart skipped a beat, and a tiny spark of excitement ignited within her breast. She glanced aside, half-afraid all the desperate hope in her entire world must be standing in her eyes. None of the previous betrothal offers had sounded near as solid, as well deliberated, as this one.

None save the relentless endeavors of a chinless apparition of a lordling whose name she'd long forgotten.

Ne'er would she forget Magnus MacKinnon's name.

Truth to tell, it'd been engraved on her heart since girlhood, and sailed through the cold and empty dark of countless lonely nights now that she was a woman.

Pushing aside every warning bit of her good sense, she scrounged deep for the courage she needed to *believe*. To trust that, like her brothers, she, too, could find happiness.

A purpose in life beyond slinking about her childhood home, useless and pitied.

Welcome, aye, but not truly belonging.

A wildly exhilarating giddiness began spinning inside her, a dangerously seductive sense of *rightness*. Lifting her chin before she lost her nerve, she sought Donall's eye. "The old laird believes Magnus will want me?"

She had to know.

"On that I give you my oath," Donall said without a moment's hesitation.

Amicia's heart caught upon the words, her suspicions and wariness falling away as if banished by a gust of the sweetest summer wind.

"Old MacKinnon even sent you his own late wife's sapphire ring to seal the pact," Iain spoke up. He dug in the leather purse hanging from his waist belt, then plunked a heavy gold ring on the table. "Sore-battered by ill fortune as the MacKinnons have been in recent times, you'll ken he wouldn't have parted with such a fine bauble unless he truly wished to see you wed his son."

"'Tis been long in coming, but you needn't suffer doubts this time." Iain's wife, Madeline, gave her a warm smile.

Amicia nodded her thanks, her throat suddenly uncommonly thick. *Hot*, too. As were her eyes. Blinking furiously, for she loathed tears and e'er sought to avoid shedding them, she snatched the ring off the table and curled her fingers around its comforting solidness.

Wee and cold against her palm, it meant the whole of the world to her.

"So-o-o, what say you now?" Donall leaned back in his chair, folded his arms.

Tightening her hold on the little piece of shining hope already warming in her hand, Amicia gave voice to the last of her doubt. "Tell me first why there must be a proxy wedding if Magnus is expected to arrive on MacKinnons' Isle within the next fourteen days?"

"Only because he is returning from Dupplin Moor," Iain answered for his brother. "'Tis the old laird's hope that having a bonnie new bride to greet him will sweeten his homecoming."

"Come you, Amicia," Donall urged, leaning forward to replenish her wine cup. "I swear to you for here and hereafter, I would not give you to MacKinnon did I not believe he will be good to you."

Amicia drew a deep breath, straightened her back. She didn't doubt Magnus MacKinnon would treat her well.

She wanted him to *want* her.

To love her with the same fierce intensity her brothers loved their wives.

Reaching for her wine, she tilted back her head and downed it in one great, throat-burning gulp. She looked around the table, half-expecting to see disapproving glances aimed her way, but saw only well-loved and expectant faces.

"Well, lass?" Donall reached across the table and nudged her arm. "Will you wed MacKinnon?"

Amicia looked down at the sapphire ring in her palm. It had the same deep blue color as Magnus MacKinnon's laughing eyes. Dashing a fool trace of moisture from her own, she leveled her most earnest gaze on her brother and prayed to all the saints that her voice wouldn't crack.

"Aye, I will, and gladly," she said, her heart falling wider open with each spoken word.

And if by chance he didn't want her, she would simply do everything in her power to make him.

Many days later, on the mist-cloaked Hebridean isle known as the MacKinnons' own since time beyond mind, Magnus MacKinnon paced the rush-strewn floor of Coldstone Castle's once-grand laird's solar, sheerest disbelief coursing through him.

Crackling tension, tight as a hundred drawn bowstrings, filled the sparsely furnished chamber and even seemed to echo off its pathetically bare walls.

An even worse tension brewed inside Magnus.

His brows snapping together in a fierce scowl, he slid another dark look at his hand-wringing father. "I will not have her, do you hear me?" He seethed, pausing long enough in his pacing to yank shut a crooked-hanging window shutter. "Saints, but I'd forgotten how draughty this pile of stones can be!"

"But, Magnus, she is a fine lass," his father beseeched him. "Mayhap the fairest in all the Isles."

Magnus swung back around, and immediately wished he hadn't because the old man had shuffled nearer to a hanging cresset lamp, and its softly flickering light picked out every line and hollow in his father's worry-fraught face.

Magnus's frown deepened.

"It matters not a whit to me how bonnie she is," he snapped, and meant it.

The saints knew he'd had scarce time for wenching in recent years. And now, since the horrors of Dupplin Moor, he had even less time and inclination for such frivols.

In especial, *wifely* frivols.

Setting his jaw and feeling for all the world as if someone had affixed an iron-cast yoke about his neck, he strode across the room and reached for the latch of another window shutter. This one kept banging against the wall and the noise was grating sorely on his nerves.

Truth be told, he was tempted to stand there like a dull-witted fool and fasten and unfasten the shutters the whole wretched night through.

Anything to busy himself.

And help him ignore the sickening sensation that he'd been somehow turned inside out.

That the sun might not rise on the morrow.

His father appeared at his elbow, his watery eyes pleading. "The MacLeans—"

"—Are well-pursed and rightly so," Magnus finished for him, turning his back on the tall, arch-topped window and its sad excuse for shuttering. "*They* ken how to hold on to their fortunes."

" 'Fore God, son, set aside your pride for once and use your head. Her dowry is needed, aye, I willna deny it. Welcome, too, but that isn't the only consideration." Clucking his tongue in clear dismay, his father set to lighting a brace of tallow candles, his age-spotted hands trembling.

Magnus glanced aside, ran an agitated hand through his hair. He would not be swayed by pity. And ne'er would he take a wife to fatten coffers he'd failed to fill.

Not Amicia MacLean.

Not any lass his stoop-shouldered da cared to parade before him.

And if they all came naked and bouncing their bonnie breasts beneath his nose!

The back of his neck hotter than if someone held a blazing torch against his nape, he strode across the room and snatched the dripping candle from his father's unsteady fingers.

"Mayhap your father's idea isn't such a bad one," Colin Grant broke in from where he rested on a bench near the hearth, his wounded leg stretched toward the restorative warmth of the low-burning peat fire. "I wouldn't have minded going home to have my da tell me he'd procured a fine and comely lass to be my bride."

At once, sharp-edged guilt sliced through Magnus, cutting clear to the bone. Colin, a friend he'd made on the tourney circuit and who'd fought beside him on the blood-drenched banks of the River Earn, didn't have a home or family to return to.

The Disinheriteds and their Sassunach supporters had burned the Grants' stronghold to the ground . . . and Colin's kinfolk with it.

Naught remained but a pile of soot and ash.

That, and Colin's unflagging determination to rebuild it as soon as he'd recovered his strength. But even if he could, which Magnus doubted for Colin's coffers were as empty as his own, Colin's loved ones were forever lost.

They couldn't be replaced by all the coin in the land.

"'Tis well glad I am to be home, Da, make no mistake," Magnus said, deftly touching the candle's flame to the remaining unlit wicks . . . without spilling melting tallow all o'er the table and onto the floor rushes. "But I see you've gone a mite addlepated in my absence. I do not *want* a wife."

"I pray you to reconsider," his father said, his tone almost imploring. He tried to clutch Magnus's sleeve, but Magnus jerked back his arm.

"There is naught to think over," he declared, laying a definitive note of finality onto each word. "I'll have none of it."

Resuming his pacing, Magnus tried not to see Colin's sad gaze following his every angry step.

Nay, Colin's *reproachful* gaze.

He also strove not to notice the chamber's sparseness, tried not to remember how splendidly outfitted it'd been in his youth . . . or think about how much of its former glory he could have restored had the fortune he'd amassed over the last three years not been stolen from its hiding place whilst he'd fought a vain battle against the English on Dupplin Moor.

He slid a look at his father as he marched past Colin, and hated to see the old man's misery. But it couldn't be helped. With time and hard work, he'd set things aright again.

He'd also rebuild his da's proud fleet of galleys . . . even if he had to work his fingers to the bone and scrape the very sides and bottom of his strongbox to make it happen.

"You need heirs. I . . . I am not well, son."

His father's voice brought him to an abrupt stop.

Magnus swore beneath his breath, squeezed shut his eyes. "I will take a wife and sire bairns *after* I've regained our fortunes," he said, thick-voiced. "You have my oath on it."

"Well you say it, but I . . . I fear—"

"You fear what?" Magnus's eyes flew wide. He wheeled toward the old man, found him hovering on the solar's threshold, his rheumy gaze darting between Magnus and the gloom-chased corridor yawning beyond the solar's half-open door.

Gloomy and shadow-ridden because the once-great Clan MacKinnon could no longer afford to keep their stronghold's many passageways adequately illuminated.

A sorry state made all the more glaring by the light, hesitant footfalls nearing from the distance.

His father blanched at the sound and crossed himself. "Oooh, sweet Mother Mary preserve me," the old man wheezed and pressed a quavering hand against his chest.

Magnus shot a glance at Colin, but his friend only shrugged his wide-set shoulders. Whipping back to face his father, he was alarmed to note that his da's face had gone an even starker shade of white.

"What is it?" Magnus demanded, the icy wash of ill ease sluicing down his back, making his words come out much more harsh than he'd meant. "Are you taken sick?"

Purest dread, nay, *panic,* flashed across the old man's stricken face. "Aye, 'tis sick I am," he said, raising his voice as if to overspeak the fast approaching footsteps. "But not near so much as I'm about to be."

Magnus cocked a brow. Something was sorely amiss and he had a sinking feeling it had to do with his father's determination to marry him to the MacLean heiress.

Almost certain of it, Magnus folded his arms and fixed

the older man with a stern stare. "Does your *illness* have aught to do with my refusal to wed the MacLean lass?"

A sharp intake of breath from just beyond the doorway answered him.

A *feminine* gasp.

And an utterly shocked one.

But not as shocked as Magnus himself when the most stunning creature he'd e'er seen stepped out of the vaulted corridor's gloom.

'*Twas her.*

Amicia MacLean.

He hadn't seen her in years, but no one else could be so breathtakingly lovely.

Even as a young lass, the promise of her budding beauty had undone him. Saints, her presence at an archery contest had once distracted him so thoroughly, his arrow had missed its target by several paces.

Her presence now, here in his father's threadbare solar at Coldstone, undid him, too, but for wholly different reasons . . . even if some boldly defiant part of him fair reeled with the impact of her exquisiteness.

"Christ God and all his saints," his father found his voice, and promptly crossed himself again. "I meant to tell you, son, I swear I did."

"Tell me what?" Magnus demanded, though deep inside he already knew.

The pallor and shock on Amicia MacLean's bonnie face told the tale . . . as did his mother's sapphire ring winking at him from the third finger on her left hand.

The lass herself squared her shoulders and lifted her chin.

She met his stare unblinking and her courage in a moment he knew must be excruciating for her did more to soften Magnus's heart toward her than if she'd thrown open her cloak and revealed all her dark and sultry charms.

Stepping forward, she reached for his father's hand, lacing their fingers. "I suspect your father has not told you that you already have wed me, Magnus MacKinnon. We were married by proxy a sennight ago," she said, just as he'd known she would.

Magnus's jaw dropped all the same.

His *heart* plummeted clear to his toes.

Her heart stood in her eyes and seeing it there unsettled him more than any deadly arcing blade he'd e'er challenged.

The image of serenity and grace, she'd wield her weapons with even greater skill. That he knew without a shred of doubt.

And worst of all, his damnable honor wouldn't let him raise his own against her.

Chapter Two

❖

"*WIFE.*" Magnus MacKinnon spoke the word as if its mere utterance might bring jeopardy to his soul. Looking anything but a man renowned for his charm and wit, he rammed a hand through his hair and muttered a curse. "Saints cherish us—married by proxy."

Disbelief almost visibly coursing through him, he did not so much as glance at Amicia. Instead, he looked up at the water-stained ceiling for a long, uncomfortable moment before leveling the whole of his astonishment at his father.

To Donald MacKinnon's credit, he met his son's stare unflinching. "Aye, by proxy—to . . . to lend ease to your homecoming," he faltered, the waver beneath his words spearing Amicia's heart. "'Tis as binding and valid as any other marriage unless—"

"Unless it is not consummated. And let it hereby be known that I have no mind to—" Magnus broke off, his color rising. He blew out a quick breath. "God's bones, did you think these tidings would gladden my heart? A wife? Now, when I have nary a *siller* to my name and naught to credit me save a badly notched sword and a well-dented shield?"

Listening to him, Amicia struggled to ignore the rush of shivers spilling down her spine, but the bitterness in his tone, so different from the husky-sweet voice of his youth, sent edges of empty cold spreading through her as one by one his objections extinguished the light and warmth of her carefully nurtured hopes and dreams.

I have no mind to. . . .

The words hung like ice chips between them, chilling her every indrawn breath. Mortification spinning turmoil in her breast, she rubbed her thumb over the heavy sapphire ring on her left hand. His mother's wedding band, and now hers.

Her ring, and her comfort.

Her strength through all the long nights she'd lain awake, awaiting his return.

His return, and his pleasure.

Not repudiation.

Yet it was repudiation that poured off him in waves. And each damning surge made her heart clutch, threatened to undo her best efforts at remaining calm.

Faith, but the backs of her eyes burned—so badly that her face hurt with the effort to suppress the stinging. Surely he would not deny their union? Refuse to make her his? Her blood froze at the very thought, even as a hot-pulsing heat began throbbing at her nape.

She blinked.

Hard, for MacLean women did not cry.

From time immemorial, they braved the sorriest plights, faced their most formidable foes, and weathered darkest nights of wind and rain, dauntless and unwavering.

And she, Amicia MacLean, would be no different.

So she swallowed the thickness in her throat, held fast to the old laird's hand, and was careful to keep her chin proudly raised. Thus steeled, she centered her most unflinching gaze on the hard-set face so irreconcilable with the bonny, smiling-eyed countenance she'd carried in her heart for so many endless, stretching years.

Since the day in the summer of her thirteenth year when she'd strayed from the tourney ground at a gathering of the Hebridean clans, only to lose her footing on a slick patch of peat moss and turn her ankle. Not wanting to heed her pain, or admit she'd lost her way, she'd hobbled about fighting tears until *he'd* loomed up before her and gallantly tucked a sprig of bell heather behind her ear to make her smile.

His own smile dimpled and bright, he'd bent to place an arm behind her knees, then swept her high against his chest and carried her across the rough moorland to her family's tent. But upon arriving there, he'd been recognized as a MacKinnon, her clan's then-time foe, and Iain, her quick-tempered brother, had promptly called him an up-jumped lout who did not know his place in the world.

A slur that earned her brother a split lip and bloodied nose; Magnus, a swollen eye; and Amicia, the distress of losing her youthful heart to a bonny bronze-maned lad her clan would ne'er deem worthy.

Hoping he would not see her distress now, either, she stared at him, determined to ignore the skitter of nerves fluttering in her stomach and praying she only imagined the slick clamminess damping her palms.

Taller, wider of shoulder, and more powerfully built

than in younger years, Magnus MacKinnon could no longer be described as merely bonny. Nay, he'd grown full magnificent.

Achingly so, as every shred of her yearning acknowledged.

Almost as if he knew her mind, he looked at her then, his clear blue gaze locking deep on hers, and she melted, the whole of her running liquid despite the awkwardness beating all around them, the disappointment squeezing her heart.

She waited, fixing her attention on him rather than her own mounting ill ease. At some point during his time away from MacKinnons' Isle, he'd abandoned the wild, wind-tossed mane of his youth and now wore his hair clipped. The glossy locks did not quite skim his shoulders, but the color was the same rich chestnut she'd e'er admired. Indeed, each strand gleamed with remembered luster and still made her fingertips tingle with the urge to touch and relish.

But nary a spark of good-humored light danced in his eyes, and the dimples that had so captured her girlish heart had deepened into twin creases that now bracketed the tight, forbidding line of his unsmiling mouth.

Moistening her own, Amicia gave him her bravest smile. "I rejoice to see you, Sir Magnus. Praise God you are returned well and whole," she said, dipping in a polite half-curtsy.

The best she could manage, clinging as she was to his father's hand and with her knees so jellied, she wondered her legs didn't buckle and land her sprawled on the rushes at his booted feet.

Under different circumstances, she would have appreciated the irony of such ungainliness. Her awkwardness would be an oddly fitting reminder of the long-ago day they'd first met—if he even remembered.

But to her dismay, her hard-met attempt to crack his stony expression only brought a further darkening of his handsome features.

"*Whole,* you say? And *well?*" He eyed her, his hands fisted at his sides. The entire imposing length of him, rigid. "My lady, do you not ken there are wounds that even the most discerning eyes cannot see?"

"I see much, my lord."

He quirked a russet brow. "Truth tell?"

Amicia inhaled to speak, intent on asserting that not only did she speak true, she also knew much of such wounds. The saints knew she bore a few herself—ones he'd inflicted on her, however unwittingly. But before she could form any such rebuttal, he stepped back, edging ever away from her until the sleeping bulk of Boiny, the old laird's equally ancient mongrel, stayed his retreat.

Caught off guard, he near tripped headlong over the calf-sized beast.

"Saints of mercy!" he called out, arms flailing. "Forby, but here is something I should have expected." He cast a dark scowl at Boiny, readjusted the plaid slung so casually across his mailed shoulder. "That wretched beast e'er reveled in bedeviling me."

But some of his ire slipped away even as he said the words and he reached down to scratch the dog's scruffy gray-tufted head. Boiny, not to be disturbed, peered up at him with one milky but adoring eye and thumped his scraggly tail against the floor.

Looking more than a little defeated, Magnus straightened, but kept a keen eye on the dog until the tail thumping ceased and soft canine snores once more filled the looming silence. Then he dragged a hand down his face and released an audible sigh.

A ragged, weary-sounding one.

"May the Fiend take me, lass, but I swear my ill humor has scarce little to do with you. To be sure, it doesn't." He came forward to brush his fingertips down the curve of her cheek, a decidedly regretful expression in his eyes. "Pray put any such thought from you and forgive me if it appears otherwise."

Amicia flicked a speck of lint from her sleeve. "Mayhap the apology of others, and to you, would be more fitting."

The words out, she glanced aside. His light stroking of her cheek sent tremors of an entirely different sort tingling all through her. A vulnerability she'd rather he did not see—for the moment.

Seeking to shake off his spell, she willed her heartbeat to slow, then bit back a sigh of regret when he took away his hand.

"It will be my endeavor that no further cause for grievousness shall arise from this"—he dropped a quick glance at her ring—"situation."

Amicia gave what she hoped would appear a carefree shrug. "I but wished to bid you welcome. You will know your own mind as to how warm a one you desire."

He pinned her with his hot blue gaze, a strange light in his eyes seeming to shine clear into her soul. "What I desire, what I have e'er desired. . . ."

Amicia narrowed her own eyes at once for something in his words made her heart jump. Faith, even the silence, after he'd let his voice tail off, thrummed with unspoken meaning.

She arched a brow, hoping to encourage him to finish

the sentence, but at his stubborn silence, she bit her own tongue as well.

It would scarce do to tell him he suffered a far greater need of healing than forgiveness.

That much was plain to see.

The truth of it stood writ in every line marring his handsome face.

Another truth, namely his impotent resentment at discovering himself burdened by a wife he hadn't sought, sent wave after wave of apprehension washing over her. A raw, gnawing dread snaked round her rib cage, winding ever tighter until she could hardly breathe.

Afraid her voice might break if she spoke again before her throat ceased trying to close on her, she focused her gaze on the nearest window embrasure. The one with the crooked hanging shutters that her proxy-wed husband, descendant of an illustrious line of great fighting men and widely renowned in his own right, had tried in vain to secure.

Cool, moist air poured through the unprotected opening and thin curtains of damp, eddying mist could be seen gathering beyond its narrow arch. She took solace in the sight, for concealing as the drifting fog might be, it could not undo the beauty of MacKinnons' Isle.

The mist only veiled what lay beyond the window.

It could not steal away miles of sand-duned shores, rugged promontories, and fine, deep-watered bays. Couldn't mar the awe she'd felt upon first glimpsing the burnished gold beaches rimming the isle or ruin her appreciation for the ridge of high, cloud-wreathed hills rising from its interior.

Just as Magnus MacKinnon's frowns and fulminations

did not diminish the worthiness of the man hiding beneath them.

The man she wanted.

Had always wanted . . . despite years of silly clan feuding over supposed slights and nefarious doings the origin of which no living person could recall—save that it had something to do with a stolen bride.

But their clans had been friendly in recent years, and she was anything but stolen. Nor was she unwilling, and she knew they could find joy and bliss together—if only he would give her a chance.

So she squared her shoulders and turned back to him, as determined a warrior as any to e'er set foot on a true field of battle.

"My sorrow that you could not have been told sooner," she loosed her first assault, the cold trembling of Donald MacKinnon's aged fingers helping her maintain an air of dignity and grace.

She let her gaze light over her husband's rumpled traveling clothes. Dried mud crusted the leather of his worn-looking boots and her pulse quickened, her heart catching, at the darkish smears on his ragged-edged plaid.

Ominous stains that looked suspiciously like blood.

A rash of chills slid down her back and her stomach wrenched at the grim reminder of the horrors, the grinding defeat he'd seen at Dupplin Moor.

"You have only just arrived and are full weary," she said, pouring compassion into her words. "I vow it no great wonder you'd chaffer upon learning—"

"I've learned naught but what canna be undone," Magnus jerked, not letting her finish.

The words rang hollow, as if he'd pulled each one

from the dredges of his soul. "A marriage needs a bed-going to be sanctified. A dowry can be returned unspent. A bride, unsullied."

"Of a certainty, my lord, and well I know it," Amicia granted, refusing to acknowledge the tight knot pulsing ever hotter at the back of her neck. "But—"

"For truth! What's keeping Dagda?" This time, the elder MacKinnon cut her off. Yanking his hand from hers, the old laird cast a desperate glance at the opened door.

But Dagda, Coldstone's redoubtable female seneschal, aptly named after the formidable and quite masculine chief of the mythical race of Irish gods, the *Tuatha dé Danann,* was nowhere to be seen.

Naught lurked in the gloomy corridor save a musty-scented chill and the wispy smoke haze of a guttering wall torch. And rather than Dagda's approaching foot-falls, the only sound to be heard above the patter of rain was the breaking of waves on the not-too-distant shore.

"Devil take that she-goat's cheeky hide if she doesn't hie herself in here with refreshments, and before long!" Donald MacKinnon scolded, swaying a bit on his feet.

At once, Magnus thrust out a quick hand to steady him. "Unless her knees have grown less creaky in my ab-sence, she'll be needing time to make her way up from the kitchens."

"Faugh!" The old laird shook off his son's hand and aimed another pointed stare at the dark-yawning pas-sageway. "She gets about well enough when she wishes to poke her nose where it don't belong."

Magnus drew a deep breath. "That may be so, but you needn't have troubled her with fetching aught for me. I've no stomach for drinking healths this night." He paused to glance over his shoulder. "Though I'll wager Colin would welcome a wee posset to aid his sleep."

"A posset?" A richly masculine voice rose from the shadows near the hearth. "What man worthy of the title would long for a posset when such fairness stands before him?"

Her attention arrested, Amicia turned toward the voice, watched as a swarthy-looking man of about the same number of years as Magnus carefully heaved himself off a low, oaken bench.

Nigh as fine on the eyes as Magnus and equally mud-splattered, he came forward with slow, purposeful strides. But a thin line of white around his lips and a not-quite concealed wince undermined his best attempts at hiding the pain each movement cost him.

"Please, sir, you are injured. Keep your seat, I pray you," Amicia urged him, her heart twisting at the way he favored his right leg. She tried to wave him back, but he came ever onward, his hands extended in such sincere welcome her breath caught with emotion.

Would that Magnus had greeted her half so warmly.

"Guidsakes, you witless lout—where are your manners?" The swarthy man, clearly a fellow knight, clapped a hand on Magnus's shoulder as if in scoffing reproach, but his white-knuckled grip indicated he had sore need of the support.

His chivalry required no such bolster. "Pay my good friend no heed," he advised her. "The great lump is but too stubborn to admit that your beauty would banish the cares from the most troubled of brows."

Sweeping her the best bow he could, his injured leg considered, he captured her hand for a featherlight kiss.

"Colin Grant of . . . och, just Colin Grant, fair lady, and I am yours to command."

A blush blossomed on Amicia's cheeks. "I thank you, noble sir, and I shall honor your friendship." She slid a sidelong glance at Magnus, noted the tight press of his lips, the muscle jerking ever so imperceptibly at his jaw.

Could he be jealous?

Her pulse leaping at the possibility, she smiled at the goodly man who'd so valiantly offered to champion her. "Aye, but it is as a leal friend I would see you, Colin Grant, ne'er a servant, for your gallantry lifts you high in my esteem."

"As you wish, my lady." Colin inclined his dark head. Magnus frowned all the blacker.

He cleared his throat . . . a mite too loudly. "You will have scarce time to attend her wishes or be her friend, leal or otherwise," he intoned, a thread of irritation in his voice. "The Lady Amicia shall be returned to her brothers as soon as her coffers of coin and sundry other dowry goods can be loaded onto the next passing galley our signal fires can draw to a halt."

"Young Magnus! How are you faring?" A tall and strong-backed older woman surveyed him from the doorway. "Tsk, never you mind," she added, running a shrewd gaze over him. "I can see with my own two eyes that you've a long, hard road behind you."

"I am well enough, or was—" Magnus caught himself. He would not add insulting innocent women to his growing list of faults.

Though from the way the Lady Amicia straightened her spine and drew back her shoulders, like as not she knew exactly what he'd been about to blurt.

Feeling ridiculously guilty, he opened his mouth to say

something—*anything*—to erase the hurt she tried so valiantly to hide, but Dagda spoke before he could.

"You won't be needing to set any signal fires," she announced. "'Tis onto a fine new galley of your own you can soon put your bride if you truly wish to make a blithering fool of yourself. But like it or no, her strongboxes have already been well-emptied."

The old woman sailed past him, her black skirts swishing, a tray of a cold-sliced seafowl and crisp-baked bannocks with honey clutched in her hands.

"Or did you not come by way of the landing beach?" She plunked the tray on the room's sole table—a roughhewn, wobbly-legged one of age-blackened oak.

Turning, she dusted her hands. "Dinna tell me you haven't asked where your brothers be?" She slid an accusatory glance at the old laird. "Has himself there not told you those two rascals and every man with good arms has been working day and night to rebuild your lost fleet?"

Magnus all but choked. "I know nothing of this," he spluttered when he could find breath. "Other unexpected matters kept me from enquiring of Hugh's and Dugan's health . . . or their doings."

His stomach, queasy already, tied itself into knots. "The MacDonald galley that bore my friend and me passage dropped us by the cliffs, at the sea gate. They did so at my behest—I couldn't bear to see the wreck-strewn shore of the landing beach."

Dagda snorted. "Those wracks be long gone, never you mind," she declared, smoothing her palms on the stiff black linen of her widow's skirts. "We had need of the wood for fuel and repairs round about the keep." She nodded to Amicia, her taciturn features softening for a moment. "Thanks be to your new bride, a score of fine, new galleys will soon be moored off MacKinnons' Isle."

"By the Mass! No-o-o." The denial burst from the heart of Magnus's smashed pride. "Our fleet should have been rebuilt with MacKinnon coin and none other." He shook his head, striving to control his features. "This is not to be borne. I cannot allow—"

"You are letting the pain of recent days blind you to what is wise and right." Colin clamped iron-tight fingers around his arm, squeezing hard for emphasis. "And you are doing hurt to those who should be cherished and protected from such outbursts."

That last, a barely audible whisper close by his hot-burning ear.

Jerking free of his friend's grip, Magnus swiped the back of his hand across his brow. Sakes, but his forehead was perspiring. As was all of him . . . icy cold rivulets of sweat streaked down his back in torrents.

And the truth of Colin's reprimand only increased the copious flow.

As did his father's mumblings about being *an auld done man.*

Feeling quite old and done himself, he shot a look at Amicia and knew an immediate jab of guilt upon noting the sudden pallor of her cheeks.

His da received a savage glare. "You are behind this," he rapped out, his ire laying a more bitter edge on his words than he would have wished. "I vowed when I left that I'd make things aright, and I would have. Even now. And at the soonest!"

"You do not ken the ill winds that have been sweeping o'er this isle," Donald MacKinnon insisted, his voice catching. "Troubles where'er we . . ." He trailed off, hunching over as great, rasping coughs seized him.

When they subsided, he straightened, a shaking hand pressed to his chest. "Donall MacLean has proved himself a strong friend," he got out, speaking with effort. "He sent us enough good Scots *siller* to commence work even before the Lady Amicia set foot on MacKinnons' Isle."

"This has naught to do with MacLean's generosity. There is none in all the Isles who'd deny he is a good and honorable man, a fine laird. I mean no ill to him." Magnus paused, blew out an agitated breath. "I would only that you'd waited until my return."

Donald MacKinnon plucked at his lower lip, a flush staining his cheeks. "Nay, nay, nay, laddie," he said at last. "We couldna done. Not with your lady's dowry coming to us, a gift from the heavens."

He stared at Magnus, his expression an odd mix of defiance and . . . dread. "We could not wait another day, see you. The cur—"

"God's eyes!" Magnus's patience snapped. "The only curse e'er visited upon this isle is the inability of its keepers to hold fast to their fortunes," he declared, not troubling to lower his voice. Bile rising in his throat, he swept everyone in the room with a heated stare. "That is the truth of it—I promise you!"

"Nay, you mistake. A shadow has lain across us longer than time can remember," his father minded him, belligerence in his reedy voice. "For sure since the day the first laird, Reginald of the Victories, set the foundations of this stronghold."

"Reginald of the Victories, whom God rest, made his own fate—as do we all." Magnus flung out an arm to take in the whole of the solar's pathetically bare walls. "No powers of darkness e'er railed against him or these stones, never you fear. Naught clouds the fortunes of the once-great Clan Fingon but our own wretched ineptitude."

His own inadequacies clawing at his innards, Magnus smoothed a hand over his tight-pressed lips and began pacing the solar. But his foul humor tagged after him, its cloying grip too firm to outmaneuver.

Sakes, the chamber's very emptiness of furnishings mocked him. And the few remaining amenities only underscored what little comforts Coldstone Castle could offer. A lacking that would pain him all his days if he could not soon amend it.

Not at all sure how he meant to do so, he passed one of the wide arched window embrasures and a chill blast of damp, salt-laden air hit him full in the face, making him shiver and worsening his mood.

Scowling, he drew his plaid closer about him and glanced into the shadowy alcove, glared at the useless, rain-warped shutters. But it was the two flanking benches of the deep embrasure that drew his eye.

Stripped to the naked stone, they met his wrath face on. Twin-staring slabs of cold gray, full of silent accusation and seeming to follow his progress around the room, aimed recriminations at him that proved every bit as damning as the distress in his father's eyes.

The disappointment on Amicia MacLean's lovely face.

The pity in the sad shake of Colin's head, and the tsk-tsk'ing reprimand of old Dagda's sharp-edged tongue.

Wishing he'd held his own, he wheeled about to face his father. "Ne'er would I censure you for believing such foolery—God kens enough storms of plaguey fortune have washed o'er this isle throughout the centuries for any man to call us Devil-damned, but I'd wished to have done with it myself, see you? Without outside aid. Not Donall the Bold's. Not his undeniably fetching sister's. Not any man's. I—"

He broke off, his voice cracking in his vexation. Determined to spare himself further humiliation, he made straight for the door, intending to absent himself with all good haste, but a gentle hand lit on the mail of his sleeve.

"A word with you, sir."

To his surprise, or perhaps not, that one touch, and the caring in the Lady Amicia's deep brown eyes, proved as mighty a hold as Colin's most steely-fingered grip.

Instinctively distancing himself, he waited, but she only gave him the faintest smile. A wee, hesitant one as if she, too, bore her own vexing cares.

As if she might need him.

A notion too dangerous to ponder.

So he pushed it away, and found his voice in the doing. "Aye?"

"Can we not share a walk?" she wanted to know, the soft lilt of her Isleswoman's voice as seductive as the compassion warming her black-lashed eyes. She pressed his arm. "Mayhap up on the ramparts where we may speak privily and unguarded?"

Magnus shook his head, tried not to inhale her warm, womanly scent. "There is scarce little to be said before I have had time to consider this . . . this *state of affairs*, and what can be done about it."

Lifting her hand from his sleeve, she smoothed the backs of her fingers down his cheek. "You are sure?"

"Never more so," Magnus blurted, feeling her touch ripple in too-pleasurable waves over and through the whole of him. "Walking with you on the battlements would not allow me the peace I need to think."

And for very different reasons than she suspected!

"Very well." She dropped her hand. "But allow me one observation, please."

"So long as you are here, you may speak your full mind." He aimed a sidelong look at his father and Dagda. "I do not hold much with intrigues and secrets."

"Then know that I saw you shiver when you strode past the opened window," she began, her features carefully schooled. "Consider, too, good Magnus, that even as a chill breeze brings gray clouds, so can that very wind banish the darkness so the sun can warm all in its wake."

Magnus stared at her, wordless.

Wholly lost, he found himself overcome by an irrepressible urge to draw her to him and drink in her sweetness and warmth until he fair drowned in the good of her. But any such indulgence would only make it more difficult to send her away, so he held his silence.

His father suffered no such affliction. "Heh, heh!" He crowed with righteous glee. "See what a fine bride I found you," he declared, jabbing the air with a knotty finger. "She is not only pleasing to look at but wise . . . as you'd be if you'd heed her wish and take the air with her."

A sage nod from Dagda and the narrow-eyed urging on Colin Grant's face unhinged Magnus's tongue. "The only taking I'll be doing is to my own good bedchamber," he said, turning on his heel. "I've sore need of rest. Whate'er needs to be yet discussed can be done on the morrow."

"Your bedchamber?" Donald MacKinnon's brief burst of high humor vanished as if it'd never been. "You canna sleep there—we've readied the old quarters of Reginald of the Victories for you . . . for you and your bride. She is already settled there."

"My room will serve me well enough."

"But—"

"On the morrow, Da." His mind set, Magnus strode from the solar.

"Saint Columba—save us! Ooooh, blessed martyrs . . . !" the old man cried after him.

Ignoring his father's haverings, Magnus stalked down the gloom-chased passage, making straight for the turn-pike stair.

But try as he might to seal his ears, his da's gabblings echoed through the shadows, craftily using the wan light of the smoking wall torches to find every wee crack in Magnus's armor.

And to his worst horror, the most disturbing objection of all found his ear just as he reached the upward-winding stairwell.

"Your old room is no more, laddie. The power o' darkness snatched it away—"

Half-convinced his exhaustion and ire had conjured the absurd words, and not his babbling sire, Magnus took the stairs two at a time all the same.

At the second landing, he sprinted down an even mustier-smelling corridor, but knew a great sigh of relief when he spotted the familiar oaken door to his boyhood bedchamber at its end.

Feeling much the fool for letting the old man's ravings get to him, he yanked open the chamber door . . . and near stepped into a black-yawning abyss.

"A mercy . . . !" Clinging to the sooty doorjamb, he stared in disbelief at the gaping darkness that had once been his room. His da had been right. . . . The chamber no longer existed.

It had indeed been snatched away as if by some evil enchantment.

Or an ancient curse.

Not much later, a stealthy darkness crept over the neighboring isle of Doon, cloaking not just the coastline but sweeping land-inward until even the loneliest moorlands and peat hags lay silent and deserted in the black, bewitching night.

Doon's Islesfolk slept as well, lulled into deep slumber by the comfort of their turf fires and the quiet of the chill Highland night.

Aye, they slept . . . all save one.

Devorgilla, Doon's resident *cailleach* since longer than stones were old, tossed and turned within the thick, white-washed walls of her thatched cottage. And as ne'er before, her pallet of dried heather and bracken proved too lumpy to spend her aged bones a good night's rest.

Blowing out a frustrated breath, the crone rolled onto her side and flung a knotty-elbowed arm over her grizzled head. Truth be told, there was naught wrong with her bed. Were she honest, she doubted the finest high folk in the land slept more comfortably than she did on her bed o' heather.

Nay, it was the eerie, dark green shadow she'd spied lurking over MacKinnons' Isle earlier in the day that stole her sleep and prickled her nape.

Out gathering herbs and other vital ingredients for her potions and charms, she'd glanced across the sea and seen the strange darkness swirling round and o'er the other island like some vile and pulsing dome of sheer, living evil.

Ne'er in all her years had she looked on such malevolence.

And though she mostly used her skill for the beneficence of the good folk of Doon, she knew enough of her art to recognize dark powers.

Her teeth chattering, the *cailleach* pulled her well-worn plaid up to her ears, and only her fearsome stubbornness kept her from yanking the threadbare blanket over her head.

Nor was she about to admit that a cold much deeper than the chill autumn night had seized hold of her weary bones.

By sheer force of will, she sent a glance beyond the haven of her bed to the two deep-set windows. Soundly shuttered, they kept out the worst of the night wind just as her door, carefully shut and barred, would thwart the attempt of anyone foolhardy enough to seek uninvited entry.

Not quite satisfied, she peered through the half-dark, turning a critical eye on the cottage's central hearth fire. All knew, if e'er such a fire extinguished, the very soul would go out of the people of a house. But the clump of peat she'd tossed onto the hearthstone before retiring smoldered with pulsing warmth, and hazy-blue wisps of sweet-smelling peat smoke curled upward toward a soot-blackened hole in the roof.

All was as it should be.

Even her little brazier of hot-burning sea coal, a much-appreciated gift from Donall MacLean, still glowed with soft red light and threw off welcome, soothing heat.

Yet she froze as if gripped in the teeth of the blackest

winter gale, her very marrow iced by a chill coming not from without, but from the cloying vestiges of the unholy darkness she couldn't put from her mind.

A rank foulness she'd almost swear had slid across the night-bound waters to howl around her cottage walls.

Ashamed of her ill ease, for she refused to name it fear, Devorgilla flounced onto her back. For good measure and in utter defiance of the shivers snaking up and down her spine, she folded her arms and stared up at the low, black-raftered ceiling.

Bunches of dried herbs hung there, each precious bundle affixed with tireless, loving hands. They comforted and reminded her she still had a wee measure of the sleeping draught she'd whipped up earlier.

Potent goosegrass tisane.

Mayhap a dollop or two would make short shrift of this troublous night. In especial, if she washed down those dollops with a full-brimming cup of fine and frothy heather ale.

Devorgilla's own special brew, and the best to be had in all the Isles.

Her heart lifting already, she threw back the covers and heaved herself to her feet. Blessedly, with a minimal amount of bone creaking. A throaty meow greeted her from near the softly hissing brazier, and her spirits soared all the more.

"Heh, but you shall have a wee helping of ale, too," she promised Mab, her stalwart companion since longer than mortal bones need to turn to dust.

Or so Devorgilla imagined as she pressed a hand to her lower back. She waited for Mab's stiff-legged gait to carry her across the short distance between them, then leaned down to stroke the tricolored cat's silky-warm fur.

"You have no taste for those who stalk about in gloom and shadow, either, do you, my sweet?" she crooned in a singsong voice reserved for Mab alone.

"We want naught to do with the like o' such debased cravens," she vowed, straightening. "Come, let us chant a word or two to hie those dark shadows back to the ill bounds whence . . . aiiieeee!"

Clutching her heart, Devorgilla reeled backward, her eyes full-wide as she stared at the broad, masculine back of the mailed warrior standing before her. Nay, not quite standing, for the braw knight she recognized as Magnus MacKinnon clung fiercely to a doorjamb.

And, Mother of the Moon preserve her, but she could see right through him!

A black abyss yawned at his feet, deep as the night and vast enough to swallow the familiar surroundings of her cottage's homey interior.

Devorgilla stared, her heart thumping hard against her ribs. An all-encompassing void shot through with eerily glowing threads of vilest green whirled all around her, its evil almost crushing her.

And then the knight vanished, the whole of his vision-self gone as quickly as he'd appeared, but the darkness remained. It crept ever forward, eating up her tidily swept floor until the crone and Mab, too, teetered on the very precipice of Doon's most treacherous cliff top.

Whitecapped combers broke on jagged rocks far below her and a bitter cold wind tore in from the sea, its deafening roar more earsplitting than the crash of the waves. In the distance, MacKinnons' Isle rode low on the horizon, its dark mass almost obscured by roiling clouds of sickliest green.

"Goddess have mercy," Devorgilla breathed, snatching up Mab before the racing wind could whisk the poor creature over the cliff to certain doom.

Then the ground shifted beneath her feet and before she could blink, she found herself on lower, gentler ground . . . the MacLeans' own boat strand. A haven of calm, and as far from the storm-chased cliff she'd just stood upon as her wee cottage was from the moon.

But the eerie glow accompanied her. Great sheets of it swirled about the shingled beach, even blotting out the massive curtain walls of Baldoon, the formidable MacLean stronghold rising above the far end of the cres-cent-shaped strand. Only the castle's topmost turrets pierced the shifting mass of luminous green.

A soft, iridescent mist that now grew steadily lighter, and much less ominous.

Devorgilla continued to mumble her prayers of pro-tection nevertheless.

Through a rift in the mist, she caught a glimpse of the Lady Rock, a black-glistening tidal islet of great menace and dread. A constant bringer of strife to the Isle of Doon.

Or so tradition claimed.

The crone snorted.

She held such notions for lack-witted prattle. Non-sense and babble put about by the unenlightened.

Naught ailed the land hereabouts or elsewhere . . . and even perilous rocks thrusting up from the sea had their place and reason for being.

Nay, man alone spread ill will, and wrapping that truth about her aged bones, Devorgilla lifted her somewhat bristled chin and peered through the mist to see what the old ones wished her to know.

But Mab saw her first, the cat's deep purring signaling the presence of a friend. Squinting, Devorgilla strained her eyes until she, too, caught sight of the *gruagach*, a mostly benevolent female spirit, perched high atop the Lady Rock.

Sad-looking, the *gruagach* simply sat there, seemingly oblivious to the strange night and the heavy seas all around her. With her head slightly turned to the side, she toyed idly with the strands of seaweed tangled in her wet, unbound hair.

Leaning forward, Devorgilla peered harder, almost mistaking the winsome creature for one of the merfolk or *selkies* said to ply Hebridean waters. But the pale glimmer of green surrounding the *gruagach* revealed her for what she was . . . though some might dub her an angel.

Devorgilla knew better.

Thought to be the spirits of mortal women who had died in childbirth or fallen under some fey enchantment, *gruagachs* clung to places they'd once loved and saw their duty as guarding the well-being of those who remained.

Some even influenced crops or a cow's ability to give pure, sweet milk. Indeed, so often as her aches and her duties allowed, Devorgilla made the long trek to Doon's *Clach na Gruagach*, or Stone of the Fairy Woman, to pour an offering of finest cream onto the stone.

And to pay her respects . . . for Devorgilla suspected the *gruagach's* earthly identity.

But even now, the creature's image was fading, washed away by the spume breaking ever higher upon the Lady Rock, the buffeting of the waves. Then she was gone, and the crone knew a pang of deep regret, for this time she'd almost caught a full-on glimpse of the *gruagach's* most-times averted face.

Her gaze still on the black-gleaming rock, Devorgilla

heaved a weary sigh, filling her lungs not with chill, moist air ripe with the tang of the sea, but with close, almost stuffy air heavy with the smoky-sweet smell of peat.

Blinking, she looked at her feet, not surprised to see them no longer standing on rain-damp shingle or even her own stone-flagged floor, but tucked soundly beneath the familiar warmth of her plaid bedcovers!

And dear Mab still slept curled in the ruddy glow of the brazier.

Too old to be cozened by the vagaries of magic, and too wise not to respect its powers, Devorgilla settled back on her pallet, content to watch tendrils of thin blue smoke from her peat fire snake along the ceiling rafters.

She also breathed a word of thanks to the ancient ones for giving her the foresight to work a wee bit of her own spelling before Amicia MacLean e'er set sail for Mac-Kinnons' Isle.

Dark forces lurked there, that she knew.

Aye, 'twas good she'd taken precautions.

She only hoped they'd be enough.

Chapter Three

❧

"SO YOU *ARE* BACK!"

Magnus jerked, his fingers tightening on the soot-smeared doorjamb of his now-vanished bedchamber before he wheeled about to face the second fetching young lass he'd have to disappoint that night.

"Praises be!" His cousin Janet MacKinnon stood before him, all gleaming silver-blond hair and rosy-flushed cheeks. "I prayed God every night that He keep you safe," she breathed, one hand pressed to her breast. A teensy package, she beamed up at him, her great blue eyes alight with adoration. "Faith, I can scarce believe it is you."

"Och, 'tis me, sure enough," Magnus said, waves of shock still coursing through him. "And come home to more surprises than I have known for long."

Janet's face clouded. "Would that it were not so," she said, glancing aside before he could catch and hold her gaze.

Even so, Magnus eyed her sharply, discomfort coiling in his belly, for the sudden petulance of her tone and the fading of her smile revealed more than her words.

But the taint of cold smoke permeating the dank passage vexed him in a far worse way.

Aggrieved as seldom before, he tossed another quick glance at the charred devastation of his former bedchamber. "Blood of Christ—the entire east tower is naught but a burned shell . . . all floors, gone."

Though clearly months had passed since the fire, he could almost feel blistering heat pouring off the blackened stones, even taste the coppery stench of fresh-spilled blood on chill, acrid air. His stomach churned with the well-remembered reek of burning flesh. Horrors he'd hoped he'd left behind him on the red-stained banks of the River Earn.

Shuddering, he pushed all thought of Dupplin Moor and its appalling ruin from his mind. "The fire, were there any . . . did anyone . . . ?"

Janet shook her fair head. "There were no injuries," she said, understanding. "Nothing was astir in this part of the keep that night."

Magnus released the breath he'd been holding.

But a good deal of his tension remained.

He had yet to see his brothers.

"Hugh and Dugan kept quarters in the east tower. Just below mine," he minded his cousin, the travails of recent weeks letting his every nagging doubt roll off his tongue far too easily. "Their chambers are as gone as mine."

Janet drew a cautious-sounding breath, her attention on a deep-splayed arrow slit cut into the passage's thick walling. "It saddens me that I must be the one to tell you of these ill happenings," she said, finally looking back at him.

Something in her tone prickled the fine hairs on the back of his neck and he studied her face in the flickering torchlight, looked for signs that she sought to cushion a blow.

"Your brothers are hale and unscathed." She took his dread, deftly displaying her unsettling ability to ken his mind. A talent he'd found plaguey annoying in their youth but welcomed all the more now, this moment.

"And where are they?" That came gruff. "Do you know?"

Janet nodded. "They are with the other men, working with the shipwright, down on the boat strand. The lot of them toil by pitch-pine torches until the small hours," she told him. "And you needn't thank me for telling you," she added with a glimmer of the cheekiness he'd so cherished in her as a young lassie.

A sassiness that, in recent years, had sadly given way to moon eyes, pouting lips, and fluttering lashes.

Soppy silliness he'd ne'er had time for in any female, least of all one he loved as a sister.

And as if she'd probed his mind yet again, her expression sobered. "You need not grieve for them or anyone else within these walls. No one suffered aught in the fire. Naught save the scrapes and bruises we harvested afterward, clearing away the rubble."

She looked away again, this time peering past him into the shadows of the ruined tower. "It happened during the Yuletide celebrations, see you?"

"So?" He didn't see at all.

A fire was a fire was a fire . . . and a *life* was a precious and fragile thing, its breath and pulse snuffed out in less than the blink of an eye.

That much he'd learned.

At the latest, after seeing Scotland's finest spill their life's blood beneath a hailstorm of English arrows.

"I dinna see what Christmastide revelry has to do with sparing men the warmth of a raging inferno."

"And I say you should." She flipped her braids over her shoulders, gave him a challenging look. "Or have you not done any carousing on the tourney circuit, Magnus MacKinnon? Have you forgotten that nights of chaos and conviviality often leave the best of men not just reeking of stale wine and light-skirted kitchen lasses, but also sleeping openmouthed on the floor rushes?"

"Christ in hell." Magnus swallowed the bile rising in his throat. "Are you telling me the men of this household lay about beneath the trestles—*drunken*—whilst the whole of the east tower went up in flame?"

Janet peered hard at him. "Would you rather they'd been asleep in their beds? In that selfsame tower?"

She had him there.

Magnus clamped his jaw, gave her a stiff nod. "You are right, to be sure," he conceded. "But it is still shameful. A sorry business."

"A sad affair, aye—but caused by a lightning strike. The most alert guardsmen could not have prevented it. Though some say the old curse guided the bolt's path."

Magnus snorted. "Pray, spare me such foolhardiness. I have no wish to hear it."

Half-turning aside, he stared into the wildly sparking flame of the nearest wall torch. Nigh guttered, its hissing lent a macabre note to their discourse, but he strove to ignore the infernal crackling . . . just as he paid no heed to Janet's fully inappropriate adulation.

In an effort to restore the easy camaraderie they'd shared as children, he swung back around and reached a quick hand to tweak her nose. "And you, cousin mine, have too good a modicum of wits to let such prattle as ancient curses and predictions of doom pass your lips."

"You ken how tongues will wag." She shrugged. "The lightning did strike the very tower Reginald of the Victories' lady wife is said to have jumped from."

"Hoary maledictions and stones that bear such sorrow they canna even warm beneath a summer sun's sweetest heat!" Magnus shook his head. "'Tis all twaddle spun by the *seannachies* on cold and dark winter nights and naught else, I swear you."

"Never you mind what the storytellers put about," Janet said, her lilting voice going breathy. *Excited.* "All will be good now you are here again." She reached for him, gripping his hands despite the sooty grime on them. "Tush, but it is overlong you were away. Aye, here is a grand and notable night."

Schooling his features lest a smile encourage her or a grimace tread too heavily on a heart he'd rather not injure, Magnus disentangled himself from her grasp. "And you are looking bonnier than ever, *Cousin*." He laid especial emphasis on their blood connection, however remote it might be. "It grieves me that I have not done better for you."

"Oh my soul! And you say I speak babble and nonsense?" She waved a dismissive hand. "The bards have been singing your praises throughout the Isles these past years," she countered, tipping back her head to stare up at him. "The tales are innumerable. All are in awe of your prowess on the tourney field . . . your feats of valor at Dupplin Moor."

"Nevertheless, I stand before you without a handful of silver to call my own," Magnus said, the weight of what he must tell her heavy on his tongue. "The modest fortune I'd amassed in ransoms and prize goods on the tourney circuit was robbed from its hiding place while I fought a battle doomed to failure before any of us could shout our war cries."

He rubbed the back of his neck, wished he had not just sounded like an embittered, battle-weary graybeard.

"Hear me, lass, I even bartered my best jousting mount to pay mail to more black-hearted cateran toll collectors than I care to remember." He did not mention that the fine-blooded beast had been his *only* such mount. "The last of my coin went to a lesser MacDonald chieftain for passage on his galley."

Janet didn't flinch, but a trace of sympathy flickered across her pretty face. On seeing it, Magnus knew a near-irresistible urge to throw back his head and roar with impotent fury.

Instead, he ran sooty fingers through his hair and took a deep breath of stale, dank air that still smelled thinly of smoke and burned timber.

"God's eyes," he swore, glancing up at the corridor's stone-vaulted ceiling. It, too, bore greasy streaks of thick black soot. "Do you have any idea what those thieving clansmen charge for the privilege of crossing their Highland territories?"

He clenched his fists, blew out a hot breath before he looked back at her. "Do you not see? Saints, had I not been in possession of such prime horseflesh, like as not, I'd not be standing here this moment."

"But you *are* here . . . and well."

Magnus pinched the bridge of his nose. A persistent ache pounded behind his forehead, and if one more person, man or beast, gave voice to how well he appeared, he would not be responsible for his actions.

Thinking he heard footfalls, or mayhap the telltale click-clicking of a dog's nails, he stared round, scrunching his eyes to peer into the darkness, but naught moved in the long passage save inky shadows and the intermittent burst of sparks from the smattering of poorly burning wall sconces.

His scalp prickled nonetheless. Turning back to Janet, he let out his breath on a long, weary sigh. "See you, lass, I lost the moneys I'd hoped to use to dower you," he blurted before he lost his courage as well. "Nary a *siller* remains."

To his amazement—or mayhap not—she evinced nary a sign of dismay. Indeed, she stretched up on her toes and gave him a quick peck on the cheek!

Magnus lifted a hand, wiped away the moistness of her kiss. "A God's name, Janet, do you not ken the gravity of what I am telling you?" He tried again. "I do not have a crust of bread to bribe a beggar to wed you much less a man worthy enough to call himself your liege husband."

"It matters not," she said, shrugging again.

Magnus stared at her, now wholly convinced his world had run mad. One woman, and a most desirous one at that, had been set in his lap with more gold-filled coffers than he could hope to win in five years of tourneying, yet he wanted nary a coin of her riches.

And the lass whom he had so hoped to dower came up empty-handed and claimed not to care!

Cooing and petting him she was, her face all aglow

like a room full o' candles. "Never you worry," she said, her tone almost coquettish. "Your fortunes will change now that the MacKinnon fleet will soon be plying the waves again." She threw her arms around his neck, pressed so close the small rounds of her breasts mashed hotly against the hard links of his mailed shirt. "To be sure, all will soon be well."

"I shall endeavor to make it so," Magnus agreed, setting her from him. "So soon as I—"

Feel a man again, he'd almost said.

"You shall feel better after you have had a bath," she encouraged, echoing his thoughts again—if only superficially. "That is why I came looking for you." Her eyes lit at the notion. "Dagda ordered bathing tubs filled for you and your friend in the kitchens, near the warmth of the cook fires. She will tend your friend, and I—"

"*You* shall bathe Colin. He is more in need of gentle hands than I, and will welcome your attentions," Magnus amended her plan. "Dagda can assist me . . . or better yet, I shall see to my own needs."

"But I have always helped you bathe."

"Not since I was a beardless stripling, you haven't," he reminded her.

She drew herself up to her full, unimpressive height. "You would rather have *her* wash you."

Och, but you err greatly, lass. Amicia MacLean is the last woman whose hands I am about to let light upon my naked flesh.

Knowing the unspoken words must surely be stamped in glowing red letters across his forehead, Magnus folded his arms and waited.

And not for overlong.

The slight narrowing of Janet's eyes revealed how

swiftly she'd read them. "You ken I would ne'er wish to make trouble for you," she purred. "But neither do I see why her concerns matter . . . considering you will soon be sending her away."

"I have not yet decided what to do with her." The confession startled Magnus as much as it appeared to vex his cousin. "As for you making trouble for me, I vow you already have," he added, seeing no point in telling her he'd just caught sight of a tall, lithe form slipping from the shadows at the far end of the passageway.

His proxy bride had shot one hurt-filled glance his way before vanishing into the blackness of the turnpike stair.

The look old Boiny had aimed at him before traipsing after her did not bear recounting.

Feeling utterly wretched, Magnus MacKinnon, paladin of the lists and poorer than a pauper's emptiest purse, had just been demoted to the level of a lowly earthworm.

Of a surety, mayhap he'd no longer need to convince the lass of the futility of staying.

Good were the chances she'd leave anon, and of her own good devices.

Pondering such an outcome, Magnus didn't know whether he should laugh or cry.

Someone else suffered no such difficulties.

They enjoyed his misery.

For long after Janet left him, the future MacKinnon laird remained rooted to the spot, staring in turn at the smoke-blackened walls of the vaulted passage or the great empty void that had once been his bedchamber.

"Sweet Christ God!" His voice cracking at last, he

gave full rein to his frustration and kicked the charred door frame.

His distress caused a malicious smile to curve someone else's lips as they watched from the shadows.

Vengeance tasted sweeter than imagined.

Aye, 'twas a rare delicacy, and one that would only improve if someone's suspicions proved true and Magnus MacKinnon's pride was all that kept him from rejoicing in his fool sire's choice of a bride.

Someone's keen eye and ever-alert ears had gleaned what few kent: MacKinnon the Younger had been sweet on Amicia MacLean since long afore his voice broke and deepened!

And even if the lass had naught to do with a certain someone's need for revenge, she would make a fine instrument to gain blissful recompense.

A fine instrument, indeed.

High atop Coldstone Castle's crenellated parapets, Lady Amicia paced the wall-walk, her new fleece-lined cloak clutched tight about her. Rain clouds were racing in from the west and a knifing wind stung her cheeks, but its chill blast did not gust powerfully enough to chase Janet's words from her heart.

The roaring of her own blood in her ears had kept her from catching more than a few snatches of the younger woman's breathy cooings, but what little she had heard only sealed the opinion she'd been forming of the fairy-like blonde who clearly fancied Magnus MacKinnon for her own.

Blood cousin or no.

A bath, she'd crooned, batting thick, gold-tipped lashes at him.

Why I came looking for you, she'd simpered as she'd twined her arms around his neck.

And most damning of all: *But neither do I see why her concerns matter . . . considering you will soon be sending her away.*

Those last words laid weighted fetters on Amicia's every breath. Worse, they undermined her faith in her ability to win a place in her husband's heart.

Increasing her step, she tried to close her ears to the echoing litany, to unhear the silky purr of her rival's voice. Tail of the devil, just remembering the woman's blatant coyness made her want to give a loud huff of indignation that any man of sound wit would fall for such artful conniving.

Like as not, she would have hooted with laughter right there in the dank passageway had that man been any other than Magnus MacKinnon.

But it *had* been him, so she'd held back any such urges. And now she made do with grinding her teeth and taking ever-longer strides along the deserted battlements. She'd pace even faster if her new mantle, a wedding gift from Devorgilla, Doon's venerable wisewoman, didn't prove so cumbersome. But its heavy folds warmed her and, the saints knew, she was built sturdy enough to carry its weight and more.

Much more . . . as she meant to prove to a slip of a chit half her size.

To that end, she drew a deep, cleansing breath of the chill night air.

Air heavily laced with the scent of the sea and cold, damp stone.

Old stone, and peat smoke, and *family.*

Air so like that of home, her eyes watered . . . or

would have if she'd been of a mind to allow such an indulgence.

And of a certainty she wasn't, so she leaned against a
square-toothed merlon in the parapet walling and blinked
back the hot sting of tears before they could fall.

Beside her, Boiny dropped to his haunches and gave a
deep-chested, elderly-dog grunt. He leaned heavily
against her, well-pleased to sit even if his milky gaze revealed his sympathy for her troubles.

Fighting the hollow feeling inside her, Amicia stroked
the dog's soft, floppy ears and stared out to where the
moon cast a silvery pathway over the night-blackened
sea.

That was what she needed . . . a magical path out of
the darkness she'd awakened in. A path she'd need to
forge for herself, that much she knew.

But how?

Her new husband was loath to keep her.

And a wee wisp of a fawning she-cat was bound and
determined to keep him!

"You will soon be sending her away. . . ." Amicia
mimicked Janet's trillings, her cheeks hot as flame despite the night's cold.

She looked down at Boiny, knew heart-swelling gratitude for his company. "Did you hear her?" she asked him,
her hand moving to knead the loose skin of his rough-
coated shoulders. "Have you e'er seen such a display of
well-honed wenchy wiles?"

Her pulse kicking up in agitation, she fussed with the
fall of her cloak, silently cursed its heaviness. Pest and
botheration, ne'er could any female save an undergrown,
great-eyed beauty of delicate, nymphlike proportion pull
off such an exhibition without appearing ludicrous.

Ire churning inside her, she leaned harder against the icy-cold granite of the merlon. Constricting bands of ne'er before experienced doubts and inadequacies clamped fast round her rib cage, squeezing with a vengeance.

Over and over again, the younger woman's simpering echoed in her mind, taunting her.

"A plague on her," Amicia mumbled, frowning out at the tossing seas.

Faith, with her *handsome height and bold form,* as her brothers were fond of describing her, she could never coo and simper at a man—any man—without looking, and feeling, an utter fool.

An ungainly and awkward fool.

Sighing, she dashed a stray raindrop from her cheek. How could she compete with a nemesis whose waist she could span with her own two hands?

By being yourself and trusting your heart, the wind seemed to whisper, pausing in its racing fury to caress her cheek most gently.

Amicia blinked.

She tilted her head to listen, but naught else came. Too much of an Isleswoman to discount such an urging, however faint or fleeting, she lifted her chin, shoved back the hood of her cloak. The wind, once more speeding across the ramparts, tore at her hair and cooled her flushed cheeks, its buffeting might a welcome relief to the hot MacLean blood coursing through her veins.

A legacy she held in tight rein . . . most times.

Curbing it now—as best she could—she trailed her fingertips along the cold, damp stone of the crenel's edge and considered her options.

Since time beyond memory, MacLean men were

known to be blessed with all manner of traditions and enchantments to smooth their way to finding the ladies of their hearts.

MacLean women enjoyed no such boons.

They had to craft and hone their own devices.

They had to be strong.

So Amicia stiffened her spine. Without doubt, nary a one of her ancestresses would have cowered before the silly posturings of a wee snippet of a lass who ought have a care lest a good Highland wind blow her from the field of competition.

Feeling better, she pulled in another great, greedy gulp of the bracing night air, savoring its salty tang. She might be made to walk along a black precipice, but she would not tumble over the edge.

And if any fool sought to accost and push her, *she* wouldn't be the one to lose her footing.

"Nor will I be set aside," she announced to Boiny . . . and the plaudits of the keening wind.

"And I, my lady, have not yet decided aught about a-setting you anywhere."

Amicia's heart near leapt from her throat. She spun around, spied *him* standing just outside of the faintly lit arch of the tower doorway. He came forward with long strides and she nigh swooned at the sight of him . . . despite the unsmiling grimness of his handsome face.

He'd bathed, and his damp hair gleamed in the moonlight while the wind lifted the lower edges of his clean, newly donned plaid, each sweet glimpse of his legs revealing how powerfully muscular they had grown in the years since she'd last seen him.

Not that they'd not been well-muscled enough to melt a lass even then.

Most unnerving of all, the gusty wind carried his scent, teasing her with tantalizing little whiffs of damp leather, peat smoke, and whate'er unidentifiable soap he'd used. Traces of the wild night clung to him as well, and a wee touch of pure and earthy maleness.

Just enough to make her senses whirl, set her stomach all aflutter, and send her resolve to stand proud before him flying to the stars.

"A good eve to you," she managed at last, raising her voice above the pounding of her heart. "I am pleased you came to join me."

"As well that I did, I am thinking—if only to encourage you to abandon such an inhospitable corner of this cold, wet night and seek your bed, my lady," he said, stepping up to her. "Though I will not lie to you . . . I did not come here seeking you. I simply felt a sore need for solitude."

The words no sooner left his mouth than a burst of chill, damp wind hit Amicia full in the face, its wet slap underscoring the wisdom of doing exactly as he'd urged. But her MacLean determination held her in place.

"You are full blunt, my lord." She met his gaze straight on, blinked a few raindrops from her eyes. "Know you, I value honest words and set them high above *affected* speech, however sweet upon the ears such might fall."

"Saints be praised for that," he said, ignoring—or mishearing—her true meaning, that of the wee jab at Janet that she couldn't keep herself from saying.

"To my sorrow," Magnus resumed, "I am not as adept with words as my youngest brother, Hugh. He has the golden tongue of the family as you have surely noticed if he still strolls about with his lute slung o'er his shoulder. I am none so gifted, but I try to speak my mind."

Pausing, he glanced up at the night sky overspread by heavy, fast-moving clouds. "Just because I sought a quiet moment does not mean I am not gladdened to find you here."

Amicia hugged herself against the cold, couldn't stop one doubtful brow from arching. "So you could hasten me to my bed?"

"Hear me, lass, for I would not unduly hurt you," he said, his ill ease almost pouring off him. "What you saw . . . or heard about my bath . . ." He broke off, rammed his fingers through still-damp hair. "Janet means naught to me. Not as you are thinking. I esteem her greatly, aye, and I owe her loyalty and more, for she is kin. But I love her as a sister only, that I swear to you."

His bath.

A soothing pleasure aided by Janet's delicate hand.

At the thought, green-tinged chills stabbed up and down Amicia's back. Sweet Mary Mother, of his sincere-sounding speech she'd heard scarce little beyond those two damning words.

A hot-glowing flush sprang onto her cheeks. "If you would not hurt me, then do not send me away," she stressed, disregarding her pride even if he wielded his own like an impenetrable shield. "I pray you, do not suffer me the shame or anguish of returning me to Baldoon."

He raised a brow at that, but glanced aside, his face set as if carved of the same cold granite as his castle home. A long, awkward silence stretched between them, broken only by the soft patter of rain on the stone flags of the wall-walk and the hollow whistle of the wind.

"The only shame is mine to bear, my lady, for it will take me overlong to repay your brother the dowry moneys already spent." He kept his gaze fixed on the distant horizon. "As for suffering, Doon is a well-favored isle, Baldoon one of the finest strongholds—"

"I bid you to honor my own perception of shame and suffering," she countered, deflecting his objections as ably as a well-practiced knight parries an opponent's sword thrusts. "Would you but know me better, you'd see the folly of your words."

Magnus swallowed, moistened lips gone suddenly dry. "But I am thinking of you, lass," he said, and hoped the words didn't sound as insipid to her ears as they did to his own. "I would not keep you here, bound to a man without enough coin to feed you properly much less—"

"I will not go back." She folded her arms, her dark eyes flashing rebellion.

Drawn by that fire, and the underlying note of desperation she couldn't quite disguise, Magnus cursed himself for a fool, enchanted, when he should have been mightily vexed.

Ne'er had any female spoken thus to him, but the slight quaver in her voice and the rapid-beating pulse at the base of her throat belied her mettle, and saints help him, but he wanted to cradle her against his chest and comfort her.

Her scent—warm, womanly, and laced with a faint touch of heather—made *him* long for succor.

The dark, languorous kind he hadn't enjoyed in more years than he cared to admit.

Mayhap never, were he honest.

He frowned, tried not to inhale too deeply. Or note the agitated rise and fall of her breasts. *Notably lush breasts.* Even the heavy lie of her cloak couldn't hide their bounty. Magnus stifled a groan. Keeping her would prove a greater trial than any he'd ever faced on the tourney field.

Her indisputable charms would not be so easily ignored as the dubious offerings of the less than savory light skirts e'er so eager to spread their legs for jousting champions or, truth be told, any knight or lairdling with a *siller* or two to spare.

As if aware of his quandary and the power she held over him, she moved closer, her imploring gaze searing his soul. Sakes, he couldn't budge a muscle if his life depended on it—she befuddled him beyond all good reason.

"I appeal to your knightly honor, sir," she said, not batting an eye. "Please reconsider your desire to nullify our marriage."

Magnus near choked. She had no idea of the kind of desire she unleashed in him.

"It is *because* of my honor that I would see you returned," he said, lighting his fingers to the glossy black braid coiled over her ear. A grave error in judgment, for the cool silkiness of her hair launched an immediate assault on his fortitude. "I may be sore weary from what transpired at Dupplin Moor, but I am ever yet a man. Think you I could know you beneath my roof—as my own lady wife—and not touch you?"

She stepped closer. A ploy that worked, for those scant few inches of nearness and the dangerously seductive sensuality flowing out from her set his body on fire and had him beyond all coherent thought.

"You are much mistaken if you believe I am asking you not to touch me," she was saying, her clean, heathery scent stealing his breath. "I only plead you not to shame me by sending me back."

"I—" Magnus broke off at once and frowned. Now he could not even get words past his fool tongue!

"Or would you risk rekindling our clans' old enmity by shunning me?"

The softly spoken words split through the sensual haze that had been fogging his wits. "'Twas a stolen bride that began the feud between our families, not a *returned* one."

"A shunned bride is the greater insult, is it not?"

A surge of ill ease crashed through Magnus. He blew out a frustrated breath. Where he'd only hoped to soothe, he now stood on thinnest ice. There *had* been strife off and on between their clans for centuries—even if no one could say which clan originally stole whose bride.

The tradition had been born and every hundred years or so, a MacKinnon—or a MacLean—bride or betrothed found herself snatched away in the dark of night, ne'er to be seen again until her belly swelled with her captor's get.

And so the feuding would begin anew.

"You are neither stolen nor shunned," Magnus said, a great weariness settling on his shoulders. "Your brothers know that. They will not be looking to violate our truce when I but seek to uphold your honor."

"My honor or your pride?"

Magnus could not answer her.

"There are other reasons I would ask you not to send me away," she said after a few moments of silence. "I would appeal to you to spare me a future as a smiled-upon-but-pitied clanswoman at another woman's table. I would have . . . I only wish a husband and family of my own."

When he still did not answer, she peered at him, earnest challenge all over her beautiful face. "In return for keeping me, you may touch or have me any way it pleases you."

This time, Magnus did choke. "This is madness . . . allowing you to stay," he spluttered, seeing his doom in the quick flash of triumph in her eyes. "Purest folly."

"Then you will not send me away?"

Wordless, Magnus shook his head.

"I thank you, sir." She beamed at him, and even old Boiny, the mangy turncoat, looked pleased. "You shall not regret your decision, I promise you."

His decision?

Magnus almost snorted. Instead, he merely inclined his head, and hoped it appeared as a tired nod rather than a defeated one.

"Dagda tells me she's been planning a celebratory feast," he said, hoping to regain some semblance of control in a world spinning fast out of his grasp. "Once it is held, I will join you in old Reginald's chambers of a night, and you shall serve as Coldstone's chatelaine. As befits my wife. If any question your position, I shall have words with them. But between us, my lady, in the sanctity of our bedchamber, I pray you not to expect much of me."

"You are a true knight," his newly accepted wife said, not needing many words.

A blind man could see that she reveled in her victory.

And that she wholly expected to tear down whatever safeguards and boundaries he'd just attempted to erect.

"Then I shall bid you a good night, fair lady." He took her hand and brushed a light kiss across her knuckles before he strode for the tower door.

It took all his strength not to run.

But once he'd stepped into the enveloping shadows of the stairwell, and knew himself shielded from her dark, all-seeing eyes, he gave in to his frustration and descended the downward winding stairs at a most *un*-knightly pace.

Chapter Four

❦

$\mathcal{H}$E'D STEPPED INTO THE WRONG GREAT HALL.

Or he hadn't, and the transformation leaping out at him from every nook and cranny was the reason his da had dragged his feet and muttered imprecations beneath his breath every step of their way down the winding turnpike stair.

Frozen by disbelief and no little irritation, Magnus stood in the shadows near the stair-foot and surveyed the early morning scene. As in every hall at such an hour, men sat huddled in plaids around the crackling log fire, its reddish glow illuminating their sleep-bleary faces.

Others yet sprawled upon their pallets while not a few still lolled at the trestle tables, their heads resting on folded arms. Or, in some cases, in pools of spilled and soured ale. Someone somewhere plucked at the strings of a lute.

His brother Hugh, no doubt, though he could not be sure as too much darkness yet filled the smoky hall for him to pick out his youngest sibling amongst the gathered kinsmen.

Nevertheless, enough pitch-pine torches sputtered and hissed in their iron-bracketed holders along the walls for him to well assess the damage.

Even if some would call the differences . . . *improvements.*

Sensing movement, Magnus shot out a hand and curled firm fingers around his father's elbow, deftly staying the old laird's feet before he could slink back up the stairs.

"What folly is this?" Magnus cut the air with his free hand, indicated the vastness of a hall he scarce recognized as being theirs. "Saints of glory, but I have now seen it all. This is too much . . . !"

Donald MacKinnon gave an uncomfortable shrug. "The years have not been kind to us, son. Can you not see the changes as long-needed enhancements?"

Magnus said nothing. God helping him, the only *enhancement* he could endorse was the layer of pleasantly scented meadowsweet someone had sprinkled atop the newly spread floor rushes.

Everything else he could do without.

Even the pleasing aroma of wood smoke.

His temples beginning to throb again, he drew a deep breath and released it slowly. He *liked* the choking sting of smoldering peat. Relished it, in fact. He'd cut his teeth on its smoky-sweet bite and ne'er resented that, save on rare celebratory occasions, log fires proved too dear for Clan Fingon's thin-sided purses.

But the log fire wasn't all that vexed him.

New tapestries hung everywhere, jewel-toned colors screaming their worth, while scattered groupings of heavy silver candelabrums, each one topped with real wax tapers, crowded the long tables.

Of such luxurious fripperies, he wanted naught.

Not when the plentitude had been paid for with *merks* taken from the Lady Amicia's overflowing coffers.

And without doubt they had been.

The guilty flush stealing across his father's face confirmed it.

"I cannot condone this." Magnus frowned, each colorful thread in the new tapestries, each eye-catching gleam of silver glinting off the candlesticks, a dirk thrust in his pride. "We can ne'er repay such splendor."

"You needn't glare holes in me," Donald MacKinnon defended the opulence. With a show of strength that would have delighted Magnus at any other time, he shook himself free of his son's grasp.

Belligerence sparking in his eyes, the aged laird thrust out his chin. "Nary a coin from your lady wife's dowry went toward any of this," he declared. "'Tis wedding gifts you're a-looking at—all of it. From the MacLeans, and from their sundry friends and allies throughout the Isles. Even the high table—"

"The high table?" Magnus started at once for the raised dais at the upper end of the hall.

"Aye, so I said—the MacLeans gifted us with a new one, complete with a finely carved laird's chair." His father hurried to catch up with him. "They even sent along a matching chair for your lady."

Magnus could only grunt in response. The neck opening of his tunic suddenly proved too tight for him to press a more coherent reply past his throat.

Mmmmmph would have to suffice.

That, and a good dark scowl.

Furtive glances slid his way from those men already awake and breaking their fast, but each time he glanced in anyone's direction, the offender made a great show of buttering a bannock or leaning down to offer a tidbit to one of the many hounds begging about the hall.

Other eyes observed him, too.

Eyes well-hidden in shadow so none would notice the simmering malice a certain someone couldn't quite tamp down since the MacKinnon heir and his dastard father had emerged from the stair tower—for their appearance gave irrefutable confirmation that the morning's attempt to have done with the ever-greedy lairdie had met failure.

"I kept my own chair," Donald MacKinnon prattled, giving his son a sidelong look. "It is no so fine as the new, but will serve for the now."

"The *whole* of the old table would have served," Magnus snapped, stepping around a sleeping clansman. "A mercy, Da, that table has stood on the dais since before your grandsire's day. Christ's wounds—what happened to your sense of family tradition?"

"The only tradition this clan has hanging 'bout its neck is that damnable curse," the old laird muttered as they made their way past row upon row of bench-lined trestle tables.

New trestles and benches, Magnus noted, the discovery causing the throbbing at his temples to increase to a most disagreeable hammering across the whole of his forehead.

"The old table had to go, and none too soon," his father insisted, puffing out his cheeks. "Its wood had grown wormier than a lochan's bank in spring."

"I dinna care . . ." Magnus froze, his heart slamming

hard against his chest. "Saints alive—they are grown men!"

His jaw dropping, he stared toward the magnificent new high table but saw only the two strapping young men slouched fast asleep across its black-gleaming surface.

His younger brother, Hugh, snored, his head resting mere inches from a platter of untouched oatcakes. Hugh's burnished auburn hair, so like Magnus's own if a wee shade lighter, glinted gold in the candlelight.

Dugan, his middle brother, and dark as Colin Grant or any MacLean, slept too soundly to snore. He'd cushioned his strikingly handsome face on arms that looked every bit as well-muscled as Magnus's own.

The transformation clutched hard around Magnus's rib cage and made breathing difficult. Saints, where had the time gone?

"God have mercy," he got out at last, his deep voice thick with emotion. "They are grown men," he said again, and ran a none-too-steady hand through his hair.

A few short years on the tourney circuit and his spindly-legged little brothers now looked to match him in size and brawn. Dugan even sported a lush and curly beard!

Magnus scrunched his eyes, blinked a few times, half-expecting these two strangers to be miraculously restored to the smooth-faced, skinny-shouldered youths he remembered. When next he looked, though, no such change manifested.

"Hech, laddie," his father snorted, lowering himself into his chair. "Did you think to come home and find your brothers yet beardless?"

"I thought . . ." Magnus shook his head, blew out a quick breath. "I canna say. I do not know what I thou—"

"You ought think of the depredations this household has suffered and be glad-hearted to have a bride able and willing to help you out of these ill-plagued times." Dagda plunked two wine flagons on the high table, then poured a brimming cup for Donald MacKinnon.

Leveling a stern look at Magnus, she clucked her tongue. "Consider the good it will do your brothers to have a new fleet of galleys to command. They are men full seasoned now, both too old to waste their days lolling about this broken-down pile o' stanes with naught to do but sing verses to moonbeams and swing their swords at dust motes."

Magnus smiled at her—one of the rare times he'd smiled at all in recent weeks, and of a certainty, his first since setting foot on MacKinnons' Isle.

He also noted the increased number of silver strands in the dark braids wound tightly around her head. And there was a new, ne'er-before-there puffiness beneath her eyes.

Looking at her, something hot and jabbing caught at his throat. Far from young before he'd left, Coldstone's e'er-capable seneschal had aged much in his absence.

"Ah, but you speak from my heart, dear Dagda," he vowed, purposely laying on a light tone. "I, too, would see my brothers well-occupied and know this holding in finest order . . . including its once-great fleet." He accepted the wine cup she offered him, took a sip. "I would but see to these ambitions with my own good coin. There alone we differ."

"I warned he would see this proxy marriage as an ill-advised adventure." Janet stepped from the shadows, a large platter of green cheese and hot, crusty bread balanced against her hip.

She slid a heated glance to the window embrasure

across the hall where Lady Amicia sat listening to Colin Grant strum tunes on Hugh's borrowed lute.

Following her gaze, Magnus's brows snapped together. His wife—wanted or nay—had removed her cloak, and torchlight spilling into the deep-set alcove caressed each one of her lush curves and cast a high shine onto her glossy, black-gleaming braids.

Most annoying of all, she was beaming at Colin Grant!

His jaw clamping, Magnus turned back to the high table. He'd have a word with his womanizing friend later.

Battle-injured or nay.

". . . Magnus will soon be sending her away," Janet was saying, her voice ringing with pettiness. "Their marriage is not legitimate without a proper bedding, and he does not want her. Not her riches or her . . . her body!"

Magnus near spewed his wine.

His wife's delectable body had occupied him far longer than any present would guess.

Truth was, were he made differently, he'd march across the hall this minute, flip up her skirts, and show the world just how much he wanted her! How very able he was to enjoy the bounteous charms his lute-strumming friend ogled so freely, damn his serenading hide.

Janet set her platter of cheese and bread on the table. "Without a bedding—"

"Bedding?" Dugan's eyes snapped open. "What fair maid is in need of a tumble?" Sitting upright, he glanced round. "I shall tender my services to any lass in need thereof!" he announced, a roguish grin spreading across his face . . . until his gaze fell upon Magnus.

"By the Rood—Magnus!" Leaping to his feet, he bounded around the table to throw his arms around Magnus in a bone-crushing hug.

After a moment, he stepped back to give his older brother a thorough and sweeping scrutiny. "Sakes, but it is good to see you . . . even if I can scarce keep my eyes open to look upon you at this scourge of an ungodly hour."

"I'll second that about the hour," Hugh broke in, pushing to his own feet. But he flashed Magnus a broad smile as he came forward, his arms opened wide in welcome.

Grown just as tall and broad-shouldered as Dugan, he clasped Magnus to him in a fierce embrace. "Aye," he declared, releasing him, "much as it pleases me to know you home, I could have done without Dagda awakening us in the middle of the night, claiming you would have important words with us, and then you taking forever and a day to hie yourself down here."

Magnus cuffed his youngest brother on the shoulder. "If I mind aright, we e'er broke our fast before sunrise. Mayhap you ought retire a bit earlier of a night and not be out and about until the small hours?"

Hugh blinked, couldn't quite stifle another yawn. "We have not been idle. There has been good reason to—"

"I ken what you've been about. But for now, I am thinking a bit of fresh air will help chase the sleep from your eyes." Crossing the dais, Magnus threw open the shutters of the nearest window.

At once, damp, gusty wind swept in to whip the edges of the newly hung tapestries and gutter not a few of the finely tapered beeswax candles lining the high table.

Enjoying the little disturbance more than a grown man should, Magnus cleared his throat and hardened his jaw—cautionary measures to hide the satisfaction he took in the blustery weather squelching even such ineffectual evidence of his trampled pride.

Flemish wall rugs and candles so delicate they could not withstand a wee breath of fine Highland air!

"Guidsakes, where were you, man?" Dugan caught his ear. Scratching his beard, he gave a great stretch. "We sat here like dolts for well over an hour."

"Ho, Dugan! You have not touched a single oatcake," their father cut in, sliding the platter of bannocks toward his middle son. "Eat some afore you stop growing."

Dugan hooted. "Not so! I ate six of 'em, each one smeared with butter and honey—and I would have wolfed down more had I not fallen asleep waiting on you and Magnus to show your faces."

"Men have things to do of a morning, never you mind." The old laird snatched up his wine cup, tossed down a hearty gulp.

"What things?" Hugh wanted to know. His gaze on their father, his russet brows drew together. "I ken that look on you. Something is amiss here and I would know what it is."

Hugh's clear blue eyes narrowed. "Aye, I would hear the whole of it, and so would Dugan. We are no longer wee bairns to be spared ill tidings."

Donald MacKinnon's face turned mottled red. "It was nothing and I forbid anyone to speak of it." Slamming down his wine cup, he glared round the table.

Even Dagda and Janet received a glower fierce enough to scorch blood.

"Now I know something is underfoot." Bracing his hands on the polished surface of the new high table, Hugh leaned forward to within inches of his father's tight-lipped face. "I will not leave be until—" Hugh broke off at once, sniffing the air as he straightened. "Lucifer's knees, when was the last time you had a bath?" he demanded, clenched fists on his hips. "You smell as if you've been sleeping in the cesspit."

The red stain on Donald MacKinnon's face deepened to purple.

When their da replenished his wine and sloshed more of it onto the table than into his cup, Magnus clamped a firm hand on his younger brother's shoulder.

"Have done with your badgering, Hugh," he said, tightening his fingers in additional, silent warning. "The matter is of no import—"

"*Of no import?* Hah, I say!" Their father half-rose from his chair, his flushed features working. "'Tis little wonder I reek of the cesspit when I could well have drowned in it!" He gripped his wine cup so tight his knuckles gleamed white. "'Twas the curse again, I swear it."

His outburst over, he sank back onto his chair, aiming one last pointed glare at Hugh. "And that, laddie, is the reason your brother and I were late getting down here."

"Tsk, tsk, tsk. Here is no way to talk," Dagda soothed, stepping up behind him to knead his knobby shoulders with strong, work-toughened hands. "You ken there is no such thing as a curse hanging o'er this household. Ill winds blow through here at times, to be sure, but no ancient curse."

The old laird sniffed and sipped his wine.

"So-o-o . . . what does the cesspit have to do with your great tardiness this morning?" Dugan slung an arm around Magnus's shoulders. Ever in high spirits, he wriggled his brows. "Did Da take a wee swim in the morass?"

"Nay, but he may well could have if he hadn't wedged himself in the latrine chute," Magnus said after a space. "The seat cracked beneath him and he fell into the shaft—had it been a wee bit wider, he would've plunged straight through to the cesspit. As is, he got stuck after falling but a few feet. Even so, it took a while to free him."

All humor left Dugan's handsome face.

He exchanged a glance with Hugh. "That canna be," he said, shaking his dark head. "Hugh and I replaced the seats in all the privies not longer than a fortnight ago. We used the finest, sturdiest oak. It would ne'er have given out under Da's weight, not when we—"

"Aye, and I agree," Magnus cut him off, nodding almost imperceptibly at Janet.

The lass hovered near, her bonnie face tinged bright pink. Dugan's meaning was clear enough without words. Both he and Hugh had grown into towering, well-muscled men. If Coldstone's privy seats supported their hulking frames, their father's slight one should ne'er have posed a problem.

Not if, as Dugan claimed, they'd used the best timber.

A scarce commodity on MacKinnons' Isle, fair as its sandy bays and rolling moorlands might be.

So where had his brothers gathered enough of the *finest, sturdiest oak* to waste on lowly privies?

Magnus compressed his lips. He'd wager anything he already knew.

But to be fair, he turned to Hugh, the brother most likely to give him a swift and straight answer. "Are you certain you used good-quality oak?"

His younger brother shuffled his feet, but nodded. "The best to be had—straight from the well-timbered shores of Loch Etive on the mainland."

"I thought as much." Magnus pinched the bridge of his

nose, drew a long breath. "Paid for out of my bride's dowry, no less?"

Looking uncomfortable, Hugh inclined his head again. Wordless, this time.

"And how else were we supposed to pay for two shiploads of prime boat-building material?" Donald MacKinnon shot back, his voice rising. Low murmurs and scuffling noises accompanied his outburst, rippling the length of the hall as curious gazes turned toward the dais.

"Best timber, wool and flax, tallow," he went on, looking from one of his sons to the other, his agitation palpable. "All the cordage we need—everything. The MacLean arranged delivery and gave his lairdly word he would see more supplies sent if—"

"To be sure he will," Magnus said, feeling older than his black-frowning da. "Donall the Bold is renowned for his generosity. Nevertheless, we shall impinge on his goodwill no further. Make wise use of whate'er materials he has thus far provided and be glad for them for they will have to suffice. It will be difficult as is to make adequate restitution."

Dugan was about to object, Magnus could see the protests forming on his tongue. Forestalling any such opposition, he raised a silencing hand.

"Do not press me, brother, or I would see all that he has already sent returned whence it came. That I do not, it is only because I would not deny you the experience of building a galley, seeing one come to life beneath your hands."

And because, as the good king Robert the Bruce once sought aid from his friend Angus Og, I fear this realm will yet again look to the Isles—and leal Islesmen with swift-

sailing galleys—if e'er Balliol and his Disinheriteds are to be routed once and for all.

Biting back the niggling threat of danger yet uncoiled, lest he overburden his brothers' young hearts, Magnus curled his hand around his low-slung sword belt and gripped hard, clenching and unclenching his fingers on its smooth-worn leather until the tension began sliding from his shoulders.

"It is scarcely a noble course to decline wedding gifts," Dugan blazoned forth, his tone and the way he toyed with his curling black beard indicating he meant anything *but* shiploads of timber. "Many are the men who would gladly relieve you of such a . . . *bounty.*"

"And are you declaring yourself such a man?" Magnus shot back, but his blood cooled upon seeing the amused twinkle in his brother's dark eyes.

"I thought that was the way the wind blows." Dugan gave him a playful punch in the arm. "I am pleased to see it."

"As am I," Hugh agreed, a dimpled smile lighting his face.

At the end of the table, their father harrumphed. "Dinna be smiling too fast," he admonished his younger sons. "If the curse addles your brother's brain, there is no telling what foolhardiness might please him. Or what new ills might descend upon us. Already—"

That did it.

"A God's name! I have had enough of curses," Magnus roared, lifting his voice so everyone in the hall would hear him. Even those hunched sleepy-eyed in the most far-flung corners.

In especial, any whiling away the morn in the cozy confines of a window embrasure.

"It is infinitely sad that Reginald of the Victories' fair lady wife took her life by leaping from the east tower of this castle," he rapped out, pacing between the dais table and the opened window. "But the circumstances of her death did not call down a curse upon this house, that I swear."

He shot a narrow-eyed glance at his da. "And if any seer of olden times truly claimed such a malediction existed, and could only be lifted so long as we keep a mighty fleet of galleys, then I say that soothsayer had a keen interest in selling us timber!"

He paused by the window, let the gusting damp cool his heated brow. A much-needed measure with *her* striding his way—and on Colin Grant's gallantly proffered arm!

That great oaf had an annoyingly wry smile playing at the corners of his mouth, and only his limp saved him from a hot glare, for the lout carried not only Hugh's lute but Lady Amicia's fur-lined mantle as well.

Like as not, he'd charmed her out of it.

And with the single-minded purpose of parading her full *cloakless* beneath Magnus's nose!

No doubt so he could not help but admire her glossy black braids, hanging loose as they did this morn. Two thick plaits of well-sheened ebony, they fell clear to her hips and looked luscious enough to make his mouth run dry.

Before all the heavens, the lass had the kind of lustrous tresses a man ached to run his hands through, burned to see spilling unchecked over gleaming white skin.

Naked skin.

And if he didn't mind losing his soul, just the sort of

glossy skeins a man might bury his face in, to drown happily.

The heady bliss of nuzzling his face into her *other* hair, without doubt an equally enticing notion, didn't bear consideration.

A tiny muscle began to jerk in Magnus's jaw.

Aye, with surety, Colin Grant meant to torture him.

And most dastardly of all, having held a privy ear to Magnus's secret delights and lusts over the years—intimacies regrettably divulged during too-long nights of endless boredom on the tourney circuit—the cheeky whoreson now used his privy knowledge to maneuver the lass forward so that she had no choice but to pass through the chill wind pouring through the opened window.

A decidedly clever coup, for with her low-cut gown of finest linen already clinging to her supple curves, a few scant steps through the rain-misted air was all it took to plaster the thin cloth of her bodice to her breasts—and tighten what appeared to be exceedingly large nipples.

A delicacy Magnus relished . . . as he'd once revealed to Colin when both men had been so deep in their cups they'd had no better topic to pass the evening than an earnest discourse on the various delights of female anatomy.

His blood running hot, Magnus strove to tear his gaze from the bounteous swell of his wife's bosom. And in especial from the twin dark-tipped rounds thrusting so provocatively against the near-transparent linen.

Seldom had he seen such generous areolae.

And ne'er had he been seized with such an irresistible urge to throttle a friend!

"A good morrow, my lady," he managed to his wife. Colin, he purposely ignored. "I trust you slept well?"

She inclined her head with a smile, giving him the polite response he'd expected . . . until a determined gleam entered her dark eyes.

A seductively wicked gleam.

"As you will soon see, my lord, our chamber is well-appointed," she said, her voice as smoky-rich as her other attractions. "The bed in particular lends itself to all good comforts of the night."

Magnus drew a quick breath. Truth be told, he near swallowed his tongue.

Colin hooted a laugh and gave him a bold wink.

His father cackled with glee. "Ho, but she calls to mind your mother in her time!" he called out, his face lighting.

Fixing a sharp gaze on Magnus, he slapped the table with the flat of his hand, his vexation of moments before forgotten. "Be glad the wedding feast is but in a few days' time, my son. Such fire ought not be allowed to cool."

"And if Magnus canna keep it ablaze, I'm volunteering my *hardest* endeavors!" a deep voice rose from one of the long tables near the back of the hall.

Assorted agreement and guffaws followed, coming from all corners as men everywhere joined in the merriment. Dugan and Hugh indulged with gusto, laughing long and loud, and even Dagda's tired eyes sparkled with mirth.

Only Janet's face darkened, her lips tightly pursed as she bustled about replenishing wine cups and making ever-louder clattering noises.

Turning his back on the lot of them—his bonnie-nippled, serene-smiling bride in particular—Magnus strode back to the window, where a single ray of watery sunlight sought to pierce the day's gloom.

Frowning at it, lest he be minded of how easily Lady

Amicia could have dispelled the darkness from his heart if only he could have taken her to wife under more favorable circumstances, he waited for the jollity behind him to lessen, then spun around, his gaze seeking Colin.

"The weather is clearing, my friend," he said, amazed by the calmness of his tone. "If you would try the wonders of the Beldam's Chair, we'd best be off before the rain worsens again."

"The Beldam's Chair?" Donald MacKinnon's bushy brows shot upward. "Tscha!" he cried, slapping the table again. "You spurn my belief in old Reginald's curse, call me a fool for claiming I've seen a ghost galley plying our waters of late, yet you would see your friend hie hisself across the bogs and moor to seek a cure in a magical chair?"

Throbbing heat inched its way up the back of Magnus's neck, and he took several deep breaths before answering. His gaze strayed to Colin's injured leg. "I ne'er said I believe in the chair's curative powers, though I will not deny I am wishing to see a wonder worked for my friend—that hope is why I brought him here."

"And her?" Janet appeared at his elbow. "Are you now keeping her?"

Never one to lie, Magnus nodded. "It would seem so."

His cousin's blue eyes narrowed, perturbation hovering in their depths. "You still needn't . . . take her—even if you have to get through a sham wedding feast."

"Ah, fair lass, but the wedding feast shall be true enough," Colin put in, seizing her hand for a kiss as he joined them. "As will be the bedding ceremony thereafter—I shall personally assure that it is so."

"And how, my friend, do you think to do that?" Magnus demanded the instant Janet flounced away, anger peppering her step. "Do *you* plan on doing the . . . honors?"

Colin shook his head. "Of a certainty, nay. That bliss shall be yours alone, my good friend." A slow smile spread across his handsome face. "I but mean to claim that vow you swore to me at Dupplin."

The words out, Colin's slow smile cracked into a full-fledged grin.

Magnus felt the floor open beneath him.

"Not *that* vow?"

"None other," Colin assured him, taking Magnus's elbow to lead him from the hall. "The oath you gave me when, after the battle, you awakened to discover I'd carried you from the field—despite my wounded leg."

"But—"

Colin glanced at him as they neared the hall's arched doorway. "You promised any boon I desire, even swore on your honor. Or do you deny it?"

"Nay, you ken I would ne'er unsay a vow," Magnus said, opening the door. "It is just that—saints, man—we never specified what that boon would be."

"Exactly," Colin agreed as they stepped out into the blustery morn. "We did not. And I now know what boon I desire of you. I want you to bed your wife."

A short while later, mayhap even before the young MacKinnon laird-in-all-but-title and his limping-legged friend had trotted their garrons through Coldstone's gatehouse, a certain someone stood in the hall's blackest shadows and watched the pestiferous person of Donald Mackinnon sip his wine.

Choking on a much ranker brew, the dastard ought be

about now . . . afloat and glassy-eyed on a sea of foulest muck.

Ne'er again to glimpse the rising sun.

That he'd been spared such a fate, rankled deep.

But there were other ways to see justice served—more means than a plunge into the cesspit to perpetuate that sniveling weathercock's faith in maledictions and doom.

Indeed, with his recent claims of demon-driven ghost ships no one else e'er saw, mayhap his own increasing addlepatedness would bring about his demise.

Either way, the fool's days were numbered.

"A curse on you, Laird MacKinnon—my curse on you everlasting," the shadow-cloaked figure snarled, drifting ever deeper into a dark recess in the walling. "I will purge these isles of you and yours if it costs me my last breath."

Nothing was surer.

Chapter Five

✦

THE PLACE HELD MAGIC.

Or so some believed.

Magnus had ne'er been sure, but now, under a brooding sky and with the runic-carved stones of the Beldam's Chair looming a dark, wet-gleaming gray before him, he could almost put faith in the ancient tales.

Especially with the chill wind howling around his ears and masses of dense clouds swirling overhead. Aye, he would not be hard-pressed to believe the stories. Just looking at the great cairn of stones and its hoary relic sent a shiver sliding down his spine.

The stone-heaped burial mound, a sepulchral memorial of the distant past, made a sight eerie enough to twist the guts of the most stout-hearted of men.

If, unlike him, they allowed such stuff and nonsense to bother them.

Even so, he adjusted his plaid more securely about his shoulders and let its familiar warmth comfort more than his physical body. Then he squelched the scowl threatening to darken his features.

A wise man, even a somewhat doubting one, knew better than to frown in such a venerated place.

Thus bolstered, he kneed his shaggy-maned garron past a series of peat bogs and small tarns, reining in near an outcrop of jagged, upthrusting boulders.

Keening wind moaned about the rocks, its high-pitched wail lifting the tiny hairs on his nape, but the day was not yet come when he'd fall prey to the mind ravings of his da and start seeing otherworldly menace crouched behind every stane to dot the high moors.

Ancient family curses and ghost galleys, indeed!

Nay, he was more plagued by thoughts of connubial four-posters and large, sweet-puckered nipples a-winking at him from behind layers of thin, mist-dampened linen!

His newest personal demons they were, and already nestled snugly amongst the army of other assorted torments and responsibilities encamped on his shoulders.

He almost swore.

Instead, he bit back the blasphemy, set his jaw, and stared hard at the concentric rings, arcs, and zigzags incised on every inch of the Beldam's Chair. Ancient Celtic symbols, their original purpose and meaning forever lost to the mists of time.

Only the chair's reputation for lending succor remained.

And since time was, the *seannachies* of Clan Fingon contended that anyone who sought ease in the throne-like chair could absorb the healing power and protection infused in the living rock from which the seat of stone was hewn.

Set deep in the north-facing side of a burial cairn, clan tradition claimed the sacred chair once belonged to the half-mythic female healer thought to lie within the pile of carefully mounded stones.

"*That* is your Beldam's Chair?" Colin drew up at last, halting his garron beside a black-surfaced bog pool not far from the cairn. "The miracle-spending wonder chair? I' faith, with all those runic carvings, it looks more like to damn than cure me."

"You shall see," Magnus said with a shrug. "There are those in my clan who swear by its powers. And not just the graybeards from whom you'd expect such faith. The chair's powers are renowned far and wide."

Colin looked anything but impressed.

Indeed, he appeared decidedly *un*impressed. "Each to his taste, I say."

Ignoring him, Magnus glanced up at the roiling heavens, a fierce tic working at his jaw despite his best efforts to hold fast to his composure. A losing battle he'd been waging ever since waking to hear his da's frantic cries emerging from the latrine shaft earlier that morning.

His brow dark as the day, he swung down from his saddle, dropping lightly to his feet. "Say of it what you will, my friend. For the nonce, you deserve no better." He cast a sidelong glance at Colin—just to make certain the skirt-chasing knave hadn't lost his footing upon dismounting onto the boggy, moss-slicked ground.

But the cheeky varlet stood tall and steady, his dark gaze darting about, and Magnus didn't know whether to be relieved or annoyed.

Opting for annoyance, holy ground or nay, he jerked his attention from his fast-recuperating friend and stared out across the high, rolling moorland. Frowning openly now, he raked a hand through his hair and took in the vast expanse of heather, peat hags, and countless brown-watered lochans.

A vista he loved with the whole of his heart and ne'er wearied of drinking in. Even on the darkest, most windswept of days. Mayhap especially then. The landscape, unchanged for centuries, stretched away in all directions and, of a certainty, looked wild and primal enough to encourage belief in all manner of far-fetched tales.

Myth, legend, and high-hung hopes.

Not that he'd e'er again give heed to his own.

Colin started toward the cairn, his handsome face a mask of skepticism. "An unholy place you've brought me to, my friend. Without light and . . . yieee!" he cried out, slip-sliding on a patch of oily black peat mire.

Sprinting forward, Magnus snatched one of the lout's flailing arms, righting him before he could plunge headlong into the bog. Already, he'd sunk in above his ankles.

"Have a care," Magnus warned, helping the other to step clear of the mud. "It is said the ancient ones do not care for doubt."

More than full of himself despite the muck slapping loudly around his boots, Colin's dark eyes danced with challenge. "And are you not in danger of being owl-blasted yourself for daring to tread their sanctum in such a cross-tempered mood?"

"I am not cross-tempered."

"Then what are you, my friend? Jealous, perchance?" Colin arched a brow. "Mayhap because the Lady Amicia complimented my singing voice and the skill of my fingers? Plucking only lute strings, that is—never you worry."

Magnus pressed his lips together, unwilling to dignify such flummery with an answer.

"Aye, I do believe that is it," Colin asserted.

Taking ever-longer strides, Magnus kept walking. Wordless, he skirted a thick-growing cluster of whins and broom bushes, and made for the cairn, leaving Colin to limp after him or stay where he would and spout his nonsense.

"I would think you'd be grateful," came Colin's deep voice at his elbow, the persistent oaf clearly bent on making a nuisance of himself. "I've given you the perfect way to keep your bride and save your pride . . . or did that one wee glimpse at her feminine accoutrements not whet your appetite?"

The reminder, even said in jest, stopped Magnus in his tracks.

Lifting a hand, he rubbed the back of his neck and drew a long, deep breath of the cold, earthy-smelling air. Then, with careful deliberation, he rolled his shoulders, refusing to let them tighten in agitation.

He would not be goaded.

Not for whatever misguided reason Colin Grant seemed so determined to make an arse of himself.

"There is naught amiss with my *appetite,* never you fear," he declared, pushing the words past gritted teeth. "And be assured that my wife's *accoutrements,* however delectable, are none of your concern."

"Ho! *Your wife,* you say?" Colin's roguish smile flashed. His amused gaze not leaving Magnus, he lowered himself into the Beldam's Chair. "It gladdens my heart to hear you call her thus. At least you admit you are well and duly wed to her, proxy marriage or no. Aye, there is hope for you yet, my sour-faced friend!"

There was that word again.

Hope.

Magnus's stomach clenched around the wretched term and all its empty implications. His hopes had been cast so soundly to the four winds, he doubted if even the e'er-quixotic Colin Grant could gather the remnants.

Well aware he must look soured indeed, but unable to do aught about it, he fixed his most level gaze on his fool-grinning friend.

"Aye, she is my wife," he said, the words like cold ash on his tongue. "And though, for a surety, I was not looking for one, it appears as if that is what I've been handed . . . and with all sundry comforts. Thanks to you!"

Colin's lips twitched in a pitiful attempt to hide another smile. "And will you be keeping that vow you made me, MacKinnon?"

"For good or ill, you ken I ne'er break my word," Magnus jerked, nigh having to force himself to breathe. Saints, just giving voice to the admission jellied his knees.

Would that any lass save Amicia MacLean would open wifely arms to him! Then he could have done with the task and mayhap even convince himself it had ne'er happened.

Or transpired out of mere duty.

Even pure base lust.

But lying with Amicia would cost him far more than his seed, and once the deed was done, he'd be forever lost.

"I am well-pleased to hear you will . . . er . . . *stand* to your vow," Colin was saying. Truth be told, he looked supremely content.

Disgustingly so.

"And," he droned on, settling back in the Beldam's Chair, "I suspect you will thank me in earnest once you've pushed past your pride, for I would wager my sword the lass favors you greatly."

Magnus's heart gave a quick bound at his friend's words, but he only made a noncommittal grunt.

The orchestrator of his doom brought steepled fingers to his chin. "Aye, I am quite certain of it. She is sore smitten with you, laddie."

"And if that were so, you honor your friendship to me by spiriting her into a dark window embrasure and using my own brother's lute to serenade her with love songs?"

"Ahhh, but you wound me." Colin placed a hand over his heart. "I but wished to keep a certain flaxen-haired vixen from sinking her talons into the lass. *That one* favors you, too, I have seen. And more than is good. Her bright blue eyes talk quite loudly and she is none too pleased about your marriage."

"Of that I am aware, but her displeasure has no grounding." Magnus glanced to the side, smoothed a hand down his chin. "Janet has trailed after me like a puppy since we were bairns. Nevertheless, she is sorely mistaken if she e'er understood my regard for her to be more than I would feel for a sister."

"You are a fool if you think she esteems herself as your sister."

"She is kin, man—my cousin."

"A not-too-near one, I am betting?" the long-nosed knave pursued, tracing a slow finger round and round one of the concentric circles carved on the chair arm.

"Kin is kin." Magnus let out a long sigh. The black-guard was pushing him over and beyond his patience. "Sakes, Colin, she is the one I spoke to you of months ago . . . the cousin I meant to dower with some of my tourney winnings."

Turning aside, he pressed his fingers against his temples. "Do you not see I have failed her, too? She is a bastard, see you? No man will have her without a notable dowry. And now—would that it were otherwise—it would seem I must hurt her heart as well as leaving her dowerless."

"*I* would take her. Dowered or no."

Magnus swung back around. "And her bastardy?"

"Traitor, thief, advantage-taking sorner . . . those are the titles that carry shame, my friend." Colin eyed him, his expression bitter earnest. "On my soul, if she would have me as I stand before you—my lands burned, my keep in ruin, and no family to welcome her to their hearth, then I am telling you I care little if she is a by-blow . . . and even less whose!"

"And that she fancies herself . . . I mean, you care not that—"

"That she thinks herself taken with you?" Colin finished for Magnus, his roguish smile beginning to spread across his face again. "Guidsakes, MacKinnon, think you I could not turn her head if I put my mind to it?"

Magnus hesitated, his gaze on the dark, lowering clouds. Of late, there was scarce little he cared to put his faith in—even Colin Grant's redoubtable skill at charming women.

Whole legions of them the last time Magnus bothered to notice.

"She but needs a bit of wooing," Colin expounded, clearly warming to the notion. "She is a fine and high-spirited lass—a meet bride to walk beside me on a path that will prove anything but smooth."

"She is notable strong-willed," Magnus argued, nudging a spongy clump of red-brown sphagnum moss with the toe of his boot. "Do not think I am not fond of her, but I would be honest with you. Her tongue—"

"Devil take me, but I am betting her tongue could make the hardest man beg for mercy." Colin released a low, appreciative whistle, slapped his good thigh. "I' faith, the mere thought of such sweetness is a nigh unbearable incitement."

His jaw near hitting the squishy ground, Magnus stared at his friend. "Sakes, you have naught else on your mind? In these sore times?"

"I would rather dwell on bliss-spending thoughts than otherwise."

Magnus suppressed a derisive snort.

His own thoughts went to his friend's empty coffers, the rubble and waste of his once-proud holding. The injured leg that, unless healed properly, would hamper him for life. Truth be told, the list of woes and misfortune plaguing them both could be recited until the morning broke.

Magnus's head began to ache.

"I canna believe you would obsess yourself with wenching when your prospects are more bleak than mine," he said, pinching the bridge of his nose. "At least Coldstone Castle is yet standing—such as it is."

Colin's good humor faded, but only for a moment. "The lass has a lusty touch, see you? It took all my strength not to run full-stretch when she was a-washing round my ballocks yester eve," he confessed, having the decency to appear a wee bit abashed as the admission left his lips.

"But never you mind her sweet-stroking fingers." He

leaned forward, looked directly into Magnus's eyes. "Do you not ken what a boon having such a braw lass at my side would be for me—facing what I must?"

Well-chastised, Magnus nodded. What else could he do? Already, he could feel the heat inching up his neck to tinge his cheeks.

The inference behind Colin's words could not have been more plain if he'd held a gazing glass before Magnus's nose.

Ten gazing glasses!

Still, their plights could not be compared.

His was . . . *different*.

Colin took life too lightly, lacked Magnus's deeper-sitting beliefs and values.

His abiding sense of responsibility.

Even so, the lout had made him feel every inch a stone-hearted buffoon. Magnus cleared his throat, ready to apologize—even if he knew himself in the right.

"I did not mean—"

"I ken what you meant," Colin said, all smiles again. He waved a careless hand. "As for wenching, so long as my obsessing is but to lay claim to one bonnie piece, what can be the harm in it?"

Magnus rubbed his throbbing forehead. Now he *did* feel the buffoon. "And here I'd been thinking—"

"That I would use the shadowy confines of a window embrasure to coax a kiss from my best friend's wife?" Colin made a wry face, but his tone conveyed he bore no ill feelings.

And if Magnus yet harbored any doubts, Colin's broad wink allayed them.

"Discredit my honor if you must, but 'tis well you aught ken my taste in women," he minded Magnus.

"Have we not enjoyed enough shared evenings of, shall we say *fair entertainment,* for you to recall I have e'er looked to abscond into the heather with pale-haired maids?"

"Och, to be sure, I remember well," Magnus agreed. Indeed, the image of Colin with a veritable parade of Janet look-alikes on his arm tramped across his mind's eye. "You e'er sought wee slips of lassies with corn-colored hair and huge blue eyes."

Colin nodded, looking pleased. "Aye, so I did—and still do, I vow! Just as you e'er looked to lose yourself in the arms of sultrier beauties with well-rounded curves."

"Your observation skills serve you well," Magnus conceded.

Looking down, he made a pretense of studying his knuckles rather than risk letting his astute friend glimpse the damning truth behind his fascination with raven-haired women.

His pitiable penchant for painting another woman's face on every dark-haired lass who'd e'er deigned to hitch her skirts for him.

Amicia MacLean's face.

The one he'd carried in his heart for more years than he cared to remember.

Disaster and havoc.

Nothing left but a few scattered stones . . . the dust of your bones.

Tears, lamentations, even a falling upon your knees will not avail you.

The malice-filled recitations came with the turn of the tide, the wind and the sea echoing each hate-filled cry and carrying their wrath from the bowels of Coldstone's most secret heart to a place enfolded by a quiet too deep for human ears—a lone tidal islet too forsaken for even hermits and holy men to seek a foothold upon its jagged, black-glistening surface.

The Isle of Doon's accursed Lady Rock.

A threshold to another world, and where things have no reckoning of time, though none would suspect the like—none save Doon's own blessed *gruagach*.

A benevolent female spirit, older than the ages, she whiled on the islet now, toying with the ropey strands of seaweed tangled in her unbound hair, her very presence making her an interloper in time. A trespasser in a world she'd walked often and in many guises, some of them human.

A world that, at times, she'd held more dear than had been good for her.

In recent years by earth reckoning, she'd thought she'd found peace at last, believed she'd addressed and attended the duties gathered during her last sojourn upon Doon's fair shores.

But certain tasks yet bound her, in particular the malevolence of a vengeful soul soiled by irrevocable darkness.

So she returned again and again, braving the loneliness of her perch in the sea, and scarce noting the waves, breaking high and icy cold against the islet's treacherous rocks.

With an ache in her heart, but a purpose unbending, she endured the lashing wind and steady drizzle, her gaze ever fixed on the massive walls of Baldoon, mighty stronghold of the MacLeans and her last home in a world she'd not quite been ready to leave.

In that short mortal existence, she'd been Iain

MacLean's first bride. Fated to perish at the hand of a greed-consumed kinsman for the good her passing would eventually bring the clans whose well-being she was destined to guard.

And now, in her true form once more, she sheltered them from every dark wind and sought to keep them from harm for so long as they walked the earth.

Her great love for them welling in her heart, she watched Baldoon's silent walls and sent those within all her goodwill and strength. Welcoming light shone from a few of the castle's narrow-slit windows, the golden warmth beckoning fiercely, but only as echoes of another time.

Precious memories of days gone by, each one caught up by the wind and hurtled through the night as swiftly as they'd come. Bittersweet moments vanishing without a trace, just as the dark one's rantings just now, had struck and then sped past her. Each malediction barreling onward to plague and unsettle other hapless souls who, like her, ought better be at rest.

So she tore her longing from a place she'd best tread no more, and made cause with the windy night . . . with the powers imbued in her present state.

By a softly muttered incantation or two, and a fervent belief in the good of her work, the *gruagach* summoned a fine and luminous mist of green.

Just enough magic for the whisper of a sigh to whisk her from the wave-splashed rocks of the tidal islet, so bound to her by fate, to the comforting hearthside of a trusted friend—the cozy thatched cottage of Devorgilla, Doon's e'er-dutiful and revered wisewoman.

Not that the *gruagach* sought a fireside blether this darkest of nights, nor even a taste of the *cailleach's* famed heather ale. Truth be told, Devorgilla slept . . . if her intermittent snores and wheezes were any indication.

For a good long while, the *gruagach* peered down at the old woman, then gave a light wave of her hand, filling the room with a soft, shimmering mist of palest green. A wee precautionary measure to keep the crone lost in her dreams, and to win herself a few unobserved moments to look about and see if her quiet urgings had been heeded.

Or if a stronger, more forceful intervention would be required.

Hoping not, the *gruagach* paused beside Devorgilla's central hearth fire, turned a lingering glance on the soft-glowing clumps of turf. Acknowledging a weakness she usually suppressed, she allowed herself one deep-drawn breath of the homey, peat-scented smoke, savoring its heart-piercing familiarity before she moved on.

Before she regretted her chosen path.

But the smoky-sweet smell of the burning peat clung to her, its wispy blue curls seeming to follow her across the tidy, stone-flagged floor. Her throat tight—far too tight for one such as she—the *gruagach* ignored her yearning, and hastened toward a rough wooden shelf running the length of the far wall.

The *cailleach's* stock of spelling goods was kept here, and somewhere amidst its clutter ought be the object she sought: a small vial of precious content—sacred earth collected from the grave of Eithne, mother of Saint Columba. And known by all to have miraculous properties.

A more powerful protection could scarce be had . . . not that the *gruagach* would e'er tell Devorgilla any such thing. The *cailleach* could work wonders of her own with her fossilized bat's wings and powdered toe bone of toads.

It just wouldn't hurt to see a bit of stronger magic, tactfully presented as earth snatched from beneath a slumbering *tarbh uisge,* slipped in with the rest.

In especial when one's opponent walked in such hate.

Aye, to be sure, no one would frown on her for claiming the earth came from the lair of a water bull—the most feared of all creatures to dwell in Highland lochs.

Old Devorgilla herself had been known to twist the truth a time or two. Albeit only for the benefit of those who depended on her skill.

Thus satisfied in her wee deception, the *gruagach* searched amongst Devorgilla's treasures until she happened upon her own contribution to the crone's supply of charms. And to her great relief, the vial she'd slipped amongst the clutter proved empty. Only a residual glimmer of soft, luminous green remained.

A faint glow at the bottom of the vial.

The crone had taken the bait.

Her heart much lighter, the *gruagach* dropped a kiss on Devorgilla's furrowed cheek. Then she smiled. A wan smile and far too fleeting, but a *sweet* smile nonetheless.

And one that, if only for a moment, made her look almost as real and lovely as she had in her most fondly remembered guise.

The one just past, when she'd been the young bride of a braw MacLean man and gone by the name of Lileas.

"One-and-twenty, two-and-twenty, three-and-twenty . . ."

Panting in a manner that could nowise be called feminine, Amicia paused for breath on the twenty-third step, one hand pressed to the curve of her hip, the other planted firmly against her breasts.

A scowl dark as the rainy night soiled her sweat-dampened brow, and her spirits, usually high, were in grave danger of swinging as foul as the musty air in this forsaken, out-of-the-way stair tower.

"I' faith!" she gasped, speaking to Boiny. Though, at the moment, achy-limbed and exhausted as she was, she'd shout her frustration to any who'd lend her an ear.

"Death itself would be kinder than traipsing up and down these stairs yet one more time," she told her tongue-lolling companion.

Wisely supine on the next landing, just two circular steps above her, Boiny cocked a canine brow, fullest sympathy in his milky-brown eyes.

She ought to be so sensible.

Ought to still be sitting straight-backed at her place at the high table . . . ignoring Janet's sullen-eyed glares as best she could. Or better yet, safely ensconced within the sanctuary of her own bedchamber, abed and sleeping.

Blessedly oblivious to her cares and the terrors of never-ending spiral stairs.

The rigors of mounting, descending, and reascending them.

A torture she'd engaged in every evening for the last three nights. Each time, she'd escaped the high table by pleading a wish to retire early. Then, with old Boiny trotting along at her heels, she'd made for the most remote turnpike stair in Coldstone Castle and used its smooth-worn steps to pare her well-fleshed form.

To *hopefully* whittle down her welling curves.

And, since her husband would ne'er have desired her enough to *steal* her as his more romantically inclined ancestors had been known to do, to better her chances of at least being an *un*shunned wife.

But even now, after days of tedious, ongoing labors, she could not detect a hint of improvement in her generously curved hips. Not one wee indication that the full-rounded swell of her breasts had diminished.

Far from it, they pressed damp and heaving against her straining bodice . . . large and cushiony-seeming as always.

Infinitely annoying.

Swiping the back of her hand over her perspiring brow before another bead of stinging sweat could roll onto her eyelashes, she gritted her teeth and prepared to climb and descend the stairs one last time.

Only through persistence would she succeed at making *less* of herself.

Succeed at making herself more appealing for Magnus MacKinnon.

Making herself more . . . delicate and nymphlike.

More like wee tiny-bosomed Janet.

A maid he clearly favored despite his firm denials.

"We've seen them kiss, haven't we, lad?" She leaned down to stroke Boiny's gray head as she passed him on the landing. "And the way he looks at her, speaks to her! As if she'd melt unless treated with fullest care . . . fair smothered with charm."

Her ire mounting, Amicia climbed to where the next wall sconce flickered, pausing just long enough to choke on its smoking torch flame before she wheeled about and began her final trek down the dank-smelling stairs.

"That teensy-waisted viper has coldest steel flowing in her veins, I vow it," she huffed, not bothering to speak softly.

Nor to keep the bitterness from her tone.

No one could hear her save old Boiny, the damp walls, and the constant patter of rain on stone.

Or so she thought until the swish of heavy skirts and a not-so-discreet cough told her otherwise.

Feeling as if a storm of ill fortune had just unleashed its wrath upon her, she looked down the stairwell to see Dagda peering up at her through the gloom.

Coldstone Castle's self-proclaimed seneschal stood beneath an arrow slit window not four steps below her, a small but well-burning torch clutched in her hand. The fair Janet hovered just behind her. A beam of moonlight coming through the window slit fell slantwise across the younger woman's face, emphasizing her ethereal beauty and glossing her flaxen braids to purest, shimmering silver.

A hot-pulsing ache, deep and tight, began spreading through Amicia's chest. Even worse—because she couldn't conceal it—a bead of sweat rolled down her forehead and dropped off the end of her nose.

Ne'er had she felt more ungainly.

Less a lady.

A stricken moan rose in her throat, lodging there, for she wasn't about to let such an audible admission of distress pass her lips.

So she allowed herself the most manly gesture of swiping her sleeve across her damp brow—then sought to salvage her pride by drawing herself up to her full, lofty height, the minuscule Janet be damned.

Squaring her shoulders, she broke the silence at last. "A good eventide to you."

Dagda's brow lifted. "We thought you had gone

abovestairs, my lady," she said, her expression a strange mix of surprise and thoughtful, almost motherly concern.

"And so I did—but I ne'er said what tower I meant to climb," Amicia blurted, too unnerved by Janet's stare to bite back the tart response.

"Well met," the old woman shot back, surprising her. "You have a quick wit—that is something you will have cause to make good use of in this household."

Amicia nodded, not quite sure what to say.

Closing the short distance between them, Dagda held up her torch and peered closely at Amicia's face.

"When you were not in your chamber, we fretted you had lost your way in the dark passages," she said, the concerned tone back again. "This keep is nowise so large as your Baldoon, but it has its hazards," she added, sliding a glance at Janet.

That one, all round-eyed and gawking, looked anything but concerned—save mayhap for fear that, in her wild-looking state, Amicia had run full mad and might spring upon her lily-white throat any moment.

Or unsheathe her talons and do serious damage to the rose-petal skin of her oh-so-finely-boned face.

Amicia almost hooted.

Little did the fragile-looking beauty know that her very delicateness struck dread in Amicia's heart.

Dagda reached to smooth a strand of damp hair from Amicia's brow. "No one e'er treads this corner of Coldstone . . . none save bats and mice, I'd reckon." Lowering her voice, she angled closer. "Some, like the old laird, even claim the spirits of restless MacKinnons walk these stairs. Is that what you were about, my lady? Wandering the dark, looking for Coldstone's ghosts?"

"I—" Amicia began, but shut her mouth again as quickly.

She could not think of a single logical reason for stomping up and down the turnpike stair of the castle's most remote tower.

Moistening her lips, she glanced around, sought an answer in the shadow-hung stairwell. Had she known Coldstone was thought to be haunted, she would have grasped any ghost—MacKinnon or otherwise—as an excuse.

As was, she had none.

Until she spotted her dear Boiny making his lumbering way down the stone steps, padding ever nearer, his raggedy tail swishing in affectionate greeting.

Upon reaching her, he nudged her side, leaned hard against her. And just the feel of him, his freely given strength and devotion, warmed her through and through.

Enough so to give her the cheek to lie.

"I was looking for Boiny," she declared, dropping a hand to rub behind his ears. "He was missing from my chamber, so I set off to find him. . . . Obviously, I have."

Dagda gave the dog a skeptical look. "That old beast scarce leaves the hearthside," she said, doubt lacing her words. "But he does seem to have taken to you. . . . Mayhap he was seeking *your* company and lost his way?"

Amicia shrugged, feigning nonchalance.

Lifting her chin, she leveled an earnest gaze at the seneschal, asked the question she'd nigh forgotten, flummoxed as she had been until Boiny's timely appearance.

"What took you to my bedchamber?"

A defiant jut to her own chin, Janet stepped out of the shadows. "No one knows Magnus better than I do—he is a braw man and has many . . . *needs*," she said, her tone iced politeness. "Since he has decided to keep you, I but sought to assure your chamber is appointed to his tastes."

"This keep boasts no finer quarters," Amicia gave right back, for once gladful of her overflowing coffers and the many MacLean luxuries she'd brought with her. "Now I am here, my husband's comforts and needs shall be tended by my hand, never you worry."

Emboldened by the way Janet gaped at her, Amicia opened her mouth to embellish her warning, but before she could, the younger woman gathered her skirts, spun on her heel, and fair flew down the curving stone stairs.

Dagda gave a snort of approval. "That one needed a dressing-down. E'er too fond of herself, she is."

And looking quite taken with *herself,* the old woman gestured to the down-winding stairs. "Be you ready to quit this musty tower so we can retire to your bedchamber?" She cast a dubious glance at Boiny. "With your friend, if it pleases you."

Amicia blinked. *"We?"*

"There you have the rights of it," Dagda said, already starting down the stairs. "With your lady mother having passed when you were but a bairn, I thought a wee discreet talk might be in your good interest."

"In my good interest?" Amicia echoed, catching up with her.

Surely the woman didn't mean what Amicia thought she meant?

But the incongruously dreamy look lighting the seneschal's face said she did.

Gruff-voiced, stern-gazing old Dagda wanted to speak to her about . . . *that.*

The bedding ceremony and what came on its heels.

Amicia swallowed, seeing no way to refuse the offer without giving offense.

Aye, she had no real course save to tag along back to her quarters, settle herself before the hearth fire, and dutifully listen to Dagda's advice.

So long as she managed to hide what she already knew—the deliciously wicked knowledge she'd used all manner of bribes and threats to pry from her good-sisters' reluctant lips—all should be well.

Such things were best kept to herself until she chose to reveal them . . . to her husband, one tantalizing gem of wisdom at a time.

If she could scrounge up the nerve.

Chapter Six

❖

$\mathscr{A}$FTER A LONG TREK THROUGH COLD and draughty passageways that smelled of mold and worse things Amicia didn't care to identify, she paused at a heavy oaken door and waited for Boiny's stiff-legged gait to bring him to her side before setting her hand to the latch and freeing the way into her bedchamber.

Handsome quarters that had once belonged to her husband's much-sung ancestor, Reginald of the Victories, the builder of Coldstone Castle. A legend in his day and, could prattling tongues be believed, so revered that, after his death, his chamber had stood empty and unused for centuries.

But a faint air of sadness permeated the room, and as she always tried to remember to do, Amicia offered a silent prayer for the good of Reginald's soul as she stepped across the threshold.

Pale moonlight slanted through tall, arch-topped windows set into shallow recesses along the opposite wall and, as usual, the air in the chamber struck her as colder than it ought to be. The shutters stood open, allowing a breeze to circulate, but even the cold damp of the salt wind could not account for the bone-deep chill that seemed to come more from the tower's thick walling than the blustery night.

Chiding herself for harboring any such foolhardy notion, Amicia scanned the chamber before moving deeper into its dimly lit depths—a precaution her father, and then her brothers, had e'er drilled into her, claiming what a tempting ransom prize she'd make with her high looks and generous MacLean coffers just waiting to be emptied for her release.

She took a deep breath, the irony of her fate squeezing her heart.

A fate that had her standing disheveled and shivering on the threshold to a room filled with every frippery MacLean coin could procure, bride to a man who wanted neither her wealth nor her supposedly bountiful charms.

A man who had ne'er wanted her despite the many times she'd tried to win his regard and favor in their youth.

And now she knew why.

It was not because their clans had oft been at odds over the years. Nor because her own father supposedly charmed and soiled a MacKinnon beauty only to abandon her to marry Amicia's long-dead mother—a charge her da had refuted to his dying day.

Nay, her failure to attract Magnus MacKinnon's eye was because he was a man whose tastes ran toward the dainty.

The delicate and golden-haired, not the dark and well-rounded.

Annoyance pulsing through her, Amicia bit back an

epithet she did not want to let loose with Dagda hovering so close at her side. She noted that someone had placed another brick or two of peat on the hearthstone, and her throat thickened at the gesture, her irritation fading.

Her husband's people, with one notable exception, had welcomed her, allowing her into their hearts and showing her naught but kindness.

Vowing to repay them a thousandfold—and hopefully win her husband's love in the process—she willed her own heart to stop flipping so foolishly. She rubbed her arms against the cold and stared across the room at the slow-burning turf fire.

Recently tended, the peats glowed a fine deep red and their smoking warmth gentled the worst of night's chill, while a small charcoal brazier hissing in one corner provided additional comfort.

Intent on seeking his own, Boiny made a low, rumbling sound deep in his chest and nudged past her into the room, heading straight for the hearth, where he circled a few times before settling himself with a well-contented old-dog grunt.

Dagda sniffed.

The noise startled Amicia. She blinked and swung around to face the older woman, remembering with some embarrassment why the seneschal had elected to accompany her to her chamber.

"Did I not tell you that great beast is e'er betaking himself where it's warm?" Dagda eyed Boiny, her face a mask of light and shadow, uplit by the sputtering rush dip still clutched in her hand.

"Warmth and . . . *softness*," the seneschal declared, thrusting the torch into an iron wall bracket near the door. "While life is in me, I swear such is all men want save a full belly and an occasional excuse to swing their swords and bellow at each other."

"You know much of men?" Amicia tried not to appear doubtful.

"Enough to ken that one"—Dagda jerked her chin toward the dog—"will scarce be leaving this room with such fine new trappings to wallow in."

Amusement playing across her usually stern-set features, the unlikely seneschal used the toe of her black-booted foot to lift the edge of one of the many luxuriously furred skins spread upon the floor—just one of the MacLean luxuries Amicia's brothers had sent along as part of her bridal baggage.

"No man, four-legged or otherwise, will seek his comforts elsewhere if such succor awaits him at his own hearthside," Dagda said with another sidelong glance at Boiny.

Her point made, she turned a shrewd eye on Amicia. "A prudent woman will assure that her husband's needs are well satisfied. In especial, the fleshly ones."

Amicia gave a quick nod of what she hoped would appear as polite appreciation. "To be sure, I will heed your advice," she said, fighting the urge to squirm beneath the other's penetrating stare.

"See that you do, and you will ne'er sleep in a cold bed," Dagda advised in a brisk tone.

Amicia moistened her lips. "I ken what to expect," she said, praying her flushed cheeks didn't reveal just how much, or the *sort* of things, she knew.

But Dagda's snort allayed any such fears. "Knowing what happens when a man and a woman join has scarce little to do with the satisfying part."

Shaking her head, she gave Amicia another narrow-eyed stare, then began bustling about, busying herself lighting candles and assuring the hanging cresset lamps held enough sweet-scented oil to burn until the small hours.

"Aye, lassie, there is much I could tell you about a woman's duties—and how to please a husband above and beyond them," she said as she fluffed the pillows and bolsters at the head of the great four-poster bed.

She slid a conspiratorial look in Amicia's direction. "Give me a moment to see that the fire's been tended with proper care, and then we will have our blether," she said, anticipation glowing on her face.

Amicia stared at her, watching as she jabbed an iron poker at the smoldering peat. Blessedly, her dreamy expression, however absurd-looking on such an age-furrowed brow, went a long stretch in helping Amicia tamp down her earlier agitation.

Even so, Dagda's persistent babble about *amorous concerns* made her stomach flutter and her palms dampen—despite the sound counsel her brothers' wives had given her regarding such privy matters.

Truth be told, she suspected her belly plagued her *because* of the things they'd shared with her!

Things that, in her heart of hearts, she had to admit warmed and excited her.

In earlier years, Magnus MacKinnon could charm the birds from the trees with one dimpled smile and a toss of his bronze-maned head. Should Magnus-the-man e'er reclaim and make use of such skills, she'd melt all over herself.

Half-afraid her wanton musings and most cherished wishes stood etched on her forehead, she turned aside, hiding her face from the other woman's sharp perusal.

Feeling both wicked and exhilarated at the same time, she hastened to the chamber's largest table, an elaborately carved affair of blackest oak, and with a slightly trembling hand, she poured herself a measure of fine Rhenish wine—yet another token of her brothers' largesse.

Her gaze on the windows and the dark, wet night looming beyond them, she lifted her cup in silent toast to her good-sisters' sage advice.

Bold and thrilling advice.

And now old Dagda with her hawkish stare and the wart on her chin sought to instruct her as well.

Shuddering—or mayhap simply a-shiver from the room's persistent chill, she tossed down her wine in one throat-burning gulp, not knowing whether to laugh or grimace.

So she opted for something in between and summoned an expression that she hoped would appear neither mocking nor incredulous.

Then she turned around . . . and saw her failure at once.

It stared back at her in the angle of Dagda's head and the slight narrowing of the older woman's eyes. Indeed, it crackled in the cold air between them.

"You think it folly for me to speak of men and their needs."

"I think you . . . mean well." Amicia spoke the truth, knowing a lie would be pointless.

"Och, but I do, never you doubt it." The wistful expression back again, Dagda plunged her poker into the peats with renewed vigor, thrusting deep until fine blue wisps of earthy-sweet smoke began curling upward. "There is not a day what begins or ends that does not see me striving to do my best for those I hold dear—even if some will ne'er thank me."

She looked up from her task just long enough to send Amicia a piercing woman-to-woman stare. Not that Amicia paid her much heed for the seneschal's previously uttered words still echoed in her ears.

Men and their needs, she'd said.

A braw man with many needs, Janet had cooed on the turnpike stair.

Similar words, but with her husband's fey-like cousin fashioning hers as barbs, then using the softest of innuendo-laden purrs to send debilitating poison straight into Amicia's heart.

And ooooh, but the little she-cat had found her target.

Suddenly more chilled than yet before, Amicia leaned against the table, needing, blessing, its firm support. Faith, just recalling the implied intimacy of Janet's taunt watered her knees.

The other's measuring glances, and the malice e'er lurking behind her innocent-seeming blue eyes, had little flickers of ill ease tripping down Amicia's spine.

But worst of all, her rival's fragile loveliness sent sharp-edged shards of jealousy jabbing into the soft, most vulnerable areas of her heart.

"I was not always as I am now . . ." Dagda poked a sudden finger into Amicia's arm. "Tush, lass—many were the suitors who came chapping at my door."

Amicia jerked, nigh tipping over the wine ewer she'd left sitting precariously close to the table's edge. Saints, she hadn't even noticed the old woman cross the room.

"I know you were married," she said, her gaze flitting to the other's stiff black skirts.

"Aye, and to the finest man in the Isles," Dagda sighed, a faraway look on her face. "Bonny, he was, too—as was I." She touched a hand to the silver-shot braids wound so tightly about her head. "Niall loved to comb my hair, loved to—"

"Dagda, please, you need not speak of your marriage," Amicia cut in, not missing the sheen of moisture in the old woman's eyes. "I would not see you troubled."

"I be fine, lass, never you worry." Dagda swiped the backs of her fingers across her cheek. "I lost Niall and . . . *och,* 'twas long ago. I but meant to tell you my hair was once as black as yours—Niall even composed a song of praise for its color. He likened the shade to a raven's wing. And his own hair . . . mercy, but just looking at it would steal my breath away."

She paused to pour herself a cup of wine, took several long sips before she spoke again. "His hair was the same dark russet shade as your Magnus's. A deep burnished copper, it was, and so thick and glossy." She sighed, remembering. "In a good summer, if he stood in the sun, it would gleam with the finest streaks of copper and gold. Ooo, but I was e'er putting my hands to that mane of his, and he . . . he used to bathe in mine."

"Bathe in your hair?" Amicia blurted before she could stay her tongue.

Dagda nodded. "Such are the things I wish to speak to you about." She cocked her head to one side, fixed Amicia with a shrewd, almost cagey look. "Did you ken a man can be brought to his knees if a woman allows him to bury his face in her unbound hair?"

Aye, she *had* heard the like—from her brother Donall the Bold's lady wife, Isolde. But rather than reveal any such knowledge, she feigned a look of astonishment and shook her head.

The bait taken, Dagda angled closer, lowered her

voice. "If you truly wish to have a man at your mercy, you will let him scent you."

"*Scent me?*"

This time, Amicia's perplexity was genuine.

The old woman glanced about as if she feared the walls would sprout ears. "*Give him your scent,* lass." She spoke so softly Amicia scarce heard her. "That is the way of it . . . letting him breathe in the scent o' you. And from where'er he wishes."

Amicia gulped.

Audibly.

She had a very good idea of exactly where Dagda meant. "You let your Niall do . . . *that?*"

"Och, aye, and many a fair night, too," Dagda revealed, her lower lip wobbling a bit on the admission. "There is hardly a more potent way to bind a man on you than to brand your scent on him."

"Men like that?"

Amicia could scarce believe it.

But Dagda bobbed her head. "The most braw amongst 'em will drop to his knees and beg, once he has . . . eh . . . *nuzzled* you that way."

"Why are you telling me this?" Amicia asked, no longer feeling anywhere near as worldly-wise as she'd done upon awakening that morn. She swallowed, willed her heart to cease thumping so hard against her ribs. "Why do you care how we . . . er . . . *fare together?*"

Dagda made a wry face. "See you, I ken your Magnus over well. He is braw and well-lusted, even if he is a mite sore-battered and foul of temper since his return from Dupplin. His current state is only the more reason to heed my advice—he will need powerful incentives to push past all that troubles him." She looked down, brushed at her skirts. "I would know you prepared when the time comes for him to bed you."

Dagda then glanced up, leveled a steady gaze on Amicia. "I tell you, too, because he has e'er minded me of Niall when he was young. If you ken how to properly please him, and bind him to you rightly, he will love you for all his days."

"And that would please you?"

"Naught would make me happier." Dagda tipped her wine cup to her lips, drained it. "It would do my old heart good to see that fine laddie as besotted with his good lady wife as my Niall was with me—and I with him," she said, her eyes misting. "Niall used to say he needed me like the air he breathed. And me, I'm still a-needing him that way. Even with him gone all these long years."

Amicia looked toward the windows, caught a glimpse of the moon through the rain-filled mist. "You have cause to miss him greatly," she said, sorrowing indeed for the other woman's loss. "I am sorry."

"And I thank you, but there is not much good it may do me—your sorrow or my own." Dagda drew a long, quivering breath. "A fever took Niall—and my two bairns with him. Naught can return them to me. Not prayers, not rantings, not even the most infinite regret."

Biting her lip for she truly didn't know what to say, Amicia took a step forward and would've drawn her into a sincere if somewhat awkward embrace, but the old woman sidestepped her with surprising agility.

"I told you, there be no sense in rueing what is past and canna be undone." She cut the air with a dismissive wave of her hand. "I have had my work here to content me. Niall and Donald MacKinnon were kin, so the old laird gave me a roof o'er my head when I had nowhere else to go, see you."

Turning aside, she pretended to pat her hair, but, in truth, she swiped at her eyes again. "Donald's three lads needed mothering," she went on, surreptitiously wiping her hand on her sleeve. "And with me having lost my own two, my coming here served us both better than well."

But not well enough to obliterate the soul-deep ache inside you.

Keeping the observation to herself, Amicia went to stand in the chamber's only window embrasure. Her heart wrenched for the older woman, for she understood only too well the need to put a braw face to the world. To preserve dignity at all costs and forfeitures, lest others think you weak.

She'd done the same for many a year and only recently changed her views . . . deciding to abandon decorum in favor of desire.

With more of a jerk than she'd intended, she threw open the shutters and welcomed the in-sweeping rush of the cold night air, the moon-silvered glint of falling rain. Bracing her hands on the icy-damp stone of the window ledge, she stared out across the night-darkened sea and imagined a faint glimmer of luminous green flickering on the distant horizon, but when she blinked and looked again, the strange light was gone.

Only the sorrow remained, the chamber's own and the sharper pain pouring off Dagda to flood the room, much as the old woman sought to hide her hurt behind posturings and bluster.

Amicia took a deep breath, drew in the scents of wet stone and the sea. Familiar scents. Well-loved. Sighing, she rubbed her thumb across her sapphire ring, savored the warmth of its heavy gold band, the satiny smoothness of the large cabochon gemstone.

Her own little piece of shining hope.

An ever-constant reminder that life was far too short and dear, too easily extinguished, for anyone not to be courageous enough to chase a dream.

Behind her, a not-quite-muffled sniffle broke her reverie . . . and set her course.

E'er one to suffer her own pains much better than she could bear seeing others enduring theirs, she stiffened her back as best she could and sought hard for some light-toned banter to toss the other woman's way.

Regrettably, the only thing she could think of was Magnus MacKinnon scenting her!

Nevertheless, she turned, prepared to blurt . . . something.

Anything.

But Dagda had moved back to the door and was examining Amicia's new fur-lined mantle. It hung on a wall peg—exactly where she intended it to remain, for Devorgilla, bless her good heart, had fashioned a garment sumptuously warm, but of a far-too-cumbersome weight to be practical.

"'Tis of great richness," Dagda said, fingering the cloak's fastenings. She lifted a fold, peered hard at the pattern of black flecks scattered across the lining's soft, yellowish-white fur. "Be that ermine? Niall was e'er promising me a fine fur-lined—"

"Aye, ermine, it is," Amicia cut in before the old woman could wax on about her late husband again, distressing herself. "My brother received ells of it in trade some while ago. But, Dagda, I would know more of

Reginald and his lady . . ." she began, her voice trailing off at a clamor outside the chamber.

Heavy, fast-approaching footsteps, the chink of metal—a single swift pause before, without so much as a knock or warning, the door swung wide, and by no means gently.

Magnus burst into the room, his brow fierce, every fury-driven inch of him clad in full knightly regalia.

"Saints o' mercy!" Dagda cried, a startled hand flying to her breast.

Amicia's breath caught in shock. Heart in her throat, she stared at him, too stunned for words.

By the hearthside, Boiny gave a hackle-raising growl until he recognized the commotion's perpetrator. His curiosity thus assuaged, he dropped his bulk back onto the rushes and returned to sleep.

But Amicia stood transfixed, her gaze latching on the wicked-looking battle-ax clutched in her husband's powerful, white-knuckled hand.

Nor did she miss the flash of mail beneath the voluminous plaid slung so proudly over his shoulder. He'd girded on his sword belt, and, even now, in the quiet confines of her chamber, his free hand hovered perilously close to the hilt of his death-bringing brand.

Breathing hard, he stared at them, his expression black enough to curdle blood. Wordless.

Amicia began to tremble. "For truth, here is a . . . surprise," she gasped, digging her fingers into her skirts to hide their shaking.

"Aye, and a most foul one, I'll be bound!" he rapped out, looking past rather than *at* her, his heated blue gaze sweeping the room. "Praise the saints naught has befallen you."

Her own mettle recovered, Dagda grabbed a fistful of his plaid, gave it a healthy shake. "Sons o' Beelzebub, laddie!" she scolded. "Are you ale-witted this e'en? Or have you lost your wits completely to come pounding in here armed to the teeth and spitting fire at two innocent women?"

Ignoring her, he jerked his plaid from her grasp, then swung round to glower at the opened door. Amicia stared at it, too, quite certain the heavy oaken panels still vibrated from being flung against the lime-washed wall—a wall that now bore a notable dent where the iron door latch had crashed into it.

"Why wasn't the door bolted?" he demanded.

Amicia moistened her lips, curled her fingers deeper into the folds of her skirts. "Here, sir? In your home?" Her voice sounded hoarse even to her own ears. "I do not know why it should have been?"

"Neither do I, my lady, and that is the problem," he gave back, raking a hand through the deep chestnut waves of his hair. Some of the bluster appeared to slip from him, only to return with a vengeance the instant his gaze lit on the door's unused drawbar.

He stepped toward her and placed one ever-so-firm hand on her shoulder, looked deeper into her eyes than anyone had ever done. "The Fiend take me if I e'er catch you behind an unbarred door again, do you hear me, lass?"

Amicia stared at him, sore tempted to brush aside his demand. But, to her own surprise, she found herself nodding. "As you wish," she acquiesced, determining to do just as he'd bid.

But not because his words or even his display of seething fury had cowed her into meek submission.

Nay, she'd follow his order for one reason alone.

That reason being the unsettling thread of fear he couldn't quite keep from his deep, husky voice.

Ill ease rippled all through his great, strapping body, clouding the clear blue of his eyes and overlaying every magnificent inch of him with simmering, scarcely-held-in-check tension.

And as if he sensed she'd glimpsed it, the last of the strain vanished from his handsome face and he gave her a wan smile—if the slight uptilt at one corner of his mouth could be counted as a smile.

"It is not my wish to frighten you," he said, still peering deep into her eyes. "Just do as I ask and I promise to do my best not to plague you with such an outburst again."

A loud snort came from behind them, near the table, quickly followed by the *glug-glugging* noise of wine being poured. Dagda appeared at their sides a moment later, offering two brimming cups of the potent Rhenish wine.

The instant her hands were free, she planted them on her black-skirted hips and turned on Magnus, her dark eyes flashing. "And if you don't mean to be a-scaring the life out of your womenfolk, mayhap you ought not stomp around this pile o' stones on dark and windy nights a-warning of dangers what don't exist?"

Magnus cocked a russet brow, took a hearty gulp of wine. "And what were you doing *a-stomping* round this tower so late of a night? Keeping Lady Amicia from her night's rest on a . . . *dark and windy night*?"

"Mayhap there would not have been a cause for my visit if you would be busy about your duty keeping her warm on such nights." The mischievous glint in Dagda's eye took the sting from her tart reply.

Hitching up her skirts, she swished to the door. But she paused on the threshold, raised a forefinger. "Be sure to bolt the drawbar," she warned. "You wouldn't want old Reginald or his lady to come looking to see who's in their bed!"

And then with a knowing wink and whirl of black linen, she was gone, slipping away into the corridor's gloom without so much as a further glance or fare-thee-well.

Magnus stared after her, his brow darkening again. "That one e'er walks on the precipice," he said, swirling the wine in his cup. "May the saints be kind if e'er she takes a false step."

"I vow she has her reasons for being as she is," Amicia said, feeling a need to defend the old woman.

"To be sure," Magnus responded with equal speed.

But his eyes narrowed and he looked anything but charitable as he brought the wine cup to his lips and downed its contents in one long swallow.

He set down the empty cup with an overloud *clack*, and regarded her with sharp, measuring eyes. "Like as not, we all have justification for our actions—if only to our own good selves."

"And what are yours?" Amicia put down her own cup, the wine untouched.

She took a heavy linen napkin from the table, ran its embroidered edges through her fingers as she looked at him, waiting. Their gazes locked, and she swallowed, her mouth suddenly dry.

"Why are you here, my lord? Now, this night, before propriety deems you join me?"

At his silence, she lowered her gaze to the battle-ax he still clutched so fiercely. And the ax was by no means his only weapon. The bulk of his broadsword, its hilt and scabbard, loomed ominously apparent beneath his plaiding. She'd also counted at least two dirks thrust beneath his belt.

"I would know the truth, Magnus." She used his given name for the first time—the sound of it on her tongue both strange and thrilling.

"I simply wish to know you safe."

"Know me safe?" she echoed, sensing more behind his actions than his words revealed.

He nodded, and a nervous-twitching muscle in his jaw confirmed her suspicions.

"If I cannot greet our marriage with overweening gladness, the very least I can do is assure no harm comes to you."

She crumpled the napkin, let it drop back onto the table. "I have been looking out for myself for many years. Despite my brothers' brawn and concern."

Disillusionment and a frightening sense of hopelessness filling her chest, she struggled to keep from blowing out a breath of pure frustration. His indifference in their youth had lacerated her heart and now he would rub salt in the wound by vowing to protect her whilst *he* grieved her soul.

She appreciated his protection, but she wanted his *love*.

"There are more grave hurts than physical ones, my lord," she said, challenging him. "Would you help me to allay those as well?"

He touched her cheek, toyed with a strand of her hair. "It would be better for you if we do not go down that road, my lady."

"And if I am already more than halfway along it?"

He pressed his lips together and just looked at her.

Then he took his hand from her face and the loss of his touch, however innocent and fleeting, sluiced through her like ice water, leaving an empty, unquenchable void.

Amicia curled her own hands to fists, resisted the urge

to grab and shake him. He was beginning to remind her of her brother Donall the Bold at his vaunting best.

Or worst!

Aye, save for the bright gleam of his rich auburn hair, so lustrous in the flickering candlelight, he looked exactly like Donall in one of his *I-am-the-laird* and *no-one-ought-question-him* moods.

Beneath her skirts, one foot began to tap furiously—thanks to the thick layer of furred skins spread on the floor, no telltale *tap-tappings* sounded to reveal her agitation.

He would know her safe.

Old Dagda would see her pleasuring him.

Amicia's chest heaved, the longings unleashed by his simple touch tearing her heart. *She* just wanted a home . . . a husband to love, and love her, a hearthside to call her own, and a bairn or two to bounce on her knee within the cozy circle of its warmth.

Instead, she'd won the leal affection of a doddering old man and his equally aged dog, a fierce-eyed female seneschal with the heart of a bawd, and a husband who'd rather skulk about encased in mail and suspicion than climb into her bed, wearing naught but his fine dimpled smile and the desire to make her his own.

Determined to claim that smile *and* the pleasure any way she must, she indicated the battle-ax, which, to his credit, he'd rather sheepishly laid upon the table when she'd turned a disapproving stare on the weapon.

"From whom would you keep me safe, good sir? The fierce Norsemen of old have not threatened these waters in centuries and we are at peace with all our nearest neighbors." She reached to trail one finger along his mailed sleeve, gave him the best little smile she could muster. "Or do you wish to protect me from the ghosts of the fabled Reginald and his lady? They are the ones of the curse, are they not?"

The quick snapping together of his brows told her they were.

"I have yet to hear their tale," she went on, hoping the recitation of the legend might prod him out of his tight-lipped silence . . . urge him to open up to her. "Will you tell me of them? Dagda—"

"Is that why she was in here? Filling your head with her crazed tales of ice-cold stones and lost love?" he jerked, staring at her. "Heed not a word of her prattle. And that is all the great MacKinnon curse is, I promise you—foolish prattle," he vowed, his deep voice vehement. "A fireside tale for a long and dark winter night, naught more. The day centuries-old sorrows and walking ghosts harm a hair on any living soul's head is the day a cow will fly to the moon."

"But there *is* something amiss. You would not have stormed in here tonight, girded for battle, were that not so." Amicia folded her arms, lifted her chin. "I would know what that something is. A nameless foe cannot be fought."

"Think you I do not know that?"

"I am sure you know much, my lord. And of things I would enjoin you to share with me," she said, leveling her gaze at him.

His gaze slid downward. Following it, her heart leapt to her throat, for her crossed arms had lifted and plumped her already generous breasts and the clinging linen of her gown drew especial emphasis to their welling fullness.

Worst of all, the upper rim of her dusky right nipple peeked above the dip of her low-cut bodice. Nay, truth be told, fully half of her good-sized areola showed! One deep breath and the whole nipple would pop into view.

Uncrossing her arms at once, she tugged the gown into place. "As you can see, sir, I am not a wee and delicate flower afraid of a bit of wind and rain. You needn't shield me. I will not melt if you tell me what troubles you."

He lifted his gaze from her breasts at once. Faith, his face glowed brighter than the brazier! And Amicia had a sneaking suspicion she knew why.

The thought sent a riptide of sparkling pleasure shooting through her, even warming her *there* in the sweetest, most secret part of her lower belly, but she'd test the notion and its possibilities later—in a more auspicious moment.

For the nonce, she contented herself with tilting her head to the side and studying him through carefully lowered lashes. "I ask you again—why are you here?"

He cleared his throat. "Unexpected tidings brought me here, my lady," he said, his flushed cheeks proving just as unsettling as his frown.

"What tidings?"

The scowl returned. "Sakes, but you are a persistent wench," he said, ramming a hand through his hair. "'Twas the privy seat if you must know."

"*The privy seat?* The one that collapsed beneath your da?"

Magnus nodded. "Aye, the very one."

She opened her mouth to ask him what the broken privy seat had to do with his skulking about of a night, armed to the teeth, but before she could, he swung about.

Crossing to the door in three long strides, he closed it and slid home the greased drawbar in one smooth movement.

Her wide-eyed gaze not leaving him, Amicia snatched her *arisaid* off the back of a chair and swirled its soft woolen folds around her shoulders, shielding her dishevelment and, above all, any wayward-inclined nipples from view.

But when he wheeled back around, he wore an expression so bitter earnest she doubted he would have noticed if *both* of her nipples sprang free to wink at him.

Mayhap not even if they spoke up and said him a fine and merry good-e'en.

Indeed, he drew a deep breath and stared at an undefined spot somewhere across the firelit chamber, his gaze strangely inward-looking.

He patted the hilt of his sword, then lifted the silver-linked hem of his mailed hauberk. "You would know why I burst in here garbed for battle, and so I will tell you," he said, his face granite-set. "My father's plunge into the latrine chute was no accident. See you, I sent a few lads to retrieve the privy seat. I just had an uneasy feeling. A hunch. If you prefer, call it a cold prickling along the back of my neck."

He paused, drew a long breath. "The cesspit was long overdue for a good scouring, so it would not have been a waste of anyone's time. Either way, the lads brought the seat to me a short while ago."

Now he turned to her at last, his gaze steady and penetrating. "The seat had been sawed in two," he said. "And very neatly."

"*Sawed in two?*" The suggestion stole Amicia's breath. "As in a-purpose?"

He nodded.

"That will have been the way of it, aye. Someone wanted Da, or whoe'er happened to use the garderobe, to drown in the cesspit."

Chapter Seven

❧

AMICIA STARED AT HIM, not quite certain she'd heard aright.

Regrettably, the tension hanging thick in the air about him and the hard, firm set of his jaw said she had.

Still, it wouldn't hurt to be sure.

"Are you saying someone deliberately cut through the privy seat?" She pressed the words past lips gone dry with shock. *"A-purpose?"*

He'd been standing before the table, staring down at his discarded battle-ax, but now he turned. "So I have said," he confirmed, his expression like granite. "Would that it were not so."

Amicia blinked, even though his answer did not surprise her. Neither his words nor her own body's reaction to having his looming so tall before her.

So near and imposing.

Soft light from a suspended cresset lamp spilled across his head and shoulders, glinting in the rich chestnut strands of his hair and gilding the silvery rivets of his mailed shirt. The gold-flickering glow also illuminated the disquiet marring his handsome brow.

Her pulse quickening, she studied him through lowered lashes. His proximity and even the simple act of breathing in the same air undid her. The heady masculine scent of him, an appealing mix of clean linen, leather, and polished steel, sent long, liquid pulls through the deepest part of her stomach and watered her knees.

Warmth began pulsing through her and everything around them seemed to fade away while her focus on him sharpened to brilliance. Just looking at him branded possession. Even without the dimpled grin and merry eyes of his youth, he made a compelling presence. Strength and irresistible vitality thrummed through him, tantalizing and drawing her despite his dark frown.

Mayhap even because of it.

Truth be told, in his discomfited state, he exuded a smoldering appeal that caught at her heart, filled her with a welter of emotion and unleashed an overwhelming urge to skim her fingertips along the tight-set contours of his face. To smooth away each line of hardness with the gentlest caress.

But nagging memories of reaching out to him in the distant past, and being rebuffed, slid through her, shading and curbing any such compulsion. So she simply smoothed her skirts and contented herself with her determination to claim such liberties soon.

With the good saints on her side, and a wee bit of MacLean daring, mayhap even sooner than she'd dared hope.

Her heart lifting at the possibility, she cast a glance between him and the bolted door. "What you are saying would mean treachery within these walls, my lord."

"Aye, like as not that is the way of it." He sounded as if his very soul quailed at the thought. "Try as I might, I can think of no other explanation." He squeezed shut his eyes for a moment, tunneled his fingers through his hair. "We have a devil supping amongst us, lass. But who?"

Amicia held back for a moment of maddening indecision. She had a very good idea of who could be the instigator behind such vindictive doings. But now was not the time to voice her suspicion—unless she wished to mark herself a jealous shrew.

So she swallowed the accusation and prayed he would not see it in her eyes. "You truly believe so?"

"Och, but I do—regrettably." He glanced down, trailed a finger along the handle of his battle-ax. "I will tell you, too, that I do not believe in curses or ghosts," he said, pinching the wick of a guttering candle before returning his gaze to her.

"It would take an arm almost as strong as my own to saw through well-seasoned oak—an arm attached to a living and breathing person. Someone who is bold, foolhardy, or comfortable enough to move about these walls at their will and leisure."

The implications of his words beat through her but did not lessen her distrust of his cousin. The wee snippet could have cajoled any besotted fool from the garrison to do her will.

Almost certain of it, Amicia cleared her throat, blinked against the smoke rising from the snuffed candle.

"Can the wood not have cracked of its own? A natural fault . . . mayhap rotten inside?" She clutched at other possibilities, however remote. "Once, at Baldoon and in the midst of the Yuletide carousing, a trestle board split clean in two. Could not—"

"Nay, lass, there can be no doubt." He shook his head. "The cut edges bore the marks of the saw's fury. The knave who did this was not only stout-armed, but driven by white-hot rage."

His face grim-set, he went to the window embrasure where he ignored the twin-facing benches, newly adorned with plump, finely embroidered cushions. He stood with his back to her, staring out at the swirls of eddying mist drifting past the window arch.

The night breeze, heavy with the smell of rain, riffled his hair. Firelight from a nearby torch picked out the brightest strands of gold, and Amicia's fingers itched to test the silkiness of those bronze-gleaming highlights. A near all-consuming urge stoked through countless nights of youthful longings.

Shaking off the spell of him, she clasped her hands together and drew a great breath before she spoke. "If this is someone of such a twisted heart, I pray you discover his identity with all haste. For the good of us all."

"Never you worry, I shall," he said without glancing round. "The dastard will soon find himself clapped into Coldstone's deepest pit and regretting the day of his birth. Or mayhap I shall put him to the cliff—let him plunge headlong into the sea as he'd hoped to see one of us hurtle into the cesspit." His hands clenched to tight fists. "On my soul, Amicia, I swear I will let no harm come to you."

Amicia's heart dipped at his use of her name without the formalizing *lady* prefix. A first, and a triumph she seized with gladness. Sweetest pleasure spiraled through her, too, at the fervor in his voice as he'd vowed to protect her.

"I have fullest faith in your ability to safeguard me," she said, melting, a flood tide of preciously guarded images whispering across her heart. "Mayhap I should not tell you, but the truth is, I have long admired your strength and skill, Magnus MacKinnon."

Now he did look over his shoulder. "I—thank you for that," he said, an odd thickness to his voice.

The glow from the brazier revealed a faint tinge of pink stealing onto his cheeks. Perhaps an indication of how uncomfortable her compliments made him—or mayhap how much they pleased him.

And that second notion pleased her.

Inordinately so.

Her sapphire ring seemed to warm on her finger as she looked at him. The possibility, real or imagined, made her heart smile. "See you, I remember from early on, how you e'er won the day at the competitions of strength our clans participated in," she minded him, encouraged.

She circled her thumb over the ring as she waited for his reaction, drew courage—and boldness—from the stone's satiny, almost pulsing warmth. "I vow you e'er left the field as champion."

"Och, nay, lass. There you mistake," he said, turning back to the window, the darkness of the mist-hung night. "I once lost an archery contest by badly overshooting the target. But that was many long years ago and no longer of import." An odd touch of melancholy threaded the softly spoken words.

"For now, in *this* pass, just know that I will guard your safety with the whole of my strength and all the breath in me. That is so sure as night follows day."

His vow, and even more so, the tinge of regret edging his husky-smooth voice, lifted the fine hairs on the back of Amicia's neck. In truth, even whilst flattering, she did not want him to fight for her. She wanted to protect him. To know *him* safe from all darkness and danger. And she loathed the notion of being a responsibility.

Another burden placed upon his shoulders.

She burned for one thing only.

His love and adoration.

A chance to win his heart.

With effort, she tore her gaze from his broad, plaid-draped back, shivers of regret slinking down her own. Unless her eyesight had weakened since her arrival on MacKinnons' Isle, there was now a decided slump to his shoulders and, damn her clumsy-tongued hide, but she feared something she'd said might be the cause of it.

Or mayhap the moon eyes she'd surely been making at him since he'd burst into the bedchamber—despite her best efforts to maintain a composed, *ladylike* demeanor.

To control the yearnings that raged inside her with enough passion to set all the heather ablaze.

Her throat tightening, her eyes filming with sheerest frustration, she turned back to the table, glared down at the gleaming ax blade. The polished steel shone over-bright in the candlelight and the sharpness of its edge left nary a doubt to the damage it could wield.

As could the broadsword hanging at his side, the wicked-looking dirks thrust beneath his waist-belt. Faith and mercy, he even had one sheathed in his boot!

She slid another look at him, eyed the weapons—a veritable arsenal—and tight bands of trepidation coiled around her chest, obliterating all her other emotions.

Her own now paltry seeming concerns.

All save one.

She glanced back to the securely bolted door.

Did he mean to sleep here? Mayhap even in their fine four-postered marriage bed—at her side?

Her heart pounding, she stared at him for a long moment before taking the first step across the skin-strewn floor.

She had to know.

Even if the discovery found him shunning her. The warm-pulsing weightiness spreading through the lower-most reaches of her belly at the thought of lying with him demanded she learn his mind.

So she let the urgently pleasurable sensation spur her forward, toward its braw and bonny source, one brazen footfall after the other.

Fitting or no, the timing propitious or nay, the gnawing need inside her stamped out every last flicker of propriety.

Not that a MacLean e'er walked the earth who'd let seemliness—or risk—bar the way to their deepest desire!

And she was a MacLean—through and through.

Bold and resolute, even if her knees trembled just a wee tiny bit.

She moved closer, chin lifted and shoulders straight, her heart thundering against her ribs. Faith, she could even hear the blood roaring through her ears!

Even Boiny, until now deep in his canine slumber, raised his shaggy gray head to peer at her—his rheumy gaze curious, as if he, too, could hear the insistent hammering.

Only Magnus appeared oblivious.

He stood at a slight angle, the whole strapping length of him silhouetted against the tall, gray arch of the window, his profile silvered by moonlight, softened by shadow.

For one shattering moment, the strange half-light of the embrasure erased the tight lines of strain carved into his face and let her glimpse the Magnus of old—a beautiful lad of spirit and vigor. The dashing young champion with the roguish grin, who'd charmed all the lassies and laid fast claim to Amicia's affections.

A forever claim that had burned all the brighter with each passing year.

An unspoken bond that now consumed her.

Almost upon him, she slowed her pace, savoring the remembrances stirred by his moonlit image, not quite ready to break the spell. But, like old Boiny, he heard her approach and spun to face her, looking at her with eyes filled with light and laughter, and flashing his dimpled smile.

Until the ruddy glow of the firelit room undid the magic of her yearning heart.

Her breath caught at the transformation, her eyes flying wide even as his narrowed in piercing consternation.

"You've gone pale as the moonlight—even as I am looking at you," he said, something in his gaze and his voice making her tingle all over.

"Do you think to stay the night here . . . *with me*?" she blurted before the hard-won steel in her backbone could melt, slide right out of her to form a molten pool around her feet.

"I would think that was obvious," he said, stepping from the embrasure. "Why else would I have bolted the door?"

Amicia drew a breath, prayed she would not stutter in her nervousness. "My pardon. I phrased the question poorly. 'Tis where in here you think to sleep that I would know?" she asked again, this time placing special emphasis on *where*.

"Not where you are thinking," he said, his gaze lighting briefly on the massive four-poster across the room.

He placed his hands on her shoulders, and the intimacy of that small contact, even through her clothes, slid through her like a caress.

"Do not fret yourself, lass. You may be at your ease this night. There will be time anon for . . . *connubial pursuits*." He began kneading her shoulders, his gentling of her and the mention of their joining, however tactfully worded, undoing her, making her breath come in short, shallow gasps.

Then the warmth and concern slipped from his clear blue eyes and the hard, set-faced look returned. "There are enough rich trappings spread about this room for me to make a more than comfortable pallet to sleep on. I' faith, I spent most of the last three years making my bed on the rough heather with naught but my plaid to warm me."

A MacLean to the bone, Amicia seized her chance.

"You may share the bed . . . I do not mind," she heard herself suggest, scarce believing her brazenness but loving her daring.

For one exhilarating moment, giddy excitement streaked through her, but Magnus shattered her hope by stepping back to put a good arm's length between them.

"That would not be wise," he said, looking down to adjust the hang of his plaid. "See you, I shall rise before first light and I have no wish to disrupt your sleep."

"I see very well, my lord," Amicia said, embarrassment sweeping her.

Visibly stiffening, he fixed all his attention on brushing at nonexistent specks of lint on his plaid, the bright mail of his sleeve. "I warrant you see what you believe you see. That is not necessarily the truth of it, lass."

"Nay?" She cocked a brow. "Then what is, my lord?"

He drew a tight breath, clearly uncomfortable. "That I desire an early start to begin looking for the miscreant—"

"You needn't trouble yourself overmuch, I vow—it can only be Janet," she blurted, her frustration and hurt hurling the suspicion at him.

"Wee Janet?" He gaped at her, incredulity stamped all over his bonny face. "Och, but you are sore amiss, lassie, that I promise you."

To her aggravation, he nigh snorted his astonishment. "Did you not hear what I told you? Whoe'er is behind such dark deeds is fueled by hatred. Janet's worst wrath could reap no more trouble than a wet kitten."

Green-tinged heat pouring over her, Amicia struggled to banish the younger woman's image from her mind, but the vexing likeness remained, taunting her with all its fragile loveliness and flaxen-haired charm.

"A wet kitten can have mightily sharp claws," she snapped, feeling about as frail and tender as a plow horse, with her stained and disarranged bodice, her wild and mussed hair.

"Mayhap you are the one who misjudges," she said, trying not to glare.

A shuttered look came over his face and he glanced aside. "I have misjudged many things of late, to be sure. But Janet is kin. I will not think poorly of her."

"Are there any under your roof who are *not* kin?"

That got to him. "Nary a one," he owned, rubbing at

the red-gold stubble on his chin. "Nevertheless, it is pure folly to suspect Janet."

Amicia stifled a huff of indignation. "Your cousin is sore vexed—and surely less delicate than she looks. I would advise you or anyone in the path of her fury to take fullest heed."

Magnus passed a hand over his eyes, shook his head. "Nay, I will not believe it. Not of Janet. Not of anyone of MacKinnon blood."

"Then mayhap you must indeed look to your ghosts," she said with a flare of finest MacLean temper.

"My ghosts?"

"Reginald of the Victories and his lady wife for a start," she tossed at him, too grieved to heed the tightening of his features, the twitch of a muscle in his jaw.

"Dagda tells me they favor this very room," she declared, her cheeks flaming. "Perchance here is as good a place as any to begin your search?"

She marched to the massive four-poster, flipped up a corner of the opulent coverings. "Mayhap they are hiding beneath their bed?"

"Their bed?" This time, he did snort. "Without question, that hulking monstrosity is of great age and has stood in this chamber for a good many years," he owned, speaking as if the words left a bitter taste in his mouth. "And I have no doubt Reginald would have approved of the finery adorning it since your arrival, but I'll swallow my sword if he e'er spent a single night in it. Neither with his doomed lady wife or any other lass."

Amicia let the bedcovers fall, dusted her hands. "So Dagda told me falsehoods?"

"Dagda is a prattling fool, and more the pity she wasn't born a man—with her glib tongue, she would

have made a better teller of tales than my brother Hugh!"
Magnus folded his arms, turned a sharp eye on her. "I am
hoping you have a better head on your shoulders than to
believe such belly-wind?"

"If you do not believe in the tradition, why has the fire
in this chamber not been allowed to go out since their
day? Your own da told me so—that its peats have been
kept alive even though no one used the chamber all these
centuries."

Magnus heaved a great sigh. "Last I heard, *all* hearth
fires hereabouts are kept from fully extinguishing. Or
have you ne'er seen the old women of a household skulking about late at night, burying wee clumps of live turf in
the ashes so a spark can be fanned into a blaze come the
morning?"

He had her there.

Indeed, most clans prided themselves on the claim that
their peat fires had been kept aglow as far back as family
memory could stretch. 'Twas a time-honored tradition
that the fey folk would frown on the household if a fire
wasn't kept to warm them through cold and dark Highland nights.

Aye, he'd maneuvered her into a corner. So she nodded, wordless. And let the thrust of her chin and the tight
press of her lips say what her tongue didn't.

To her amazement, rather than darkening with ire, a
glint of amusement lit in his eyes. "Just dinna mind me of
the fairy part," he said as if he'd read her thoughts. "We
both ken a body's comfort of a frosty morning is the true
reason for such goings-on."

He gestured to the hearth and its softly glowing turf
fire. "As for the fire in this chamber, I'd judge old Dagda
and my father keep the tradition not because they fear the

wrath of the wee folk, but because they enjoy believing in tall tales. *In magic.*"

"And you do not?"

"Believe in magic?" The twinkle in his eye vanished, its disappearance proving as eloquent an answer as any spoken denial.

"You brought your friend here to sit in your Beldam's Chair. You must believe in its powers?"

"Oh, I'll not gainsay the efficacy of all such wonders and ancient observances." Going back to the table, he poured himself another cup of the potent Rhenish wine. "I simply put more faith in the strength of my arm, the steel of my brand, and what I can see with my own two eyes."

"But—"

"I have *seen* magic of the Beldam's Chair, lass. That is why I brought Colin here." He rubbed a finger back and forth along the rounded side of the wine cup. "And because he has a more trusting heart than Da and Dagda put together."

"And you, sir? Do you trust your heart?"

"If you ask Colin, he will tell you he has seen enchanted isles rising from the sea only to vanish on second glance," he declared as if he hadn't heard her—or chose not to. "He'll also swear any good *cailleach* worth her salt can conjure up a storm by incantation. Call forth waves so heavy, they'll smash against the windows at the tops of the tallest castle towers."

"So you are telling me the Beldam's Chair will heal Colin because he *believes* it will?"

"Either that, or his own will to be whole again so he can pay proper court to my wee kittenish cousin." He shrugged great shoulders. "He is sore smitten with her."

Amicia bristled. "Then mayhap you ought warn him she wishes to sink her claws elsewhere?"

Spinning about before he could answer, she went to the row of tall, open windows. Behind her, she could hear him pulling coverings from the bed, imagined he meant to use them for a pallet.

But she'd be damned if she'd turn around and look.

Not after offering him the comforts of her bed—the unspoken but understood welcome of her arms.

Better to inhale deeply of the chill night air and let its cool embrace douse some of the ire streaking through her.

Extinguish the heat of her passion.

Humiliation twisting through her, she did just that, dragged in great gulps of the cold air, but the husky purr of her rival's voice grated in her ears, the other woman's carefully veiled jeers tossing handfuls of ice chips at each glimmer of warmth she'd tried so desperately to cling to ever since Magnus had burst so unexpectedly into her bedchamber.

And the moment she remembered the reason for his presence, guilt assailed her for snapping at him.

But not for resenting Janet MacKinnon.

That, she couldn't help.

Not after his second reference to his cousin as *wee*. Or more annoying still . . . a *kitten*.

Adored by Colin Grant or otherwise.

Her blood rising, she paced about the room, her nerves too flayed for her to even attempt to stand still, though *he* appeared to have turned to stone.

He'd indeed made a comfortable-looking pallet near the hearth and now stood before it, his wide-set shoulders rigid, his hands clenched at his sides.

And, may the Devil take her for noticing in such a

stress-fraught moment, but in the flickering light of the fire glow, he looked at once magnificent and vulnerable in his knightly array.

Mostly vulnerable.

Because his warrior's trappings appeared so incongruous surrounded by the domestic finery of the well-appointed bedchamber.

And saints help her, but each time she glanced at him, that air of vulnerability slid ever so deeper beneath her skin, wrapped its golden cords all the more sinuously around her foolish adoring heart.

'Twas a dangerous peril that banished her anger as quickly as it'd come and made her burn to march right back to him and have done with every bit of ludicrous-looking knightly adornment affixed to his great, strapping body!

A very unladylike moan escaped her, and she clapped a hand to her lips, praying he hadn't heard.

Not that she'd have been able to withhold the moan even if she'd tried.

The thought of him standing naked before her, knightly or unknightly, roused-to-full-stretch or otherwise, proved too potent a notion for even a feckless MacLean to bear without capitulating.

Her mouth ran dry. Saints, but she yearned to see him in all his bare-bottomed glory!

To touch him.

Put questing fingers to him . . . *there,* where he was most manly.

"Mercy me," she breathed, fanning her face with her hand as she wore a track in the floor skins.

Her wanton musings warming her more than the heat of ten raging bale fires, she swiped the backs of her fingers across her moist forehead. Then she threw off her clinging *arisaid,* tossing its woolen length onto a three-legged stool.

And if her nipples chose to pop over the low dip of her bodice edging and make another uninvited appearance, so be it!

At least she *had* nipples, and fairly good-sized ones—an embellishment she doubted her small-breasted rival could boast of.

That small triumph buoyed her until she happened to glance downward. For her low-belted gown called attention not only to the generous curve of her hips, but also the ever-so-slight roll of flesh at the top of her belly.

Forcing herself not to grimace, she pulled in her stomach. Then she crossed the room until she stood but a breath away from him.

"So you mean to sleep here?" She indicated the heap of coverlets and furs, and one pillow he'd taken from the bed.

"This night, aye. I told you—tonight you may rest undisturbed."

And if I desired to be disturbed?

Her hot MacLean blood nigh flung the words at him. But her greater wish to please won out and so she bunched her hands in her skirts and blurted the first thing that came to her mind.

"You said Reginald's lady wife was doomed. Why was she?"

Because she loved a man whose pride damned her, Magnus's heart answered.

He started, the innocently asked question hitting him like a fist in the gut.

His every instinct warned against venturing anywhere

near the old tales—the legend and the curse—but his honor would not allow him to lie to her.

"What have you heard of the legend?" He focused his attention on her face rather than the appealing flush that spread ever so sweetly across the top swells of her breasts.

"Scarce little," she said, her voice testy, an almost-rebellious glint flashing in her eyes. "No one seems wont to speak of it save to cluck their tongues or bemoan its tragedy."

"It *is* tragic. A sad and sorry tale. The hearing of it would only distress you," Magnus said, hoping to dissuade her.

But his words had the opposite effect, for she jutted her chin at him and the glint in her eyes turned fiery. "If I am to be lady of this keep, I would know Coldstone's heart. The good and the bad of it."

Then she stunned him by cupping her flushed breasts and lifting them, *offering* him their bounty—or so he thought until she indicated the dried patches of white-rimmed sweat stains marring the fabric of her bodice.

"Do you see these stains?" she demanded, her whole demeanor daring him to speak the truth.

I see the top halves of two of the largest, most delectable-looking areolae e'er to be my pleasure to gaze upon, he almost said, catching himself just in time to clear his throat and give her a nod.

"Aye, I see them—the stains, I mean. What of them?"

She took a deep breath and a wee bit more of the sweetly puckered reddish-brown flesh welled into view. At once, a sharp-gripping tightness swept across his groin, but he quelled the urgent *pulling,* banning the pleasurably insistent pulsing to a more appropriate time and place—if ever one should arise, which he sorely doubted.

"I bear these stains," she was saying, "because I was hastening about in a bit of a dither earlier." She narrowed her eyes as if she expected him to comment.

When he opted for the wisdom of silence, she went on. "Not many a lass would traipse about in such an unlady-like manner as to cause this degree of dishevelment. Nor would most high-born lasses allow themselves to be caught in an unflattering condition."

Unflattering?

Magnus near hooted—and would have, were he not in such a foul mood. She could stand before him soiled with muck and goose feathers and he'd still find her the most fetching creature he'd e'er laid eyes on.

The most desirable.

Aye, she proved an unbearable delight . . . any way she wished to come before him.

Not that he'd admit it.

"The stains matter naught." It was the best he could do without compromising his pride.

"Ah, but you err, for they matter greatly," she contradicted, her dark eyes ablaze in the candle glow. "They matter because they prove I am stout-hearted . . . *other* than most. I will not cower and tremble at your family secrets and sorrows—they can be no more grave than some lying o'er my own clan."

Magnus stiffened, not liking where she was leading him. "Say you?"

She nodded, clearly pleased.

A sickening dread began to pulse through his innards, his every instinct warning him of what she'd do with the tale once she'd heard the whole of it.

How she'd use it.

She stepped closer, all rounded curves and luminous skin, her vibrancy and lightly musked female scent proving equally potent weapons.

Sakes, if she came any nearer, all the strength would run out of him. Already he feared his knees would buckle any moment.

Her gaze saying she knew it, she traced light fingertips down his mailed chest. "Will you tell me?" Her voice held a full woman's sensual caress, its soft Highland lilt besotting him as soundly as the tempting swells of her breasts. "Tell me of your ancestor and his lady?"

Magnus didn't even try to smother his groan. "Aye, to be sure," he agreed, the tops of his ears beginning to burn. "But only after you've taken to yon bed and I have settled myself on my pallet."

"As you wish." She accepted his concession with an almost-too-casual shrug.

But just as he pulled in a breath of relief, she undermined his small victory by setting surprisingly deft fingers to the lacings of her bodice. And, merciful saints, loosened and low-dipped as it'd already been, she had it gaping open before he could even exhale.

Another moan rose in his throat, louder and more ragged than the first. Hearing it, she pinned him with a knowing stare and eased the gown off her shoulders until it bunched about her waist.

"I told you I am mostly in good heart," she said, reaching for the delicate straps of her camise. "As you can see, neither am I timid. Be assured there is naught you can tell me, or require of me, that I shall find . . . *off-putting.*"

Magnus inclined his head—his throat, and certain other parts, too thick and tight for him to comment.

"I would deny you nothing, sir."

That enticement shimmering in the air between them, she slowly peeled down the wispy covering of her under-gown until nothing touched her magnificent breasts but the brisk night air and his riveted gaze.

Full, large-nippled, and gleaming beautifully in the glow of the hearth fire, they swayed a bit from the swift workings of her fingers. And they swayed even more when she lifted her hands and began pulling the pins from the glossy black braids coiled loosely above her ears.

The tantalizing motion sent bolts of sheer, white-hot need pounding into his loins, her every movement stealing his breath and setting him like granite. Her nipples began to contract, the large rounds of her areolae crinkling and drawing deliciously tight beneath his stare.

"Jesu God," he ground out when the hardened tips lengthened, stretching toward him as if begging for his caress, his kiss.

Half-afraid *he'd* soon be reduced to begging, he bit down so fiercely on the inside of his cheek that he tasted blood. But the saints took pity on him at last, for the very urgency of his desire ripped through the spell she'd cast over him.

The knowledge that he was a mere hair's breadth away from dragging her against him and taking her, mayhap even in standing, braced against the cold, hard edge of the table, restored his sanity as naught else could have.

His lesson learned, he began stalking about the chamber, snuffing the candles one by one. He slid a hot glare at the night taper, flickering innocently on the small bed-side table. That flame, too, would meet its end—but only after Lady Amicia was securely ensconced within the massive, canopied bed.

Meantime, he doused every other source of illumination, plunging the room into ever-greater shadow until only the soft glow of the peat fire and the tiny coal-burning brazier lit the murky half-dark.

She moved about behind him, turning down the bed-covers. Something she did not seem to be doing with all speed.

And he wasn't about to glance her way to be sure. He deemed it wiser to keep pacing and simply set his jaw against the image of her voluptuous body stretched sinuously upon the linen sheets.

Blessedly, the worst throbbing at his groin receded. But one more glimpse, however fleeting, of even an inch of creamy skin not usually freely visible, and he'd find himself in fine ferment all over again.

"I am abed, sir, and . . . covered."

The words floated out of the semi-darkness, mellifluous as always but with a slight tinge of defiance.

And that wee suggestion of rebelliousness sent another hot tide of tingles sluicing across his nether parts. Had she perchance divested herself of all her garments? Would she, in her boldness, have *other* sultry delights on display for him?

Perhaps a quick flash of the sooty-black curls he imagined sprang in wild abundance between her shapely thighs?

At the thought, his tarse raged harder than the bone hilt of his dirk, but he took the bait and spun to face her—and saw at once exactly how she'd chosen to express her *defiance*.

Not that he could see much of her at all, buried as she was beneath a welter of furs and mounded pillows.

She'd extinguished the night candle, but enough of the

fire glow seeped between the parted bed curtains to reveal the lusty spark of humor in her dark-flashing eyes. Equally telling, she appeared to be biting her lip to keep from smiling.

And those brief—but startlingly revealing—glimpses of her indomitable spirit filled the cold places inside him with warmth just as glorious as the fierce heat that had swept through him upon glimpsing her naked-swaying breasts.

For one precious moment, he savored that warmth, holding it as close and dear as he'd like to hold her. Then, with a heavy sigh, he crossed the room, seeking sanctuary in the infinitely safer wash of cool, gray moonlight spilling through the opened windows.

And if the saints had any mercy at all, they'd let the patter of the mizzling rain, the hollow whistle of the wind, his own wise distance from the bed, blur the tale he'd promised to tell.

Ill ease nipping at every inch of him, he stared up at the black-raftered ceiling and began. "The first keeper of this castle, Reginald of the Victories, had but one arm," he said, his words eliciting a sharp gasp of surprise from his wife . . . just as he'd known they would.

"But I'd heard he was a great warrior," she argued from the bed. "How—"

"By all accounts he was a much-esteemed man—the most skilled warrior in all the Isles," Magnus confirmed, tossing her just the wee hint of a sad smile. "But life being as it is, there always comes a day when even the greatest amongst us meets someone better skilled. That day cost Reginald his right arm, and he never considered himself a whole man thereafter."

"Was he married when he lost his arm?" Amicia raised

herself on an elbow, peered at him through the gloom. "Is that the sadness in the tale? His wife stopped loving him?"

"Nay, far from it—she loved him deeply. That is the tragedy, for he could not believe it."

"Because his pride would not let him?"

"So tradition claims," Magnus admitted, pulling a hand down over his face. "He had only just married and was building this stronghold when his arm was sliced off in the heat of a fierce battle. Although he'd e'er been a bonny man of quick wit and a sunny nature, he quickly grew bitter."

Amicia sat up straighter, but still kept her nakedness well-hid beneath the bedcovers. "He must've kept building the castle?"

"Och, aye, that he did." Magnus stared at the falling rain, preferring not to see if the coverlets slipped. "He spared no expense or trouble, strove to build the finest stronghold these isles had e'er seen."

He blew out a frustrated breath, hating what he must tell her.

"Reginald hoped to impress his new bride, see you? He feared she would not love him unless he gave her the grandest home his coin and standing could provide."

"But you said she loved him deeply."

"And she did." Magnus sighed. "With the whole of her heart and every breath she drew."

"She didn't care that he'd lost his arm," Amicia said, making the words a statement.

"Nay, she didn't—not one whit. But she did doubt Reginald's love, even though the *seannachies* tell us he loved her endlessly." Magnus's stomach began to pitch and twist. This was the part he'd been dreading. "'Tis said he ne'er spoke his heart to her, ne'er laid bare his innermost feelings. He only devoted himself—his life—to building this castle."

He slid a glance at her, then immediately wished he hadn't, for her unbound hair now spilled in charming disarray around her shoulders. The long, black-gleaming tresses beckoned almost indecently, demanding all manner of lascivious attention even as she stared at him all *dewy*-eyed, her feminine heart most assuredly guessing the end of the tale.

"She felt unloved," she said, proving him right.

Worse, her lower lip wobbled with tears she clearly fought to keep from spilling. "She didn't ken *why* he was so obsessed with building the castle and he ne'er told her."

Magnus pressed his fingers to the icy-damp stone of the window molding and a great shudder racked his spine. "Every new day saw them loving more, yet growing further apart," he said, borrowing one of Hugh's descriptions of the pair when his own words failed him. "With each new stone laid, each new comfort provided, rather than showing the appreciation and devotion Reginald hoped to win from her, his lady—Margaret was her name—only became more sad-eyed."

"Did she not *tell* him how she felt?"

"More times than there are stars in the sky." Another of Hugh's quotes. "But each time she did, or begged him to reveal *his* heart to her, he would either plunge himself into some pressing castle-building task, or fall into an exhausted sleep from having done so."

A sniffle came from the direction of the bed.

Magnus suppressed a groan . . . and an urge to smash his fist into the chamber's cold, arras-hung wall.

"So Reginald of the Victories could not see his greatest victory of all." The statement came on a long, quivering sigh. "He ne'er knew that it was not a proud and mighty castle his lady wife so desired—she wanted only his love," Amicia concluded.

"That will have been the way of it, aye," Magnus agreed, bracing himself to tell her the rest, wishing she hadn't proved so persistently curious.

So persuasive.

"And loving him as she did, life without his love held no meaning for her."

At his words, all color drained from her face. "So that is why you called her doomed. She took her own life, didn't she?"

Magnus nodded. "Hers, and surely Reginald's, too, for from the day she let herself fall from the parapet walk, he is said to have grown ever more bitter, believing until his death that she'd taken her life rather than endure being bound to a man who was not whole."

"Oh, dear saints . . ." Amicia gasped, dashing silvery tears from her cheeks with trembling fingers.

Furious with himself for distressing her, and equally frustrated with her for giving him scant choice, Magnus stared out at the dark, impassionate night and pulled in a great, spine-stiffening breath of the chill air.

When he trusted himself to speak again, he turned back to her. "There is more. The reason many believe a pall—or curse—lies over all who live within these walls. Would you truly know Coldstone's heart, my lady?"

She nodded, her eyes still misting but with a decidedly belligerent spark beginning to replace the tears.

"Then know you that from Margaret's death onward, the stones of this castle turned cold—so frigid that even the brightest summer day cannot warm them. Hence, the name Coldstone," he told her, his nape prickling at the way her chin thrust higher upon each spoken word.

"Some say their ill-fated love yet lives—remaining as a clear memory to this day, ever locked within the chill damp of Coldstone's walls."

Her eyes fair blazing now, Amicia regarded him long and hard. "Then I would say it is well past time for someone to release them."

Magnus blinked. He had no answer to that.

But for one breath-catching moment, something inside him leapt and brightened; then the sensation passed as quickly as it'd come.

So he strode for his pallet in silence and thought, stripping off his knightly accoutrements as he went, leaving his wife to stare after him . . . or seek her slumber.

He also tossed aside her fool notions.

Impossible, dangerous notions.

Delving too deeply into romantic old tales best forgotten would mean exposing his own heart.

And that was something he had no intention of doing.

In especial, not to her.

Chapter Eight

✦

'TWAS THE SMELL THAT AWAKENED HIM.

"Saints of glory!" The imprecation burst from Magnus's lips, the stench's bite watering his eyes.

Rank and penetrating, the foul miasma weighted the air and invaded his nostrils with each indrawn breath. Too sleep-fogged to think clearly, he cracked his eyes to merest slits, half-expecting to find himself adrift in the cesspit.

Blessedly, the dull gleam of his discarded hauberk and the pointedly closed bed hangings of the huge four-poster, outlined in shadow across the room, swiftly dispelled that particular concern.

Not quite first light, a damp, blustery wind poured through the opened windows, rippling the wall hangings and causing the hanging cresset lamp to sway on its chain. A light drizzle still fell, and its soft splatter on the stone window ledges heralded the start of another wet, gray day.

Blinking, he rubbed at the crick in his neck. That pain, and the acute throbbing at his temples, attested to a poor night's sleep . . . a chaste one spent on his pallet of rumpled furs.

Much as he'd rather it'd been otherwise.

In especial, he could have done without the firm press of Boiny's shaggy back against his side. Or even more vexing, the dog's noxious emissions poisoning his lungs.

Wincing, he pushed up on an elbow and glowered menace at the sleeping dog. "You chose an inopportune moment to rekindle our affection, old lad," he grumbled, reaching to tousle the beast's floppy ears nonetheless.

Stench cloud or nay.

Who was to say what less than appetizing habits he'd develop upon achieving his own gray-bearded years?

So he settled for a grimace and his wince, and saved any further harsh words for a soul more deserving of them.

Another sidelong look at Boiny, and he stood. Stiff and sore from the too-short night, and trying not to breathe too deeply, he moved about, snatching up his scattered clothes.

He tugged on his braies, eager to be gone, and Boiny seized the moment to claim the pallet's warmth. Making it his own, the dog sprawled full-length across the mounded skins and borrowed blankets, seemingly content to wallow in his wicked, odorous fumes.

Indeed, Magnus scarce had time to don his boots before another sharp wave of offensiveness rose up to taint the chill morning air.

Pulling a face that would have sent the Devil running, he thrust his arms a bit more roughly than need be into the sleeves of his under-tunic and yanked it over his head.

He swiped his sword belt off the table, girding it about his hips as he hastened for the door.

But as he slid back the drawbar, his frown deepened. Had he truly been dreaming of the sweet press of his lady's warm, well-rounded bosom? The imagined thrust of hardened nipples against his naked, slumbering flesh?

And, most stirring of all, the curling squeeze of inquisitive fingers stroking up and down his eager, sleep-swollen shaft.

He paused on the threshold, the notion sending liquid fire through his veins. Aye, he had enjoyed such dreams and the vivid images were yet fresh in his mind, still potent enough to rouse and enflame him.

Especially the one with the full shapeliness of her lush body rubbing against his as, skin to damp skin, heat to lower heat, she'd begged him to take her.

And how, in his dream, at least, he'd gladly acquiesced.

His senses storming, he opened the door. His raven-haired bride would never know how swiftly he would relent now, this very moment, if she would but throw open the bed curtains and crook just one finger in sensual invitation.

But a last glance over his shoulder proved the futility of any such possibility. The heavily embroidered hangings remained closed and naught but thick silence came from within.

An impenetrable barrier best left intact . . . just as any rises beneath his braies were better ignored—at least for the nonce.

Too many other duties called him.

Important issues he meant to attend alone. And well

before the castle stirred and his long-nosed kinsmen could question his purpose.

No one need know he'd been sneaking to the isle's sandy, windswept dunes of a morn. Or that, once there, he'd crouch amongst the thick-growing machair and bracken and cast surreptitious glances at the boat strand.

That he'd look on with heart-lancing pride as men rushed about on the damp, glistening sand, his bride's mountain of *siller* being put to good effect as they painstakingly rebuilt the MacKinnon fleet—one fine galley at a time.

Nor would it be wise to let anyone guess he'd made a few visits of his own to the Beldam's Chair. That he hoped its supposed powers might lessen some of the cold, heavy weight on his heart and perhaps mend a tear or two in his sore-battered spirit.

Aye, too much of the puissant Reginald's blood flowed in his veins for him to risk looking a fool.

So he slipped from the room on quiet feet. But the moment the door latch dropped into place, he abandoned his caution and thundered down the draughty corridor, his mood as dark as the poorly lit passage.

Driven by his most persistent demons, he did not slow his steps until he'd hastened through a little-used passage around the great hall and strode out into the thin drizzle of the inner bailey.

And the moment he did, a diminutive cloaked figure emerged from the deep shadow along the tower wall and hurried forward across the rain-damp cobbles.

"Magnus!" Janet cried, rushing him, her arms extended in greeting.

"Ho, lass, before you slip and crack that pretty head of

yours," he warned, reaching for her when she would have launched herself at him.

She clutched at his arms, panting. "Praise God you are out and about," she said, the words echoing in the empty courtyard. "I would—"

"And I would ken what *you* are about at this hour? Traipsing around in the rainy dark . . . alone." Magnus took gentle hold of her, set her from him. "Did you not hear my orders that none of the womenfolk are to venture out on their own? There are dangers about, lass. I would know you safe."

She looked down, fidgeted with the heavy, rain-misted braid hanging over her shoulder. "I did not think you meant me. I was in the kitchens, helping, and only stepped out to get away from the cook-smoke for a few moments."

Magnus captured her chin, turned her face back to his. "But there is more, is there not?"

"I"—her voice faltering, she indicated a cloth-covered basket resting in a sheltered corner of the bailey wall—"I was returning to the hall with some of Cook's fresh-baked custard pasties."

The slightest of smiles flickered across her lips. "Your friend Colin favors them."

"That great lout is a man of hearty appetite."

Magnus angled his head, just now catching the faint kitchen smells drifting on the damp morning air—the tantalizing aromas of woodsmoke and roasting meats, fresh-baked breads and frying dough.

Rich fare for a household that would suffer a diet of dry oatcakes and watered ale were *his* coin stocking the kitchens.

With the morning going rapidly sour, he leveled a

piercing gaze on his cousin. "Be advised that Colin favors all manner of . . . *delicacies,*" he told her. "The daintier the sweetmeat set before him, the more the knave's mouth waters."

Janet began winding her single flaxen braid around her fingers. "I have noticed he seems to have a taste for . . . such," she said, a bit flat-voiced, her expression wistful. "Some of the kitchen lasses are wagering who will claim the first kiss from him. A kiss and . . . more."

"Something tells me they will still be wagering when my firstborn son grows a beard." Magnus reached to give her arm a light, encouraging squeeze. "But have a care, I beg you, lass. I would not see my friend take a false bite—would not see either of you take to your bed with a turned belly."

"Never you worry. I cannot foresee him making such an error," she said, smoothing her sleeve when he released her. "But I will heed your words and assure he does not receive anything that might ill become him."

She looked down again, fussed with her cloak. "For myself, I am ever cautious."

"I am glad to hear it." Magnus folded his arms. "And now I would know the rest. You are troubled—I see it all over you."

Janet shifted. "Your father has been ranting about the ghost galley again. He swears he saw it heading for our shores, hell's own fiends at the oars, only to vanish into the mists right before his eyes."

"Did anyone else see this devilish craft?"

"Your brothers were with him at the time, but neither saw anything."

Magnus let out a long sigh. "My father's wits are waning by the day." He turned his head, stared at the dark bulk of Coldstone's keep. "Even so, I do not think my da and his ravings have much to do with what is eating at you."

He looked back at her. "Now tell me what it is."

Janet blinked, a spark of some indefinable emotion flaring in her eyes. "Very well, but do not think I disesteem your . . . your *lady*. I but bear grim tidings about her. To my sorrow!"

"Ill tidings?" Magnus arched a brow. "Then have out with them, for my patience has already run mighty thin this morn."

"You had a . . . tedious night?" she probed, looking almost as if she wished he had.

Nay, I had a wondrous night spent lusting after the tight-puckered flesh of my wife's deliciously large, hard-budded nipples.

Then I ran hard as a jousting lance trying to decide if her lower hair will spring as sleek and lush as I am hoping!

Half-afraid his frustration had shouted the words, Magnus sharpened his gaze on Janet, but far from looking shocked or vexed, she appeared to be preening like a cat before a bowl of cream.

Suspecting the reason for the look, Magnus took a step backward, putting ample space between them. "I had a *trying* night and a less than pleasant morning," he said, swiping at a few rain droplets that had settled on his brow. "But my dark humor has naught to do with my wife—should the thought cross your mind."

"Lady Amicia is much on my mind," Janet gave right back, her efforts to keep her face expressionless almost pitiable. "She is the reason I must speak with you, and alone."

"We are alone." Magnus looked about him. "What have you to say that you cannot voice here? Save the mizzle and a few wispy threads of mist, our privacy is secured."

She gave a little shrug. "It would grieve me to see you shamed if my words fell on the wrong ears."

"Shamed?"

Janet nodded, threw a glance at the high bulk of the tower wall. Glimmers of light were just beginning to flicker in some of the narrow slit windows.

"Let us be gone from here," she urged. "Please. . . ."

Not waiting for him to answer, she slipped her arm through his and tried to maneuver him into the shadowed arch of the gatehouse's tunnel-like pend.

Magnus shook himself free. "Speak here, or leave me be, lass. I have much to do this morn."

She flicked her braid over her shoulder. "I hope you are not growing over-fond of her? If you are, it shall grieve me all the more to distress you."

"Come you, distress me—out with it."

"As you wish. I am here to tell you she is crazed," she blurted. "Feeble in the head."

"Feeble? I'd vow there isn't a feeble bone anywhere in her body," Magnus said, shaking his head. "And crazed? The Lady Amicia? Nay, I do not think so."

"I would swear at a sword's point that she is full mad. She is not like . . . most."

Nay, she is not. She is a woman like no other. Her own precious self, and in the most delightful ways—as she proved to me last night!

Magnus's heart, all his deepest longings, roared the words.

The longings he'd kept hidden since the long-ago day he'd first glimpsed her limping about in the heather.

That bittersweet day, and all the ensuing ones, an exquisite torture that mocked him, he pinned a narrow-eyed stare on his pouty-lipped cousin. "What is the substance of your suspicion? Tell me true, lass, for you make a grim accusation."

"I am not speaking out of due. Dagda and I caught her in the old tower yester eve. She was barreling down the turnpike stairs."

Janet sniffed, as if that explained everything.

Now Magnus did hoot.

His first true laugh in many a day. A great rollicking one that reached to his toes and made his belly shake.

"Guidsakes, but I am glad you did not see me tearing through the keep just now." He swiped at his eyes. "If you had, you would be calling me just as addled."

"Nay, you mistake the heart of it. She wasn't just charging *down* the stairs. She was racing back up them, too. Over and over and over again."

Magnus's laughter withered and died.

"Over and over and over again?" A sickeningly hollow feeling began to spread through his stomach.

"Dagda and I both saw her."

"I will speak to her." Magnus pulled his plaid tighter against a sudden gusting of chill, wet wind. "There is sure to be a sufficient good reason."

Janet shrugged. "For your sake, I pray that is so," she said, then strode off to retrieve her basket of custard pasties.

Watching her go, Magnus hoped so, too.

Saints, did he ever hope so.

*   *   *

Hope.

A sweet golden band of it circled Amicia's finger, warming her against the gray morning light filtering through the tightly drawn bed curtains.

Truth be told, hope had accompanied her all through the night, spooling out from her deepest dreams to caress and cloak her. Even if she'd spent those fitful hours alone, tossing on cold and empty sheets when she'd rather have been held and adored in her husband's embrace, giving full and unrestrained rein to her passion for him.

Aye, hope had wooed and encouraged her. It'd sung to her from behind his carefully guarded expression, melted her with each declared vow to protect her, and blessed her in the sounds of his restless slumber.

Telltale tossings and turnings.

Each one assuring her he'd rather have spent the night in her arms. If only she dared believe. And she almost did, so she stretched and allowed herself a hearty yawn. A bold welcome-to-the-morning smile.

He was still fretting about.

His stirrings and unrest had wakened her.

And men were . . . *needy* . . . of an early hour.

Her good-sisters had sworn it.

And the thick bulges she'd inadvertently glimpsed at the groins of slumbering kinsmen, on the rare occasions she'd passed through Baldoon's great hall before anyone else had wakened, confirmed those claims.

Warming at the thought of Magnus's morning *bulge*, and fully prepared to seize the advantages it might provide, she deliberately let her camise stay bunched about her waist, where it'd been throughout the night, and, sitting up, grabbed hold of the bed hangings and yanked them open—only to have her high spirits shattered as soundly as if someone had dumped a creel of cold and slimy fish over her head.

Week-old and rotting *dead* fish!

The bonny Magnus and his hoped-for bulge were nowhere to be seen.

Nor old Boiny.

Only Janet.

Amicia's undersized rival stood in the middle of the chamber, gaping at her. Drop-jawed, wide-eyed, and wholly disapproving of the fully exposed nakedness of Amicia's large, free-swinging breasts.

"You!" Amicia cried, too startled to think to cover herself.

"And a fine good morrow to you, too, my lady," the other gave back, two bright spots of color on her cheeks.

Pulse pounding, Amicia fumbled for the straps of her camise. "What brings you into my chamber at such a young hour?" she demanded, struggling to get her arms through the delicate loops.

Janet flashed hot blue eyes at her. "Dagda sent me with fresh bedding and candles." She indicated the clean-looking linens folded over a chair back, the small wicker basket of fine wax tapers resting on the table. "I am e'er about before cockcrow, see you. My services are much required—unlike yours."

"Unlike mine?" Amicia spluttered, too bleary-headed from sleep to conjure the sharp retort the prickly little *kitten* deserved.

Undisguised malice shimmering all over her, the teensy piece slid a pointed look at the mussed pallet, her meaning clear as a bright summer day.

Amicia blanched.

At once, everything in the room faded to insignificance, falling back into the murky morning light until only the pallet remained. Each crease and lump in the jumble of furs and blankets took on brilliant clarity, the whole of it jeering at her in all its very-much-used glory.

A flicker of purest animosity playing across her face, Janet went to the table and trailed her fingertips over the well-polished silver of a heavy candelabrum—a MacLean heirloom.

One of several scattered about the bedchamber.

"You've filled this room with so much finery," Janet commented, now fingering the edge of one of the many Flemish tapestries adorning the walls.

She gave a breathy sigh. "It won't do to have such a splendid chamber in disorder. I will tidy Magnus's bed pallet and save you the bother," she declared, releasing the tapestry.

Before Amicia could blink, the younger woman plucked a length of plaid from the floor and gave it a brisk snap. She looked at Amicia as she folded it, wordless—but with an expression that spoke worlds.

Amicia bristled. Heat shot up the back of her neck. And, saints help her, even her nostrils flared! Seized by rabid indignation, she opened her mouth to protest, to shoo the little vixen from her sight, but her voice choked in her throat.

All her sweet bravura of moments before dwindled to a tiny, hard-spinning lump somewhere behind her ribs.

A hot-burning, *painful*, cut-off-her-breath kind of lump.

Dread laming her, she watched the younger woman tidy the pallet. Unthinkable, should Magnus prefer such sleeping arrangements every night.

And a thousand damnations on her own fool self for not clearing away the evidence of just such a disaster before his fey-like cousin could slip into the room and waylay her!

Dance light-footed all over her hopes and dreams.

Reeling, she relinquished her battle with her tangled camise straps and faced defeat. Since her fingers seemed to have taken on the shape and dexterity of fat sausages, she made do with simply jerking the bedsheets over her bared breasts.

"You needn't shield your mother-nakedness before me," the kitten cooed at her, a falsely sweet smile curving her lips. "I have seen the unclothed entirety of much older and *stouter* women than you. Having me see you shouldn't be as daunting as having Magnus gaze upon your . . . fleshiness."

That did it.

Something inside her popped . . . and whatever it was, it sent thousands of white-hot splinters jabbing into her heart.

Clutching the covers hard to her breasts, she glared her fury. "And if you'd eat more than a bird's portion of slaked oats and pottage, mayhap you'd win a few curves of your own!" she snapped, looking the other woman up and down. "By all that's holy, there is scarce enough flesh on you to keep you grounded in a good wind."

To Amicia's astonishment, her outburst seemed to hit her rival like a fist in the gut. With all care, Janet smoothed the last of the mussed furs that had been Magnus's bed pallet.

"'Twas e'er a dream of mine to be tall and sultry-like," she said, straightening.

Her task completed, she moved toward the door, looking smaller with each stilted step she took.

Small, and annoyingly forlorn.

The hot-stabbing needles beneath Amicia's ribs slowly retracted their points. But they left a cold, dull-throbbing ache in their place.

This new sensation proved just as unpleasant as the other, but in a wholly different way. Moistening her lips, Amicia opened her mouth to speak, to say *something,* but her voice lodged in her throat. So she looked on, watched the other woman pause at the clothes peg to stroke Amicia's ermine-lined cloak.

"You have many bonnie things and I envy you the lot of them. Magnus most of all," Janet said, her tone empty . . . *wistful.* "I had such hopes that he would take me to wife."

Amicia pulled in a harsh breath on the word *hope.*

Hope was *her* word.

All she had to hug close to her.

She didn't want to hear about Janet's hopes or troubles.

"You are his cousin," she pointed out, her voice cooperating again. "He would ne'er have considered a marriage to you."

"We are *distant* cousins and even that cannot be known for sure. But he was e'er good to me—kind, see you?" Running both of her hands over the cloak's furred lining, Janet turned a glittery-eyed gaze on Amicia.

"With all others rumpling their noses at me, and Magnus so big-hearted, I e'er fancied he'd be the only one who would consider having me," Janet said in a voice scarce to be heard. "Now you are here, and—"

"And I have nary a notion what you are chaffering

about." Amicia scrambled to her feet and crossed the room, trailing bedsheets as she went.

Holding one of them fast about her, she fixed a you'd-best-tell-me-all stare on her no longer quite so formidable rival. "What havers are you tossing about you? What men would turn away from you?"

Janet sniffed.

A wet, sniffly sniff this time.

"Not havers, my lady," she said, dashing a tear from her cheek. "The simple truth that I am base-born. I thought you knew."

Amicia shook her head, not trusting herself to speak. Something nibbled at her, at the very fringe of her mind—and then she remembered.

"Magnus wanted to dower you," she said, her thoughts in a whirl. "He would not have done so if he didn't believe he'd find a viable husband for you."

Another tear leaked from Janet's eye and she blinked, clearly trying to stop the flow of more. "You do not know him as I do. He is . . . big-hearted. Did you not hear me say so?"

Turning away, Janet opened the door, but kept her fingers curled around the latch as if she needed its support. "To be sure, he believed he'd find someone who would have me . . . a bastard unable to even lay a firm claim to being a *Clan Fingon* bastard. My true origins are that obscure."

"Magnus looks on you as kin. He's told me so."

"Aye, he does," Janet agreed. "That truth, and knowing how he's e'er lusted after tall, well-made lasses with hair the color of midnight should have kept me from being surprised at seeing *you* set foot here, and as his proxy-wed bride."

Amicia swallowed the gasp rising in her throat.

Her heart lurched.

And the sharp, little, green-tinged shards returned with a vengeance. Only now, rather than Janet's delicate-fingered hand, each hurtful jab was aimed and driven by a blowsy, raven-haired rival without a face.

An endless stream of them.

A great shudder tore down the length of her and she reached for the door edge, grabbing hold of it just as fiercely as Janet's fingers curled around the latch.

"You mustn't trouble yourself—be glad-hearted he favors stout, dark-haired women," Janet said, the comment lacking even the slightest hint of a taunt. "His passion for them will make it easier for you to lure him off his bed pallet!"

Aye, nary a hint of malice tinged Janet's words.

Only well-meant if poorly chosen comfort.

For long moments after Janet took her wee self into the shadowy passage whence she'd come, Amicia remained frozen on the threshold, her fingers clenching and unclenching on the edge of the door.

And feeling anything but comforted.

"So-o-o, here we are at last," Donall MacLean said after tramping up four full stories to the stair-head of Baldoon Castle's loftiest tower.

He cast a stern eye on the grizzled old woman cradled in his arms. "I vow you have sound reason for seeking an audience here rather than in the warmth of my solar? Not that I have e'er had cause to doubt any contrivance you've tossed at me."

That drew an indignant snort from his featherlight, black-garbed burden. But Donall the Bold, proud laird of the great Clan MacLean and doughty holder of their mighty stronghold, Baldoon, ignored the snort.

He also excused the wee cackle that followed it, and set down the crone with the same great care he'd just put into carrying her up more winding steps than he cared to count.

Not that Devorgilla's slight weight would overtax a flea.

Nonetheless, he took some pains to exhibit a respectable degree of *exertion*. He also schooled his handsome face into a formidable scowl.

Stretching his arms, he flexed his fingers and glanced round, let the freshening wind catch and toss his plaid, riffle his dark, shoulder-length hair.

A fine drizzle misted the air and lowering clouds of deepest gray muted the roar of the sea, even as roughcrashing swells threw white spray high up the tower walls.

Several guardsmen clustered about a tiny brazier set in the lee of a little gabled cap-house at the far end of the parapet-walk, but a single jerk of his head sent them scurrying off to hold watch over some other corner of the blustery morn.

Satisfied, he rocked back on his heels and stared up at the dull gray sky. "Aye, old lass, most good men would not venture from their hearthside on such a wet, dreary day. . . ." He let the words tail away, made a bit of a show of his fierce grimace of displeasure.

Another *contrivance*, to be sure, but an expected part of old Devorgilla's pleasure.

The *cailleach* would not part with a single glimmer of what troubled or excited her unless she first be paid proper court. And Donall MacLean knew her ways over-well.

As did his brother, Iain, just now emerging from the torchlit stair tower, his face as black-frowning as Donall's . . . save that Iain's glower appeared a mite more authentic than his lairdly brother's.

Striding up to them, Iain jammed fisted hands against his hips and looked down at the teensy, bird-like crone. "Sakes, Devorgilla, what foolery are you about this time? Having us hie ourselves up here into this swirling soup?" He emphasized his point by swatting at the thick swathes of chill gray mist drifting across the ramparts.

Devorgilla clucked her tongue, tilted her cowl-covered head. "For shame, laddie, are you doubting me?" She touched a gnarled finger to the bright-gleaming quartz crystals set into the clasp of his sword belt. "*You,* of all men?"

"Och, nay," Iain assured her, lifting his hands, palms out. "I would ne'er doubt a single word to fall from your lips. Nothing is more sure." Looking duly contrite, he took her hand and pressed a light kiss to papery-skinned knuckles. "I would but hear what you wish to tell us that could not have been broached below?"

"Not vain puffing words, I promise you," she said, her cheeks turning pink from his kiss. "'Tis not so much what I can tell you, but what I would have you see."

She cast a shrewd glance at Donall. "Something you both ought see."

"Then show us quickly for I'd return to my wife's side anon—she is feeling poorly this morn," Iain returned, his grousing earning a swift glare and an elbow in the ribs from his brother.

Devorgilla sniffed. "Your fair lassie will be suffering through many such a morning afore she finds her peace again," she prophesied, a mischievous smile playing about her lips.

Now was not the time or place to tell him what she'd long glimpsed in her cauldron's rising steam . . . that his lady wife would prove a fine breeder of many healthy sons, the first one already growing sweetly beneath her heart.

For the nonce, other, more pressing cares required her attention.

Dire ones.

Lifting her arm, she pointed at the faint glow of vilest green shimmering through the storm clouds lining the far horizon. There, where MacKinnons' Isle rose low and dark from the tossing sea.

"See you that tinge of green?" she prodded, hoping their hearts would be able to see what the rolling curtains of mist hid from mortal view.

"Green-tinged mist?" Donall's tone revealed what *his* heart couldn't.

"Aye, green and . . . fiendish." Devorgilla tried again, this time jabbing her finger in the direction. "O'er Mac-Kinnons' Isle," she said, raising her voice above the screaming seabirds wheeling and gliding round the lofty parapet tower. "Look hard—and with more than your eyes."

The tight, concentrated line of Iain's mouth, as he peered through the fog, encouraged her. But not over-long, for his dark brows quickly snapped together.

"I see naught," he admitted. "But I'll trust it to be there. Sakes, I would believe a host of *selkie*-folk were cavorting across yon waves, if you said it was so, old lass."

Pleased for that small mercy, Devorgilla rubbed her

hands. "If you have such faith, I would ask a boon of you."

"A boon?" That from Donall. He did not attempt to hide his wariness. "What would you have of us?"

"Naught that would cost you greatly. I would see you send a score of able-armed sworders to strengthen Magnus MacKinnon's garrison," she voiced her desire. "Evil lurks o'er his isle and, braw warrior or nay, he will be needing help to safeguard your sister."

The brothers exchanged looks.

Not quite doubtful looks . . . but *stubborn*.

Either way, Devorgilla did not care for them.

She huffed a breath. "Have I e'er led you wrong, laddies?" she asked, seizing her one remaining advantage. "Either of you?"

Silence and the screech of the gulls answered her.

That, and the slide of Donall's boot sole as, looking down, he poked his toe at a sodden gannet feather sticking to the wet stone flagging of the wall walk.

Iain spoke first. "Magnus MacKinnon is no hand-wringing bampot. If aught is amiss on his isle, he will see to the trouble with all haste."

"He would ne'er let any harm come to Amicia. Of that, I am certain," Donall put in, leaving the stone-clinging feather for some other fool to prod and worry.

He patted the crone's arm, placating her as if she'd only yestereve learned of the power she could wield with a few muttered incantations or a simple brew of liquefied toad spittle.

"Magnus is a well-seasoned fighter. A great knight. He survived Dupplin, did he not?" he minded her, all laird now.

And grating sorely on Devorgilla's patience.

"But he will be hurting inside, see you? That is why his father wanted Amicia there before his return—so she could comfort him. We—"

"She will not be doing much soothing at all if she's cold in her grave!" Devorgilla waggled a finger at him, glared at his brother for holding his silence.

Donall pulled a hand down over his face. "On my honor, were Amicia in any other's hands, I would fill our whole fleet of war galleys with my best men and send them speeding to her aid," he said. "But MacKinnon swings a daunting blade and has a strong arm and good wits to go with it. Whate'er plagues him, he will not look kindly on intervention. Ours or anyone else's. I ken him that well."

"Donall speaks true." Iain sided with his brother. "Magnus is proud . . . *a man apart.*"

Parted from his new wife afore he's even tasted sweet bliss with her, Devorgilla mumbled beneath her breath.

The brothers received a scalding stare. Devorgilla's best.

"Be that your last word, laddies?"

Iain nodded, but had the good grace to look unhappy about it.

The *laird* blew out a slow breath, and looked . . . resigned.

"Magnus refused my offer to lend him our most skilled shipwright, preferring to use the aged man who worked for his father. And just recently, he turned away the last galley-load of supplies I sent him. It would be unwise to tread further on his pride."

Devorgilla pursed her lips. "So be it," she said, flicking a raindrop off her sleeve.

She tamped down the burning urge to transport them

both right smack into the middle of a patch of stinging Highland nettles—and send them there full naked!

But she was wise enough to ken when to concede defeat.

Or, at least, when to *appear* to do so.

Turning away, lest her dark side get the better of her, she stared out across the sea again—or rather, at what little of its rain-pitted surface glimmered through the thick fog.

"I shan't darken your door about this matter again," she murmured, more to herself and the wind than to them. "There are . . . *others* who ken the danger and would help me."

"Others?" the brothers spoke in chorus.

Little good it did them.

Devorgilla's audience had ended.

Lifting her chin, she pressed her lips together and shuffled to the stair-head door. Iain had promised to carry her down, and vexed or no, she wasn't about to forgo such a treat.

Three great strides brought him to her side, and with a bit of a styled flourish surely meant to appease her wrath, he swept her into his arms for the long trek down the winding stairs.

But at the first landing, he paused to look down at her. "What jabber was that about *others*?"

"Never you mind," Devorgilla evaded, clutching fast to his broad shoulders. "This danger, too, will pass. With or without your help. Sooner or later, all winds fall and every cloud rises."

With a good moon and a bit of meddling and magic, we'll just hope the two of you won't be caught without your plaids when it happens.

Chapter Nine

✦

"*PSHAW, LADDIE—are you going to be a great gowk and deny the curse now?*"

His face flushed with triumph, Donald MacKinnon stood behind his laird's chair at the high table and aimed a victorious, I-told-you-so stare at Magnus.

"'Tis a belly-turning sight, eh?" Jutting his bristly chin, the old man pointed at the almost-dead adder dangling from his middle son, Dugan's, dirk blade. "God kens, a limpet would own to the truth—admit what I've been telling you. We've been set upon by forces darker than the crack o' the Devil's own behind!"

Magnus eyed the writhing creature with distaste. "Belly-turning, to be sure," he agreed, ignoring the rest.

His innards churning indeed, he scanned the faces of his fellow clansmen. Surging forward in a great crush, they elbowed their way from every corner of the huge, groin-vaulted hall, pressing near to gape and stare. They crowded the dais, grave-faced to a man, each one stunned into silence.

Chill gray light slanted in on them through narrow, high-set windows to illuminate their ill ease—their fulsome belief in Donald MacKinnon's nonsensical ravings about curses and suchlike devilry.

Magnus frowned.

The discovery of the adder, and the superstition clouding his kinsmen's eyes, laid a pall over an afternoon he'd already been dreading for days.

And now it'd gone from bad to worse.

Clearing his throat, he eyed his ashen-faced clansmen, forced himself to swallow the bitter taste in his mouth. "My sorrow that our minds run so wide apart," he said, steely-voiced. "But I say you, the only fiend of hell who had aught to do with bringing yon adder into our midst is a flesh-and-blood man walking amongst us—not some nebulous creature from the hoary realm of the dead or the secret land of the fey!"

His pronouncement made, he folded his arms and let his gaze rake each man.

To his relief, he caught a few nods of accord from within the circle of gawking men. But only a few. Most turned away to reach for the nearest ale cup or scratch with furious intent at sudden-appearing itches. A curious affliction that seemed to ripple through the entire ranks of MacKinnons gathered in the hall.

Bothered by nothing of the sort, Donald MacKinnon all but snorted.

He flashed a defiant glare at Magnus. "You needn't glower at the rest of us, laddie," he said, his tone cantankerous. "I vow you'd be equally loath to doubt had you not been away all these years, if you'd seen the stress and strife we've suffered."

"I have seen my share of suffering, never you doubt it." Magnus smothered the images before they could take form, closing his mind's eye to the sight of mangled bodies and torn flesh, his ears to the soul-splitting screams of men in mortal agony, his nose to the stench of freshly spilled blood.

Glancing at the smoke-blackened ceiling, he pinched the bridge of his nose until the memories receded.

"'Tis the goings-on and turmoil on this isle, I meant, and well you know it," his father groused. "Our trials have been great, our sorrows endless."

Loud cries of assent greeted these words. Shouts accompanied by the stamping of not a few booted feet and the jabbing in the air of more than one clenched fist.

Spurred on by his kinsmen's support, the aging laird banged the hilt of his dirk on the table, silencing the men he'd just rallied. At the ensuing quiet, he clutched the back of his chair with a white-knuckled grip and fixed a hot blue gaze on Magnus.

"If you doubt me and these men of your own good blood, ask your lady wife. She has seen enough to fill your ears for days," he said, his stare a snapping challenge. "'Tis a wonder she hasn't hied herself straight back to Baldoon and its curse-free, snakeless comforts! Aye, be glad she is abovestairs tending her ablutions or whate'er it is womenfolk are e'er about, and didn't see . . . this! And on the very day of your wedding celebration revelries."

His piece said, he swayed a bit on his feet and, seeming to sink into himself, began mumbling inanities.

Blessedly inaudible ones, too low-voiced to be understood.

Not that Magnus needed to hear them.

The increased mottling of the old man's face spoke loudly enough.

As did the renewed unrest sweeping the length and breadth of the crowded hall.

"Hear me, good men," Magnus called out to them. "Such talk serves nothing. Senseless beating of the air brings naught but wasted breath. But, aye, I agree. This"—he jerked his head toward the adder—"reeks of someone choosing the day with care."

That last got his father's attention. "So you admit the snake didn't slither in here on its own to say us a fine g'day?"

Magnus hesitated, choked back a groan. "Nay, there, at least, we stand in fullest agreement. I hold that it was indeed deposited here—just not by unworldly powers."

"So says he of little faith!" His father threw up his hands. "Faugh and bother! There be more to this world than cold steel, coin, and what we can see with our naked eye," he railed. "Some things a man just kens with his heart, laddie. You would be wise to learn that."

"And how say you, Dugan?" Magnus rounded on his brother, slid another half-fascinated, half-repulsed look at the dangling adder.

Dugan shrugged. Standing alone, for no one seemed wont to seek his company, he held his arm extended well before him, his swarthy features working with clear distaste.

"I say it scarce matters how the thing came to be here. Only that we found it before . . ." Dugan let the words trail off, looked across the torchlit hall to where their youngest brother, Hugh, sat on a trestle bench, a knot of cooing womenfolk gathered round him.

Magnus followed Dugan's gaze. "Nay, my brother, it matters greatly. Hugh could have been bitten—reaching for his lute and finding an adder coiled beside it!" he said, turning back to eye the snake again.

"Think you I dinna know that!" came Dugan's hot rebuttal, but Magnus scarce heeded him, his attention on the snake.

Skewered through the middle, it twitched and jerked in the last moments of its venomous life. Fire glow caught on the adder's scales, turning the pale gray skin a bright-gleaming silver, while the black zigzag running down its back and the beady red eyes showed the creature to be a male.

A blessedly dead male . . . and soon to be roasted.

Cursing under his breath, Magnus crossed the dais with great strides, and snatched the dirk—snake, and all—from Dugan's hand.

Before his brother could even think to form a protest, much less splutter one, Magnus hurled the dagger and its grisly victim into the hearth fire. Whirling back to Dugan, he unsheathed his own dirk—his best one—and thrust it, hilt first, at his brother.

"Keep it—with my gratitude," he said, his voice a shade huskier than usual, his throat over-tight at what might have happened to Hugh. "Like as not, you saved our brother's life."

Dugan fingered the dirk, looked undecided. "Think you I would stand by with that . . . *thing* coiled and ready to sink its fangs into Hugh's hand?" He lowered his voice. "He froze, I tell you. There was naught to do but knock him aside and kill the wretched creature. I just ne'er meant to shove Hugh so hard he'd stumble and fall."

"A hurting arm is nowise so dire as a body filled with poisonous snake venom," Magnus said, his voice pitched equally low.

"Aye, true enough, but . . ." Dugan blew out a long breath. "It still waters my bones to think what could have happened."

Magnus gripped his brother's arm, squeezed. "But it didn't—as shall naught else."

"I pray God you have the rights of it," Dugan said, his brow still knitted as he peered down the hall again. He had yet to sheath the new dirk.

Taking it from him, but gently this time, Magnus tucked the dagger beneath the other's belt. He gestured round him then, waving a hand at the arras-hung walls and the many long tables already groaning with viands and wine and ales, all in preparation for the night's feasting.

"If I am expected to accept such plentitude without a flinch, you can receive my dirk as a token gesture of brotherly appreciation, can you not?"

"Hugh would've done the same . . . for me, or any of us," Dugan countered, but patted the dirk hilt all the same, at last looking a bit pleased.

"So what are we going to do about the dark powers a-slinking about within these walls?" Their father's voice rose above the chaos again. He stared at them from the high table as he tipped a leather-wrapped flagon of *uisge beatha* to his lips for a long, throat-bobbing pull of the fiery Highland spirits.

"My bones tell me there will soon be even more ruination coming down o'er our heads," he vowed, glaring belligerence. "In especial, now that the adder failed to do their fiendish handiwork and devil ships are plying our waters! No telling what will become of us if e'er that ill craft chooses to set ashore!"

Magnus drew a great breath, pressed fingers to his aching temples. "We redress the balance is what we do," he said with all the patience he could muster. "With the adder, this was a close strike—we dare not let any such danger come so near again," he added, harboring no illusions of the difficulty in avoiding blows from an unseen foe.

A fiendishly clever foe.

But one he'd find—even if he had to overturn each stone of the castle, search every Devil-damned bog on the island.

An endeavor he would embark upon that very afternoon.

Hot gall thick in his throat, he tossed another glance at Hugh. His youngest brother had rolled up his sleeve now, and Dagda appeared to be clucking like a mother hen as she rubbed salve on Hugh's fast-swelling elbow.

Seemingly oblivious to the chaos, Colin paced back and forth in front of Hugh, his gait nigh as smooth as before Dupplin, and chatting up a storm. No doubt sharing commiserations with Hugh upon the travails and hardships of assorted bodily injuries.

Only Janet stood a little apart, her troubled gaze fixed on Hugh's reddened elbow, her pretty face a whiter shade of pale than Hugh's own pain-pinched features.

Somewhere behind Magnus, someone opened the shuttering in one of the hall's deep-set window embrasures, letting in gusts of damp, freshening wind.

The chill breeze brought the smell of rain and the sea,

but also the odor of the burning snake. Magnus's stomach pitched at the pungent smell, and he snatched up someone's forgotten ale cup and tossed its contents down his throat.

He shuddered. Unthinkable, had Hugh not seen the adder before closing his hand on the lute. He wanted to tune its strings before the evening festivities—the celebratory wedding feast.

Slamming down the cup, Magnus wiped his mouth on his sleeve and pushed that last from his mind. He'd set sail on that jabbly sea when its waters began swirling round his ankles and not a moment before.

For now, a silent prayer of thanks for his brother's life would serve.

If the good saints would hear him.

And thanks were due indeed—whether his voice was recognized or no.

Magnus would have had to bear the weight of knowing Hugh had met his untimely end in an effort to ready himself for his role as sole entertainer at Magnus's own wedding feast.

A wedding for a night only.

If he had aught to say in the matter.

But a night he'd ensure would be one his bride would ne'er forget—even if she did relish traipsing up and down dank stairwells!

Aye, for the hours of this one night, he would love her well and truly. With the deepest part of himself and setting aside his pride and frustration, to give her the wedding night she deserved.

His honor would not allow otherwise.

And something in the raised flesh at the back of his neck told him whoe'er had sought to ruin the day knew fair well that he would put his all into assuring his lady's pleasure.

That he would be *her knight* in the fullest—if only just this once.

An all-too-fleeting joy someone meant to steal from him.

But just when the hazy suspicions tiptoeing along the edges of his mind began to loom clear, a sharp tug on his sleeve chased the fragile inklings right back into obscurity.

"By the Devil's slippery tail, son, just how do you mean to *redress the balance* when the Fiend hisself is after us?" Donald MacKinnon clutched at him, the glimmer of fear in his *uisge beatha*–bleared gaze belying his earlier belligerence.

And landing another smashing blow to Magnus's pride.

"Well?" The old man poked a finger in Magnus's ribs. "Have you lost your tongue . . . or are you still thinking up a plan?"

Magnus shoved his hair back from his forehead, bit back a snarl of frustration. He'd already taken more precautions than if they were in danger of a siege, up to and including the barring of all gates and doors—even in daylight hours.

Yet all his efforts thus far had served but ill.

"I dinna blame you, laddie," his father said on a grieved-sounding sigh. "I could ne'er think of ways to outmaneuver the curse, either."

Magnus opened his mouth to speak, but before he could, the old man shuffled back to the high table, one hand pressed against his hip as he went.

"I will set double guards," Magnus called after him,

hating the resignation he'd glimpsed on his father's face, the sag to his thin shoulders. "I am even patrolling myself," he added, lifting his voice. "Through the night, early mornings, in the emptiest passages of the keep . . . in especial those!"

"We are signed and sealed to our fate, lad," his father declared without turning around, his thin voice somehow cutting through the din.

Magnus stared after him, watched him pick his slow way through the crowd. "God aiding me, an end will be put to this. I promise you. . . ." He had raised his voice again, trying to comfort, but broke off because the words sounded so empty.

So useless and ineffectual he almost wished he hadn't voiced them.

His father looked back at him. "Your keenest vigilance will avail nothing," he claimed, his voice weary now. "A malaise has e'er hung o'er this house. The man has yet to be born who can guard hisself against a curse. To be sure, I e'er misliked it myself, but I learned to live with it. Not that I'd care to tumble down the latrine chute again. Nay, I—"

Tumble down the latrine chute.

The words leapt at Magnus, shooting round his chest to squeeze so tight he could scarce breathe.

Troublesome words that clamped even harder the moment his da lowered himself into his chair at the overladen high table. With surety, the massive oaken piece could not have weighed much more were it carved of granite . . . and that, fully unadorned.

At present, it groaned beneath the weight of more heavy-silver platters, candlesticks and candelabrums, and other assorted feasterly trappings than Coldstone Castle had likely seen in centuries.

If ever.

And once the coming night's revelry and carousing began in earnest, and his kinsmen reached the depths of their cups, every one amongst them who could yet stand would rush the dais to drag Magnus and Amicia above-stairs. Each man, and even some of the bolder women-folk, would vie for the privilege of stripping them for the bedding ceremony.

A ribald and raucous undertaking, the bawdy rituals of which he could do without.

Aye, the coming night would prove a challenge to be suffered through—lest some dark-hearted soul had ven-tured into a secret vault beneath the dais end of the hall and meddled with the workings of an ancient trapdoor that one of his more dastardly-minded forebears had built into the floor beneath the high table.

One touch to the triggering mechanism, and anyone sitting on the wrong side of the dais table would vanish into a supposedly bottomless pit—trestle bench and all.

A convenient way to dispose of an enemy.

Or, with a wee bit of devious contrive, a whole horde of carousing revelers.

Laird, family, and kinsmen alike.

Plunge down worse than the latrine chute, you will, you stoop-backed bastard! A certain someone stood swathed in the hall's blackest shadows and glared the threat at Donald MacKinnon, even as he lowered his bony bottom onto the padded seat of his laird's chair.

The pestiferous old goat needed cushions to sit upon—frail and feeble as he was. Not that his scant weight would keep him from falling all the harder into his own keep's deepest pit!

Aye, hearing mass on his knees for a thousand years wouldn't save him.

Him, his fool sons, and—would the gods of wrath and vengeance be kind—as many MacKinnons as the gaping dais floor could swallow.

A pity the eldest son, great champion of the field and unwilling husband, hadn't the wits to recall his dastardly forebear's favored means of having done with those who displeased him.

A greater shame that no MacKinnon chief since those times had thought to take an ax to the rusty but still-functional triggering mechanism hidden away in a dank, cobwebby corner of Coldstone's deepest, least-visited undercroft.

Melting out of the darkness, a certain someone took especial care to blend into the milling throng, and even to offer Hugh a few words of solace on his busted elbow.

But urgent matters needed attendance, so the vengeance-seeking figure pushed with ever more determination through the smoke-hazed hall, cutting a path through boisterous clansmen and scurrying servitors.

Eager to slip from view and mind, Clan Fingon's faceless foe sought the blessed shadows. And savored the anticipation, basking in the glory of knowing fullest retribution would soon be had, and not long thereafter nothing would disturb the desolation of MacKinnons' Isle save the sound of the sea and the cry of seabirds.

Lips twisting in a grim smile at the notion, someone finally reached the sheltering gloom at the lower end of the hall, only to spin around, eyes flying wide at the sudden commotion on the raised dais.

Hands curled in tight, white-hot fury, that same someone looked on as Magnus barreled his way through startled-looking kinsmen. He burst onto the dais, plucked his spluttering da out of his laird's chair, then tossed the old he-goat over one shoulder and leapt off the dais before anyone in the hall could even draw a breath.

A great ruckus ensued, shouts and outcries ringing all around, the confusion so great, not an intelligible word could be understood.

Not that everyone present required an explanation for the laird-in-waiting's odd behavior.

Frowning blacker than the coming Highland night and muttering damnation, the figure slipped from the hall, alone and unobserved.

Old MacKinnon's tourneying son did indeed have his wits about him. A surer method of having done with Clan Fingon would have to be found.

If sawed-through privy seats, poisonous adders, and ancient trapdoors proved to no avail, more drastic methods would be employed.

Or aimed at softer, less-suspecting targets.

He'd given an oath and was a man of honor.

Magnus would not lose his head and rail at the evidence that his express orders had been so baldly ignored.

Thus determined, he repeated the words to himself as, much later, in the gathering dusk, he stood in shadow and watched *her* creeping through the even darker shadows of the stables.

Old Boiny's presence should have warned him, though. The calf-sized beast lay snoring before the stable door, his great and shaggy bulk sprawled across the threshold and blocking the entry.

Magnus blew out a breath. He'd only wanted to stroll about a bit, examine the curtain walls and mayhap ride around the outer perimeters, looking for a newly dug tunnel or any such hidden means into the stronghold, when he'd noticed wisps of pungent smoke drifting out from the stable door.

A door that stood ajar . . . curling threads of smoke he had no explanation for—until now.

The smoke tendrils came from the small torchlight she held in her hand as she poked about where, regardless of what she sought, she'd find little more than dust, cobwebs, and a pitiful few underfed garrons.

Beasts who seemed to have given her their trust as wholly as old Boiny, for nary a one of the sturdy little horses so much as neighed protest at her intrusion.

Only *he* objected.

And to more things than discovering her thrusting her pretty nose into every dark corner of his lowly stables.

Aye, he must be in high favor with the gods indeed to live in a land of lochs, bogs, and rough moorlands and ne'er be able to take a step without one fetching raven-haired lass forever rising up out of the mists to plunge his life into turmoil.

As if sensing his stare, or mayhap his thoughts, she suddenly froze in her furtive exploration and whirled around. "Oh!" she gasped. "W-what are you doing here?" Her chest heaved, and a moth-eaten saddlecloth was clutched in her free hand. "I was told you were off making your rounds outwith the castle walls."

Magnus had to smile.

At least the lass was honest.

"Do you always inquire of my whereabouts and undertakings before you set off on your own, my lady?"

She lifted her shoulders, had the grace to color. "I had reason to look in here," she said, nipping the little hand-held torch into an empty wall bracket. "I also did not want my . . . eh . . . search to upset you needlessly. There are already so many things weighing on your mind."

"The time is long past to consider whate'er might be on my mind, wouldn't you say?"

Magnus regretted the words as soon as they left his tongue, but, as so often in his life, the Lady Amicia brought out the worst in him.

As if to prove it, he stepped over Boiny's sleeping form and strode through the darkened stables to stand before her. "You could lend my mind ease if you tell me what you hoped to find in here, my lady."

He ran his fingers along the rough wood of a stall partition, the movement releasing a puffing trail of dust. "You could comb through this stable from now until the edges of doom and find nary a purse full of silver or a single length of fine braid," he said. "Nary an ell of dearest cloth. Nothing at all to catch a woman's eye and fancy."

Her blush deepened and she glanced aside, her fingers still digging into the ancient saddlecloth. "I believe you ken such frippery holds little appeal for me, Magnus MacKinnon."

"Aye, I do know it," he said, stepping so close the heat of his body warmed her. "So what *were* you hoping to find?"

Amicia felt her cheeks flame, more with his proximity than what she must tell him, so she peered into the deep shadows of a nearby stall and answered him.

"'Tis glass shards or narrow, sharp-edged pieces of metal I was seeking," she said, meeting his eye—and not at all surprised to see the shock there. "That, or perhaps an overlong thorn or two," she added, making it worse.

"I warrant I know you well enough, too, to trust that such objects were not sought to bring about my demise," he said grimly. "Nor anyone else's, aye?"

Amicia nodded.

"I wished to avert someone being hurt—including these dear beasts," she said, casting a quick glance at a swaybacked mare watching them patiently from a nearby stall.

"And what kind of . . . *harm* did you think to prevent?" he wanted to know, sounding and looking as if he already did. "What made you think of such a danger?"

Scrunching the saddlecloth in her hands, Amicia sent up a silent prayer that he would not think her as prone to fanciful imaginings as his father. "I saw a dark-cloaked figure scurry in here earlier," she said, kneading the rough, scratchy cloth. "Whoe'er it was, they darted from shadow to shadow, or crept along hugging the tower walls, until they reached the stables and slipped inside."

She looked at him, letting her eyes dare him to believe her. "Just watching chilled my blood, and then I remembered my brothers speaking of a friend's anguish when he lost a prized steed because an enemy slipped a thorn beneath their friend's saddlecloth. The moment their friend mounted his horse, the thorn was driven deep into the horse's back, plunging the beast into madness. The young man was thrown—he could have suffered grave injury or worse but took only bruises. Regrettably, the horse broke a leg in the frenzy and had to be killed."

"And you feared I would face such a fate tonight?"

"I thought it possible."

"Then I must thank you, my lady. And count myself blessed to have such an astute bride."

Amicia's blood quickened at the underlying softness beneath his simply spoken words. "I did not find anything," she blurted, her pulse beginning to beat a fast rhythm. "I may have let your father's chatter get the better of me."

"Whether you were right or not scarce matters." He walked a few steps away from her, stood looking toward the light gray outline of the open door. "'Tis that you cared to come looking that I am thanking you for."

Thanking her.

Magnus MacKinnon was thanking her.

And she wanted so much more.

But a thank-you was a thank-you, and *any* emotion was better than indifference.

Much better.

So why did the backs of her eyes ache with a jabbing, scalding heat, and why had her throat gone so frightfully tight she could scarce pull air into her lungs?

Digging her fingers ever deeper into the smooth silk of the saddlecloth, she fixed her burning gaze on him, stared oh-so-hard at his bonny young face, *willed* him to look her way.

She wanted to give him her favor.

The fine length of jewel-studded silk her father had given her a fortnight ago, claiming the precious cloth held all the colors of the sun.

She thought the silk a perfect match for Magnus MacKinnon's wild mane of lustrous bronze-colored hair.

And she wanted him to have it as a token of appreciation for helping her when she'd hurt her ankle at a similar gathering of the clans a year before.

A token, too, of her affection, for she'd given him her heart that very same afternoon. But telling him so could wait . . . or would have to.

She could not do or say anything to him if he ne'er bothered to look her way.

Biting her lip, she lifted her arm and waved the silk high above her head. Fine and light as it was, it snapped and rippled in the wind at once, and she was sure he'd notice.

Tears of frustration began filming her eyes, blurring her vision, but she kept her arm in the air, holding up her favor until her shoulder burned as hotly as her eyes and her arms and fingers began to tingle.

And still he did not look.

"Hell's damnation," Amicia hissed beneath her breath, venting her misery with one of her brothers' curses.

It felt good to at least curse since she could not call out Magnus's name. To do so, him being a MacKinnon, would have her father dragging her off the games field by her ear and mayhap even forbidding her to return the next year.

So she kept brandishing her shimmering gold prize, praying he would see and come for it—for if he did, especially as a much-loved games champion, even her da would not be able to keep her from presenting it to him.

To do so then, with all the clans looking on, would be a gross breach of Highland etiquette.

So she hoped and waved and stared his way, silently calling his name as loudly as her heart would let her.

But he stood, turned halfway from her, almost in full profile, and so hemmed in by clamoring, clutching maidens, her hopes of catching his eye grew slimmer by the moment and the archery trials were about to begin.

Crying inside, she drank in his golden beauty, branding him onto her memory so she could relive, at will, each precious moment of looking at him. Each dimpled smile he flashed at someone, every bonny twinkle in his laughing blue eyes. Even if his smiles and laughter weren't meant for her.

In her dreams, she claimed them.

Saw again her young Caledonian god, standing in half-profile to her, so proud in the sunshine of a fine Hebridean day, with the wind tossing his gleaming bronze mane, his handsome face shining.

His refusal to accept her favor as sad as the way her beautiful silk banner turned old and scratchy in her hands, its cool smoothness forever gone, the teensy seed pearls and gemstones adorning its edges now only irritating bumps of itchiness on a tattered and smelly saddlecloth.

The saddlecloth!

Jerking, Amicia flung it from her, her heart still splitting with the anguish of her memories. She swiped the back of her hand across her cheeks, not surprised to find them wet, as she peered frantically about the darkening stable, once more looking for Magnus.

Once more having to note that he'd gone, left her behind, just as he'd done in her oh-so-vivid dream.

But then she saw him, still there, and her heart bounded. He stood in the deeper shadows near the door and was watching her with the strangest, most intense of expressions.

His eyes almost blazed in the darkness, and were she

one to believe in wonders, she'd swear a passion as heated as her own flared in those magnificent blue depths.

Turbulent emotions roiling just beneath the surface of his carefully checked control.

Emotions she intended to unleash.

And now, unlike all those years ago, she possessed the will and backbone to run with her heart. Even better, there was no one around to drag her off by her ear and deny her what she wanted so badly.

Their clans no longer feuded. And, blessing of blessings, even embraced their union.

Now everything had changed.

And she meant to seize the advantage.

Chapter Ten

✦

$\mathcal{L}$ATER, AS NIGHT BEGAN TO FALL and its darkness curled round the castle walls, Amicia made her way down the winding turnpike stair, a colorful entourage of comely, well-rounded beauties trailing in her wake.

Not the chattering, eager-faced maidens who'd fought her for Magnus's attentions in younger years, but ripe-bodied, raven-haired lovelies who kept annoying pace with her, tagging along no matter how she hurried.

They joined her, too, in the maze of dimly-lit passageways leading to Coldstone's great hall.

The great hall, her wedding feast, and the magnificent full-grown man her bonny young champion had become. The husband she meant to claim and had no intention of sharing with a bevy of clinging, eyelash-batting light skirts.

Remembered, imagined, or otherwise.

Everything inside her warring at the thought, she passed through a particularly dank stretch of corridor where the stone-flagged floor proved more damp and slippery than elsewhere. And with each forward moving step, she struggled harder to squelch her resentment.

Saints, but she wanted Magnus with a desperation that verged on all-consuming—and if the deep emotion she'd glimpsed stirring beneath the surface of his intense blue gaze earlier could be trusted, mayhap her chances at winning his love were not as slim as she'd believed.

Her heart lifting, she shot a quick glance at the moon, visible through a window slit, and took strength in its silvery light. Her friend and companion through many nights of longing, the moon knew her secrets.

Tonight her old ally would smile on her triumph.

And triumph she would even if she had to use one of Magnus's best virtues against him: his responsibility to duty.

Aye, to be sure, he would make her a woman this night and perchance even seek to love her pleasingly in the by-going.

If only because pride and duty demanded he do so.

And, her pesky companions boasted with glee, because he favored the charms of dark-tressed, *over-fleshy* women.

Amicia frowned.

She didn't want any such preferences propelling him into her arms—even if she did possess both attributes in raging abundance.

A wealth of raven-black hair and enough fleshly delights to please any man fond of filling his hands with a woman's warm and generous curves.

Aye, in that, at least, the future laird of Clan Fingon would not be disappointed.

Their physical joining could be a beginning.

Hopefully, a propitious one.

Feeling a bit better, she snuggled deeper into the soft embrace of her fur-lined cloak. Cumbersome or no, its warmth staved off the cold and saved her the shame of entering the great hall with chattering teeth and all a-shiver.

MacLeans, too, had their pride.

And steel in their blood—something the *cailleach's* gift seemed to remind her each time she swung its warmth around her shoulders. Almost as if the crone had cast an enchantment over each stitch her gnarled hands had put into the exquisite if awkward-to-wear mantle.

Sending Devorgilla a silent nod of thanks in case she had, Amicia hastened her step. The great hall loomed around the next curve and already she could hear muffled voices, the faint strains of lively music.

Here, so close to the feasting, more than the usual number of wall torches had been lit, each one spewing choking smoke into the chill night air. Despite her cloak, she shivered, for the flickering light, if welcome, cast weird shadows and picked out the dark blotches of dampness staining the stone walls.

Stone walls that moved!

She froze.

The unseen beauties fled, vanishing as swiftly as if they'd ne'er been there to plague her.

Her blood chilling, she almost wished them back. Light-skirted conquests, like as not long dismissed from her husband's mind, were a much preferable terror than undulating walls.

And they *were* undulating . . . every blessed stone!

A scream locked in her throat, she looked on as the wall came to life. The damp stones vibrated as if they breathed, some even seeming to groan darkly on the exhale.

Scarce able to breathe herself, her eyes stretched full wide, muscles she hadn't even known she possessed tensed in sheer, laming horror.

"Oh, dear saints," she gasped, finding her voice at last—and blessedly, her feet, too. But before she could take more than two backward steps, the wall's moans became an ear-splitting *screech*.

Worse, the shifting stones sprouted an arm.

A very masculine arm, oddly familiar, if not quite well-muscled enough to be her husband's.

The accompanying hand held a vicious-looking morning star flail—a knight's weapon of choice for fierce, oft-times less than noble, close-range fighting.

Gulping, Amicia stared at the flail, at the iron macehead flanged for optimal destruction and capable of rendering crushing blows sure to kill or, at the least, sorely maim the unfortunate recipient of its deadly strike.

"Sweet Mother in Heaven!" she cried, pressing a hand to her breast as the wall moved again, this time swinging back into a hellishly dark recess to allow the arm's owner to step through the opening.

And when he did, relief flooded her at once—even if Dugan's dark-frowning visage revealed him to be in anything but a good temper.

"*Roast the Devil on the hottest hob o' hell* would be more fitting, my lady," he said, looking furious enough to attempt such a feat. "And Magnus will roast *my* hide for bursting out of this hidey-hole in front of you."

Straightening his plaid with a quick jerk of his free hand, he stared at her, his gaze so black and piercing, her insides quivered.

"W-what were you doing in there?" She tried to peer around him, to see into what she now recognized as a secret passage cut into the wall. Although Dugan was not as tall and powerfully built as Magnus, he proved quite strapping enough to block her view.

He reached to jiggle one of the stones in the wall. "What was I doing?" he echoed as, with the same eerie groans, the wall swiveled back into place.

"Naught that my brother will be pleased to hear," he finished as soon as the wall settled, the stones ceased juddering.

"Is there aught he has been pleased about of late?" The words leapt from her tongue before she could stay them.

But to her surprise, Dugan crooked a lopsided smile.

"There is much he *ought* to greet with pleasure, I'd judge," he said, his countenance lighting. "Aye, save for a few wee troubles, that knave can count himself a greatly favored man."

Heat blooming on her cheeks, Amicia touched her fingers to the cold, damp stone. "And this secret passage plays a role in what plagues him?"

Dugan's gaze grew guarded. "In part," he said, clearly not keen on telling her what he'd been about in the damp-smelling recess.

"I am not unaccustomed to intrigue or danger," she told him with a glance at his mace. "Aye, even within one's own good walls."

She fixed a level gaze on him, let her tone and the glance indicate she knew full well that good men did not roam their own keep's passageways armed to the teeth unless they had serious reason.

"I did not come here to run from whate'er ills Magnus

carries on his shoulders. I would much rather face them head-on and at his side."

Dugan blinked but recovered quickly. His smile flashed. "I knew you would make a meet bride for him."

"That is my greatest wish, but one I cannot fulfill if I am kept in the dark about Coldstone's secrets."

The guarded look returned to Dugan's face. "Not secrets, lass. Nor mere haverings, either, I will admit. It is only that he would not see you troubled on this of all nights."

Pulling on his dark-curling beard, he peered toward the hall. "Magnus didn't expect you belowstairs so soon," he said, apparently trying to change the subject. "He meant to send someone to fetch you when all had been made ready."

"I finished my ablutions an hour ago and wearied of pacing the chamber." She touched an encouraging hand to his arm. "It matters naught to me if the hall has been festooned nor even if we feast on simple bannocks and watered-down ale."

Now Dugan *did* look distressed.

"That is not the kind of readiness I meant." He regarded her with an expression that swung between sympathy and a barely-veiled urge to bolt.

"Then what did you mean?"

He blew out a breath, shuffled his feet.

Amicia bit back a smile. She'd won.

"Christ on the Cross, Magnus will have my hide," he burst out, confirming the victory. "Even now, he is in the hall ordering every able-armed man to help him cart the high table to the lower end of the hall. The high table and everything else set upon the dais."

This time, Amicia blinked, wholly confused.

But the answer came with all speed. "He wishes to clear the dais for musicians? Or dancing?"

Dugan shook his head. "He wishes to avoid having anyone plunge to certain death should the ancient trapdoor beneath the high table give way during the feasting. That is the way of it, naught else."

But there *was* something else.

She was sure of it and wasn't moving until she had the answer to that as well. "And the wall passage? The flail? What do they have to do with all this?"

Dugan glanced down at the deadly mace, tucked its long shaft beneath his belt. "Magnus sent me below to smash the workings of the triggering mechanism," he said, patting the mace. "He ordered the high table moved lest someone had rigged the trapdoor in a way that would let it fall open even if the usual trigger had been made ineffective."

Shivering anew, Amicia posed her last question. "What happened to make him think something so dire might occur? Did someone fall into one of the privy chutes again?"

"Nay, but what happened could have been as tragic. Come," he said, taking her arm. "I will tell you along the way."

"I would rather know now."

"Very well." Dugan released a resigned-sounding sigh.

Amicia waited.

Clearly purchasing time, he stared up at the damp-streaked ceiling. "This morning, our brother Hugh nearly fell prey to whate'er darkness stalks these walls," he said, looking back at her.

"He could have suffered an adder bite—even died of

its poison. Had he not seen the snake first, he would have surely plunged his hand straight into its lethal coils."

"Dear saints!" Amicia stared at him. "But how did it happen? Adders frequent the moorlands and are scarce seen save on rare sunny days when they bask on rocks or sun-warmed peat banks. Besides, wasn't Hugh in the great hall this morning? How—"

Her breath catching, she paused, a sickening dread spreading through her. "Dinna tell me the adder was in the hall?"

To her horror, Dugan nodded. "Aye, bold as day. And the whole of it is even more unsettling."

"What can be worse?"

"The place in the hall where the adder was found." Dugan glanced away, fixed his gaze on a shaft of moonlight streaming through an arrow slit. "Hugh serves as *seannachie* for Clan Fingon, see you? Our coffers have ne'er been full enough to employ a true bard as most clans do. Not that we mind. Hugh's voice is purest gold, his words treasured by us all."

"But what does Hugh's silvered tongue have to do with the adder being in the hall?"

"Everything, my lady. Hugh discovered the adder when he went to fetch his lute. He wanted to tune its strings before playing this evening."

"The snake was near his lute?"

"Coiled right next to it," Dugan confirmed, his voice grim. "That is the damning part—the snake being with Hugh's lute proves without doubt that a blackguard of the most cunning sort walks amongst us."

"I see," Amicia said, not seeing at all.

"Nay, my pardon, lass, but you cannot. Not until you hear the significance of it."

"Then what is the significance?"

"Hugh's lute is of rare value—a fine instrument of too great a worth to be left lying about when he isn't strumming it," Dugan explained, flicking another glance down the passageway. "Because he e'er frets something could happen to it, he keeps it locked inside an *aumbrey* near the high table."

Amicia swallowed.

The floor seemed to tilt beneath her feet.

Now she understood.

She'd seen the cupboard Dugan meant. A safe storage place for valuables and always kept under key, its door firmly closed. Indeed, at first glance, only a keen eye would even note its existence, so seamlessly was it fitted into the dais wall.

"A snake could ne'er have gotten inside the *aumbrey*," she said, her blood running cold. "Not unless someone put it there."

"There you have it," Dugan agreed, his fingers curling around the haft of his flail. "Whoe'er is responsible knew Hugh would be retrieving his lute. With the wedding feast set for this night, nothing is more sure."

Amicia pressed a hand to her cheek, wordless.

Dugan cleared his throat. "Lady, my brother will miss your presence, but he will understand if you would now prefer to bide awhile abovestairs before joining him," he said, looking so miserable at the suggestion, the queasy roilings in Amicia's belly turned to steel.

Hard, well-tempered MacLean steel.

"I thank you, but I will go to him now." She lifted her chin. "I will not hide away from whate'er troubles face my husband."

"Magnus is a reasonable man . . . for the most." Dugan tried again. "He will—"

"And I am a resolute woman," she cut in, red-hot daring pulsing through her.

Its ferocity—and the emboldening thrill of it—amazed and enlivened her. Even if her brothers would swear a more headstrong lass ne'er walked these Isles.

She knew the truth, knew the doubts that e'er gnawed at her heart, robbing her sleep and chasing her through her dreams.

Tonight she meant to challenge every one of them.

"Your brother will need me this night . . . if only to wear a joyous, untroubled face before his people," she asserted. "Do you not see? The dastard behind these attacks will be there tonight. Waiting, watching, and hoping to see us cowering in fear."

Staring at her, Dugan started to shake his head, but then an ever-broader smile began sneaking across his face.

"By the Rood, I knew you'd make my brother a fine bride," he said, offering her his arm with a bit of a flourish.

"Then let us hope he can be convinced of that as well, good sir," Amicia gave back, linking her arm in his.

Feeling bold indeed, she let him escort her forward, toward the great hall and her waiting husband.

And each step of the way, she drew Devorgilla's cloak a bit more securely about her shoulders.

Just for good measure.

Amicia clutching the cloak was not lost on a certain someone observing the fine lady's arrival. In the secrecy of shadow, a far better cloak than any fur-lined mantle however dear, someone allowed a wee smile to tug at lips too long set in lines of vengeance.

The night was yet young and fresh, but Clan Fingon's doom inched ever near. And just as the new bride's richest raiments couldn't keep her from shivering, neither would dragging tables and shoving benches from one end of the hall to the other stop someone's boiling wrath from crashing down upon their unsuspecting heads.

And all the fool precautions they attempted would prove fruitless.

Someone's machinations and wit would e'er besiege them until very soon, in the hour of their greatest need, they would be brought to their knees.

One by one, if need be until the earth had been cleansed of their scourge and every last MacKinnon awakened to find himself on the hither side.

Aye, their end approached.

Tonight was the beginning of it.

Amicia paused just inside the hall's arched entrance, her breath catching at the transformation of its mosttimes silent and grim vastness. Though the choking bite of countless pitch-pine torches stung and watered her eyes, the difference couldn't be denied.

Nor the splendor.

Silver branches of fine-burning candles lit every trestle table, and not the lesser-quality tallow candles most often found throughout the MacKinnon stronghold. Nay, these were fine tapers of purest beeswax, and the dazzling array of victuals they illuminated would have received *oohs* and *ahhs* at the noblest of tables.

Aye, for this one night, Coldstone Castle seemed to

have set aside the burden of troublous days and truly out-
done itself.

Someone had spread sweet-scented meadowsweet
atop the floor rushes and that delicate scent pleased the
senses even as the richer, heavier aromas of well-roasted
meats and seafowl hung in the smoke-hazed air, tantalizing the taste buds and making mouths water.

Amicia caught her lower lip between her teeth,
pleased beyond measure. Ne'er had she seen a more im-
pressive display.

Even with the somewhat disconcerting circumstance
of the high table no longer gracing the raised dais at the
other end of the hall, but in such close proximity to the
main entry door she'd almost walked straight into it.

Nevertheless, the scene before her stole her breath.

In especial, the sea of staring faces turned her way.

Shining faces filled with warmth and welcome.

The fleeting glimpses of recovered pride touched her
deeply. The manifestations of pride ran rampant throughout the hall, visible in the upright posture of those lining
the trestle benches and in the unmistakable spring in the
step of those not yet seated.

"I' faith!" she managed to gasp—just before her throat
locked on her.

Too stunned to do much more than stare, she dug her
fingers into Dugan's arm lest he urge her any farther into
the thronging masses of more MacKinnons than she'd
known existed.

"They are here to greet you," he told her, correctly
guessing at least one reason for her gasp. "You haven't
seen them before now because they've been toiling at the
boat strand day and night, rebuilding our fleet. They are

there at earliest cockcrow and do not return until long after you've sought your bed."

"There are so many." Amicia stood as if frozen to stone, keenly aware of countless sets of eyes turned her way, each pair scrutinizing, even if in friendly and warm regard.

Dugan patted her hand. "You needn't fret, lass. They are pleased to see their future laird's bride." He slanted her a look of brotherly encouragement. "Magnus's bonnie, raven-haired bride."

"Raven-haired?" Amicia shot him a quick glance.

If one more MacKinnon called attention to the sootiness of her hair color, she'd shave off the whole of it.

Everywhere!

"Well, you are—are you not?" Dugan teased, winking at her.

He lifted a lock of his own black hair. " 'Tis a bonny enough shade, I'd say."

Amicia shrugged one shoulder, not wanting to dwell on her coloring.

Not now.

Not this night.

"Dinna look so troubled. 'Tis a good thing you are not fair-haired or flame-topped, never you worry." Dugan took her hand, kissed the air above her knuckles. "My brother has e'er had a taste for sultry lasses. You will have him on his knees and begging your favor before you can say, 'Coldstone Castle.' "

A stab of sharp green *ache* shot through her upon his words. "At the moment, I would be well-content just to see him smile." She tightened her grip on his arm when he made to lead her forward.

She wasn't taking another step until she'd assured herself nary a one of those blowsy, black-tressed phantoms hadn't used Dugan's innocently hurtful words to slink close to her again.

Nay, she wasn't budging.

Not before she'd had time to regain the strength of her MacLean blood.

Its steel.

An advantage she'd sorely need to face and claim the magnificent man pacing in front of the hearth fire.

Not that she couldn't look on him until her eyes ached!

She stared across the hall at him, her heart thundering, the nervous flutters in her stomach underscoring the thrall he held over her.

Heads taller and more powerfully built than any other man she'd ever seen, Magnus MacKinnon didn't notice her at all. Truth to tell, he didn't appear to notice . . . anything.

But hard lines of strained concentration stood etched into his handsome face and each one suggested the reason for his preoccupation. As did his over-long strides and the fierce passion blazing in his eyes.

A heated fervor she suspected had scarce little to do with the charms of lushly curved lasses, sultry or otherwise.

Even so, just seeing such passion—*any shade or flavor of it*—burn so brightly in those clear blue eyes of his made her heart pound all the same.

A soul-deep sigh rose in her throat. Faith, but she yearned to see those gorgeous eyes alight with an obsession of an entirely different sort.

She was more than obsessed.

Not that she cared.

Far from it, she'd swim the deepest Highland loch,

climb the steepest brae, brave the fiercest north wind, and even shout her sheer, raging *want* for Magnus MacKinnon to all the world and the entirety of the heavens—and do so gladly, if only such a spectacle would help her win his heart.

His love.

The deep abiding kind she'd harbored for him since all time was, and for as long as time would e'er continue to be. A love that swelled her heart until she'd swear she could touch the wind and sea and sky.

A passion that, if e'er released, would shake the hills—should she put any faith in such romantic notions.

Possible or nay, such had been the shape of her every dream too long for her not to take full advantage of any crumb of opportunity he tossed her way.

So for the moment, she ignored the stir all around her and simply drank in the glory of him, let his heady male beauty melt her. Garbed in full Highland panoply, with his plaid slung proudly over one shoulder and his mailed hauberk gleaming in the torchlight. Just looking at him heated her in places a more timid lass would ne'er acknowledge.

But for the nonce, she forced herself to stop thinking about the welter of kisses she burned to light upon every inch of his great, braw-muscled body!

"I told you he'd be well-occupied," Dugan said, his voice scattering the tingles, restoring her wits.

He latched a strong hand around her wrist, began dragging her forward, apparently having decided that it was time for Magnus to own to his bride.

Whether he wished to or no.

A notion circling through Magnus's own mind—lay-

ing bright golden bands about him, a new one for each
nearing step *she* took toward him.

It was time to face his fate.

Without dark scowls and evasions, and making use of
every shred of charm he'd e'er been credited to possess.

If he hadn't forgotten what to do with them.

And if his new bride didn't find the nonsense that
opened each MacKinnon wedding feast so off-putting,
she truly did seek return passage to her fair isle of
Doon—a place where he doubted such folly would be tol-
erated.

"Ho, Magnus! I bring you a meet bride," Dugan called
out, propelling Amicia toward him—just as ritual demanded. "Will you claim her? Or would you relinquish
her charms to me, as next in line to represent this great
and worthy house?"

"What?" Amicia's wide-eyed glance shot to Dugan's
bitter earnest face, *her* face having gone a flattering
blanched-white upon hearing his words.

Magnus stood still as stone, hating to see his bride's
dismay, but secretly pleased by her reaction to the nonexistent possibility of finding herself as Dugan's bride.

Catching that one's eye, Magnus squared his shoulders
and gave the expected response.

"I will surrender her to none," he said, speaking to
Dugan but looking at his wife. "That I swear!"

He swore, too, to change the tradition that forbade
him—or anyone—to warn her about this ritual test of her
affections, her loyalty.

Aye, a change would be the order of the day once he
became laird in truth. But for now, he contented himself
by trying to reassure her with his eyes.

Let her know by his expression that she needn't fret—

that he wasn't about to give her over to Dugan or any man. And that he'd have done with this buffoonery as swiftly as circumstance allowed.

Circumstance, and the scores of MacKinnons savoring each moment of the much-anticipated ritual.

A silly custom if ever there was one, dreamed up by some long-dead ancestor—like as not when the lout had been too drink-taken to occupy himself more wisely.

"So that is the way of it—you desire her. I have feared as much." Dugan rubbed his chin. "And if there is someone here who might wish to challenge you for her favor?"

Magnus dropped his hand to his sword hilt, withdrew the blade to half its gleaming length. "Any insolent cockerel who'd dare attempt to win her shall leave here with his tail between his legs like some whipped cur," he vowed, summoning his darkest mien. "Of that, you may be sure!"

"By all God's wrath, what *is* this?" Amicia demanded, her initial shock swinging into a bold display of the famed MacLean temper.

With two spots of bright red coloring her cheeks, she glared at him, at Dugan, and even at those hapless clansmen who just happened to be standing close enough to catch the heat of her stare.

And, saints preserve him, but Lady Amicia in full, fiery temper proved more fetching than he would have thought possible.

Indeed, he found her so glorious that, for a moment, he forgot his own cares and knew his first true lift of the heart in longer than he could recall.

Knew, too, a hot stirring beneath his braies.

"Well, MacKinnon?" she demanded, glittery-eyed. "I asked you what this is about?"

Damning tradition, he mouthed one wee warning: *'Tis only the begin of MacKinnon Claiming Ceremony. . . .*

Regrettably, even as he formed the words, his kinsmen chose the moment to voice their good cheer.

"Hech, hech, but she's a fiery piece o' womanhood!" a deep male voice called from somewhere in the hall.

"Aye, the sparks will be a-flying tonight!" another agreed, hooting with glee. "Would that I could be a shadow on their bedchamber wall this e'en!"

"Would that *I* were less gray-topped," an older clansman burst out, thumping his chest. "I'd lay claim to her myself, by God!"

Her eyes now at fullest stretch, Amicia wheeled to level a stare at the snaggle-toothed graybeard before turning back to aim the entirety of her incredulity on Magnus.

"For truth, sir . . . can it be the whole Clan Fingon has run craven?"

The fiercest urge to agree with her swept through Magnus, but duty bound him to ignore her protestations and follow the course of the fool ceremony.

He *did* rake his kinsmen with a warning stare—the fiercest he could muster.

Their peace thus assured, he pressed a hand to his heart. That, too, being part of the ceremony.

The part he most dreaded.

"Be on with it, Magnus—or shall I say the words for you?" a gravelly-voiced clod of a clansman with a bushy red beard put to him. "I'll fight you or anyone here for the lass—and give you my last *siller* for her, too!"

"Very well . . . so be it," Magnus said more to himself than anyone.

"Lady Amicia is mine," he declared, lifting his voice. "And I am hers. We belong to each other," he rushed on, nigh shouting the remaining words. "Now. This night. And forever more . . . if she will have me."

A throbbing hush spread through the hall, all gazes shifting to Amicia.

Magnus hesitated but a pulse beat, just long enough to swallow the tight knot in his throat. "Lady, will you show us where your heart lies?" Somehow he got the words out. "Is it your will to be my lady wife? To share my hearthside and bed, mother my bairns?"

Her dark eyes shining, Amicia nodded. "I have always willed it—such has e'er been my deepest hope," she responded at once, rubbing her thumb over her sapphire ring as the words spilled from her heart.

Her answer unleashed raucous cheers as, throughout the hall, clansmen banged flagons and dirk hilts on the long tables, stamped their feet until the floor shook.

The fervor in her voice and the light in her eyes as she'd said the words unmanned Magnus, scouring him with a hot-burning pleasure that had naught to do with the rousing draw of her warm, womanly appeal, her earthy sensuality—much as he desired her.

Nay, it was the implied pride in being *his* and her unabashed delight in that state, that undid him. The knowledge knocked great gaps in his defenses until he had the uncomfortable sense of standing naked and vulnerable right smack in the crossroads of his destiny.

Most unsettling of all, he found himself glad to be there.

"Then go to him, my good-sister." Dugan's voice rose above the jubilation of their kinsmen. He gave a nudge to the small of her back, urged her forward.

Not that she needed any such assistance.

Abandoning all pretense of ladylike reserve, she

launched herself at Magnus, throwing her arms around his neck and twining her fingers into the thick waves of his hair.

"Whoa, lass . . . my precious lass," Magnus heard himself say as he steadied her, the endearment a truth he could no sooner have kept to himself than stop breathing.

He *did* settle his hands on her shoulders, holding her back just a wee bit so he could revel in just looking at her, *savor* the glory of her. How disarmingly *alive* she was. *How alive she made him feel.*

Aye, she undid him entirely, marched hot-footed over every defense he'd thought to erect against her. Ne'er had he beheld a more stunning woman, a more desirous, utterly *female* one.

He looked at her, allowing himself for the first time since his homecoming to truly lose himself in the pleasure of simply gazing on her.

The lass who'd chosen him above all others.

The woman he would have made his long ago, had the fates been kinder.

Firelight cast a golden glow over her face and reflected in her hair, making her glossy raven braids glisten like moonlight on night-blackened water. She'd coiled them above her ears again, had woven pretty blue ribbons into the plaits, and he burned to undo them. Toss aside the ribbons and let her unbound hair spill through his fingers like finest watered silk.

Her mad dash into his arms had set her magnificent breasts to swaying, and even through the folds of her cloak, he could feel their fullness swinging against the insides of his forearms as he held her. The erotic contact, both exquisite and maddening, tantalized him beyond endurance.

"You are lovely," he told her, lifting a hand from her shoulder to feather a caress along the curve of her cheek, touch awed fingers to the cool silk of her gleaming braids.

One glossy tendril had slipped free from the artfully coiled plaits and he reached for it, let the silky strands curl around his fingertip. "Sweeting, I must ask you—you ken there can be no retreat from this point?"

Especially not for him.

Not now.

Not after she'd declared herself so beautifully in front of God and all his kinsmen. And especially not after he'd known the gift of her lush curves straining against him—and that through the folds of her ridiculously voluminous cloak!

He'd lose his soul when the time came for them to stand in a full-naked embrace.

He blew out a gusty breath, knew himself already lost.

"Well, lass?" he probed, toying with the glossy black curl, *praying* she'd not disappoint him. "You ken tonight's significance?"

She nodded, wordless, but her magnificent eyes brimmed with glittery starlight—the brightness of unshed tears and newfound hope.

Hope, acceptance, joy, and . . . aye . . . a desire that surely burned bright as his own.

And seeing those emotions shining all over her beautiful face nearly brought him to his knees. Still, his honor forced another question from his tongue.

One for her ears alone.

"You are aware of what next transpires when we are escorted abovestairs?" He near choked on the words, hoped her boldness wouldn't abandon her now. "In especial, what will happen *after* our kinsmen leave us?"

Taking her lower lip between her teeth, her only outward sign of nervousness, she nodded.

Then she drew a long, quivering breath. "I have e'er yearned for this moment," she said, her dark eyes luminous. "Be assured that I will revel in what happens when we are alone. There shall not be a moment of it that I have not dreamed of for long."

She took her hand from behind his neck just long enough to swipe at the moisture shimmering high on her cheek. "Far longer than you know," she breathed, her voice hitching.

"*Lass. . . .*" Magnus could say no more, the thickness swelling in his own throat refused to let out the words he burned to say.

And as well, for his gawking kinsmen had edged near, the whole long-nosed lot of them tilting their heads and cupping their ears to try and catch whispered intimacies he wasn't about to share with them.

His bride showed much less reluctance.

Smiling triumphantly, if a bit wobbly-lipped, she lifted her chin for a kiss . . . letting the seductive brush of her curves, still rubbing so soft and yielding against him, *demand* he give her one.

Trying not to hear the ribald shouts erupting all around them, Magnus swept his arms around her, dragged her flush against him. Lost, he arched her voluptuous body until they stood lips to toe, so close they almost melded together.

A throaty *purring* sound escaped her as she stretched her fingers into his hair, caressed his nape, her touch sending delicious shivers rippling down his back.

"Are you not going to kiss me?" She parted her lips in an invitation no man would even think to deny.

"Aye, I am going to kiss you indeed," Magnus vowed, holding her gaze, reveling in its smoldering intensity.

I shall kiss you in ways you ne'er dreamed of, sweet lass.

Raw desire pounding through him, he lowered his head, intending—for now—only to brush his lips over hers a few times, but she slid one hand down his back to cup his buttocks and—saints alive!—urged his hips ever tighter against her own.

Another deep, throaty *purr* came from low in her throat at the startling, bone-melting impact, and before he'd slid his lips but once, twice, across the yielding soft- ness of hers, she stunned him by sliding her tongue inside his mouth.

"Christ and all His saints!" he moaned against her lips, his breath mingling with hers. The intimacy enflaming him, his entire body tightened as her tongue met his in a hot, sweeping glide.

You are unmanning me, he thought he heard himself growl, not quite sure if he'd spoken the words aloud.

And even if he had, he didn't care.

Wielding her best weapons with boldest intent, she un- raveled him stroke by sweet-sliding stroke. Hot, slick, and deliciously silky, her tongue swirled over and around his in a lascivious dance that shot jolt after jolt of heat ripping across his groin.

And each lush sweep, each hot tangle of her tongue with his, claimed another never-to-be-won-back piece of Magnus MacKinnon—deftly turning what should have been a quick, perfunctory pass of his lips over hers into a breathy, open-mouthed kiss. A white-hot conflagration of sharpest, most brilliant need.

A wild slaking, a drinking in of each other's essences, that set his senses to reeling and had him so ragingly hard, so needy, he was close to tossing her over his shoulder, charging out of the hall, and tossing up her skirts to thrust himself full-tilt inside her as soon as he'd put the throng of roistering onlookers behind them.

Onlookers who, from their increasingly bawdy shouts, seemed more than eager to see him do just that.

Only here in the hall—to *their* enthralled delight!

"If she kisses him like that during the bedding ceremony, I swear I am not exiting the chamber!" a rowdy kinsman roared close by Magnus's ear.

So close the man's ale-fumed breath fanned across his cheek. Close enough for him to know the lout had already enjoyed a more than ample eyeful.

Indeed, the clansman's persistent ale fumes reminded him that not just one but *every* MacKinnon on the isle had witnessed his capitulation—a notion that doused his lust faster than if he'd poured a bucket of iciest loch water into his braies!

"By God, I'd say the lass has her heart hung on him!" another clansman bellowed the moment Magnus broke the kiss, and set his heavy-breathing vixen from him.

Nigh panting himself, hottest need still blazing inside him, he searched the hall for prattle-tongued Dagda, eager to have done with the remaining *traditions* and throw off the yoke of onlookers.

More eager still to do some serious *looking* himself— just not at an assembled mass of ugly, bearded faces!

And until he'd composed himself, he wasn't looking *her* way, either.

His blood yet burned too hot for him to risk even one glance in her direction. Even standing so near to her left him trembling in the aftermath of the riptide that had just swept him.

The aftermath of her boldness.

A brazen act the like of which she'd ne'er believed she'd perform. Moistening lips gone decidedly tender from their soul-devouring kiss, Amicia drew in small, shallow breaths. She struggled against the overwhelming need to press her hand to her breasts and pull in *great, greedy gulps* of air.

Faith, did she need them.

She'd run to within an inch of shaming herself. Nay, more than an inch. Yet even if she could retrace her steps and start anew, she'd do the same again. Mayhap even hold him tighter than she had, kiss him all the harder when he tried to break away.

There could be no shame in seizing a dream.

A happiness she'd been chasing too long not to grasp firm and glory in, now that it'd come tantalizingly close to her reach.

Nay, she would not be ashamed.

She'd only be furious with herself if she *hadn't* allowed herself such sweet, sweet bliss.

Even if now, in the afterglow of their startlingly intimate kiss, he wouldn't look at her.

Later, once they were alone and the bedchamber door's drawbar soundly in place, she'd address that longstanding habit of his. She'd *make* him look at her . . . and at places other than her peaty-brown eyes!

For now, though, she let him gaze where he would.

And following that gaze, her jaw dropped, for the jostling mass of clansmen were stepping aside, freeing a path through their midst for Dagda and the old laird. A common enough sight in Coldstone's cavernous hall—until one spied the enormous bronze drinking mazer Dagda held aloft.

"'Tis the Claiming Cup," Magnus whispered, his warm breath a caress at her ear. "A great bronze drinking vessel believed to hail from Reginald's time, and even if not, it is of great antiquity, fashioned with miniature war galleys embossed around its rim," he told her.

"All newly married MacKinnons must share of a drink from it. First the pair, together, and then the mazer will be passed to our kinsmen. Everyone present will drink from it, usually a fresh-made batch of heather ale. . . ." He paused, amazed how easily the words *our kinsmen* had rolled off his tongue.

Stunned at the way his heart warmed at the implication.

"Dagda will speak a few words, and then after everyone has had their token sip, the feasting will commence."

"And thereafter the bedding?"

Magnus nodded, unable to speak, his throat, and certain other parts of him, being too tight and swollen for him to risk forming another word.

Not if he didn't want to sound like a spluttering eunuch.

Blessedly, the approach of Dagda and his da spared him any such embarrassment. Not far behind them, Colin was making his own slow progress through the crush as well, the fair Janet hanging on his arm—*her* lips looking nigh as kiss-swollen as Magnus's lady wife's.

A condition that would explain the notable absence of the two from the hall until just now—as did the slight swagger to Colin's almost-good-as-new strides.

To Magnus's further relief, Dagda the grim wore a smile. Or rather, her best semblance of one.

Looking well-pleased indeed, she didn't even grumble annoyance when some of the vessel's contents sloshed over the elaborate rim to spill down the front of her widow's gown.

A light touch to his sleeve proved to him that he'd only fooled himself by thinking the arrival of the heavy bronze mazer would get his mind on . . . other things.

More grateful that Scots favored plaids than he'd e'er been in his life, he turned to find Amicia peering at him, her brow knitted.

"Shouldn't your da be the one to speak whate'er will be said when we drink from the mazer?"

"Da used to say the words, to be sure," he admitted. "But he relinquished the duty to Dagda years back when he began ailing. The ceremony falls within her responsibilities as seneschal, and she always seems to relish it as her part in MacKinnon weddings. With all her faults, the old lass has e'er had a soft heart for . . . young pairs."

He'd almost said *young lovers*, but caught himself in time.

Passion was well and good—a bliss he'd sorely missed in recent times. Years, were he honest. *Love*, however, was something he was not near prepared to consider.

Not even this night.

Mayhap never.

Another tug at his arm underscored the silliness of any such notion. Just how bad it stood with him. "Aye?" he asked, wishing he didn't feel as if he were teetering along a cliff-edge and about to lose his balance.

"Why is it called the *Claiming Cup?*" His wife posed the one question he'd hoped she wouldn't.

"There's a good reason for that," he said, trying to give the words a light tone. "The mazer is brought forth after the bride and groom have accepted, or *claimed*, each other. The shared drink signifies their union as one. The passing of the mazer around the hall symbolizes their oneness with the clan and . . ."

"And . . . ?" she prodded when he hesitated.

Feeling defeated yet again, Magnus reached to skim his fingertips down the curve of her cheek. *"And,"* he began, his tongue annoyingly thick, "some claim the passing of the mazer gathers all the happiness in each clan member's heart."

"But there is more, is there not?"

Magnus nodded. "The *'collecting of the clan's* goodness' is why the new couple share not only the first sips from the Claiming Cup, but also the last," he explained. "It is believed those last two sips contain joy of a brilliance to rival all the stars in the night sky. And that, fair lady, is Clan Fingon's gift to each new married pair we welcome into our midst."

She sniffed at that.

Sniffed, and glanced aside.

But Magnus could see she was blinking furiously.

Still, true to her MacLean heritage, she recovered with all speed to pin him with a most penetrating gaze.

"Is all well with you, my lord?" she wanted to know. "You sound rather . . . *pained.*"

"Och, to be sure, I am fine," he said, laying on a deliberate bluster, lying through his teeth.

He wasn't well at all.

Or mayhap he was.

More well than he'd e'er thought to be again.

Chapter Eleven

✤

CANDLELIGHT GLEAMED on the Claiming Cup, turning its gilt-bronze to shimmering gold. In especial, the embossed war galleys circling the mazer's rim shone with eye-catching brilliance. Each galley boasted a sail crafted with a different inlaid gemstone and these flashed colored sparks of light as Dagda carried the ceremonial vessel around the great hall, making certain each clansman partook of the ritual sip.

The sharing of his heart's gladness and joy.

A spectacle Magnus watched with mixed feelings from his place at the high table.

The sadly displaced high table.

A botheration he'd sworn to keep from his mind, if only for this night, but an annoyance nonetheless. And one that had returned with howling vengeance the moment he'd escorted his lady to the table's temporary place of eminence at the lowest, most humble end of the hall.

"It matters not." Amicia leaned close, her words and

the press of her hand to his sleeve letting him know how well she read him. "I would savor this night were the high table placed in the middle of the wildest moor and with a fierce black wind raging all around us."

Magnus looked at her, found her watching him with an expression that made his heart clutch. Not trusting himself to speak, he patted her hand, gave it a warm squeeze.

A wee concession she topped by trailing the fingers of her free hand along his jaw in the lightest of touches. Sweet, feathery caresses that sent small ripples of sensation all through him.

Clearly bent on pursuing her advantage, she gave a soft little sigh . . . just the kind of feminine *purr* guaranteed to slip beneath a man's skin and melt his bones.

"Aye, sir, that would please me well—a table beneath the moon and stars . . . just for us. I would relish such a celebration," she said, her voice low-pitched, smoky. "I wouldn't even mind if we dined on simple pottage."

Magnus stiffened, her well-meant assurances dashing cold water on the languor she'd stirred in him, each word a lance thrust to his pride.

Simple pottage washed down with watered ale would be the kind of fare she'd have to tolerate were her coffers not so bottomless—did her brothers' largesse not provide every tempting morsel set before them.

Set before every hungry mouth in the MacKinnon hall.

Including the black-hearted dastard whose penetrating stare and malice he could feel coming at him in rank waves ever since he'd claimed his seat.

He could also sense the miscreant's smirking pleasure in his own discomfiture—yet every time he glanced round, he saw only the benign-smiling faces of his kinsmen.

"You do not believe me," Amicia was saying, taking her hand from his arm, the thread of hurt in her voice a hard fist in his gut.

Magnus made a noncommittal sound, for a moment, not quite sure what she meant. But then he remembered—dining in the heather and sating oneself on starlight.

A foolishly romantic notion she could almost make him believe in.

"Nay, there you err," he said. "I do believe you, and fully."

That is the great tragedy of it.

He was the one who would see her spared a plaguey life marred with cares and too little meat. But now, after holding her, after tasting her kiss . . .

"But you are . . . displeased," she said, her eyes bright.

"Amen to that—the stubborn fool," Colin put in, leaning around several clansmen to level a stare at Magnus. "Mayhap 'tis you who ought to seek healing in your Beldam's Chair. Perchance it can restore the wits I suspect you left on the banks of the River Earn."

"Aye, mayhap I should." Magnus returned Colin's stare with one of his own. "Your visits certainly have honed the edge of your tongue."

He raised his ale cup. "Here's to the Beldam's Chair! May its curative powers aid the weary and the damned for all time."

But he slammed down the cup a mite too loudly. Truth was, he *had* been sneaking alone to the sacred stone chair. Though the saints knew what he hoped to accomplish by going there.

He'd just felt a . . . need.

He stared out into the smoky hall, his gaze latching on

Dagda. Looking well-pleased with herself, she was giving a great bear of a red-bearded kinsman his obligatory sip from the Claiming Cup.

And getting frightfully close to the high table.

Magnus drew a deep breath, looked back at his wife. "See you, I would only . . . ah, lass—" he broke off, gestured to the opulence all around them. "Funding such splendor would have been a drop in the ocean had I not lost my fortune—the tourney winnings and booty that were stolen from their hiding place when I fought at Dupplin Moor."

"You can be proud you were there that day," she said, a dangerous glint in her eyes. "My heart swells with pride that you were—that you stood fast to defend this land. And you did so when it must've been apparent before the first English arrow flew, that defeat would be inevitable."

The heat in her eyes softened to a heart-melting warmth. "Aye, you can be proud. Honor is the most noble cloak a man can swirl about his shoulders. The lost riches matter not a whit—not to me."

A goodly portion of the ice coating that had slid round his heart cracked and fell away, but not nearly enough. His pride still pulsed with agitation regardless of how uncomfortably tight his throat had gone at her words.

Snatching up a freshly-topped ale cup, he tossed down its contents in one long swill. "It matters to me."

Undaunted, his bride slid a pointed look at the well-laden tables, but Magnus knew that she meant to indicate the clansmen crowding them and not the succulent viands.

"This time it is you who mistake," she said. "Take a good look at your kinsmen. All that matters is the light on their faces—their restored pride. Not the wealth lining those tables. Only the men sitting at them and the renewed purpose shining in their eyes."

Pride and purpose he should have put there.

Not the gold coin he'd married.

And that knowledge sat like a cold, immovable lump in his gut.

As did the glaring bareness of the raised dais. The hall's once-pulsing center gave itself as a grim reminder that beneath the night's raucous celebration, all was not well within Coldstone's thick gray walls.

Far from it, an invisible pall hovered over every crowded table, thick as the haze of the smoking peat fire and every bit as choking.

A sad and sorry state made all the more notable in the frequency with which many clansmen refilled their ale cups and the furtive glances they sent into the hall's shadow-deep corners.

And that, despite the jovial grins pasted on their faces.

Magnus grimaced. The necessity of such ill ease in one's own hall galled him, but he'd be damned if he'd allow a faceless coward to mar what little jollity his people had seen in years.

Nor would he let it ruin the one night he'd sworn would pass in naught but his wife's pleasure.

His pleasure in *her.*

With the blackest weather keeping her clan from attending the festivities, Magnus wished doubly hard to make this night memorable for her.

So he thrust back his chair and stood, reaching a hand to his bride as a great hush fell over the hall.

"Dagda! Make haste and hie yourself over here," he called, eager to move on to the more *enjoyable* part of the evening.

"Son of Clan Fingon!" The seneschal played her part, hurrying forward to plunk down the Claiming Cup. *"Drink, and be as one!"*

Magnus glanced at Amicia, meaning to reassure her that this foolery, too, would quickly pass. But the words lodged in his throat when she stood and her cloak slipped from her shoulders.

Thus bared, and with her braids coiled above her ears, naught but flickering candle glow stood between the lush swells of her breasts and any eyes that cared to relish the view.

Indeed, her gown's bodice dipped lower than any Magnus had yet to see her wear. And thanks to his great height, he was gifted with the best view of all.

Worn off the shoulder, the gown was crafted to delight any man of height who might happen to stand close and cast a downward glance at the inviting expanse of exposed flesh.

For if he did, as Magnus was now doing, the tall man could view much more than the top crescents of her areolae that sometimes peeked above the rim of her gowns.

Nay, *tonight,* the tall man could peer down and view the entirety of each nipple.

And Magnus MacKinnon was a very tall man.

Tall, and with a down-directed gaze.

Over-large, darkish, and relaxed, his wife's nipples stood fully free within the bodice's artful gap, each one deliciously puffed, though already beginning to pucker and tighten beneath the heat of his stare.

Magnus tightened as well, and only with great effort tore his gaze from his wife's now boldly-thrusting nipples.

But not before he lowered his head to whisper in her ear. "You are not wearing a camise."

She drew back to glance at him, a tiny smile playing at the corners of her lips. "It seemed expedient not to . . . this night."

"Shall we proceed?" Dagda spoke up, a knowing gleam in her eye as she slid the Claiming Cup across the high table. "There will soon be time aplenty for you to savor . . . other pleasantries."

Somewhere close by, someone chortled—by the wheezy sound of it, his da. "I knew the lass would please him," the same thin voice declared, indeed his father's. "Ho! The laddie will ne'er suffer a cold Highland night again with yon lassie a-warming his bed!"

Secretly glad to see his da enjoying himself for once rather than grousing on about dark powers and curses, Magnus schooled his features into an appropriately solemn expression.

"My wife and I will receive Clan Fingon's blessing with much favor," he said, giving the seneschal the expected answer as he lifted the drinking vessel in toast to those gathered in the hall. That courtesy done, he turned to Amicia.

Locking gazes with her, he tilted the Claiming Cup first to his own lips, then offered the heavy mazer to her, taking care not to look any lower than her face as he held it for her.

"Hail to the new lady of Coldstone Castle!" Resounding cheers thundered through the hall before he even took the vessel from her lips.

"Aye, she is the new lady of the keep. Let none forget it!" Magnus lifted his voice above the shouts of acclaim and thrust the empty Claiming Cup above his head, upturning it to prove that nary a drop remained in its depths. "I thank you, Clan Fingon! For the gift of your hearts' happiness—for your claiming of my lady as your own."

"Hail to Sir Magnus and Lady Amicia!" the clansmen roared. "May your hearts e'er be filled with gladness, your joys never end. This night and ever after."

"Hail Clan Fingon—may you e'er be strong and thriving!" Magnus returned, slamming down the mazer. He grabbed Amicia's hand and raised it high so all could see their linked fingers.

"My good MacKinnons and friends, we salute and thank you," he finished, lowering their hands. "It has been a long day and longer evening. I invite you to partake of all that is set before you. Aye, I say, let the feasting commence."

At once, men settled in to the more serious undertaking of filling their bellies and slaking throats parched from cheering. But a new hum of exclamation rose as not a few voices clamored for entertainment—a tale from Clan Fingon's own silver-tongued bard.

Yielding to their encouragements, Hugh heaved himself to his feet and reached for his lute. He sketched Amicia a gallant bow. "For your honor, fair lady. What would you hear?" he asked her, already strumming a quiet tune, setting the mood that had many clansmen already sitting forward, watching and listening in rapt attention.

Amicia slid a glance at Magnus. "Is there a clan favorite?"

At once, Magnus's brows snapped together. He held his tongue, but hoped Hugh would not mistake the warning.

A certain one-armed ancestor with too much pride had plagued him enough of late.

But Hugh merely gave a lighthearted shrug. "Many and varied are the tales we enjoy," he said, ever the smoother of rough waters.

"Would you hear a tale of high valor on the field of battle? Or mayhap one more suited to the night—a tale of beauteous women and chivalrous knights, filled with yearning hearts, lost love, and haunting romance? The endless tragedy of what-ifs and might-have-beens?"

" 'Tis the story of Reginald and his lady she might be wanting to hear," Dagda suggested from where she hovered near the far end of the high table.

"The Devil take Reginald," Magnus nay-sayed her choice. "My wife has already heard his tale."

"Then what would you hear, my brother? As honored groom of the day?" Hugh waited.

Magnus frowned.

There wasn't a tale worth being told that did not hold enough tragedy to pierce a heart of stone: griefs that could ne'er be healed, losses that could ne'er be replaced, yearnings and aches that would ne'er be assuaged.

Such were the hearthside tales that fired every Highlander's romantic heart and spoke deepest to their loyal-bound souls.

His own, too.

All the more reason to avoid hearing them!

Still, he probed his memory for a tale to recommend—any tale.

But then a sparkling torchlight caught and gleamed on Hugh's bright-shining auburn hair and inspiration seized him.

"Will of the Bright Sword!" Magnus blurted, regretting his choice before the echo of his words could fade from his ears.

He opened his mouth to unsay them, but shut it again as quickly. Calling undue attention to the tale would only have his lady more determined to hear it.

Will of the Bright Sword, indeed.

Only Reginald's tired yarn would have proved a worse choice.

But wave after wave of reaction swept the hall as though a dam had burst, each man present clamoring for the well-loved tale.

The choice made, Hugh began to stroll through the rows of long tables, strumming his lute as he went, waiting for the din to lessen.

And when it did, he began his tale.

"Many are the legends spawned from our beloved hills," he said, pausing beneath a well-burning wall torch so its flickering light could add to the drama. "Some of our stories are great Celtic fables known and loved by all, and some ... the rare and little-told tales ... have the power to leave memories like no other."

He started walking again, sipping from proffered ale cups, and letting the mood ripen. For the moment, the stage was conceded to the gusting wind and the soft crackle of the hearth fire.

Such sounds, too, were inherent to the Highland night. They possessed the power to stir and rouse Celtic blood.

"He is good." Amicia tilted toward Magnus, squeezed his hand.

If fate is kind, he will have forgotten the words, Magnus muttered beneath his breath.

"Aye," Hugh was saying, "some stories reach deeper and one such tale comes to us from remote times and mayhap the loneliest of our shores—the tragic tale of

Will of the Bright Sword and his beloved Mariota, a fair maiden of high rank but doubting heart."

Against his better judgment, Magnus slid a glance at his wife. Like his kinsmen, she stared at Hugh, a wistful smile curving her lips. The dewy-eyed expression proving that beneath her fiery MacLean spirit, there beat a soft and tender heart. One that wouldn't fail to be moved by the sad ending to Will and Mariota's story.

Theirs was just the kind of tale that would make a lass's eyes mist with unshed tears and have her snuggling closer to her own true love, seeking the comfort of his arms and more.

Such was the power of Will and his fool bright sword.

As if to prove it, she turned a damp-eyed gaze on him and . . . sniffed. "I am thinking your brother has the true gift of the *fili,* studied bard or nay."

"M'mmmm." Magnus gave a noncommittal grunt, not failing to notice that *her* voice held a smoky warmth every bit as soothing as Hugh's.

His blood beginning to burn hot and fast again, he turned his attention back to his brother, leaning dutifully forward and pretending enthrallment when, in truth, he'd fixed his gaze on a conveniently-placed window splay just across the hall.

". . . and so it was on *Eilean Ma-Ruibhe,* a wee isle in the middle of Loch Maree," Hugh was saying, "that a tragic ending came to two young lovers, as a pair of very ancient gravestones standing side by side in the island's small burying ground will attest."

He paused to take a long sip of frothy heather ale. "Aye, my friends, Loch Maree is blessed with a haunting beauty scarce to be matched in all the land, but the mortal dust lying in unsleeping watch beneath those two gravestones marks the sadness of a great love that ne'er reached full bloom."

As if he sensed his inattention, Hugh slid Magnus a pointed glance. "Will of the Bright Sword was a warrior of great acclaim, his sword arm and war skills prized by many," he went on, continuing the tale. "E'er desirous to help those in need, he found himself off on various war expeditions more often than he was able to visit the fair Lady Mariota on her lonely isle of *Eilean Ma-Ruibhe,* called the Isle Maree by some."

His gaze once more fastened on the window splay, Magnus snatched up his own ale cup and hid his frown beneath its rim—a wee cautionary measure should Hugh happen to look his way again.

He would not be caught tight-lipped and flush-faced when Hugh recited the most damning part of the fool-hardy tale.

"Plagued by Will's ever-increasing absences, Lady Mariota endeavored to test his affections—test them most severely, and to lamentable end," Hugh explained to his hushed audience.

"The moment Will's war ship was spotted sailing up the loch, his lady love had herself rowed out to meet the approaching galley—to meet it with her appearing to lie dead within her own small vessel. She had her maids aboard and had instructed them to pretend to mourn over their 'dead' mistress's prone and lifeless body."

Another sniffle sounded beside him and Magnus risked a glance at his wife, caught her dabbing at her eyes with a linen napkin.

His watery-eyed da did the same. And from the as-sorted shifting and soppy-sounding noises rising from the long tables, a fair number of his clansmen had succumbed to a similar affliction.

Immune himself, and with his own eyes unblinking, Magnus kept his ale cup in place and fixed a narrow-eyed stare on his brother's back as he strolled through the middle of the hall, strumming plaintive chords on his lute—letting his listeners wallow a bit in the sadness of the tale.

Not about to be lulled by such a ploy, Magnus set down the silly ale cup with a purposely loud *clack* and leaned back in his chair . . . determined to remain demonstratively unaffected.

". . . Poor Will of the Bright Sword, pleased beyond measure to see his Mariota coming to greet him, finally noted her condition, saw her lying still and pale within the nearing boat." Hugh glanced over his shoulder again, sent Magnus another telling stare. "Overcome with grief, Will called to his lady's handmaidens begging them to deny that his love had perished, but under their mistress's strictest orders, they confirmed her supposed death.

"Upon hearing the despair in Will's voice, Mariota's heart swelled, for she now knew without doubt that her beloved loved her true. But just when she meant to scramble to her feet and call to him, her little boat drew alongside Will's galley, and upon looking down and seeing her lifeless form, Will's grief overcame him and he whipped out his dirk, plunging its blade deep into his heart.

"Mariota's eyes snapped open in that very moment, and agonized by her own piercing anguish, she leapt over the low-slung side of Will's galley and, before any could stop her, pulled the dirk from his dying body and thrust it into her own."

Hugh paused as everyone in the hall held their breath and leaned forward in anticipation of the story's end.

"Aye, my friends, such was the tragedy of Will's and Mariota's love," he began again, his voice rising with every word of the tale's climax. "The two gravestones marking their end bear no names, each one only having a faint cross incised upon its age-pitted stone. But those who hear and see with their hearts know Will and his lady lie buried beneath those stones, for time has caused the stones to lean upon each other, allowing them to be united in death as they ne'er were in life.

"And to this very hour, *Eilean Ma-Ruibhe's* silence shelters them as, together, they walk its distant shores . . . gazing out across the still waters of Loch Maree. And they await the day their sadness can be assuaged by knowing a thousand and one pairs of young lovers have heard the telling of their sorrowful tale and, through it, dared to cast aside their own hearts' doubts and live joyously, filling each new day with happiness, loving and being loved. . . ."

For long moments, no one spoke. Hugh's tale, his deep, rich voice, and the mournful chords of his lute's melancholy tune seemed to linger in the smoke-hazed air.

But then the first thick-voiced cry of appreciation rose from the crowd, and Hugh made his way back to the high table amidst the plaudits of all.

And only later, when the mood in the hall swung from sentimental to ribald again, and the first raucous shouts for the bedding ceremony began to shake the walls, only then did Magnus realize that he'd been affected indeed.

So much so, that, unbeknownst to him, at some point in the telling of the silly tale, he'd slipped his arm around his wife, pulled her close, and—saints preserve him!—had been gentling kisses across her brow!

Much to the amusement of those sitting about who weren't yet too drink-taken to cast a clear-eyed glance in the direction of the high table.

Truth to tell, those hardy souls now surged forward, eager to hasten the laird-to-be and his lady abovestairs for the most rousing part of the evening's entertainment.

And none amongst the revelers, who were half-dragging, half-carrying Magnus and Amicia up the winding turnpike stairs, looked forward to the bawdy ritual more than a certain hungry-eyed individual caught up in the very heart of the gleeful carousers.

It'd been a long time since a MacKinnon had suffered such passion for his lady—even if this one tried to hide it.

Not that it mattered.

A certain someone could tell.

And meant to use that passion to unleash the wrath of vengeance long overdue.

The bare-fleshed and lascivious delights of the bedding ceremony were all that would be needed to undo the last vestiges of Magnus MacKinnon's waning restraint . . . and smooth the way to his crushing devastation.

'Twas only a pity the lass would have to be sacrificed to achieve it.

A certain someone had grown rather fond of her.

Chapter Twelve

❖

*L*ADY, *I* MUST HAVE *words with you . . . at the soonest.*

The hushed female voice tried to find her ear, but when Amicia looked round, she saw only ale-flushed faces and swathes of disheveled plaid. The boisterous troop of clansmen who saw it as their duty to hustle her and Magnus ever higher up the curving stairs to her bed-chamber.

Nevertheless, she kept searching.

Scarce louder than a sigh, the hurriedly whispered words had come from close behind her and were spoken in greatest urgency, the voice sounding much like Janet's.

If indeed she'd heard anything.

With the smoking flames of the wall torches tossing in the night draughts and constant sprays of fine damp mist gusting through the arrow slits, like as not she'd simply heard the cry of the wind and imagined spoken words.

The saints knew on such a wild night, and with her

emotions in a whirl, no one could fault her for hearing voices where none had been lifted.

Or so she thought until the jostling throng neared her bedchamber door and she caught a quick glimpse of Janet's fair head in the crush.

". . . would e'er be a burden on my heart if I did not . . ."

And this time Amicia *did* hear the words—if only a snippet of them before Janet fell back, her odd message and her hurrying feet no match for drink-taken clansmen set on reaching their laird-to-be's bedchamber and the finest entertainment of the evening.

The seldom-offered opportunity to tease and heckle their future chief without having to suffer for it. And the undeniable boon of catching a wee look at their new lady's full exposed plentitude.

A ritual nuisance Amicia determined to endure with dignity.

Much worse could befall her.

Aye, were she honest, Janet's queer behavior unnerved her more than the thought of a few scant moments spent standing unclothed before a clutch of ale-addled but good-hearted Islesmen who'd like as not have no true recollection of all they'd seen, come the morning.

Islesmen who were grinning foolishly as they kicked open the door and surged into her room. They tossed Magnus onto the great four-poster bed, some of the most ale-headed amongst them falling onto the mattress with him.

"Remember my words, lassie." Dagda appeared at her elbow, Amicia's fur-lined cloak draped over her arm. She leaned close, her dark eyes glittery with excitement. "You must make him want you."

Amicia jerked, all thought of Janet's strange whisperings evaporating as a flood of intimate images sailed through her mind.

She slid a glance at Magnus, her heart thundering even though he was still fully clothed. He sat on the edge of the canopied four-poster, an expression of tolerant good humor on his handsome face as two red-bearded kinsmen struggled to yank off his boots.

Someone had pulled back the bed hangings and the glow from the hearth fire threw dancing patterns of shadow and light into the bed's curtained interior. The pristine white of the bridal sheet gleamed bright and beckoning, its significance sending a cascade of heat streaming through her.

By sundown on the morrow, that same sheet would have been paraded throughout the castle and held under the noses of every MacKinnon old enough to appreciate the reddish smears that, by then, would mar its snowy weave.

"Make certain he catches your scent," Dagda persisted, dropping her voice. She tap-tapped a finger on Amicia's arm to make her point. "Mind you well if you wish to besot him."

"You are kind to share your . . . wisdom," Amicia said, tearing her gaze from Magnus and praying no one else had heard the woman.

Feeling naked already, she indicated her cloak. "Thank you for bringing my mantle abovestairs," she blurted to deflect the seneschal's interest from carnal activities. "I should not have left it behind in the hall."

Dagda stroked the mantle's ermine lining. "Och, to be sure, such a fine cloak ought not to be left about. Not at Coldstone. . . ." Letting the sentence go unfinished, she turned aside, all bustle and business, to hang the cloak on its peg by the door.

"Off with you, you great clumsy-fingered oafs!" Magnus half-roared, half-laughed from the bed. "I can undress myself, and in half the time!"

The words were hardly spoken when, one by one, his boots hit the floor with two loud *thuds*.

"See you," he said, pushing to his feet, "a man ought to ne'er allow another to do what he can best do hisself!"

Amicia straightened her back, wet her lips. She, too, would soon be disrobing. The act was upon her, for Dagda had ceased fussing with the mantle and was striding forward, her purpose writ plain upon her face.

She'd coiled her silver-shot hair at the nape of her neck, braiding it with shiny black ribbon in honor of the occasion. At first glance, this gave the impression of glossy-bright dark hair unmarred by the coarse gray threads that marked her advancing years.

The many candles someone had troubled to set ablaze flattered Dagda as well, their soft golden light smoothing the lines and furrows in her most-times tight-drawn face.

For one eerie moment, Amicia's breath caught. Even the old woman's step seemed more brisk and sure than usual. Something about her gave the unsettling sensation of glimpsing the seneschal as she must've been as a much younger woman.

A strikingly handsome one who'd suffered great tragedy and loss as the severe planes in her face and the silvery gleam of age-grayed hair at her temples once more attested.

Shivering, and not because of the room's cold, damp air, Amicia blinked a few times until the clansmen's high spirits and ribaldry reclaimed her attention and all vestiges of long-lost youth slipped from the old woman's countenance.

"Be you prepared?" Dagda was asking, her voice carrying in the crowded chamber—the suddenly quiet chamber.

Crackling anticipation stood on every staring face as the seneschal placed two sturdy hands on Amicia's shoulders, holding her so that her back was turned to Magnus.

"You need not flush so. He is not yet fully unclothed," Dagda said, her gaze sharp. "He stands beside your bed clad in his braies, thin though they be," she revealed, the twinkle in her eye turning mischievous. "Tradition deems that you must watch his men remove his braies and he, then, must look on as I disrobe you."

"The way I mind it, tradition demands we must *all* look on," a drink-slurred voice burst out from near the door.

"And decency deems we keep those looks to a minimum—and fleeting," Hugh spoke up. "I'd mind you not forget it."

The man gave him an owl-eyed stare. "Faugh, Hugh! Do you ken how long it's been since I—" he started to protest but then lifted his hands in mute surrender as he sagged against the doorjamb.

Ignoring him, for the man was clearly too ale-headed to cause a disturbance even if he wished to try, Dagda aimed a censorious stare at Janet and Colin.

They'd seized the slight furor to begin moving around the chamber dousing candles until naught remained to light the room save the reddish glow of the peat fire and the thick waxen night candle burning on its pricket beside the bed.

Amicia silently blessed them, her heart warming ever more toward her husband's bastard cousin.

Dagda cleared her throat. "I ask you again," she began anew, "are you prepared to have your husband look on your nakedness and judge you worthy . . . or nay?"

I ache for him to look on my nakedness!

I burn to see his.

Amicia almost cried out the words.

But she kept her secret wishes to herself and simply nodded, her stomach fluttering and her mouth going dry despite her mounting excitement.

"A nod will not suffice. You must speak the words we rehearsed earlier."

Amicia drew a long breath. "Aye, I am prepared to inspect my husband's nakedness and have him do likewise of mine," she said, her cheeks flaming hotter with each spoken word.

"Then turn and behold him." Dagda deftly maneuvered her to face him.

Embarrassed or nay, a thrill of pure, hot-streaming desire shot straight to the deepest reaches of her female heat.

Faith, but he took her breath away.

Tall, broad-shouldered, and golden, his magnificence wrapped itself around her, igniting her senses and sending the most delicious sensations winding all through her.

Even just glancing at his well-muscled calves, so powerful and pleasingly-formed, their shape well-defined and pressing against the light linen covering of his braies, made her mouth run dry and her heart skitter out of control.

An insistent pulsing began low by her thighs and an exquisite heaviness started spreading through the lowest

part of her belly as every inch of her tingled with aware-
ness.

Saints of mercy, she scarce had need to *see* her husband's bare-bottomed virility—sheer and vibrant masculine
power pulsed and throbbed along the whole glorious length
of him.

Towering over his kinsmen any hour of the day, standing amongst them *near naked* and with the fire glow casting a luminous sheen across his wide-set shoulders and
handsome brow, his sheer presence dwarfed every man in
the room . . . even the brawniest, toughest-looking souls.

A gasp of awe slipped from her lips . . . a soft, little
ooooh, which brought hoots and guffaws from the clansmen.

"Noble and puissant, eh, lass?" a great bear of a black-
bearded Islesman teased, wiggling his ears at her.

Amicia flushed, well-versed enough in fleshly matters
to ken exactly what part of her husband's body the well-
girthed giant meant.

Magnus only arched a russet brow, his clear blue gaze
decidedly pleased.

Or amused.

He stood looking at her with his arms folded across his
chest and his legs braced slightly apart. A slight upward
turn at the corners of his mouth allowed a faint hint of his
dimples to wink at her, enchanting her in ways just as
heart-catching as the gleam of well-toned muscles and
manly brawn.

His eyes seemed to darken as he watched her with a
heavy-lidded, hot-smoldering gaze that sent little flames
of thrilling desire licking across her every nerve ending.

Truth be told, she was melting.

He appeared thoroughly at ease, both in his near nakedness and with her perusal of him.

Indeed, the slight jerking of a muscle in his jaw proved the only outward sign that he found any part of the proceedings not wholly to his liking.

Not that she could have stopped looking at him even if she'd wanted to—which she didn't.

So she continued to study him, her most private place tingling and throbbing when her gaze lit and lingered on his chest.

Ne'er had she seen a more fetching one.

A light dusting of red-gold hairs spread across his chest muscles and down the center of his hard-slabbed abdomen to vanish beneath the rolled waistband of his braies—and *oooh* did she ache to explore those wee fine hairs.

They glistened like spun gold in the firelight. And just *thinking* about touching them, mayhap rubbing her cheek against them to test their friction against the smoothness of her own skin, made her heart pound and intensified the hot-beating pulse drumming so fiercely between her thighs.

Aye, everything about him inflamed her—and he had nary a need to be *examined* for proof of his virility.

The most tantalizing allure poured off him, his masculinity so pure and strong, anyone who'd dare question it would surely put themselves at risk of being struck down by the wrath of some furious Celtic god.

Nay, his manhood stood without doubt.

In especial, there, beneath the thin linen of his braies where the heavy bulge of his sex was clearly defined. Blessedly, *not* standing, but imposing all the same. The power of its potency came to her in great, bone-melting waves and overlaid the whole of the room with a musky-dark masculine aura of power.

Power, and barely contained . . . desire.

Her desire.

Her sudden and indescribable need to see more—to see all of him.

"I'm a-thinking it's time to test the lad's mettle," an older clansman declared, stepping forward.

Tossing back his mane of coarse, steel-gray hair, he fixed a piercing stare on Amicia even as he reached for the waistband of Magnus's braies. "Ha, Magnus! Let the lassie see—"

"My wife can see all she desires and more," Magnus said, seizing the graybeard's wrist before the man's stretching fingers could get anywhere near the rolled waistband. "But I shall do the disrobing myself."

From the corner of his eye, Magnus caught Colin slip from Janet's side to snatch Magnus's plaid from where it lay, rumpled and discarded on the bed.

And bless the knave's well-loved hide, he also shrugged off his own plaid, holding both at the ready as he came forward to stand slightly to the left and behind Magnus.

Far enough away not to interfere with clan tradition, but close enough to lend Magnus and his bride a much-appreciated act of true and knightly comradeship.

Settling his own hands upon the top band of his braies, Magnus slanted his friend a sidelong look of deep-felt gratitude, then turned back to his wife.

She'd been over-bold throughout the wedding feast, her daring and charm pleasing him beyond measure—but he knew her to be virtuous, could almost scent the tremulous edge of a maiden's anxiety skimming along just beneath her brave veneer of daring.

Forcing himself to harness his own thrumming tension, he let out a long breath. "You have naught to dread—not from me or the traditions that shape this evening. We will soon be alone," he promised her, voicing the reassurance he hoped would settle the jittery pulse fluttering so rapidly at the hollow of her throat.

"See you, this night"—he paused to glance round the circle of his staring kinsmen—"*this night* we shall forge a few traditions of our own."

Some men arched brows at that, or exchanged nervous glances. Others pulled at their beards or flicked at invisible specks of lint on their plaids.

No one looked pleased.

Donald MacKinnon gave a loud harrumph. "Clan Fingon tradition is best kept, son. Have you not yet seen what happens when fools dare to tweak and prod?"

Magnus curled his fingers more deeply around his waistband's rolled edge, cast a quick, lowering glance at the thin cloth yet shielding his maleness. "Is *this* not bowing to tradition?"

"I dinna see you strutting bare-bottomed before her yet!" a bold-faced clansman called from the shadows near the hearth. "Damn me for a plaguey pest, but the only full-naked MacKinnon I see about is yon sleeping mongrel," he finished, jerking a thumb at old Boiny, the great shaggy bulk of him curled as ever before the hearthstone.

A flurry of bawdy comment and encouragement stirred at once, especially from those deepest in their cups, but a raised hand from Magnus and quick-flashed warning quelled their ribaldry.

"She, and you, my kinsmen, shall judge me now . . . and forever after hold your clacking tongues unless you wish them cut from your mouths."

To prove his willingness, Magnus shoved down his linen underhose and kicked them aside to stand fully naked in the center of the room.

Not taking his gaze off his wife, and praying he'd not harden—not yet anyway—he spread his legs just enough so that his shaft and ballocks could dangle fully exposed, hanging free to the curious stares of any who cared to examine him.

"Further," he began, hooking his arms behind his neck so the muscles of his upper body, too, could be better displayed and inspected, "a man's ability to take his ease can be observed in the swelling and lengthening of his shaft. That's a feat I hereby deem best accomplished and tested when looking upon the nakedness of his own good lady wife and not, as MacKinnon custom has e'er demanded, by having some sloe-eyed kitchen lass pinch his hardness and poke at his testicles!"

Again silence answered him.

Silence, and slack-jawed stares.

His clansmen surely knew he'd make short shrift of them if they dared let more than a perfunctory glance light where men's eyes had no business lingering. They knew, too, they'd best not allow more than a rapid flicker of a quick-eyed gaze touch his lady's vulnerability.

By comparison, *her* gaze was all over him.

She'd lowered her lashes, but the smoldering burn in their rich-brown depths shone through all the same. And the longer she stared at him, especially like *that,* the more difficult it would be for him to remain at ease.

An aching tightness already coiling through his groin,

he cleared his throat and spoke the words he hoped would bring a swift end to the spectacle.

"Lass, bare yourself so we may be done with this buffoonery," he ground out, the words coming more gruff than he'd intended.

Before I am undone.

A distinct and pressing possibility with surge after surge of welling heat sweeping across his loins.

"Take off the gown," he said, his voice tight. "You can undress yourself, can you not?"

She slid a look at Dagda. "But your traditions. I would not breach them. Isn't Dagda supposed to undr—"

"A pox on tradition!" Magnus closed the distance between them in three swift strides, his nakedness forgotten. "Did you not hear me?" He forced himself to keep the heat from his voice, trailed a finger along the high, smooth curve of her cheekbone, then down and across the fullness of her sweet lips, noting their slight tremble beneath his touch.

"This night *we* make the traditions. Now, this moment, you and I are Coldstone's legends—naught else."

Touching her own finger to her lips as if she still felt his touch there, she nodded. "With surety, I can remove my gown," she said, her voice surprisingly firm. "I shall do so with pleasure."

"With all speed—if you will, lassie," an ale-addled clansman bade her, the loon clearly having noted the slight twitching of Magnus's semi-aroused shaft.

" 'Tis for the best—unless you wish his ballocks to run blue!" another cried, and slapped his thigh.

Magnus grimaced.

He'd not only forgotten his nakedness, he'd forgotten to school it!

Much to the hooting glee of his kinsmen.

"Aye, from the looks of him, he canna wait much longer," a bald-headed kinsman agreed, the observation and the ensuing guffaws from others confirming indeed that the long-nosed bastards were sneaking glances where they shouldn't.

"Shall I help you, lady?" Janet pushed her way through the throng, her face discreetly averted from Magnus's nakedness, the flush on her cheeks as red and glowing as Amicia's own.

"Nay, 'tis good, but . . . I thank you," Amicia said, even as she lifted her hands to unfasten the side lacings of her gown.

She must've loosened them earlier, for a few quick jerks with nimble fingers were all that was needed for the bodice to fall open. With serene determination, she eased her arms from the gown's sleeves and pushed down the wide-gaping bodice until her breasts were fully exposed, her nipples already drawing tight in the cold night air— or mayhap with the searing heat of her husband's gaze.

His, and every other lecherous blackguard crowding the chamber.

His jaw set so tight his teeth hurt, Magnus made a quick flicking gesture at the gown, still bunched in charming disarray about her waist.

"Have done," he jerked, the words a choked rasp. "Now."

"Och, aye, to be sure and I will," Amicia gave back, her boldness firing his blood.

Her dark gaze locked on his, she thrust her hands into the folds of deep blue linen until she found and unclasped the gold-embroidered girdle fastened low on her hips. She tossed the belt aside and raised her chin, her bared breasts all shadow and light, their curves and swells, the dark-tipped and thrusting peaks, an irresistible invitation.

For a few precious moments, no one stood in the softly-lit chamber but the two of them and the sizzling anticipation snapping between them. A keen sense of deepest intimacy so thick on the cold, rain-tinged air, Magnus would've sworn he could have cut it with his dirk.

But his were not the only eyes fastened to the heavy folds of rich blue linen yet shielding his lady's sweetest charms.

Countless others stared, too. Some in a most annoyingly penetrating manner.

His hands clenching, he tossed a quelling glance at the circle of waiting kinsmen. "Come you, lass, have off with the gown," he urged his bride. "The whole of it."

And she complied—her rich brown eyes sparking, the look in them flooding him with sensual heat as she let the gown slide the rest of the way down her naked body to form a billowing pool at her feet.

"Saints a mercy!" a deep voice groaned—one Magnus recognized too late as his own. At once, his shaft swelled and lengthened to full-stretch, and at a speed that astounded him.

Garbed in naught but candle glow and her own MacLean steel, his lady stood full naked in all her glory, the gleaming white opulence of her breasts stealing his breath, the wealth of glossy black curls at the vee of her thighs *unmanning* him.

Not that anyone would dare call the raging hardness riding hot and proud against his belly . . . man-less.

Swallowing, he tossed a glance at his brothers—Hugh,

e'er the sensitive soul, with his back to the proceedings, and Dugan already coming long-strided toward him.

"Say-the-words," Magnus snarled at Dugan, half-afraid he'd lose his seed any moment—and equally afeared he'd ram his fist into his brother's nose if the blackguard dared cast a glance at the tangle of raven curls springing at the top of his wife's shapely thighs!

"The words!" Magnus growled when Dugan's gaze indeed began to waver.

Flushing bright red, Dugan snapped his attention back to Magnus's dark-frowning face. "Sir Magnus!" Dugan began, if with a somewhat over-thick voice. "Are you satisfied with the lady's . . . good health?"

"I am more than satisfied," Magnus rapped out, his own voice rough. "I am well-content."

He knew even greater contentment when, the words spoken, Colin moved with all haste to swirl Magnus's plaid around Amicia's nakedness.

"And you, Lady Amicia?" Dugan turned to her. "Is Sir Magnus to your . . . pleasure?"

Clutching the plaid tight about her shoulders, she slid the briefest of glances over Magnus's jutting phallus.

"He is more than pleasing to me. I would want no other," she said, lifting her gaze, her voice strong, almost defiant.

Then Colin was thrusting his own plaid into Magnus's hands, thus ending an ordeal Magnus didn't ever care to repeat. His emotions high, he slung the plaid around his nakedness and opened his mouth to thank Colin, but the other man spoke first.

"I trust you will honor your word?" he wanted to know, not quite able to keep an I-knew-it gleam from twinkling in his dark eyes.

"My word?" Magnus held fast to the borrowed plaid, his fingers having proved too clumsy to knot the fool thing.

Stepping back a bit so the clansmen streaming from the chamber had unhindered access to the door, he shook his head.

"I've no idea what you mean, my friend," he said, truly puzzled.

"The boon," Colin supplied. He gave an imperceptible nod in Amicia's direction. "Your promise to bed her— you will keep it?"

At once, memory returned.

And Magnus's pride—even if its roar held all the ferocity of a newly born wolf cub not yet able to open its eyes or even stand on its feet.

"Well?" Colin persisted.

"Well, indeed," Magnus answered, letting a decidedly *wolfish* grin spread across his face. "It would seem you have bested me yet again."

"How so?" Colin angled his head, waited.

"Simply . . ." Magnus began, planting a firm hand to his friend's lower back and propelling him toward the door, ". . . that I intend to bed her very, very well—unless I've lost the art, that is."

Colin paused on the threshold, shook his dark head. "And I vow, in the tasting of yon lass's bounteous charms, you will *discover* the art, my friend," he predicted, his face lit with mirth.

Mirth that Magnus did not share.

Not a shred of it.

He only knew he wanted his bride.

And in ways that would shake every heathery hill in the land.

Chapter Thirteen

❦

"**A** GOD'S NAME, but they dragged their feet about leaving us!" Magnus stood on the threshold, fingers clenched around the door latch, Colin's plaid still clutched about his middle. Truly, he was willing his kinsmen's ankles to sprout wings as they made their bumbling way down the shadow-hung corridor.

If such faltering progress could be called movement.

Hot irritation and another, *deeper* heat made his pulse pound. He breathed a silent prayer of relief that the louts were heading away from the bedchamber and toward the winding turnpike stair that would lead them back down to the great hall.

"Ne'er has anyone been plagued by such slow-moving buffoons, I vow it!" He frowned after them, the beginnings of a tic just beneath his left eye fueling his annoyance.

Enough was enough.

By the Mass, the corridor's odor alone would have had

him striding along with the greatest of speed. The stone-vaulted passage smelled of damp cold and torch-smoke on the best of nights. Damp cold, torch-smoke, and mold on the worst of nights.

This night, it reeked of all those things *plus* the miasmic cloud of ale fumes trailing in his kinsmen's unsteady wake.

But at last, even the stragglers vanished into the yawning dark of the stair-head, the lingering echo of their bawdy ditties and trudging footfalls all that remained to mark their passage.

Their departure left him feeling more naked than naked—his last excuse for not turning to face the hot-driving lust charging the air behind him. He knew she'd see his need stamped all over him the instant he faced her.

Faced her, and delivered up his soul.

"Do you not want to shut the door?"

Her voice came from just behind him—and said so much more than the simple words.

Magnus froze, his barriers smashed, but his pride still digging sharp claws into his limbs, holding fast in one last bitter battle before defeat.

"I thought you wanted them to go?"

"Och, but I did, lass," he said, surrendering, his final defenses clearing the field. "I wished to be alone with you more than you would guess."

"Truly?" The hope in her voice grabbed hold of him, a victor seizing the spoils. "More than I would guess?"

"Much more."

"And will you tell me the ways?"

She'd stepped closer, clearly testing her win, and the soft whisper of her breath feathered across the bared skin of his back. Its sweetness sent waves of sensual heat surging into his groin until he'd run so hot and tight the intense, pulsing pleasure proved almost painful.

The kind of pain that made the heavens sing.

He turned, accepting the deep, searing need. No longer able to hide or deny its strength. "I will *show* you," he promised, tremors of anticipation rippling across every inch of him—in especial his hardest inches.

She glowed with her triumph. She looked down for a moment to adjust the plaid still wound tight around her lush-curved form, and a strange flicker of doubt flitted across her beautiful face.

"Then you are wholly consigned to what we must do here?" She slid a look at the waiting bed, left the question hanging between them.

The fool kind of query *he* would have made—were she of a less bold-eyed and daring nature.

"Consigned?" He blinked, coloring like a squire, he was sure, but, saints, ne'er could anything be farther from the truth.

Not that his fool tongue could string together what *was* the truth. Not just now. Not with her scent sneaking beneath his shattered guard and stealing his wits.

Clean and heathery, the scent floated around him, seducing his senses. It was every bit as intoxicating as the most potent heather ale.

A thousand times headier.

"The door . . . ?" She touched a hand to his arm. "Do you not want—"

"I want—" he broke off, the warmth of her fingers on the bare flesh of his arm making him ragingly conscious of his state of undress—and hers.

Most especially hers.

Saints, his wants were lodged so fast in his throat he

could scarce draw breath around them! But he knew what she meant—in his besottedness, he'd forgotten to close the door. So he yanked it tight and slid home the drawbar, locking out any wretch who'd dare seek to return.

Cheeky, long-nosed wretches in particular, but also any regrets or hesitations that might dare try to discolor the bliss he'd determined to give her this night.

The joy he meant to allow himself.

"You want . . . ?" She was peering at him, the softest of smiles curving her lips. "I am thinking I would like to hear what it is that you desire. Aye, I wish to hear the words."

Magnus swallowed, his tongue suddenly as clumsy as his clansmen's stomping feet.

Jesu, he could still hear their awkward progress— *boom, boom, boom,* came the echo of many pairs of shuffling, stumbling feet.

Just a faint echo, but persistent enough to drift back along the darkened passage and . . . disturb him.

Bedevil him.

For the echoing footfalls had some vague *something* dancing along the periphery of his memory, and he couldn't quite grasp its significance.

He only knew it unsettled him.

"Shall I tell you what *I* want?" his minx of a wife suggested, taking bold advantage of his momentary confusion by letting Colin's borrowed plaid dip low enough for the merest top slivers of her areolae to peek from above the edge of the tartan cloth. "What I have always wanted? *Desired?*"

Magnus swallowed, swirling heat squeezing his innards, snaking round the hard length of him. "Sweeting, I'll grant you my best sword that we share the same wants this night," he vowed, careful to keep one hand fisted in his own plaid lest it fall and expose his readiness too soon.

This was to be a night of slowest pleasures, each moment stretched and savored to the fullest.

"Aye, the very same wants and desires, to be sure. Merely to different purposes."

"Say you?" She let the plaid's edge slip down a bit more—only on one side this time, but enough for the hardened peak of one fine-thrusting nipple to pop free and wink at him.

She glanced down at the exposed nipple, then looked back up to stare him full in the eye as she slowly—very slowly—readjusted the plaid until he could see no more. Not even the sweet-puckered rims of those tantalizingly large areolae.

Magnus frowned, the hard length of him throbbing with almost blinding urgency.

She smiled.

Moving to the table, she began pulling the pins from her coiled braids. A dangerous move, for the table stood not far from the peat fire and in its reddish-gold glow, the creamy top swells of her breasts and her bared shoulders shone like finest mother-of-pearl.

A feast for a man's eyes, and one that made him burn to see the rest of her luscious body's curves and hollows gilded and limned by the soft, flickering firelight.

Her face glowed, too, and a rapid pulsing beat in the dip between her collarbones. It was a clear hint that her flush had more to do with excitement or agitation than the cozy warmth spooling out from the hearth fire.

"And what are those cross-purposes you mentioned?"

she wanted to know, the slight strain in her voice knocking out the possibility of *excitement*.

She'd gone very still, not moving at all except to nudge her toes at the furred skins spread upon the chamber floor.

"Aye, I think I should like to hear them," she said into the uncomfortable silence. "What purposes do you mean? Save the obvious? That we must—couple—so a bloodied bedsheet can be carried about the hall on the morrow?"

"That is part of it, aye, the bedsheet. . . ." Magnus spoke true, and regretted the words the moment they left his mouth.

In especial, when *her* mouth tightened upon hearing them.

She gave him a vexed look. "You are duty-bound to make me your wife in truth, yet you do not find the task . . . displeasing." She flicked a telling gaze at the tent-like protuberance beneath his plaid. "Nay, sir, even a less enlightened lass would ken without doubt that you do not find the task at hand in any way onerous."

Magnus cleared his throat, tried to swallow the tightness threatening to strangle him. "Rest assured I view our conjugal union as neither a burden nor a task," he said, casting a significant glance of his own at his arousal. "As you have well noted, my lady."

"Aye. So I have." She slipped the last of the pins from her hair. Her thick, shining braids tumbled to just below her waist. "So what did you wish to imply?" she asked, her fingers undoing the plaits, tugging at the glossy blue ribbons she'd used to cross-garter them. "I truly want to know."

Magnus blew out a frustrated breath. "God kens, I am not blessed with Hugh's silvered tongue, lass." He sought to excuse himself. "By *different purposes,* I but meant that while I am betting neither of us will deny a certain physical need, it is my wish to give you pleasure this night. It is the night of our wedding feast and I would know it special for you."

He paused, made a conscious effort to stop the wretched flow of words but couldn't. "And you, precious lass, will be wanting such closeness *all* nights," he said, near choking on the words. "I can see it in your eyes."

And it terrifies me more than the thought of the earth opening up beneath my feet.

"I see." She tightened the plaid around her, gathering it higher until the voluminous folds reached to clear beneath her chin.

"Nay, you do not see at all," Magnus argued, feeling as if he were sinking ever deeper into a bog patch.

He pinched the bridge of his nose, damning his fool stubborn pride. He cursed his honor for not allowing him to ply her with sweet golden untruths to smooth the furrowing of her brow.

"Will it make what must happen between us more . . . er . . . palatable if I swear to you that"—he flicked a hand in the direction of his loins—"*my desire* for you is genuine?"

To his dismay, the words he'd hoped would soothe her only seemed to upset her all the more. The sparking challenge that had been simmering in her eyes now flared to snapping anger, and the sweet flush on her cheeks deepened to the bright shining red of a woman riled.

"Ach, sir, I know well enough that your physical lust is not contrived." She trailed a slow finger along the table edge—almost as if the white half-moons of her well-kept nails were a dagger's edge drawn across a rival's throat.

Magnus swallowed uncomfortably.

Something was sorely amiss.

She reached up to tuck a silky curl of inky-black hair behind her ear. "I am dark enough, am I not?" The soft-spoken words were barely audible above the wind and rain lashing at the window shutters.

A cold dread spread through his gut as Magnus stared at her. "Why do I think we are speaking past each other?"

She shrugged a mite too casually. "I think not." Looking down, she flicked at something invisible on her bare arm. "How can we be . . . when I only meant that all and sundry are aware of your wenching tastes."

"My wenching tastes?"

Her gaze snapped back to his. "Your voracious appetite for well-fleshed light skirts with skeins of raven-black hair." She set her jaw, her flashing eyes daring him to deny it.

And he couldn't.

It was more than true—he'd just never told anyone why.

And he'd be damned if he'd tell *her.* Doing so would be selling his soul to the Devil.

Giving away the last shreds of his dignity.

So he simply stared at her, hoped the truth wasn't writ all over his astonished face. "Who told you that?"

She looked down again, this time to trace the table's wood grain swirls with her fingertips. "Everyone," she said, her gaze fixed on the table. "Janet, your brother Dugan . . . and others," she added, making larger swirls with her fingers for each spoken name.

Magnus blew out a breath, rubbed the back of his neck. Saints, the weight of an unseen iron yoke seemed to settle heavier onto his shoulders with each indrawn breath.

"Can you deny it?"

He shook his head, felt the yoke's weight increase a thousandfold. "I will not lie to you," he said, running rough fingers through his hair. "I have indeed favored well-formed maids with dark, flowing tresses."

"So it is said," she acknowledged, still not looking at him. "And that, sir, is exactly what I meant—the reason I ken you are not adverse to . . . taking me."

She glanced up then, smoothed one hand provocatively across the fullness of her plaid-draped breasts. "I must surely resemble the tourney whores you are rumored to have been so fond of?"

Nay, lass, they resembled you! That was the way of it! Magnus's heart roared the truth at her.

Years of it.

He stood dumbfounded, his tongue weighted by the strictures of his own fool pride.

"That is by with, I swear you," he jerked, keeping a careful check on his words lest the whole of it pour out like an eddy of free-flowing water. "Sakes, lass, do you not know that the true way of things often runs far deeper than that which lies on the surface?"

It was the closest he could come to spilling his heart to her.

Wishing he *could,* he turned half away from her, fixed his gaze on the windows. Hard rain hammered against the closed shutters, rattling them, and each new clap of thunder released another blinding flash of bright silvery-white light that sharpened the outlines of everything in the chamber in a quick wash of startling black and white.

And in the few moments without pealing thunder and

rapid bursts of light, an eerie greenish glow shone through the cracks in the rain-swollen shutter slats—the unholy color, a sure sign of a Highland storm the likes of which seldom had been seen.

At least not in his day.

Not that he was all too sure he'd own to having glimpsed such an otherworldly light even if he had.

Shivering, he gritted his teeth and wished he could have done with this mummery. He came close to going down on bent knee and telling her the truth . . . that he'd wanted her with the whole of his heart since he'd first glimpsed her at the ripe age of two-and-ten.

A tender age, to be sure, but enough years for even the most ambitious of lads to realize the folly of hoping to win the hand of a daughter of such a high and mighty house as MacLean.

In especial, a *feuding* clan.

Nevertheless, it was a plan he'd embarked on with all the gusto and faith of his bold, young heart—a goal he'd clung to every day upon awakening and every night before he'd succumbed to sleep.

He had contrived meetings at each gathering of the island clans. One day, he'd followed her onto the moors, hoping to please her with a bouquet of bell heather. Then she'd hurt her ankle, and after carrying her back to her kinsmen, they'd shunned and reviled him. The experience made it clear how futile his love was for her.

Thereafter, he'd avoided looking at her, the pain of doing so too deep for his young lad's heart. And the few times he'd slipped and glanced her way, some flaunting evidence of her wealth and status had reminded him of his lacking.

Even so, all through the years, he'd hoped in secret. The thought of her sustaining him until, at Dupplin, utter failure had ripped and shredded even his hardiest hopes and dreams. And then fate had given her to him at last— upon the shards of all his inadequacies.

"Be not so certain you have the fullest rights of it," she said then, bringing him back to the present, a challenge heating her voice again. "Oft-times there is much truth to be seen on the surface. The tragedy is when we fail to recognize it—or worse, when we do and then deny it."

Their eyes met and held. "Mayhap, sir, we would both be well-served to acknowledge the ripples on the surface *and* look deeper to find the pebble that caused them?"

Magnus bit back a groan of frustration.

The pebbles lining his path were the size of boulders. Mammoth chunks of granite that would break a giant's back, much less a mortal man's.

Narrowing her eyes, his long-desired bride turned a penetrating gaze on him. "I can begin by telling you I shall do my best not to mind that you desire me for my hair color and not becau . . . because I am me."

He stared at her, slack-jawed.

Could she not *see* his mind? His heart? Even if he did not speak the words?

Ne'er had he known a lovelier maid, or one more desirable.

Especially now, full naked save the enveloping folds of his plaid. Lucifer's knees, just looking at her, with the fire glow gleaming off her bared shoulders and glinting in the ebony silk of her hair, inflamed him and set his blood to heating with furious, unabated need.

The only problem was the oversized chunk of granite

looming up between them—an immovable barrier that had the words *love, joy,* and *intimacy* chiseled all over its hard-glittering surface.

The only truths he couldn't share with her.

Not if he didn't want that boulder shattering what wee bit of his pride yet remained intact.

So he would give her what he could—his body, his physical passion, and the knowledge that he indeed cared deeply.

He just wouldn't mention his true feelings.

For his sake as much as hers.

Not until he'd repaid her brothers every last *siller* and could support her from his own coffers.

"Sweet lass." He caught her hand, holding her gaze as he brought her fingers to his lips. "You are lovely as no other," he vowed, trying hard to imagine what Hugh would say in this moment, how his golden-voiced brother would weasel his way out of such a foul-reeking corner.

"To me, you are incomparable," he tried, the honeyed words sounding silly on his unused-to-tenderness tongue. "Any lass I knew before you, raven-haired or otherwise, is but a distant shadow, that I swear to you."

Drawing a trembling breath, she pulled her hand from his grasp and looked down. But not before Magnus caught the glitter of unshed tears clinging to her spiky black lashes.

The shimmering gleam of her tears were a swift kick in the teeth to his fool attempts to imitate his sweet-tongued brother.

She waved a stilling hand when he opened his mouth to recite another sonnet-like bit of sentimental nonsense. "Do you know I ought to be relieved?" she said in a small voice that made his heart tilt.

Taking the first step, he hooked two fingers beneath her chin, turned her face to him. "How so?" he asked, rubbing his thumb gently along the smooth line of her jaw. "Relieved in what way?"

"Ach"—she blinked furiously and dashed at her cheeks with the back of her hand—"see you, when I first came here, I feared you might prefer wee slips of maids like Janet, all fair and fragile." She plucked at the plaid she'd wrapped so securely about her.

In particular, at the folds covering her abdomen.

Moistening her lips, she turned a shimmering gaze on him. "Had I known you relished well-rounded, more womanly-shaped lasses, I would ne'er have spent hours marching—"

Boom, boom, boom!

She clapped a mortified hand over her lips almost as if she, too, had heard the long-faded echo of many pairs of trampling feet trudging down the turnpike stairs.

Magnus heard it without question.

But he also heard a single pair of marching feet—a most fetching feminine pair with the sweetest ankles he'd ever seen. And in his mind's eye, he saw those delightful feet not just traipsing down endless spirals of winding stone steps, but also making the journey back up the stairs.

Over and over again.

Just as Janet had reported that early morning in the rain-misted bailey.

Comprehension sluicing through him, he stared at her, his heart slamming hard against his ribs. Hoping she wouldn't notice that his hands trembled, he reached to touch her loosened braids.

"Can it be you were about to admit marching up and

down the tower stairs?" he asked, unraveling her plaits until the thick glossy strands spilled free. "And that you did so repeatedly?"

He stretched his fingers through the cool silk of her hair, savored its sweet slide across the back of his hand. Didn't dare to trust the wild hope beginning to well inside him.

"Did Janet and Dagda perchance catch you in this . . . *unusual* activity?"

She said nothing, but the way she compressed her lips and a slight tensing of her eyelids proved ample answer.

An awkward silence she couldn't keep for long.

"Botheration!" The expletive burst from her lips and she swiped another hand across her cheeks. "A grand and merry pox on whiche'er of the two told you."

Magnus folded his arms, waited until a particularly strong buffet of wind ceased rattling the shutters before he spoke. "And will you tell me why you engaged in such foolery?"

Biting her lower lip, his bonnie bride said nothing.

Not that she had need of words—the delicate flush inching up her neck and making her face glow as bright as red-burning peats screamed her ill ease with a loudness more deafening than the sharp cracks of thunder shaking the chamber's thick stone walls.

He cocked a brow, let the slightest of smiles take any harsh edges off his words—and hammer away a few more chips of stone from the mammoth clump of granite.

His smile broadening, he went on, the words flowing now. "A lass traversing a turnpike stair is none so rare a sight in any keep, I'll wager, but a fair lady occupying herself with such a task for hours on end is . . . intriguing."

And encouraging beyond measure if he was correctly guessing the reason she'd indulged in such nonsense.

He hadn't developed his physical stamina and muscular build without long hours of hardest training.

She swung away from him, tossed a sheaf of gleaming black hair over her shoulder. "There is naught *intriguing* about it," she declared, her voice ringing. "For a braw champion of the lists, you are precious dull at kenning a woman's heart if I must color my reasons for you!"

"Ahh . . . but you color so beautifully," he said, feeling almost two-and-twelve again, bursting with hope. "Saints, but you are bonnie when you glow like that," he blurted, grinning at her lovely profile. Noting well the bright red of the cheek turned his way, he wondered if a similar flush kissed the lush fullness of her breasts.

"So-o-o, you would you see me color, would you?" She whirled to face him, a blaze of MacLean fury sparking in her dark eyes. "If I say you what I was doing on those stairs, I shall flush a brighter red than a hundred Highland sunsets!"

Magnus folded his arms, waited, amazed to feel a grin crinkling his eyes and deepening the creases in his cheeks. His dimples. Mother of God, he'd almost forgotten how damned good it felt to smile.

Apparently too caught up in explaining herself to notice his mirth, Amicia snatched a convenient flagon off the table and poured herself a measure of finest *uisge beatha,* tossing it down in one choking gulp.

"Good sir, I mounted and descended those stairs so that I need *not* blush when standing before you unclothed," she announced, her voice rising as she set down the cup with a loud *clack.* "So that my . . . er . . . exertions might pare a bit of the *womanliness* from my hips."

She blew out her breath on a hot, gusty sigh. "See you, I'd hoped to rid myself of a bit of extra flesh—lest this body's roundness repel you!"

Her color deepening indeed, she threw open his plaid and flung it aside. "Look you, Magnus MacKinnon," she charged him, grabbing a barely-there roll of flesh at the top of her abdomen, pinching it hard before she let go to smooth her hands along the well-rounded curves of her shapely hips, "see my nakedness—the plumpness marring my belly, my . . . *form!*"

Magnus stared at her, too flummoxed to find words.

Did she truly not know how desirous she was?

How intoxicatingly beautiful?

Saints, the slight swell of her tummy delighted him. The luxuriant tangle of sooty curls at the tops of her thighs stole his breath, and the large, dark rounds crowning her breasts had him moistening lips run impossibly dry. Sheerest lust and raw, raging need swept through him like rivers of molten fire.

"Merciful heaven, dinna tell me you believed I'd find you displeasing?" he got out, strangle-voiced. "You—of all women?"

"And why not me . . . of all women?"

Because for more years than you know, just the whisper of your name across my heart has filled me with a warmth brighter and more beautiful than the light of a thousand suns.

Blinking, Magnus rammed a hand through his hair. Scalding heat crept up the back of his neck. Sakes, he half-expected to glance over his shoulder and discover Hugh had somehow let himself into the chamber, that his word-gifted bard of a brother hovered close behind him and had flustered the flowery sentiment in his ear.

But inside he knew.

The words dwelled in the deepest part of himself. There in the darkest, most intimate corner of his heart where they'd always been and, like as not, would e'er remain. Through this life and beyond.

Forever.

For eternity.

"Come you, Sir Magnus . . . tell me why." She took a couple of steps toward him, her breasts swaying. "I am none so fragile that I cannot hear the truth."

"The truth ought to be clear enough for you to see," he said in a voice near as tight as the hot iron hardness lifting his plaid.

He stared at her, unable to tear his gaze from her voluptuous bounty, the raven curls adorning her woman's mound. Saints help him, but a faint trace of her musky femininity wafted up from that jet-black triangle, the heady scent beguiling him.

"I need the words, my lord. My eyes see—and very well. Mayhap I see the truth. But even so, my heart would hear the words."

"I' faith," Magnus swore, the boulder making itself known again. "Could you not tell that your kiss during the Claiming Ceremony near brought me to my knees? Is that not truth enough for you? Of my desire and my . . . *affection*?"

"And do I have your affection?" She touched a hand to his chest, smoothed her fingers across the hard-planed muscles before pressing her palm over his heartbeat. "I would know. Now. Before we . . . proceed."

"Aye, sweeting, that you do—hold my affection. With all surety," he admitted, the words freeing him even if they only told half the tale. "Never you worry."

He looked at her, saw the doubt still swimming in her darkly luminous eyes.

"But I do worry, see you," she said, blessedly making no move to cover herself.

Instead, she jammed fisted hands against her hips, the movement causing her large breasts to sway to and fro, the nipples tight and thrusting in the chill night air.

Magnus groaned, no longer trying to even conceal his aroused state. Indeed, he threw off Colin's plaid, tossing it aside as swiftly as she'd had done with his.

If she wouldn't believe the truth of his words, she'd be hard-pressed to deny the rigid length of him riding hard against his groin.

But she scarce noticed, her hot gaze fixed on the peat fire, her fingers digging fiercely into the sweet flesh of her abdomen.

"How could I think otherwise when, from my first day here, Janet made it clear she was your intended and you, my lord, made it more than plain you did not want me?"

"Janet was e'er a lass with . . . problems," Magnus owned, lifting a handful of her hair, letting the silken strands spill through his fingers. "And I, lass, have been the good part of a fool."

It was the most he was willing to concede . . . the most he *could* concede.

"I think you are anything but a fool," she said, leaning back against the table's edge, her expression softening, her eyes growing misty.

Too misty for his liking.

For it was affection and a fine lusty union he meant to share with her—not moon-eyed revelations and sentimental sighs.

"Colin has asked for Janet's hand," he blustered, seeking a topic to cool the heart-fire glowing in her eyes. To save him from having his own eyes grow all soft and dewy if she kept staring at him with her heart on her sleeve.

"He is man enough to master her problems—just as I am thinking she will prove every ounce the strong lass he will be needing at his side when he leaves here."

Amicia gasped, her own cares momentarily forgotten.

She'd seen Colin and Janet together, and had harbored her suspicions, her hopes, for them both. But she hadn't heard anything beyond the usual castle prattling and blether. The most of it snatches of vague speculation amongst the tongue-waggling kitchen and laundry wenches.

"Y-you truly do not mind if she leaves with your friend?" She had to know. "She seemed so . . . smitten with you."

"For the love of Saint Columba, sweetness, have you not heard a word I've told you?" He looked at her, the blue of his eyes almost indigo in the firelit room.

"Nay, I see well that you haven't paid heed to anything I've said. Mayhap deeds will speak all the louder?" He almost growled the words, the huskiness in his deep voice exciting her—the *implication* behind his words melting her.

A most determined look coming over his handsome face, he snatched up one of the discarded plaids, bunched its soft folds into a semblance of a cushion, and, reaching for her, hoisted her onto the table's edge, thrusting the makeshift cushion beneath her to soften the table's hard surface.

His hardness caught her eye, the sight of it undoing her.

Some wee demon inside her made her narrow her eyes at him in challenge. "I ceased fretting about Janet when I learned about the raven-haired lasses. Knowing about them—"

At her words, a strangled groan ripped from his throat and he urged her legs apart, stepping between them even as he splayed his hands around the curves of her buttocks, kneaded the soft plumpness he found there.

"There-ne'er-were-any-raven-haired-*lasses,* do you hear me, Amicia?" The words tore from his throat. "Nary a one. Not in the sense you understood."

Amicia blinked, her breath quickening. She was acutely aware of the hot passion blazing in his eyes and wasn't quite sure what to make of it. "But I do not understand."

"*You* are those raven-haired lasses! Always you! They were but pale substitutes for what I could not have." He almost shouted the confession at her. "You and only you—the lass I have coveted since I first laid eyes on you. The lass I knew I could ne'er hope to possess."

"Oh, dear saints," Amicia gasped, her heart swelling with such joy she thought it'd surely burst. Her eyes streaming, she looked at him, not even trying to check the flow of hot-scalding tears. "Oh, dear saints," she said again, the words almost too wobbly to be understood this time. "Can it be true?"

In answer, he pulled her against him, lowered his lips to hers in a searing, soul-stealing kiss. A blinding fusion of seeking lips, sweeping tongues, and hot mingled breath.

Years and years of need unleashed.

Over and over again, he kissed her with a reckless abandon that melted her bones and left their Claiming

Ceremony kiss far behind. The wild tangle of their tongues watered her knees and moistened another, suddenly very damp and tingling place that pulsed and throbbed with an urgency that shocked her.

"Aye, it is true." He broke the kiss just long enough to breathe the assurance against her cheek. "It has always been about you."

Pulling back a bit more, he gave her a wolfish smile— a full, dimpled one that filled her with a golden warmth to rival the sun. "Think you I would have lost that long-ago archery contest had I not caught a glimpse of you standing near?"

"Oh!" Her heart flipped helplessly at his words, and a torrent of pleasure washed through her. Sweet, sweet bliss, the likes of which she'd ne'er thought to experience. "I—I . . . distracted you?"

Faith, she could scarce believe it.

"You, and none other," he assured her, lighting a flurry of soft, heated kisses along the slope of her neck, each touch of his lips on her flushed skin arousing sensations that set the world to spinning around her.

Dear, sweet saints, indeed, but he ignited a tempest inside her that would soon be impossible to contain. Especially where her blood burned the hottest.

He pulled back to look at her. "Then, as now, you alone held the power to stop my heart," he told her, skimming his hands along the curving lines of her body, letting them pause at the side swells of her breasts to stroke and caress with featherlight touches. "You, and no one else, stole my breath and, aye, fired my ambitions."

"Your ambitions?" She could scarce find her tongue.

"To win you," he said, his voice thick. "To work as hard as I could to make myself worthy and viable enough to seek your hand—and then, years later, when I thought I'd met that goal, and others, I—"

"Shush you, say no more." She pressed two fingers across his lips. "I am yours now, as was e'er my most fervent hope and dream. And you have proved to me that you love me with the same fervor I have e'er loved you."

Something in his face changed upon hearing her words, and her heart dipped at the transformation. Some of the tingling warmth rippling over her woman's flesh drew back to linger in a slow, tremulous pulsing deep inside her core . . . a tightly coiled *waiting*.

"You do love me, then?" she had to ask.

"I have dreamt of you every night of my life since I was two-and-ten."

He was still caressing her breasts, and now began flicking his thumbs back and forth across her nipples, tracing slow circles around their edges, the deliciousness of his touch melting her, making his *no-answer* answer fade into the oblivion of visceral pleasure spreading through her.

"You dreamt of me?"

He nodded. "Nigh every night. And if I did not, it was only because sleep eluded me. But even in those times, you were there in my heart." That, at least, was a truth he could share. He *had* held her in his heart, cared deeply for her.

He still did.

Especially now.

Leaning forward, he planted a wee tender kiss on the tip of her nose. "To be sure, my precious minx, your shadow walked beside me in my every waking hour."

She watched him from heavy-lidded eyes, leaned back to allow his stroking fingers greater access to her full, firm breasts, her body accepting what he could offer her even as the slight tremor in her voice underscored her heart's plea for more.

Her disappointment that he refused to tell her he loved her.

Truth be told, he didn't know if he did, even feared himself incapable of any emotion deeper than ambition, pride, and the hot-burning desire he felt for her.

Her vital, voluptuous womanhood . . . her bright smile and the way her dark eyes appeared to hold the very sun-fire in their depths when they glowed with excitement. Having her near made him feel *alive*.

It was enough for him.

He'd make it enough for her.

"Aye, lady mine, I have always wanted you. Never you doubt it. 'Twas only your over-flowing coffers and the emptiness of my own that had me declaring I'd return you to Baldoon."

He moved his hands to slide gentle fingers to and fro in the warm softness of her breasts' lower swells, sought to use pleasure to dispel the slight frown that creased her brow upon his mention of her coin.

"What will it take to make you realize that a deep heart holds a thousand times more worth than the deepest of purses?" she asked him, her magnificent eyes glinting with fiery MacLean heat again.

A joyous strumming began somewhere deep within Magnus's chest. Not in his heart. Och, nay, not there. But close enough to make him uneasy.

"Do you not ken I'd rather have you than all the rich-est nobles in the land combined?" she said, her voice strong and firm. "Shall I tell you that I enjoyed each shat-tered offer of marriage my brothers sought to gain for me—e'er in the hope that someday, somehow, I could be yours? Every word is true, my lord. Never *you* doubt it."

Magnus stared at her, knew without looking down that the almost-real chunk of granite sitting near their feet had just sprung a rending crack.

A deep fissure, indeed.

And one that made him highly uncomfortable, for if he wasn't careful, he'd fall right into it.

"Well?" she pushed him, reaching to light a finger through the dusting of red-gold hair on his chest. She thrust out her pretty chin, let her sheer will demand an answer. "Do you know it?"

"If I didn't yet, I do now," he said, knowing himself lost. "The saints know, I would even if you hadn't voiced the words. Your eyes talk more than plain, my lady."

She smiled at that. "So do yours, Magnus MacKinnon," she declared, eyeing him boldly. "I know you love me—even if you will not admit it."

"Then let us waste no more time and allow me to show you how very much I . . . adore you."

Chapter Fourteen

❧

GUSTS OF RAIN BUFFETED the shutters, and a cold draught swept through the narrow gaps in the wooden slatting, but the hearth fire still smoldered well enough and the peats gave off a fine, red glow, sufficiently warming the room.

Not that Amicia needed a peat fire to warm her.

Not this night.

A rapturous, languid heat spooled through her. Despite the sameness of her bedchamber, everything in her world had changed.

He was stroking her, his skillful hands melting her beneath his every caress, each light graze of his thumbs over her tightened nipples stealing her breath until it came in urgent, shallow gasps. Liquefying her.

"Oooooh, but your hands are the sweetest magic." She sighed, then bit hard on her lower lip, her cheeks heating.

"You needn't blush, minx," he said, looking up at her as he cupped and weighed the fullness of her breasts.

"Spending you bliss is my greatest wish this night and your plain speaking, your boldness, pleases me. You may always tell me what excites you—indeed, I would wish you to."

At his words, a great sigh rose in Amicia's throat, a deep and sensuous *purr,* and she closed her eyes for a moment, savoring his touch.

"And will you tell me what excites you?" She looked at him again, somehow getting out the words, the deep, throbbing tingles at the very center of her insisting she ask. "Do-o you like touching, p-playing with my breasts?"

In answer, he lifted them and began palming their hardened peaks, his heavy-lidded gaze still holding hers. "There are no words to tell you what it does to me, how much it pleases me, to hold the heaviness of your breasts in my hands, Amicia—to fondle and caress them."

"You do not . . . do n-not think my nipples are too big?" She had to know, whether the heat staining her cheeks intensified or no. She *did* have over-large nipples and they'd always . . . shamed her.

Her husband choked, the smolder in his gaze deepening to such a heated degree a flood of thrilling dampness blossomed there where she burned the hottest. Dear saints, she even caught a whiff of its tanginess—as he must've, too, if the slight flaring of his nostrils was any indication.

"They *are* big," she blurted, glancing down at her thrusting nipples, flustered even as her arousal had her squirming on the table edge.

"They are perfect, lass. *You* are perfect. My living dream—you and only you," he vowed, his deep voice even huskier in his passion, its buttery-rich smoothness rolling all over and through her, undoing her.

Still watching her, he took his hands from her breasts and licked his fingers, wetting them one by one. Then, lowering his gaze, he touched his fingertips to her nipples, let the damp ease the lascivious glide of his thumbs over the straining peaks. His own breath coming hard now, he lazily circled and rubbed, examined with careful deliberation the tight puckered flesh of her areolae.

Overwhelming sensation streaked through her. Saints, he'd fixed his hot gaze on her nipples with intense concentration, studying them as if each wee crinkle in the tight-budded rounds held the dearest fascination for him.

Oooooh, but he thrilled her. Truth be told, she feared she'd soon burst from the spiraling pleasure his every caress sent winding through her body.

She knew her heart was bursting.

His words—*You and only you*—were still sliding through her, over and over again, each sweet repetition searing itself into her soul and banishing endless nights of empty longing as easily as sunlight lifts an early-morning fog.

Faith, just looking at him left her breathless with need and filled her with the fiercest, primordial yearnings.

"Do not ever doubt my desire for you." He lowered his head, bringing it deliciously close to the top swells of her breasts. So close that his warm breath hushed across her skin.

"And be glad that you have such fetchingly large nipples, my minx, for they please me greatly," he added, glancing up at her as he toyed and plucked at them.

Amicia's breath caught at the pleasure of the insistent

little touches, the firm but gentle pullings, the quickening *want* low by her thighs almost unbearable now.

Liquid fire poured through her veins, and just looking at him set her pulse to hammering. Candle glow from the night taper shone in his auburn hair, highlighting the rich-gleaming luster of the red-gold strands.

She swallowed hard, her mouth going dry as her gaze latched onto the hard, throbbing length of him, the nest of soft, cinnamon-colored curls sheltering the heavy fullness of his manhood.

Following her gaze, he smiled at her—the most beatific smile she'd seen on him since their youth. His dimpled smile, the well-remembered creases appearing at either side of his mouth to delight her.

And she drank deeply of its warmth, for one giddy, breathtaking moment seeing nothing else, the very world around her seeming to fragment and vanish so she could lose herself in him.

"You may look and examine all you wish, lovely," he said, his own gaze lowering, drifting from her breasts to her belly and . . . lower. "I will consider myself well-blessed if you are pleased with what you see."

"Pleased?" Amicia's eyes widened, heat sluicing the length of her.

Ne'er had she seen anything more magnificent than Magnus MacKinnon in all his naked, golden glory. And ne'er had she known such a deep-burning ache to touch and feel.

"You do more than please me, my lord," she breathed, sheets of molten fire consuming her. "You . . . you *intoxicate* me."

He glanced at her, his smile going wicked. "And, you my sweet minx, besot me beyond all reason," he vowed, lowering his mouth to her breast. Groaning deep in his throat, he began flicking his tongue back and forth across her hardened nipples, swirled its velvety heat round and round, testing and savoring. "The look and feel of you, the taste of your skin on my tongue, your scent. . . ."

"My scent?" Amicia's every nerve ending snapped to attention, a floodtide of the most delicious tingles yet racing across her most private heat. Hot, rapid spikes of them, again and again.

She gripped the table edge, holding tight lest she slide to the floor and melt into a puddle at his feet. "Do you mean the fragrance of my bath? The little pot of heather-scented soap I use?" she asked, knowing full well he didn't, but needing to know for sure.

Some wild, wanton part of her burning to hear him *tell* her.

Describe in his own richly sensual voice the intrinsically feminine scent that, even now, was wafting up from her very core to drift about them in a heady, musk-tinged cloud that screamed of her desire for him.

Her arousal.

His own unabashed need pouring off him, he pulled a nipple deep into his mouth, grazing it lightly with his teeth, then sucking deeply for a few heart-stopping moments before he released it to answer her.

"I mean the scent of *you,* lass," he murmured against her breast, the heat in his words assuring her he found the musky aroma arousing indeed.

He lifted his head, pinned her with a look of darkest sensuality. "See you, that lusty scent we are now breathing is the very essence of you. Its dew gathers there where you burn the hottest and where your damp heat awaits to enchant and delight me."

Still, annoying little jabs of doubt tripped down her spine as she sniffed the chill air—sniffed as unobtrusively as she could with his hot blue gaze on her.

But blue stare or no, her sense of smell did not desert her. The scent hung thickly in the lust-tinged air, its musky tang proving not unpleasant but *pungent* all the same.

And base enough to have her cheeks flaming despite her excitement.

"Do you truly . . . eh . . . like the scent?" Those niggling doubts wouldn't quite let her believe it.

"*Like* it?" His brows shot upward and a look of genuine incredulity spread across his handsome face. "Lass, I savor the scent of you . . . *relish* it."

Touching a finger to her lower lip, he rubbed gently, that simple gesture flooding her with sensation. "You should believe me, sweetness. Will you?" He leaned forward to nip and nuzzle the soft skin just below her ear.

Amicia nodded, emotion tightening her throat.

"Good, for I swear to you that the fragrance stirs me just as much as the sweet hollows and curves of your naked flesh," he said, the husky undertones in his voice and the way he was smoothing his hands along the lower contours of her body banishing her doubts.

"See you, a woman's scent is highly individual and a man who lov—a man who *cares* deeply for his lady will recognize her scent amongst a thousand other women," he told her, the languorous glide of his hands on her skin spilling pleasure through her.

"So, take heed, precious, and never doubt that it besots me immeasurably to breathe in the essence of you," he assured her, gently kneading the curving rounds of her hips and buttocks, then trailing the tips of his fingers back and forth across the slight swell at the top of her tummy.

"A woman's musk also reveals when a woman desires a man," he added, the intensity of his gaze and the glow of the hearth fire on his hard-muscled body making hers go even more liquid.

A little moan of begging acquiescence escaped her when he turned his attention to the outsides of her spread thighs—thighs he yet stood between and was now easing wider apart, slowly but deliberately opening her legs to their widest possible stretch.

Exposing her.

Amicia's breath caught, her already-tingling woman's flesh responding at once to this new and greater assault with astonishing intensity. "W-what are you doing?" she gasped, the words a breathless moan as he fastened his gaze on the heart of her. "Must my legs be so . . . so wide apart?"

"I am readying you," he told her, carefully urging her thighs a few inches wider. "And, aye, your legs must be opened, lass. As wide open as you can stand it, for the farther apart they are, the better exposed you are to me, and the greater will be the pleasure I can give you."

"I am already fair dying of the pleasure," she blurted, the rivers of liquid golden heat pulsing through her woman's flesh sweeping away her modesty.

"You have not yet even tasted pleasure," he swore, brushing a kiss across her lips. "See you, whether you are a bold, lusty lass or nay, you are yet untouched. I would be sure you are well roused enough before we move to the bed—and unless I have forgotten all I e'er learned about pleasing a woman, your enjoyment will be heightened if we first indulge in a bit of touching and caressing."

"And your enjoyment?" A fiercely sweet heaviness,

hot and languid, began weighing her belly. "What of making you roused enough?"

"Ah, my minx, but I told you." He shook his auburn head. "*You* rouse me—just by being you. Look down at yourself, my heart, see how beautiful you are in your arousal. Watch me touch you."

"Touch me there? *Play* with me?" she breathed, doing as he asked, the speaking of it exciting her almost as much as his intimate touch.

"Saints, yes, but I shall play with you, lovely," he growled, sliding his hands round to the tender insides of her thighs, caressing her with the lightest of circular strokes. Exploratory touches he worked ever higher until his fingertips just brushed the welter of curls between her thighs.

"Ooooh!" Amicia cried, nigh shooting off the table's edge at that first stimulating contact.

"Shush," he soothed, lightly toying with her lower hair, taking great care not to let even the tip of a finger touch the heat of her slick-dampened woman's flesh. "Be at ease, and just *feel* . . . feel my touch and get to know my hands on you."

Scarce able to breathe, she watched him, looking on as he returned his hands to her thighs. Very deliberately, he smoothed down to her knees and then back up again, each bliss-spending stroke sending a new floodtide of heated tingles ripping across the hot-pulsing flesh at her core.

"Your scent is stronger now," he said, his voice husky with his own need. "Can you tell?"

Oh, could she! The scent was near overpowering—a cloud of baseness pressing close around them.

But she nodded, the whole of her body quivering with

desire. Faith, the deep-stabbing ache of being so vulnerable, so fully open to his hungering gaze and questing explorations, almost made her delirious with hot-burning need.

But another, admittedly wee part of her cringed at the imminent execution of the very thing she found so stirring.

He was about to go down on bended knee, let his handsome face hover just above her deepest secrets, lock his blue gaze on hers and . . . scent her.

Fill his lungs with the essence of her and intoxicate himself on her musky, female scent.

Aye, that was what he was about to do.

There was no denying it.

She could see his intent written all over his bonny face. Truth be told, it stared right back at her from his dimpled, wolfish smile, the determined gleam in his eyes.

And, saints help her, but just the thought had *that part* of her flooding with a hot, wet rush of exquisitely tingling dampness! Dear Lord, but she could already feel the moisture misting her inner thighs.

"If I let go of you, will you keep your legs open as wide as they are now?" he asked, and she swallowed.

Nay, *gulped,* for the power of speech had left her.

He was toying with her nether curls again, plucking at them and brushing his fingers across their tips with the greatest of leisure. "Well?" he asked again, his gaze not on hers but upon his task. "Will you?"

She nodded, but slid a glance at the bed, her pulsing need now begging, *demanding,* the cataclysmic union she knew they'd find there.

"Your legs, lass. Will you keep them wide?"

She inclined her head again. "I told you once there is naught I would not do for you."

"Good. Then I shall do something special for you," he promised, tracing just one finger along the very center of her womanhood. "You are soft and warm as heated honey and I think, lass, aye . . . I think I must taste you."

"Taste me?"

Her heart stopped. She hadn't expected that.

He nodded. "Och, aye, minx . . . all your sweetness and then some."

Looking well-pleased, even eager, he dropped to his knees and settled himself between her thighs, just as she'd known he would. He held them apart, looked his fill of her.

"Saints, but you are beautiful." He leaned close, breathing of her, a visible shudder rippling across his broad shoulders.

"Ne'er have I seen greater loveliness," he vowed, the slight tremor in his voice assuring her he meant every word, his soft pluckings at her intimate curls unleashing a ferocious need inside her.

"You are glorious beyond my deepest dreams." He let his gaze sweep her, noted the rise and fall of her every breath, the sweet firelit flush across the top swells of her breasts.

And most delightful of all, the dark thatch of curls at the juncture of her thighs. "You are my heart's joy," he vowed, moistening the tip of one finger in the slick wetness of her arousal, then sliding that questing fingertip to the very top of her woman's cleft. There he gently stroked and circled the sensitive bud he knew would bring her the greatest pleasure.

"Oh, dear saints!" she cried, her voice breaking, glorious in her passion.

She gripped the table's edge with white-knuckled hands, her back arching, her body rocking with need. Her breath hitching, she sought his gaze, capturing and holding it, her own filled with a delightful mix of stunned wonder and mounting desperation.

The sweetest kind of desperation a man could give a woman.

And he hadn't even touched his tongue to her . . . yet.

All the want in him clenching deep, he fought for control, the need to drench his senses on her near unmanning him. But he kept his finger circling the hard little bud.

"Does this please you? Do you like having me touch you this way?"

"I cannot stand it, but, oooh, it will be worse if you stop," she gasped, her breath now coming in short little bursts, the deep red flush across her breasts shouting her pleasure.

"And when I do this?" He spread his fingers to cup the whole of her, rubbing her heated softness with slow, insistent pressure.

"Oh, aye," she moaned, her eyes heavy-lidded as she looked down to watch him caress her.

He glanced down as well, caught the drop of glistening moisture pearling at the tip of his hardness. "I cannot wait much longer," he told her, more than half-certain he'd shame himself any moment. "But I shall lick and kiss you until you, too, can bear no more of it, that I promise you."

If he didn't spill before he could finish even the first sweet drag of his tongue through her heat.

Saints, not only was he hard as granite and near to bursting, his fool limbs were trembling!

But ne'er had he been more consumed by the wish to *give* more pleasure than he took. The fire in his belly seemed wholly inconsequential next to his all-consuming desire to please, to have her writhing and moaning beneath him.

Lost and abandoned to a total knowing with her, this night and every night thereafter.

"You are my bliss," he murmured, trailing soft, searching kisses along the smooth flesh of her inner thighs, pleased beyond telling by her urgent little cries and the way she arched and stretched her body for him, the whole of her quivering with unashamed desire.

Well aware he'd lost himself, but no longer caring, he reached up to take hold of her nipples, to lightly squeeze and toy with them—the feel, taste, and scent of her stirring a hunger such as he'd never known.

She grasped his shoulders, held fast to him. *"Please . . ."*

"Och, lass, and that is my most fervent wish," he whispered. "I want naught but to pleasure you."

"And you *are*," she cried, twining her fingers in his hair. Breathing hotly, she urged his head lower and lifted her hips to his seeking mouth, unashamedly raising her heat toward the bliss she knew he was about to spend her.

"Aye, Magnus MacKinnon, you please me so much I am about to burst on the sheer glory of it."

"Not yet, my heart." He searched her loveliness, easing his hands beneath her buttocks to bring her yet closer. "If the gods are kind, we will soon shatter together. . . ."

With a ragged groan, he lowered his head, brushed his cheek against the lush triangle of her raven curls. Inhaling deep, he pulled in great, greedy gulps of her heady female scent . . . intoxicating himself on the musky essence of her womanhood.

"Ooooh . . . I cannot stand it . . . pray have done. . . ."

"Aye, and I shall," he vowed, and touched his tongue to her very core, *licked* her.

"Ach, dia!" She near shot to her feet, the whole of her body tensing like a taut-strung bow.

"Hold you, sweeting. Do not move," he breathed, moving his head sideways, letting his lips brush ever so lightly back and forth across her silky-moist heat. "Lie back and let me taste you, give you this pleasure."

And she complied, falling back against the rumpled plaid, her body limp and trembling. Soft little moans and sighs escaped her parted lips as she dug her fingers into his shoulders, holding him there where she needed him.

"Keep your legs opened wide, lass," he said, pausing to ease her thighs farther apart when she tried to clench them around him. "Let me kiss you here"—he traced her cleft with the tip of his tongue—"let me lick and savor you, and then we will move to the bed. *Then* you can wrap your legs around me as tight as it pleases you."

"Ahhhh, but I cannot wait . . ." she cried, writhing beneath him.

"Lie still, Amicia." He pressed a gentling hand to her stomach, used slight pressure to calm her. "Relax. Open your legs more. . . . yes, that's it . . . full wide so I have best access to you."

"But—"

"Shhhh . . ." He shushed her with another hot glide of his tongue.

He watched her as he licked, holding her gaze with the

same concentrated effort he used to slide the tip of his tongue along the sleek folds of her pulsing heat.

"Your womanhood is like a perfect rose, see you," he said, spacing each word between another probing dip of his tongue into her honeyed moistness. "Sweet, soft petals to beguile and enchant, fragrant and beautiful, but possessed of thorns as well."

She blinked at that, lifted her head to stare at him, her eyes widening in confusion. "Thorns?"

Damning himself for his clumsy way with words, he reached for her hand and brought it to his shaft, circling her fingers around the hot, rigid length of him. "*That* is the *thorn* I meant, sweetness." He jerked, near spilling himself when her fingers tightened around him.

"Sweet and soft as you are, delicious as is the urgency building between us, it will hurt when I enter you," he tried to explain. "That is why"—he swirled his tongue over her again—"I would know you full aroused before—"

"I could ne'er be more desirous," she countered, shuddering as she circled her fingers tighter around his hard length in a firm, clinging grip that ripped a wordless cry from his own lips.

Then she moved her hand on him, just one innocent upward pull, but torturous enough in its mind-numbing exquisiteness to rip through his last threads of restraint.

Unable to withhold himself another moment, he swept her into his arms and carried her to the bed, flinging aside the elaborate hangings to lower her onto the startling white of the bridal sheet.

Beyond words, he followed her down, stretching himself full-length above her. He reached between them to pry her fingers from his hardness, then used his own hand to rub the tip of his shaft along her slippery wet heat. Sighing her pleasure, she slung her legs around him, lifted her hips to increase the tantalizing friction of each smooth slide of his tarse against her hot, quivering flesh.

"Have done," she breathed, grinding her hips in urgent circles against him, *needing* him. "Make me yours now—this moment." She clung to him, her trembling lips begging for kisses.

"I love you," she whispered, the words a breathless little plea. A wee sound, closer to a whimper than coherent words, and almost overpowered by the lashing rain, the tears glistening in her eyes nigh undoing the last stubborn knot tied so fiercely around his heart. "I have e'er—"

"Do not speak," Magnus pleaded, the tightness in his chest near stopping his heart, his damnable pride seizing the moment to close fast around his weakness. Black and cloying, it stole his breath and used his need to seal his lips before his heart could answer her.

Hating himself for the fleeting shimmer of disappointment that darkened her eyes, he gave her what he could, and thrust into her body, muffling his groan in the cool silk of her streaming raven tresses, losing himself in the tight, satiny heat of her.

Through the haze of his passion, he felt the tearing barrier of her innocence, heard her sharp cry. Her body's one protest against this new, demanding intrusion. But then her sharp sob of pain turned to soft whimpers and she clasped her legs tighter about him, digging her fingers into his shoulders as he opened his mouth over hers, taking her cries into his own and letting their hot breaths mingle as he eased himself deeper inside her, filling and claiming her. He made her his in the only way he could, until she arched high against him, the sheer, blinding force of her fast-approaching release sweeping him over the glittering edge of his own.

The whole length of him shuddering with mindless need, he cried her name and shattered on the unstoppable tide of a white-hot conflagration so laming in its intensity he doubted he'd e'er have the strength to climb up out of its wild, whirling depths.

And somewhere in the sweet madness of it, Colin Grant's recently spoken words rose from the spinning, tantalizing brilliance to taunt him.

Only his friend had erred.

It wasn't his ability to pleasure a woman that he'd rediscovered in his lady's arms.

Och, nay, the sweetness—the joy of her—gave him something far more substantial and lasting than mere physical bliss.

'Twas the rediscovery of his soul.

Amicia woke to the furious splatter of rain, a cold, empty bed, and a dull, aching discomfort in the private place deep between her thighs. Thunder echoed and re-echoed somewhere in the distance, each deep rumble heralding the begin of another chill day of mist and rain.

But already a warm fire of freshly-stoked peat lit the room and a round wooden tub of steaming, herb-scented water welcomed her to morning.

As did the anxious-peering faces of a full score of kitchen and laundry maids.

Amicia blinked, their curious glances and craning necks dashing the last vestiges of slumber from her as soundly as if they'd thrown back the bed coverings and roughly nudged her awake.

Together with Dagda and Janet, they bustled about,

tidying the chamber and throwing open the window shutters to let in the gusty, rain-damp wind.

An urgent necessity as her first deep breath of the day proved—for the smoky-close air in the bedchamber was still heavily scented with the night's activities, the pungent smell of musk and sexual arousal firing her cheeks and filling her with keen embarrassment.

"A good morrow to you, milady," Dagda crooned, her expression knowing, and pleased.

Coming closer, she whipped back the half-opened bed curtains and the coverlet, which Amicia hadn't thought to hold tight about her nakedness.

"I see you had a fine night," the seneschal declared, her unerring gaze zeroing in on the reddish-brown smudges staining Amicia's inner thighs, the larger smears and streaks on the soiled bridal sheet.

"H-how late is it? How long have I slept?" Amicia snatched a largish pillow from behind her, pulling it round to use as a shield. "Where is my husband?"

"Ach, 'tis not long past the hour of prime," Dagda informed her, gesturing to one of the laundry maids who stepped forward to offer Amicia a small wooden cup of steaming herbal tisane.

"It will ease your . . . soreness, milady," the lass said, her cheeks flaming nigh as bright a red as her hair.

"T-thank you." Amicia tilted the cup to her lips, let the soothing brew trickle down her parched throat.

The girl nodded and stepped back from the bed, but not quick enough to evade Dagda's firm grip to her elbow.

With a jerk of her head, the old woman indicated the pile of folded linens stacked on the table. "Place the drying sheets to warm on the chair before the brazier, then help your lady to bathe," she ordered. "The sooner she's freshened herself, the sooner she can greet her lord husband in the great hall."

A sharp glance and a brisk nod at the other lasses had them scurrying forward to strip the bed, the bloodied bridal sheet the clear objective of their task.

Amicia glanced at Janet. "Magnus is belowstairs?"

Janet nodded, but didn't quite meet Amicia's gaze. "He was called below over an hour ago," she said, offering Amicia a bed robe. "One of the lookouts thought he spotted an approaching galley, but the day is yet too dark to tell for sure."

"Hech! Like as not an ale-headed loon as crazed as the old laird," Dagda snapped, aiming a censorious look at Janet. "Now, *that one* is full of himself this morn . . . strutting about the hall a-raving about ghost ships and claiming we should have heeded his warnings."

Ignoring her, Janet turned aside, as if distracted, and took an iron poker to jab at the red-glowing peats on the hearthstone.

Amicia watched her, an odd foreboding tugging her brows together as she scrambled off the bed's high mattress and slipped into the bed robe.

Of all the women crowding the room, Janet alone didn't seem plagued by blushes or the urge to aim not-too-discreet stares at the various telltale remnants of the night's *doings*.

Nor did she seem to share Dagda's obsession to get the bridal sheet yanked off the bed and hurried belowstairs where it'd be paraded about the hall like a war trophy.

Nay, Janet's pretty face bore an unusual pallor and dark smudges beneath her eyes bespoke a night as sleepless as Amicia's own.

But not a pleasant one.

"Is aught amiss . . . Cousin?" Amicia sought to win the other's confidence by using the familiar form of address, surprising herself at how easily the term left her lips.

She laid a staying hand on the younger woman's arm when, at last, the little troop of visitors began exiting the bedchamber, a smug-looking Dagda in the lead, the bloodied bridal sheet tucked securely under her arm.

Janet hesitated, then cast an almost frantic look at the backs of the other women. "I must speak with you," she whispered, the urgent plea spoken almost too low to be heard above the hard-pelting rain.

Frowning, Amicia opened her mouth to speak, but the younger woman waved a stilling hand.

"Aye, we must speak, and at the soonest," Janet urged, dropping her voice even lower. "But not here, not anywhere near the castle."

"Where then?" Amicia spoke equally low, icy chills snaking up and down her spine at the glassy-eyed fear in the other woman's eyes. "Tell me and I will be there."

Janet waited but the space of one breath. "The Beldam's Chair. Meet me there within the hour."

"The Beldam's Chair?" Amicia forgot to whisper. "But that is in the middle of the high moors and the weather is fierce—"

Growing more nervous by the moment, Janet swooped Amicia's fur-lined cloak off its peg by the door and tossed it over a chair back. "Wear your cloak and the storm won't touch you. Just come, I pray you."

Amicia glanced at the cloak, her stomach beginning to knot with ill ease.

Janet reached for her hand, squeezed it. "Be there, my lady," she pleaded. "Lives depend on it."

* * *

About the same time, but far out to sea, in the silent waters belonging to another Hebridean isle, a gentle soul sat in solitude upon the black-glistening rocks of a lone tidal islet and murmured protective prayers as she combed cold fingers through her wet and tangled hair.

Sad-eyed and cloaked in a shimmering mist of lightest green, the *gruagach* plucked at the clinging strands of seaweed she could ne'er quite get from her hair.

She could, though, do other things . . . and had.

Aye, she'd cast her every blessing around those she'd once held so dear and still did.

Something she'd done since all time was, and would continue to do forever onward so long as the sun rose upon each new day.

She only hoped she'd done enough this time, and that her warnings had been heeded.

For as with old Devorgilla's own brand of witchy magic and incantations, there was only so much that enchantments and spells could do.

The only true magic rested deep inside every mortal man's soul—and even the bitterest blackest wind would collapse upon itself and be turned away by a heart that loved true.

Her own heart beginning to beat more quickly, the *gruagach* ignored the numbing cold that e'er surrounded her and sent her own love across the tossing waves.

Her love and all her determination, for she, too, had once spent time with the steely-backed MacLeans.

A quality she hoped the Lady Amicia would make fullest use of in the coming hours.

Chapter Fifteen

❖

"*Y*OU OUGHT BE IN THE GREAT HALL, laddie."

Donald MacKinnon lowered his scant weight onto a three-legged stool in Coldstone's bare-walled laird's solar and tossed his eldest son a belligerent stare.

"You ne'er paid any heed to *my* claims that the Devil's own dragonship has been plying these waters of late—why should you believe an ale-taken guardsman?"

Pausing, the old man began to cough. Great, jerky rasps that shook his frail shoulders. But the instant the coughing ceased, he pinned Magnus with another defiant glare. "Aye, you'd best hie yourself down there. Dagda will have waved your bridal sheet beneath the nose of every kinsman in the hall by now, and like as not, she already has the thing tacked to the wall above the high table."

Magnus frowned.

"Now *that* is another fool MacKinnon tradition I swear I will have done with when I am laird," he snapped, and made another long-strided circuit of the wretched chamber, once said to be the grandest in the castle save old Reginald's bedquarters.

The very room he now shared with his lady wife.

At the thought of her sweetness, how she'd clenched herself around him in her passion, Magnus found some of the sourness had left his mood. He raked a hand through his hair, did his best to wipe the scowl from his face.

But he rankled at the knowledge that every long-nosed buffoon beneath his roof had examined and, with surety, *gawked* at the evidence of his passion and his wife's innocence.

Custom or no, it was a fool and barbaric practice.

His father clucked his tongue. "Whether you change time-honored tradition or nay, for the nonce, it is still our custom and you should be belowstairs to accept the accolades of your kinsmen," he groused, stretching his scrawny legs to the warmth of the peat fire.

"The saints know every man on the isle will be there, expecting you." The old laird cast a glance at the crooked-hanging window shutters. "With such a black storm brewing, there'll not be a soul working on the boat strand this morn."

To Magnus's surprise, the mention of the men's daily struggle and toil to rebuild the lost MacKinnon galley fleet didn't send a hot jab of vexation shooting through him as any referral to his wife's well-lined coffers usually did.

Nary a wee tweak.

Nay, his ire rose from thinking of the fool bridal sheet being inspected by all and sundry. Then he heard his father's coughing.

He stretched his arms above his head, cracked his knuckles, and blew out a deliberately gusty breath.

"Never you worry, Da. I will take myself down there so soon as we've determined if there is indeed a strange galley in our waters—and if so, whose it is and what their business might be."

Donald MacKinnon snorted. "So you do believe it?"

Magnus shrugged. He did not know what to believe. But the guardsman, drink-taken or nay, insisted his ears had caught the great beating of a gong and the chanting of oarsmen—before the mysterious vessel had vanished into the mists.

Just as his da e'er claimed.

"Think you yon men cannot spot a galley without your hulking presence looming over their shoulders?" The old man fisted his hands on bony knees, cast a glittery-eyed look toward the solar's tall, arch-topped windows and the three broad-backed men standing there. "A mercy—they've been staring holes in the horizon for hours now."

Dugan and Hugh, and even Colin, with his almost-healed but still somewhat troublesome leg, stood straight-backed and silent at the windows, peering into sheets of slanting rain and trying to catch a glimpse of the supposedly approaching galley.

A task for fools, since Magnus had serious doubts any such vessel existed.

Demon-crewed or nay.

But there his brothers and his best friend stood, uncomplaining and like as not unblinking, too.

And that, when they could be below with the others. Snoring soundly on pallets before the hearth if they so desired, or joining in the bawdy revelry that had surely erupted the moment Dagda tromped into the hall with the bloodstained bedsheet.

A harmless entertainment they no doubt deserved—whether at the expense of Magnus's indignation or nay.

"Even old Boiny would rather be belowstairs," Donald MacKinnon sniffed from his perch before the hearth fire.

Magnus wheeled around, a decided throbbing in his temples beginning to make itself known. "That mongrel hasn't budged from the warmth of the hearth—" He broke off to stare in disbelief at the dog.

Boiny, his great bulk no longer sprawled like a ratty gray carpet before the hearth fire as was his wont, paced as furiously as Magnus himself—only in front of the closed solar door and not around the chamber.

Stiff-legged and whining, the old dog had already worn a track in the sparse covering of floor rushes.

Magnus eyed him, an odd prickling at his scalp. But he shrugged off his ill ease. The dog was old, his mind surely as fogged as Magnus's father's.

"Either the beast scorns our fair company or he has his heart set on casting about beneath the hall's trestle tables for fallen scraps of last night's feasting."

A good-natured chuckle from one of the men at the windows answered him. "Boiny isn't the only one in this room who could do with some victuals."

Dugan.

His middle brother—and the one who ate with the most voracious appetite Magnus had e'er seen.

A jab of guilt plunged straight through Magnus's ribs to land a stinging blow dangerously close to his heart.

Magnus sighed, recognizing defeat.

He had enough experience being on the other side of victorious to be stubborn now.

Drawing a deep breath, he crossed the solar and clapped a hand on Dugan's shoulder. "Have done with this nonsense, then, and go break your fast." He nodded at Hugh and Colin to indicate he meant all three of them. "And take Da and Boiny with you—I will stay up here and hold lookout myself."

"And we are like to pay dearly for stuffing our faces if you miss the ghost ship's landing and a horde of banshees descend upon our shores!" His father pushed slowly to his feet, puffed his chest.

"Or worse, if you spot a MacDonald galley heading our way with shipbuilding supplies. As I know you, you'd have a score of bonfires set to warn them off before they'd even attempt to unload a single plank of wood!"

Magnus closed his eyes, pressed his temples. Then he let out a long, slow breath.

The time to show his heart had come.

"*Should* Donall MacLean have arranged for yet another MacDonald supply galley to bring us wood and other necessaries, I . . . I will not naysay the unloading or the good use of whate'er materials we might need to finish the rebuilding of our fleet," he said, each word tasting like bitter ash on his tongue.

But not nearly so unpleasant as he would have thought they'd be.

Or as difficult.

"Aye, my over-proud son e'er knows what he is at and cannot see how direly we need—" Donald MacKinnon stopped his shuffle across the room in midstride. His rheumy blue eyes nigh popping out of his head, he stared at Magnus.

"What did you say, laddie?" he demanded, his bushy

brows rising so high they were nearly indiscernible from his hairline. "Did I hear you aright?"

Dugan and Hugh stared, too. Both of them almost as wide-eyed as their da, slack-jawed and speechless.

Colin Grant burst out laughing.

And laughed all the harder when Magnus glowered at him.

Ignoring Magnus's black glare, his ingrate friend leaned back against the solar's lime-washed wall and slapped his good thigh.

"Ho, Laird MacKinnon!" The cheeky lout addressed Magnus's father. "It would seem the clandestine trips your son has been making to the Beldam's Chair have worked their magic," he roared, near convulsing in his mirth. "Either that, or a certain comely wench has washed his fool head of his wretched pride."

The old man blinked. "But what did he *say*?" He tilted his head and tugged on his earlobe as if he'd have difficulty hearing—or believing—any answer Colin might give him. "I canna think I heard him right. My hearing isn't what it once was. . . ."

Stepping forward to sling an arm about his father's shoulders, Hugh answered for Colin. "He said that *if* a galley is indeed heading our way, he hopes it will be another supply vessel loaded with the wood and other necessaries we need to finish rebuilding our fleet and"—Hugh cast a silent plea to Magnus over their father's white-tufted head—"that whate'er surplus we do not need for shipbuilding, can be put to good use in refurbishing the castle."

"Aye, that is what he said," Colin and Dugan agreed in chorus.

Donald MacKinnon's eyes grew round.

Round, and suspiciously bright.

Worse, he sniffed . . . and not just once.

"Saints o' mercy, I ne'er thought I'd see the day . . ." he spluttered, rubbing a knotty-knuckled fist across his cheek.

"And neither did I," Magnus owned, shooing them from the solar before *he* began sniffling. "Now hie yourselves belowstairs and take that fool sheet of bloodied linen down from the wall if you'd see me happy."

Not that he could imagine being any happier than he was at the moment.

Indeed, the moment they'd all trudged out of the chamber, his face broke into a grin.

And he was still grinning when he took his place at the window to peer through the rain for a galley that might or might not be making for his shores.

Truth be told, he might grin all day.

And had Saint Andrew hisself told him, he would ne'er have believed that losing his pride would feel so damned good.

Bitterest wind buffeting her, Amicia huddled ever deeper into the thick folds of her fur-lined cloak and hurried through what had to be the worst tempest to be visited upon the Hebrides in years.

Hurried *by foot,* because even the stout-hearted garrons she'd tried to saddle in her husband's stables had balked at any attempt to cajole them from the safe haven of their byre stalls.

Each beast she'd tried to encourage into the morning's wind and rain had whinnied and protested with such vehemence, she'd had to give up her hopes of a mount lest the commotion alert someone to her departure.

Blinking, she swiped the rain from her brow, silently cursing her lack of skill as a sweet-talker of horses.

And her foolhardiness in agreeing to make this journey.

But now, more than half the way there, she had little choice but to keep setting one foot before the other until she reached the Beldam's Chair—a tedious undertaking that would be well worth the effort if only Janet could indeed shed light on who was behind the troublous goings-on plaguing Clan Fingon.

That had to be the reason the younger woman had pleaded such a secret meeting.

Even so, with the journey beginning to seem endless, it took all her will not to turn back, not to abandon her wild trek across the boggy, rain-drenched ground.

A fool's expedition to be sure, with bursts of eerie greenish lightning outlining the dark mass of the hills and illuminating the broad, high moorlands. Each flash driving home not only the folly of it, but the danger.

She shivered, tried not to feel the wind tearing at her cloak or pay heed to how hard the pellets of sideways rain stung her face, striking her cheeks like a peppered onslaught of thousands of tiny needles.

Keeping her head lowered, she strained to see through the fast-moving swirls of thick gray mist—and saw naught. She began mumbling curses, aloud this time, simply because doing so made her feel better. She also drew her cloak's hood deeper onto her forehead, blessing for once old Devorgilla for gifting her with such a warm, voluminous mantle.

But when at last the burial cairn's low-mounded pile of bluish-gray stones came into view, her stomach clenched with icy-cold ill ease.

As promised, Janet waited for her. The younger woman sat stiff-backed and rigid in the cairn's runic-carved Beldam's Chair, a MacKinnon plaid wrapped around her tiny frame, one tartan fold draped over her head to protect her from the gushing rain.

Only, rather than come forward to greet Amicia or even lift a hand to acknowledge her arrival, Janet stayed where she was, her delicate features contorting into the most bizarre and terrifying expressions Amicia had e'er seen.

Half-afraid Janet had been seized by some strange malady and couldn't move or speak, Amicia hastened her step—even when a distinct voice deep inside her warned her that she ought to run back to the castle as swiftly as her feet would carry her.

But morbid curiosity and genuine concern drove her forward even though Janet was now rolling her eyes and casting panicky yet somehow pleading stares in the direction Amicia had just come. The way back across the high moors to Coldstone Castle.

Comprehension coming at last, Amicia realized that, for whatever reason, her erstwhile rival was urging her to flee.

The direness of the situation became frighteningly apparent when, not ten paces from the ancient burial cairn, a sinewy arm slid around Amicia's waist from behind, seizing hold of her in an iron-hard grip, and the cold blade of a deadly-sharp dirk pressed tight against her throat.

"Ach, lassie, to be out a-walking in this black weather, and after such a bliss-filled night."

Dagda's voice, the same yet horrifyingly *different*, identified her assailant.

"You?" Shock ripping through her, Amicia struggled against the older woman's viselike hold. Her efforts won her a stinging nick in the tender flesh beneath her ear.

Amicia stilled at once, her heart plummeting to the sodden ground, icy dread washing over her in great, sickening waves.

"Aye, 'tis me." Dagda gave a bloodcurdling chuckle. "I am the force behind the *dark deeds* and *curses* stalking Clan Fingon," she said, her voice mocking. "I'll be taking your cloak, too, though I regret the need. It will ill-serve you where you are going, but its ermine lining will fund a life for me far from these wretched shores."

Careful to keep the dirk at Amicia's throat, the old woman divested her of Devorgilla's cloak with amazing dexterity, and swirled it around her own shoulders with surprising speed, almost before Amicia could even blink a mute protest.

"She's mad!" Janet cried, finding her voice at last. Still sitting in the Beldam's Chair, her water-soaked clothes plastered to her trembling body. "Full mad, and meaning to kill us!"

Her eyes at their widest and her face blanched a deathly white, Janet looked far more deranged than Dagda. Clutching her arms about her middle, she rocked back and forth on the stone seat, wailing and sobbing her misery.

"Ooooh, milady, I am so sorry. . . . I ne'er thought it'd come to this . . . ne'er meant to—"

"Mad, am I?" Dagda cut her off. "And who would not run mad after seeing her beloved young husband put his own self to the cliff, and taking his two innocent bairns with him when he jumped?"

"W-what?" Amicia almost spun around to face the old

woman, but self-preservation and rank fear stopped her from even thinking about moving when Dagda pressed the dirk blade harder against the quivering flesh of her neck.

"Och, you thought Niall and my bairns died of a fever?" Dagda stepped around in front of her, an expression of mock confusion on her face. "Tsk, tsk! My sorrow for keeping you so ill-informed," she said, and Amicia caught the light of madness glinting in her eyes. "But never you fret, lassie. No one kens the truth, so you are not alone in your ignorance."

With a sad, almost regretful note entering her voice, she added, "My profound sorrow, too, that you must suffer for deeds that were none of your doing. I've grown rather fond of you. But it cannot be helped. Your demise will strike a much deeper grief into the heart of the MacKinnons than aught else combined."

Prickles of coldest horror tingled along Amicia's spine and she had the sickening feeling that the earth was sliding away beneath her feet.

"My demise?" she rasped, pushing the two words off a tongue gone dust-dry with fear. "But—"

Dagda snorted. "I will explain the whole of it once we reach the boat strand and you and yon lassie are comfortably secured aboard one of the new galleys—the one I've prepared for you."

"She's sawed holes in the planking and gouged out the caulking!" Janet wailed. "She means to leave us, tied and bound, aboard the galley so we'll drown when it sinks in the storm! 'Tis her revenge on the MacKinnons! Magnus will lose you and the old laird will be convinced the curse has descended with a vengeance."

"And you, you clapper-tongued strumpet, will hold

your prattle unless you wish me to bind your mouth."
Dagda's eyes flashed in irritation. "Now come here and
tie the lassie's wrists. The rope is draped o'er the litter
hidden round the other side of the cairn. And dinna think
of running away. You won't get far, and even if you did—
what do you think the MacKinnons would do with you
once I tell them how you've helped me keep old Reginald's curse alive and thriving?"

"Ooooh, Mother of God, help us. . . . I ne'er meant to
do anyone any harm. . . ." Janet moaned, leaping up from
the Beldam's Chair to dash around the corner of the
mounded stones.

She reappeared moments later, dragging a makeshift
litter behind her, the rope Dagda had requested dangling
from one hand and trailing along on the soggy ground.

Tossing a wild-eyed glance full of apology at Amicia,
Janet took Amicia's hands and managed to bind them
with surprising speed, considering her fingers trembled
so badly Amicia wondered she could even hold the rope.

"I am so sorry." She turned another pitiful gaze on
Amicia. "I only wanted Magnus, see you? I'd thought I
loved him. Now I know I ne'er did, but back then—"

"Back then, you hoped that if you helped me destroy
Clan Fingon, Magnus would be so grief-stricken and vulnerable, *you* could step in to comfort him," Dagda finished for her. "That was the way of it, was it not? Your
hope that, by helping me avenge my loved ones, you'd
make Magnus dependent on you—so much so he'd
marry you out of sheer gratitude."

"Aye, that is what I thought. Oh, God in Heaven, how
could I have been so blind?" Janet crumpled to her knees,
stared at Dagda in sheerest horror, great tracks of tears

streaming down her cheeks. "I ne'er thought you would harm anyone. Our own kinsmen!"

"*I* have nary a drop of that tainted strain running in my veins," Dagda corrected her, using the dirk to urge Amicia onto the litter. "My Niall was the one with ties to Clan Fingon. And a good thing, for I used that blood bond and the tradition of Highland hospitality to secure myself a trusted position in their household after their meddling at sea ruined Niall's fortunes and drove him to take his own life. His, and my bairns!"

"Your husband brought about his own downfall," Janet argued, showing her first bit of spine since Amicia had walked into this nightmare.

"'Tis true," Janet railed, throwing a wild-eyed glance at Amicia. "Dagda and her husband lived on the most barren of isles. After years of trying to eke an existence from the sea, he tried to better their lot by informing the English and their turncoat Scots friends, the Balliols, of any Scottish loyalist activities in Hebridean waters."

Her teeth chattering, she paused to dash the streaming rain from her forehead. "Their wee isle was little more than rock and sand, but its location gave them firsthand knowledge of any passing war galleys, supply ships, or couriers moving between these isles, England, and the Irish coast. But each time Dagda's husband arranged a secret meeting with his benefactors, he ran up against Clan Fingon galleys and couldn't perform his promised duties as an informant. Af—"

"After a while, they stopped coming. And they ne'er paid him a *siller* for his trouble!" Dagda glared her wrath at Janet. "The MacKinnons and their watchdog presence in the waters hereabouts ruined Niall's chances of making a fortune and left him seeing no way out but to widow me. Clan Fingon stole my husband and my sweet bairns . . . my life!"

Amicia shuddered on the litter. Saints, did the old woman mean to drag her clear across the moor to the boat strand? When she ordered Janet to bind her feet to the litter as well, it seemed that must be her intent indeed.

Her stomach heaving, Amicia fought an overwhelming urge to retch. Struggling to suppress it, she listened to Dagda's rantings and prayed Magnus would notice her absence—as well as Janet's and the seneschal's—and head out with a patrol to search for them.

And that if he did, he'd find them soon enough.

"Put your hands behind your back, girl." Dagda snatched the rope from Janet. "I'm going to bind them, but not so tight you won't be able to help me pull the litter to the boat strand," she explained, making short work of knotting the strong heather rope around Janet's wrists.

Apparently satisfied with her handiwork, Dagda lifted a fold of Amicia's cloak and dragged it across her forehead, using it to momentarily stanch the endless stream of rain coursing down her brow.

To Amicia's surprise, the old woman knelt beside her in the oozing peat mire, that odd look of regret clouding her dark eyes again.

"Aye, lass, 'tis sorry I am that I require your help in this," she said, a sad smile twisting her lips. "But the loss of a much-loved wife will speak louder than the burning of a thousand empty chambers and sawed-through latrine seats."

Shaking her head, she stared down at Amicia, and with each bright burst of lightning, the crazed glint in her eyes grew wilder, more terrifying.

Not that Amicia could see her all too clearly lying

prone on the makeshift litter, the lashing rain now pounding unhindered onto her face and blurring her vision. Unable to swipe at the raindrops, they gathered in her eyes, near blinding her.

But not so fully that her heart didn't freeze with fear when she caught the silvery flash of the dirk blade as Dagda raised it high above her head.

"Because I'm fond of you, I'll put you out of your misery now," Dagda said, almost as if she indeed meant to soothe. "Your whiny friend will have to suffer her fate through to the end. You will have the mercy of sleeping through yours."

"No-o-o-o!" The denial burst from Amicia's throat as the dagger swooped downward, the roar of her own red terror and a smashing pain of bright-splintering agony, ending what should have been the first day of a new and beautiful life.

Chapter Sixteen

✦

"*WHAT DO YOU MEAN she is gone?*"

Magnus stood on the threshold to the great hall, staring at Colin. Hot disbelief pounded through him, and his good humor from just moments earlier vanished like a puff of smoke.

"She can't be . . . gone." Agitation—and fear—welling inside him, he clenched his hands lest he seize his friend by the neck opening of his mailed hauberk and rattle a better answer from the lout's lying lips.

But even before his stopped heart could resume beating, Dugan and Hugh came barreling into the hall from behind him, their own blanched-white faces underscoring without words that Colin was speaking the truth.

Bitter-cold dread squeezing the breath from him, Magnus stared at the three men, razor-sharp fear twisting his gut.

Now he knew why his scalp had prickled earlier.

Swallowing against the tightness in his throat, he fo-

cused on Hugh. "Tell me this is madness . . . that it is not
true." Saints, just putting his fear to words sliced his
heart. "There must be some mistake."

But Hugh shook his head. "They are nowhere to be
found," he panted, bending forward to brace his hands on
his thighs. "We've searched every corner and cranny in
the castle—even looked behind doors and beneath beds.
They—"

"*They?*" Magnus's already-hot-burning nape flamed
with a fresh rush of scalding heat, even as his blood
turned to ice. "Who are *they?*"

"Your lady wife, wee Janet, and that old she-goat,
Dagda." His da spoke up from where he stood, wringing
his hands before the displaced high table. "The three of
them have vanished without a trace. No one's seen 'em
since earliest cockcrow."

"Christ . . . in . . . His . . . heaven!" Magnus roared,
blood pounding hot in his ears. "*My heart's treasure . . .*"
That last was spoken on a thin breath of defeat, and so
low he wasn't even sure if he'd said the words aloud.

He only knew the entirety of his world spun and
whirled around him and that he was struggling to draw air
through a throat that seemed too tight for even a sliver of
a breath to pass through.

"Why didn't someone fetch me?"

"No one went for you because we did not think aught
was amiss until just a short while ago. It was expected
they'd be found," Colin said. "Sakes, you ken they could
have been anywhere—minding women's business or
suchlike."

Magnus's stomach turned over. His heart plummeted.
It was the *suchlike* that terrified him.

"I told you to be wary," his da minded him, making it

worse. "The Devil crew from the ghost galley's done and snatched all three of 'em. I can feel it in my bones!"

His bones jellied with horror, Magnus pressed an icy-cold hand against his chest and swept the hall with a furious glare.

His kinsmen, each one looking as stricken as he felt, averted their gazes.

The remnants of their raucous fast-breaking told him why.

The evidence taunted him from the tops of trestle tables in a disorderly welter of overturned ewers, empty ale cups, and trenchers of half-eaten bannocks—puddles of spilled ale speaking the loudest.

That, and the damnable bridal sheet still tacked proudly to the wall behind the high table.

The bastards had been reveling.

The whole merry lot of them, carousing in jest and good cheer, whilst his lady and two other kinswomen had been spirited away right from beneath their fool noses!

And while he, mayhap the greater fool, had been standing watch in the lofty laird's solar, peering through curtains of rain for nonexistent ships.

"'Tis the curse again, I tell you," his father insisted. Rocking back on his heels, he stared up at the stone-vaulted ceiling. "I knew we'd not seen the end of old Reg—"

"A pox on Reginald and his curse if e'er there was one—which I still do not believe!" Magnus jerked, a muscle leaping in his jaw. "Ghost galleys and long-dead ancestors do not abduct innocent, living women."

The old man's lower lip jutted. "Then what happened to them?"

"Saints alive!" Magnus exploded. "Think you I'd be standing here like a dimwit if I knew?"

His gut tied in more knots than he cared to imagine, Magnus pulled a hand down over his face and tried to think. There had to be an explanation. Like as not, they were off in some remote corner of the castle, entertaining themselves by watching the storm. Counting lightning bolts to pass the time.

No one of any intelligence would venture out into a tempest of such gale-gusting ferocity . . . and his braw lady wife had more wits about her than most men.

Even Janet and old Dagda, vexing as the seneschal could be, knew better than to tempt fate by hieing themselves into the full fury of a Highland storm once unleashed.

So where were they?

A soul-deep ache, dull-edged and throbbing, beginning to replace his initial hot burst of fury, Magnus paced before the trestle tables, the muscle jerking at his jawline keeping an annoying rhythm with his fast, long strides.

"Think!" he groused at his brothers as he strode past them. "And you!" He shot a look at Colin. "You are e'er trailing after Janet—have you any notion what could have happened to them? Where they could have gone?"

But Colin only shook his dark head, his expression grim. There could be no help there, no spark of sudden and bright inspiration.

Colin Grant, for all his earlier jollity, looked a man suffocated by the crushing weight of his own dread and fears.

And seeing his friend's e'er-so-carefree face drawn tight and pale only increased Magnus's own alarm.

Think, he had to think.

He glanced at his brothers again. "Is it certain they are not within the castle walls?"

"We have looked everywhere," Dugan said, and Magnus's heart sank.

"Then we must search the whole of the isle—storm or no." He flickered a glance at the peat fire, noting at once that old Boiny's favored place before the hearthstone loomed empty.

He stopped his pacing at once, looked around. "Where is Boiny? Is he gone as well?"

"Och, nay, Magnus," a kinsman standing near the back of the hall called in answer. "That old cur is still about— he's just casting around for scraps. Been o'er by the door the best part o' the last hour."

O'er by the door?

At last, Magnus knew what had been nagging at him. Scarce noticing his kinsmen's stares, he tore through the hall, running for the great shadowed arch of the keep's main entrance.

The one that opened into the bailey and the rain-lashed morning beyond.

And sure enough, just as the old dog had done at the closed door to the laird's solar, Boiny now fretted back and forth in front of the keep's heavy, iron-studded door. His stumbly, hitching steps and stiff-legged gait lanced Magnus's heart, but it was the dog's pathetic whines and the look of terror in his milky brown eyes that curdled his blood.

"They've been taken," he said, his voice deadly calm and all the more dangerous for it.

Never more sure of anything in his life, he whirled to face the men who'd followed him.

"Which one of you searched my bedchamber?" he demanded, curling his fingers around the hilt of his sword.

" 'Twas me, sir." A timid-voiced laundry maid with a shock of bright red hair squeezed her way forward. "Your brothers had some of us searching abovestairs. I be the one who looked round your bedchamber," she confessed, her face flaming scarlet. "I even peeked beneath the bed, I did."

Magnus eyed the lass, tried to school his features into a less fierce scowl. "Did you notice if her cloak hung on its peg by the door? You'll ken . . . the fur-lined one she's e'er complaining is too cumbersome to wear?"

The girl clapped a hand to her cheek, shook her head. "Nay, my lord. Looking back, I don't think the mantle was there where she hangs it. Aye, I am certain it was gone."

Nodding his thanks, Magnus turned to his men. "Those of you not afeared of a bit of rain or bloodshed, buckle on your sword belts and be prepared to overturn every stone and clump of heather on this island until we find my wife and our kinswomen," he said, already yanking open the hall's massive oaken door.

A furious welter of wind and rain gusted inside, guttering torches and blowing clouds of choking smoke into the men's faces as they surged forward to scramble down the rain-slicked outer stairs to the courtyard below.

And the moment the last one hurried past, Magnus made to follow them—but not before he dropped to one knee and gave Boiny a fierce hug.

"I owe you one, old friend," he said, hooking his fingers into the unhappy beast's heavy collar until one of the more stout-armed kitchen lasses stepped forward to take hold of him.

Boiny's heart may have been burning to tear off in search of his two-legged friend, but the dog's advancing age and his weak legs would ne'er survive the brunt of the storm.

His throat tightening again, Magnus reached to tousle the dog's rough fur before he turned to race down the stairs. "Never you fear, old boy, I'll find her," he said, as much for his own benefit as the fretting dog's. "And when I do, may God have mercy on whoe'er took her."

A furious ride and much rain later, Magnus halted his garron atop the high dunes hemming the isle's crescent-shaped boat strand and . . . frowned at the hellish scene before him.

He drew a sharp breath. Indeed, if he believed in such foolery, he would have sworn some ancient Celtic deity bent on wreaking her wrath on God's good earth had conjured the morning's storm.

Ne'er had a worse fury blasted across the Hebrides—not since the raging tempest that had destroyed the MacKinnon fleet some years ago.

And if the wild-winded squalls howling around his ears were any indication, *this* storm stood a good chance of smashing the score of half-built new galleys lining the golden-sanded beach.

Hoping to find his lady down there somewhere, of her own free choosing or otherwise, he spurred down the dunes, pulling up as close to the tossing surf as his garron would venture.

He flung himself out of the saddle, straining his eyes to see through the sheets of driving rain, the prickling of his scalp and the gooseflesh erupting on the back of his neck a sure sign that she had to be near.

Somewhere.

And close.

He knew it with every inch of his body, each thundering beat of his heart. Sakes, he could *feel* the connection crackling between them—a living thing, holding them close even when he could not see her.

He just knew, and his heart gave a great bound at the surety of it.

No one else had believed him, the lot of his kinsmen charging off to the high moors, the whole fool band of them declaring the women would seek shelter in one of the many cairns and hollow-walled brochs dotting the isle's interior.

Certain he knew better, Magnus scanned the rows of unfinished galleys. Sakes, there were more than he'd realized. They littered the beach!

But with each sweeping gaze, he promised himself he'd see her, catch sight of her huddled beneath some upturned hull, shivering with the cold and rain, but safe.

Whole.

He could not, would not, lose her now.

Sweet images of her flooded his mind, crazing him as he raced up and down the empty strand, calling her name even if the wind snatched away his cries almost as quickly as they left his lips.

Not willing to lose heart, he lifted a hand to shield his eyes from the rain and stared out at the two recently completed galleys moored in the deeper water just offshore.

The first two vessels his kinsmen had built—or what remained of them—bobbed on the surf, smashed by nature's unforgiving fist.

The largest, a fine twenty-six-oared beauty, lay on her side, half-submerged beneath the churning waves, the single mast snapped in two like so much kindling to float impotent and useless in the surf.

The other, equally fine but with only twenty oars, was still afloat, but just barely. Indeed, it appeared to be sinking fast.

But of the three women, naught was to be seen.

Magnus swore, dashed the rain from his eyes for what had to be the hundredth time in mere moments.

By the living God, even without the rain coursing down his forehead, he could scarce see two feet ahead of him much less hope to spot a sooty-haired lass on a morn darker than the crack of the Devil's own arse!

"Ho, Magnus!" Colin thundered up beside him, his winded garron as uneasy as the howling storm.

"Come, let us be gone from here," he urged. "Your brothers are off on the moors, searching the heather. I say let us join them. In God's name, why would the women come here? We are wasting precious time. . . ."

"Nary a moment is wasted if it can be used to find them." Magnus glared at his friend, but Colin's own ill ease stood etched in his face, and Magnus remembered too late Colin's deep affection for Janet.

"Forgive me," he said for the second time that morning, forgetting his pride. "I know you mean well, and that it is unlikely they are here, but . . . I just had a feeling."

"A feeling?"

"Aye," Magnus snapped, his tone daring Colin to deny it. "And so long as that feeling persists, I am not riding off elsewhere."

Even if he spent the rest of his days stalking up and down the dune-lined strand calling his wife's name.

"They cannot be here, Magnus," Colin argued.

"Come, see reason. Let us be off to where we may have a better chance of finding them."

"Nay. They are here, I tell you!"

Scrunching his eyes against the rain, Magnus scanned the beach, the great rollers crashing on the shore, willed them to appear.

When they didn't, he flung an arm toward the unfinished galley hulls. "Go you, if you wish. I am staying here. To search those boats—every last one of them."

"'Fore God, but you are a stubborn loon." Frowning blacker than his beard, Colin swung down from his saddle, strode across the wet sand to grab Magnus by the arms.

"Those are empty hulls, my friend. The most of them unfinished. Do you not see? The women will not be cowering beneath one of them. Not in this storm. Had they been caught unaware, they would seek more adequate shelter, wouldn't you say?"

"And that is the heart of it, you witless dolt!" Magnus shot him an irritated look. "Do *you* not see? They were not *caught unaware*. This storm started raging last night and worsened with each passing hour. No sane person would venture out into the teeth of such fury. They had to have been taken by force, and whoe'er would do such a thing is capable of any infamy, would not care whether they were sheltered in the storm or no."

The color drained from Colin's face. "You are right," he agreed, dashing the wet hair off his forehead. He held a flattened hand over his eyes and stared out across the tossing waves. "Think you they might be aboard one of those foundering galleys?"

Magnus followed his stare. "I pray not," he said, praying indeed.

"Were they on the one already on its side, they'd have been long since swept out to sea." Colin voiced Magnus's own dread. "If they are on the second, the one that is fast sinking—"

"Then we must fetch them!"

"And how do you mean to get out there?" Colin eyed the wild-foaming surf, the high, pounding waves. "Would you swim? Only to find you'd squandered time when they are not there?"

That they could drown was left unsaid—not that Magnus cared. At least not for himself.

To lose Amicia now that he'd finally made her his would be to have the sun and all the stars extinguish. His world would lose all light and purpose—his life . . . an unthinkable grief.

"Well?" Colin stared at him through the rain.

"The currachs!" Magnus decided, already running for the nearest of the little skin-and-wicker boats.

Colin pressed his lips together, his bad leg forgotten. "A wee hide boat—a cockleshell! In those seas?"

"A currach will hold five people and is seaworthy enough." His mind set, Magnus snatched up a length of rope from the sand, secured it to his belt. "We have no other choice," he added, patting the coils of rope.

Colin heaved a great sigh, looked doubtful.

But, bless his true heart, he didn't balk.

Not entirely.

"Just do not think I'm hieing myself out there alone," he stipulated, eyeing the surging waters with more than a shade of trepidation. "I cannot swim, see you. . . ."

"We will both go," Magnus assured him, feeling better now that a plan had been made.

But the instant he curled his fingers around the rim of

the little currach, began pulling it across the sand, the prickling sensation along his spine increased a thousand-fold.

A glance at the fast-sinking galley showed him why.

Janet stood at the galley's low-slung rail, one hand raised high above her head and waving.

"By God, there's Janet!" Relief surging through him, he grabbed Colin. "See? She has spotted us," he added, his heart making a great bound.

Where Janet was, his lady and Dagda would be, too.

But only Janet stood waving from the rail.

And, bless her sweet self, but she looked as happy as Magnus. Truth be told, she *glowed*. But despite her beaming smile and the pallor of her skin, surprisingly notable at the distance, the strands of seaweed tangling her hair bespoke of a struggle with the sea at the very least.

Magnus glanced at Colin, gave the lout's arm a rough shake. "Ho, man! Your lady is out there, waving at us. . . . Do you not see her?"

"I see nothing but rain." Colin cupped both hands to his eyes, leaning forward to see better. After a moment, he shook his head. "Nay, I only see the damned empty galley."

Impatient, Magnus thrust out an arm, pointed. "Look! I tell you she is there—" He broke off at once, staring in disbelief, for Janet had vanished.

Gone, as if she'd never been.

"She was there, at the rail, waving . . . I swear it," he vowed, dragging the currach into the surf. "Come you, hurry!" he called to Colin as he hopped into the little boat, grabbed up the oars. "I know they are on that galley. I can feel Amicia's presence out there so surely as I can see your ugly face!"

"We shall soon see, my friend," Colin said, inserting himself into the bobbing craft. "Aye, we shall see—if we do not lose our own lives trying to get out there." He grimaced. "Sakes, but you made the worst possible choice of boats!"

Ignoring him, Magnus set his jaw and began paddling toward the galley. He was not about to admit that, in his haste, he had indeed seized a less than fine craft.

Already water slopped around their ankles—and not from the pouring rain. The little currach's timber frame was half-rotted. They'd be hard-pressed to reach the galley, much less use the dubious vessel to transport five adults safely back to shore if they did.

"I am paddling—*you* bail," he said grimly, his gaze fixed on the galley, not trusting himself to meet Colin's eye.

Not all of his damnable pride had left him.

"This is madness!" Colin lifted his voice above the wind, cursed blackly when a great wave crashed into the currach, near upturning it.

"The only madness is if we do not try," Magnus gritted, straining to hold their course, the oar blades effecting little against the churning seas, Colin's two-handed water-scooping efforts even less.

But, at last, the galley loomed before them and, to Magnus's vast relief, the wee boat withstood the violent crash of impact. Better yet, they'd managed to collide with the galley's low-slung midsection and not the high bow-platform or raised stern as he'd feared they might.

Whipping the coiled rope from his belt, he secured the currach to the larger vessel as swiftly as his unsteady hands allowed, then clambered over the side of the galley, Colin close on his heels.

"Amicia! Janet!" he cried, dropping to the planked deck. He glanced about, near frantic, and seeing . . . nothing.

Someone might well have upturned a barrel of ice chips over him. He'd been so sure.

"They are not here," Colin panted, sinking onto one of the rowing-benches. Rubbing his injured thigh, he cast a dark look down the narrow gangway running between the bench rows, the defeat in his eyes squeezing Magnus's heart.

His hope.

"They have to be here." He dismissed Colin's assessment with a wave of his hand. "I saw Janet. She . . . Christ on the Cross, what is *that*?"

He stared, starting forward only to have his feet slither on the slippery deck—a deck run wet with the pouring rain, sea spray, and an oddly luminescent green foam.

"That is your lady's cloak, I vow!" Colin pushed to his feet again, pointing not at the strange rivers of greenish sea foam streaming over the deck planks, but at the crumpled and ripped mantle tangled up in the galley's mast cordage.

Magnus charged forward, dread racking him when he recognized the ruined cloak as Amicia's indeed. "Nooo!" he cried, his blood chilling, waves of nausea and denial churning inside him.

He sank to his knees beside the cloak, dragged its heavy folds up against his breast, dug his fingers into the wet fur lining and a mass of hard and soft *somethings* that felt anything but pleasant beneath his clutching fingers.

"What devilry is this?" He dropped the cloak at once, stared at it in horror.

"By the Mass, ne'er have I seen the like." Colin's

voice came from behind him, the knave seemingly unwilling to come any nearer.

Not that Magnus could blame him for his own skin crawled with revulsion.

Revulsion, and fear for his lady, for the mantle's hem had torn, and all manner of *oddities* spilled from within its folds. Strange objects without description that now littered the deck, washed to and fro by the swishing foam and rain, some tumbling over the side and into the sea.

The cloak also slid overboard, but the strange objects, some might call them charms, or *spelling goods,* remained. The objects and a single line of ominously taut rope that disappeared over the rail—its implication mocking every hope he'd clung to throughout the last hours.

Colin spotted the rope at the same time, and being closer, he reached it first. "'Tis old Dagda!" He pointed when Magnus joined him. "She is dead."

Looking down, Magnus saw her, too.

Or rather what could be seen of her above the churning waves.

Horror constricting his chest, he stared down at her, disbelief crashing over him. "Jesu God, what a terrible end," he breathed, crossing himself.

The old woman must have tripped on the rain-slick deck, tangling herself in a jumble of rope and—perhaps?—the voluminous folds of Amicia's fur-lined cloak.

"And my wife? Poor Janet?" Wheeling away from the grisly sight, Magnus grabbed Colin's arms. He held his friend crushingly tight, as if by sheer force of will and strength, he could undo what seemed the cruelest of ends.

"What of them? Where are they?" His shouts rose above the wind, reverberating off the heavens that would snatch away all that was so dear. "They cannot have met the same fate." He dug his fingers into Colin's mailed sleeves. "I will not allow it! They cannot be dead."

"They are not here." The flatness of his friend's voice said *why* he believed them gone.

Colin believed the two women already at the bottom of the sea.

"You think they are dead!" Magnus shook him, fury and bottomless, white-hot pain blurring his vision. "Admit it . . . you have no hope of finding them. Not alive."

Colin did not answer him.

But his silence did.

"Noooo!" Thrusting Colin from him, Magnus spun about, bent double in his pain. "Noooo!" he cried again, clutching his middle, mind-numbing grief eating his innards and spewing fire through him, each hot blast of agony setting another piece of his soul to flame.

"Merciful saints help me. It cannot be!" He sank to his knees, hot tears scalding his eyes, blinding him. Horrible pain welled and twisted inside him; then Colin's hand settled on his shoulder and the commiserating squeeze he gave Magnus ripped away his last shred of hope.

He looked up at his friend, seeing only the tear-blurred outline of him but recognizing the sadness in the slow shaking of Colin's head, the slumping of his shoulders.

"I cannot live without her, see you?" The words came out on a ragged gasp. "S-she is not just my wife, Colin. She is my life."

Closing his eyes, his pressed the balls of his hands hard against his cheeks. "I love her, see you?" That, barely a whisper, so great was the quaver in his usually strong voice. "I have always loved her. So much. . . ."

Colin said nothing, his silence everything.

Amicia was gone.

Both women were gone, and his life had ended as surely as if he'd left it on the blood-drenched ground at Dupplin Moor.

And mayhap he'd already died and gone to join his fallen companions-in-arms because their dying moans and anguished, pain-filled cries had risen to join the roar of the surf and the keen of the whistling wind.

"Mmmmmmpphhhh!" moaned one of those unfortunates, the high-pitched voice a bit too panicky-sounding for a knight in mortal agony. Most warriors, even dying ones, kept their dignity through the bitter end.

But Dupplin had been that bad, that horrid and damning.

A defeat smashing enough to turn some men into women.

At once, comprehension washed over Magnus, hitting him as fiercely as the waves crashing against the sides of the lurching galley.

"Dear God in Heaven!" Magnus shot to his feet, almost toppling Colin to his. "Did you hear? Those thumping noises . . . that moan?" He threw back his head and whooped. "By the Rood! Colin! They are here. Somewhere. I hear them calling us!"

He glanced around, his heart soaring with hope . . . exultation.

New tears blurred his vision, but happy ones this time. That one wee moan had come from Amicia's lips. He'd know the sound of her voice anywhere. Amongst a thousand women, across every sea, and through every light and darkness.

He grinned at Colin. "I heard them, I tell you."

Colin looked at him as if he'd run mad. "I heard nothing," he said, not smiling at all. But he did blink. And so furiously that the glimmer in his eyes revealed that it wasn't just rain plaguing his vision. "I neither saw my Janet earlier, nor do I hear anything now."

"Then you are blind and deaf!" Magnus clapped the other's back, his own certainty making him jubilant. "Come, let us tear this galley apart plank by blessed plank until we find them!"

"Magnus?"

The cry, faint but too real to be any warrior knight's ghost, came from the far end of the galley and split Magnus's heart wide open.

This time, she'd called his name.

And Colin had heard, too.

Then at last he saw her, streaming wet and shivering, bruised and bound by rope to Janet. The two of them were wedged into a storage recess beneath a bench row, both women staring at him from wide, tear-filled eyes—the most beautiful sight he'd e'er seen in his life.

They lived and were hale.

The sun had returned to shine on him—and the Fiend could take him before he'd ever let it go out again.

Chapter Seventeen

✦

$\mathscr{H}$ALF-LAUGHING, half-sobbing, Magnus ran forward, dropped to his knees before the two women. "Praise the saints!" he cried, throwing his arms around both of them, putting the whole of his gladness in that one crushing hug. "We thought you were dead. Like poor Dagda—"

"Magnus, my dearest Magnus, is it truly you? I'd been praying you would come," Amicia breathed, her voice quavering. "But please—do not speak of Dagda, not yet, I beg you."

She shook her head, tears spilling down her cheeks—tears that, for once, she did not attempt to check. "Not until I have savored this moment, unmarred."

Squeezing back his own tears, Magnus made short work of her bindings, lifted her from the smallish recess, then stepped back so Colin could do the same for Janet.

"Hush you, sweeting." Magnus sought to comfort his bride. He drew her closer, smoothed his fingers over a large bluish swelling on her forehead.

Saints, just seeing the ugly knot and her pain-glazed eyes filled him with a fury such as he'd never known.

"You are hurt." He rocked her, rained kisses on her brow, her cheeks, and even her nose. "I will find whoe'er did this and make him wish he'd ne'er glimpsed the light of day. Praise God, Janet signaled to us—" he broke off, wheeled to face Colin and Janet.

"I saw you at the rail, waving to us." He stared hard at his shivering cousin, not missing how she quaked all the more beneath that stare.

He also noticed that her hair was plaited and not loose and trailing seaweed. He noted, too, that the odd green-glowing sea foam had vanished from the deck. Along with the strange flotsam of curiosities that had spilled from his lady's cloak.

All of it had vanished—or been claimed by the sea and rain. Almost as if, now that he had found her, such charms, or whate'er they'd been, were no longer needed.

A chilling mix of confusion and comprehension washing over him, he narrowed his eyes at Janet. "I saw you, I swear it—yet you were bound and tied to the oar bench. How—"

"Not now, my heart. There are things in this world we may ne'er understand, but they can be good things . . . so good," his love silenced him. She pressed cold fingers to his lips, looked at him as if he were the whole of the world for her.

And he was her world. The entirety of it—all her light and gladness. "Now, this moment, I just want to look at you," she declared, her voice breaking. "I so feared I would ne'er see you again."

That after aching for you forever, we'd been damned to have but one night of heaven.

But then she'd heard him calling to her, reaching for her through the mists that had claimed her, and she'd somehow managed to climb up out of its swirling dark and answer him, half-afraid her heart had conjured his beloved voice.

Shuddering, a great sob escaped her and she clung to him, her body trembling, rivers of tears coursing down her cheeks. The warmth and safety of his arms around her was a sweet bliss so stunning it took her breath.

"Shush, lass, I am here now," he said, wrapping a fold of his plaid around her, enveloping her in the tightest of hugs. "As are you, sweeting. Naught else matters."

But it did.

He'd lost the only two galleys his men had finished, and from what she'd seen of the storm damage to the half-built ones on the strand, many of those ships would never see completion. Not with his pride keeping him from dipping into her coffers to pay for more supplies.

She looked aside, sniffed. "You err, my love," she got out on a wobbly breath. "So much matters. . . . Your fleet has been ruined again and—and even if you wish the rebuilding of it had not yet begun, there are some who have needed . . . otherwise. Your da. Your brothers. Many others."

Pulling a bit away from him, she pressed her hand to his chest, stroking, as if her touch, there where his heart beat, could persuade him. "Will you not reconsider using my dowry coins to order more supplies?" she urged, prepared to beg if necessary. "Can you . . . can you not push past your pride just this once? For your da? For me?"

He angled his head at her. "Pride, you say? Sweet lass, what is pride to a heart that loves?"

"It would mean so much to your da, in especial. He—" Amicia's heart stopped, brilliant light and joy bursting through her darkest cares and worries. She stared at him, so afraid she'd imagined the words. "What did you say?"

Magnus drew a long breath, sating himself on the beauty of her shining eyes, the sweet quiver of her lower lip, before he answered her—savoring yet again how damned good it felt to be free of his fool pride.

How endlessly glorious it was to hold her, know her safe.

"I said, *what is pride to a heart that loves,*" he admitted at last, loving the comprehension spreading across her lovely face, the wonder of it.

"You are full right, my lady, and have been e'er long. And I—I have been a fool." He lifted a hand to her cheek, caught a spilled tear on his fingertip. "But I have made amends, never you worry. I have assured my father, and any other long-nosed louts who cared to know, that your dowry coffers can and shall be spent to the fullest—to the good of us all."

She blinked, her chest rising and falling with greater and greater rapidity. "And the last part of what you said? The love part?"

For one wee instant, Magnus's pride clamped an icy fist around his heart, squeezed so tight he could scarce draw breath. But then a great wave of stunningly bright happiness surged up from somewhere deep inside him and swept away that last stubborn bit of cold and dark.

Feeling almost giddy, he caught another of her tears, slid a glance at Colin. As he'd suspected, the knave's flapping ears were aimed straight at him. As was the worst sort of gloating I-told-you-so stare.

Not that Magnus cared.

He blew out a breath, straightened his shoulders. "The love part, lass? Well . . ."

Letting his words tail off, he crushed her to him, and cradling her beloved face with his hands, he kissed her deeply. A fierce, soul-slaking kiss, thorough and searing. A kiss that should show her without words what was in his heart.

What had always been there.

But in case she needed the reassurance, he told her. "Aye, my minx, that *love part* was my way of admitting that I love you," he said, heedless of whether Colin-of-the-big-ears heard him and laughed or nay.

"Y-you love me?" The tears were streaming now. "Truly?"

Magnus nodded. "I have done since I first laid eyes on you. At the very latest, that long-ago day when I followed you onto the moors and found you injured and stalking about in the heather, all long legs, raven hair, and de-lightful indignation."

"Oh!" That came out on a gusty breath and she flung her arms around his neck, twining her fingers into his hair, and holding him with such ferocity he feared she might never let go.

"Shush you," he soothed, stroking the back of her head, more pleased than he would have believed that his admission of love brought her such happiness, feeling as if his heart might burst with his own joy.

The rush of emotion consuming him, he tightened his arms around her, slanting his mouth greedily over hers, drinking in all the warmth and bliss she brought him.

Pulling back at last, he looked deep into her eyes, hoped every beating ounce of his love shone in his own. "All will be well, my precious," he said, gentling his fin-gers over the knot on her brow. "And you shall be fine. I will ne'er let even a shadow of harm come near you again.

Soon we will have you settled by the hearthside, warm and dry. We will speak of all this and more . . . later."

"She will be even more fine if you cease trying to crack her ribs," Colin put in. "And I fear there will be no *later,* if we do not hie ourselves to shore before this galley slips beneath the waves. The way it is tilting, I vow we shall taste the sea any moment."

And as usual—but not always!—the lout was correct.

"Saints, but you are right," Magnus admitted, "we must be gone from here at once—so soon as we have cut free Dagda. We cannot take her back with us for a due and decent burial, but we can release her to the sea. She deserves at least—"

"S-she tried to kill us!" The words burst from Amicia's lips with such sudden heat, Magnus blinked, certain he'd misheard.

But a violent shudder racked her body—he'd felt it run through her. Then she was staring at him, the remembered terror in her beautiful, dark eyes telling him he had not misunderstood.

"Dagda was mad. . . . She was the one who'd been causing s-such havoc and grief. . . . She told us ev-everything," she babbled, the words spilling forth in a torrent as if a dam had broken.

Only Janet remained silent.

Wrapped securely in Colin's arms, Janet looked on as Amicia stammered the details of their ordeal. His cousin's pretty face was twisted into such a pale-faced mask of horror, Magnus reached for her hand, squeezed hard.

"You will be fine, too, Janet," he said, hoping to take some of the pain from her eyes. "If I am not wholly without my wits, I vow you will soon be a bride after all—dowry or no."

He winked at Colin and smiled at his cousin, but to his horror, his well-meant words caused a great sob to wrench from Janet's throat.

She lowered her head, dashed frantically at dripping tears. "He will not be having me now," she wailed, looking up to fix a panic-stricken stare on Amicia. "No one will. Not after—"

"She is weary, pay her no heed," Amicia cut her off, her voice firm, surprisingly strong. "Of course, he will want you, Janet. And think how proud your grandchildren will be someday when the bards recall how valiantly you fought against Dagda when she attacked me. Och, aye, Colin Grant will have you and be proud to do so."

A watery gasp and a tear-glazed look of stunned appreciation answered Amicia, warming her heart.

But she wasn't quite finished.

She slid a look at Colin. "Is that not right, good sir?" Amicia charged him, knowing already he'd pull down the moon and the stars for the wee flaxen-haired maid.

"To be sure, it is," her husband's friend agreed, and planted a kiss on the top of his lady's head. "I love her true and would make her mine at the soonest—if she will have me."

"Then let us follow your own sage advice, pray God yon cockleshell will see us safely ashore again and then make all haste back to Coldstone, where we can recover from this madness and you can properly woo her!" Magnus declared, already climbing down into the little currach, eager to be off.

More than ready to put the chaos of the morning behind him and do some wooing of his own.

But when a short while later, Magnus and his little party approached the massive curtain walls of Coldstone

Castle and clattered through the torchlit gatehouse pend, all thought of wooing, and otherwise, took flight.

He stared at the well-burning torches, his confusion so palpable he could taste it, cold and metallic on his tongue.

It had been years since anyone had bothered to illuminate Coldstone's gatehouse, the need for rationing fuel superceding ease of passage through the tunnel-like entry.

Yet, now twin rows of torchlight ran the pend's length.

Even more astonishing, the outer bailey and inner courtyard bustled with activity as strange men hurried to and fro, shouldering great iron-shod chests and bulging leather satchels. They were apparently heeding the shouted orders of Dugan and Hugh, who stood at the center of this chaos, grinning like fools and gesticulating in so many directions Magnus grew dizzy just staring at them.

And, again here, the whole impossibly surreal scene was lit by scores of blazing torches.

A quick glance at the looming bulk of the keep showed that fire glow and torchlight flickered behind every tower window as well. Even more startling, the strange men who scurried about so industriously were no Highlanders.

Nay, they had the look of the Lowlands to them—and were far too richly garbed to be just anyone's lackeys.

And with surety, they were too fine-looking to be any distant kin or friends of his da's.

For one long-stretching moment, Magnus wondered if he'd somehow ridden into the wrong castle. Or if he, his lady, and mayhap even Colin and Janet, had indeed drowned in the waters off the boat strand and this was some crazy kind of hell he'd awakened in.

But then his brothers spotted him and their faces split into even broader grins as they hailed him, waving furiously and glowing with more exuberance then he'd seen on them since they were spindly-legged laddies e'er tagging after him, adoration in their hero-worshiping eyes.

"Ho, Magnus!" Dugan called, lifting his voice over the pounding rain and the shouts of the scurrying strangers. "Here is a fine day, I tell you! You have your lady safe and sound, I see, and . . . Da's ghost galley has landed!"

"Da's ghost galley?" Totally flummoxed, Magnus dismounted, a throbbing ache beginning at his temples—despite the goodness of the day.

The fine day as Dugan had called it.

The madness going on all about him was more *goodness* than he could swallow just now.

Especially when one of the strangers—a strapping young lad dressed fancier than an emissary from any royal court—rushed up to lift Amicia gallantly to the cobbles, near knocking down Magnus in his hurry to display his chivalry.

Frowning, Magnus swept an arm to take in the whole of the high-walled courtyard. "God's eyes, man," he said, half-surprised his tongue didn't fail him in his amazement. "What goes on here?"

"I told you Da's ghost galley has arrived," Dugan said again, laughing this time, scarce able to contain his mirth, in fact.

"And yours, too," he said to Colin, giving Magnus's owl-eyed friend a playful punch in the arm.

That, at least, gave Magnus a chuckle—ne'er had he seen a look of greater perplexity on Colin Grant's face.

"Take yourself inside, Magnus," Hugh suggested, ever the peacemaker. "Da will surely explain everything the instant his eye lights on you."

Eager for that moment, indeed, Magnus grabbed Amicia's hand and dragged her with him across the bailey and into the keep, leaving Colin, Janet, his brothers, and any richly-raimented strangers to stare after them or follow, however it suited them.

"Heighho, laddie!" Donald MacKinnon hurried forward the moment they stepped into the great hall. "You will ne'er believe our good fortune! Old Reginald has had mercy on us at last—he's done gone and lifted the curse. Aye, to be sure!"

Magnus blinked. "Reginald and his curse?" Now he was confused. "Dugan said your devil ship had landed?"

"Pschaw!" His father waved a dismissive hand. "There was no ghost galley or a devil ship either," he said, peering at Magnus from beneath bushy, beetling brows. "I am an auld done man, see you? I make . . . mistakes at times. This was one of those times."

"This?" Magnus glanced about the hall.

More strangers buzzed about here, too, just as splendorous in their garb, if a bit more dignified in demeanor. And a growing collection of ne'er-before-seen strongboxes occupied one corner.

Strongboxes that looked suspiciously like money coffers and bearing the royal seal.

Magnus swallowed, a sudden, hot-burning suspicion thickening his throat and jabbing red-hot needles into the backs of his eyes.

"Who are these men and what are they about, sir?" Amicia—bless her soul—asked the question Magnus could not get past the swelling lump in his throat.

She stepped forward, lit a hand to his father's bony arm. "And why are those coffers stacked in yon corner?"

Magnus sent her a silent thank-you, his eyes already misting, for there could be only one answer to the question his thick tongue couldn't form.

The answer he'd ne'er even dreamed would come to pass.

"Recompense, it is!" Donald MacKinnon declared, snatching up a rolled parchment, its wax seal broken and dangling.

He waved the document beneath Magnus's nose. " 'Tis from the Guardian of Scotland himself, see you? To reward you for your loyalty and valor at Dupplin—and to restore the tourney fortune and booty that were stolen from you whilst you fought for the crown."

Magnus blinked. Now he knew why the scores of men scrambling about the bailey in all their finery had minded him of Lowlanders—they were Lowlanders, and straight from the royal court.

As were the many coffers of *siller* and *merks,* the stacks of silver plate and like frippery mounding on the high table.

Wealth he had earned.

And now returned to him by a grateful Guardian in young King David II's name.

"They even brought you a horse, Magnus!" Dugan announced, joining them. "A fine beast—a tourney champion like the one you forfeited to pay passage tolls on your journey home. That loss, too, had reached the crown's ear." Dugan winked. "The animal is in the stables now, already making our garrons half-crazed and asserting his superiority."

His da waved the parchment at him again, and Magnus stared at it, dumbfounded. Saints, but his eyes stung too badly for him to make out a word of the spidery handwriting, and his throat had gone too thick even to swallow. And very soon he might shame himself, for his fool knees were about to give on him.

"Magnus! Your valor honored and your fortunes restored! Oh, how I joy for you, my heart," Amicia cried, his dear sweet wife showing no such difficulties in expressing herself.

Indeed, she launched herself at him so fiercely, they both near tumbled backward into Colin's arms.

Righting them, that one slung his arms around both their shoulders and squeezed. "So-o-o, my friends," he said, looking and sounding as mirth-filled as Magnus's brothers, "it would seem old Reginald has blessed rather than cursed Clan Fingon, wouldn't you say?"

"Blessed you, too, Grant," Hugh said, joining them.

He picked up a second parchment from the table, handed it to Colin with an apologetic glance at the broken seal. "Da could not contain himself in his excitement and opened the scrolls as soon as the courier identified himself. So he read yours, too."

"Mine?" This time, Colin blinked.

A thickset man of middle years stepped up to them, nodded to Colin. Garbed similarly fine as the other royal emissaries, this one set himself apart by his evident aura of authority.

"I am Sir Alastair Douglas," he said with a quick glance at the parchment roll clutched in Colin's hand. "Word came to the Guardian not only of your bravery on the field, good sir, and your injury, but also of the loss of your home."

Colin inclined his head, his eyes, too, suddenly overbright. He reached for Janet's hand, drew her away from the old laird and to his side. "Aye, that is the way of it, Sir Alastair," he said, his deep voice huskier than usual. "Naught remains of my home save a few scorched stones and rubble."

"And it would be an ill day for Scotland if so great a loss and loyalty such as yours was not duly rewarded," the crown's representative said, with another glance at the scroll. "Yon parchment is a charter for you, Sir Colin. It confirms the fullest possession and all rights of your former lands, restoring them to you—along with ample restitution to see your home rebuilt to its former strength."

"I—I am humbled, my lord," Colin said, sketching the courier the best bow his almost-healed leg would allow. "I do not know what to say. A mere thank-you seems—" Colin's voice broke and he blinked, swiped a hand beneath his eyes.

The man nodded, clapped a hand on Colin's shoulder. "Send word to the Guardian when you are returned to your own dominions and the funds will be delivered to you forthwith. But for the nonce"—his gaze lit on the four of them, their wet and bedraggled appearance—"I would suggest you freshen yourselves and then join us thereafter. My men are sore weary of plying your stormy Hebridean seas and will be ready for a warm fire and a night of good food and converse."

Magnus wholly agreed, but before he turned away, there was one niggling riddle that needed solving. "You have been in our waters over-long, then?" he asked, and slid a pointed look in his father's direction.

"I told you they were my ghost galley!" the old laird snapped, thrusting out his bristly chin. "And dinna you dare snigger at me—an old man is entitled to his . . . delusions on occasion."

The courier looked confused. *"Ghost galley?"*

Magnus cleared his throat. "For some time now, my father has claimed to have seen a galley approach our shores only to vanish before his eyes, disappearing into the mist. No one else in the household e'er saw this mystery vessel until a guardsman spotted yours, so—"

"You are wondering if we could have been this vanishing galley?" A smile began tugging at the corners of the courier's mouth. "Aye, like as not, it was indeed our galley your father claimed to see. We made numerous attempts to reach your isle, only to turn back when the seas ran too stormy or the tides adverse. Yours is a wild coast, my friend, and many are the hazards in your skerry-strewn waters."

"But surely an emissary of the Scottish crown would have oarsmen skilled enough to navigate the Sea of the Hebrides?" Dugan said, earning a dark look and a sharp foot-stomping from Magnus.

"Excuse him, sir," Magnus said, feeling the neck opening of his tunic tighten on him. "My brother only meant—"

Sir Alastair waved a hand. "No offense taken, my friend. And, aye, our oarsmen are experienced and able indeed. It was the prize tourney stallion we brought you that had us seeking shelter in the deep harbor and sea cave of a nearby, unoccupied isle each time the passage grew too rough."

"The horse?" Amicia flickered a glance at Magnus. "I do not understand."

"You are not a horsewoman, my lady," Magnus reminded her. "A plunging and lurching galley is no place for a high-strung steed—or even a steady-hearted garron. See you, the beasts must be secured with rope for any passage—a rough one causes them to thrash about, possibly causing hurt to themselves, not to mention the oarsmen."

The courier nodded. "Exactly. Had we wished to hold our course for your isle, we would have been forced to put the poor beast out of his wild-eyed misery and toss him overboard. We did not want to suffer you his loss, though, so we made many turnabouts, spent our nights deep inside the other isle's sea cave, soothing the poor animal. We almost did not make it here this morning, either, but this time the storm broke upon us when we were much closer to your shores than the other isle."

Magnus turned to his da. "So, Father! Now we know for certain that neither old Reginald nor the Horned One have been meaning to bedevil you."

"And I shall bedevil you if you do not take your fine lady wife abovestairs and let her freshen herself. She is wet and shivering—as is your cousin," his father declared, wagging a finger. "Wee Janet has been telling me of Dagda and I would have you fill my ears with that sorry tale as we sit at meat with these good folk. Something we cannot do until the whole sodden lot of you hie yourselves back down here in clean and dry raiment."

"We shall make haste then and return anon," Magnus said, pulling Amicia from the hall even as he spoke.

But once they reached the privacy of their bedchamber, he did not appear in all that great a hurry. Neither to see to his ablutions—or to have her tend to hers.

Nay, much to Amicia's astonishment, rather than peel off his damp garments and make good use of the wooden tub of steaming, scented water someone had thoughtfully set before the hearth fire, Magnus MacKinnon went straight to the great canopied bed, dropped to all fours, and, as best Amicia could tell, began rummaging about beneath the bed.

Looking on with amazement, Amicia listened to his muffled curses, a few grunts, and the sounds of a *thump* or two, until at length he wriggled backward, dragging an ancient-looking and quite dusty strongbox with him.

A money coffer, but one that had clearly not been opened in years.

Straightening, he set the coffer on the bed. Little puffs of dust rose from its lid and a few bits of rust fell off the hinges and onto the bedcoverings. For a long moment, he just stood looking down at it, the oddest, almost reverent, expression on his face.

Amicia moistened her lips.

Her heart began to pound and her palms dampened just watching him.

There was something very strange about the way he'd handled and was staring down at the battered and grimy coffer.

Almost as if it were his greatest treasure.

The thought made her shiver.

Apparently noticing, he reached a hand to her, drawing her near when she laced her fingers with his.

"W-what is that?" she asked, eyeing the coffer, not surprised when her voice came out sounding . . . squeaky.

"My greatest treasure," he said, mirroring her thoughts. "My heart's treasure."

Now she did shiver—a great flood of trembling ripples racking her from head to toe.

"It looks old," she got out, slipping free her hand so she could rub her forearms against the chillbumps.

"It is old, lass, and it contains nary a *siller*. That is why I want you to see it."

"I do not understand."

"Och, but I think you will when you see what is inside," he said, reaching to lift the coffer's lid.

It opened with more little puffing clouds of dust, the hinges emitting an ear-splitting screech, but try as she might, Amicia could see nothing inside.

"Never you worry, it is not empty," he said, reading her thoughts again. "It contains my dearest possession. Something I have kept safe and cherished for many long years, something that has consumed me always and—and kept my hope alive when darkness and doubt surrounded me."

Hot tears began pricking the backs of Amicia's eyes at his words, some soul-deep part of her recognizing what she had not yet grasped.

"And why do you want me to see this . . . something?" That came out strangled-sounding.

He looked at her and the warmth, the love shining in his beautiful blue eyes, made her heart slam against her ribs.

"I am showing it to you because of my good fortune, because of the wealth—my newfound wealth—swelling the great hall below. I want you to see what I value, have always valued, above all else. *Who* I have cherished above all others."

Amicia swallowed, nodding when words couldn't be squeezed past the hot lump in her throat.

"I want you to see it so that you will never have any doubt about how much I love you."

"And this . . . t-this something will show me that?"

"I believe so," he said, lifting a flat package from the bottom of the strongbox. A rectangle of time-darkened sheepskin. He laid it on the bed with even greater care and reverence than he'd shown the coffer.

"Open it."

Amicia couldn't move—her knees had jellied and her pulse was roaring so loudly in her ears she wasn't sure she'd heard him aright.

"Open it, sweet, for what lies within is yours—or was."

Biting hard on her lower lip, Amicia stepped up to the bed, reached for the packet. She touched trembling fingers to the brittle leather, untied the yellowed string holding it together.

It fell open.

The years slid away.

"Oh, dear saints," she choked, swaying on her feet as she stared down at the dried sprig of bell heather.

Dried, pitifully flat, and very brown.

But definitely bell heather.

Magnus MacKinnon's most prized possession.

Something he'd kept and cherished since the long-ago day on the high moors when he'd tucked it behind her ear.

"Oh, dear saints," Amicia said again, a sob this time. "You kept this all these years?"

"To be sure, I did," he said, sliding his arms around her from behind, nuzzling her neck. "It fell from your hair after my fight with your brother that day—when you limped away, crying. I retrieved it and have cherished it e'er since."

Amicia turned to face him, near blinded by her tears. "If only you'd known how I ached for you, how much I loved you—even then," she said, wrapping her arms around his waist, holding him tightly.

"But I know now, my minx," he murmured, planting a wee kiss on the tip of her nose. "We both know now. And nothing shall e'er keep us apart again."

"Nothing," she agreed, brushing a light kiss against his lips.

"So it will be," he promised.

"Forever?"

He nodded, gave her a dimpled smile.

"Och, aye, lass. Through all our tomorrows, unending."

Epilogue

❖

$\mathcal{M}$ANY MONTHS LATER, after a harsh winter had passed
and spring was just beginning to kiss the land, a great
gathering of the Hebridean clans came to MacKinnons'
Isle to rejoice in the restoration of Clan Fingon's good
fortune and, for those who believed in suchlike, the
swinging of an ancient curse into a blessing.

A joyous blessing.

And a goodly number of them.

So on this day of inimitable beauty and importance, no
few of the clansmen, friends, and allies crowding the
isle's crescent-shaped boat strand knew quite which
blessing to lend their most rapt attention.

Those whose hearts beat most rapidly for warring
campaigns and great deeds of heroism admired the two
score of new MacKinnon galleys heaving on the long
westerly swells, great square sails flapping in the wind,
slantwise spars and tall carved prows upthrusting and

proud, their imposing outlines against the cloudless sky boldly declaring their sovereignty of the seas.

The Grant banner flew from one of the vessels, that one a gift from the MacKinnons to Colin Grant, and it was to this galley in particular that many Islesfolk stared. For although the grand festivities had been called to hail the launching of the new fleet, the recent wedding of Colin and his Janet and their imminent departure for their own dominions stirred the blood and had many an eye misting.

Already the sweeps had been lowered and the helmsman's baton kept a rhythmic, clanging beat on the gong, each steady stroke echoing from the enclosing dunes and hillsides. From the shore, it was clear to see that the oarsmen were in their places, their deep-voiced chanting rising on the wind, in perfect timing with the beating gong.

Soon that one galley would shoot forth, distancing itself from the others in a burst of speed and sea spray to carry those onboard to distant shores.

"You were great-hearted not to reveal her part in the treachery." A diminutive figure in black laid a gnarled hand on Amicia's sleeve. "Aye, it was good of you and I would have expected no less," Devorgilla added, her shrewd gaze fixed on the Grant galley. "Inside, the lass has a shining heart and e'er did."

Amicia started, stopped feeding broken bits of honeyed oatcakes to Boiny, and gave her old friend a narrow-eyed stare. "And just how did you know about that? I have ne'er spoken of it to anyone—not even my husband."

The *cailleach* hooted, turned her own gaze on Magnus's galley as it skimmed across the waves, keeping fast pace with Colin's. A friendly farewell and salute he'd pursue until the Grant vessel moved out of MacKinnon waters.

"And no purpose would have been in telling him, either. *That* one would ne'er have believed you, for he sees only the good in those he holds dear," Devorgilla said, helping herself to one of the oatcakes piled high in the little basket Amicia held balanced against her swelling belly. "And you, lass, ought eat more of these yourself rather than feeding the whole of them to that dog."

"Do not skip around my question, Devorgilla." Amicia demonstratively gave Boiny the largest oatcake she could find in the basket. "How did you know what transpired that . . . that day?"

She shuddered, even now, not comfortable remembering.

"Tsk, lass, the same way I know . . . many things." Devorgilla hedged. "But knowing 'em or nay, a prudent heart ne'er *discusses* them. Some things just are and ought be accepted as such."

"I am sorry about the cloak," Amicia said, keenly aware of its loss now that its creator stood beside her. "It kept me warm."

The crone clucked her tongue. "Keeping you warm was ne'er its purpose. Just be glad it served you so well."

Amicia nodded, snuggled deeper into her *new* cloak, a much lighter one, and also crafted by Devorgilla's own true hand, if not so fine and splendorous.

"Even so, I regret the loss of the other," she said after a while. "The ermine lining was dear."

And it must've pleased the grizzle-headed crone to present her with such a magnificent gift.

That was what troubled her.

"Think you I care aught about fancy furs, lassie?" Devorgilla quipped, angling her head to peer up at Amicia. "Think you I dinna ken such frippery means scarce little to you?"

Amicia blinked, confused. "Then why bother sewing such a priceless lining into the cloak?"

"Hech, hech, it was what was *inside* the cloak that mattered, as I suspect you discovered, but I had good reason for choosing such a noble fur for you, never you doubt it," she said, a familiar twinkle entering her eyes.

A mischievous twinkle well-known throughout the Isles.

Well-known and respected, even feared by some.

"I suppose that reason, too, must remain a secret?" Amicia probed, her expression pure MacLean challenge.

Unimpressed, the crone planted her hands against her bony hips and breathed deeply of the fine spring air. *Hebridean* air, and as wise souls would say, the best in the land. "Och, nay, lassie, that I will tell you," she said at last, her wizened face splitting into an impish grin.

"'Twas for *him* that the ermine lining was meant, not you. A wee precautionary measure—should suchlike be needed."

"I do not understand." Amicia blinked at her, wholly confused. "For Magnus? But why?"

Devorgilla cackled with glee. "That wee bairn you carry is mushing your wits, lassie, if you still dinna know."

Scrunching up her eyes, the crone peered hard at Amicia. "'Twas this *second* cloak I always meant you to have, see you? I kent its good craftsmanship and durability would please you more than ells of silky fur and glittery gew-gaws for claspings. But you needed such a mantle so that when it left your possession, yon braw laddie would see how little you mourned its loss."

"Oh!" That came out on a sudden, gusty breath.

Now she understood.

"You wanted him to have tangible evidence that such finery is not what I hold most dear?"

The crone nodded, looked pleased. "Aye, that was about the way of it."

"And do you think he knows that? Do you think he knows how much I love him?"

To that, the *cailleach* threw back her cowled head and laughed—her jollity answer enough.

And full aware she'd get no more out of her, Amicia turned aside and stared out to her husband's galley, pleased when she caught a glint of sunlight on his handsome auburn head as he stood beside the helmsman.

Just that quick glimpse warmed and delighted her, minding her of how she'd slid her fingers through his silky, bronze-gleaming hair that very morning as they'd lain abed, savoring its cocooning warmth until the very last moment, their bodies and hearts intimately entwined.

So reluctant to leave each other's arms.

Even for such a joyous and triumphant day.

"You needn't wallow in such fierce longing, you know." Devorgilla slid her a shrewd glance, clucked her tongue again. "A love with the depth of yours will last the few hours until you are in his arms again."

Amicia glanced sharply at her, instinctively slipped a loving hand down to cradle the bulge at her middle, something in the crone's tone lifting the fine hairs on the back of her neck.

But Devorgilla was no longer looking at her—nor at

the silver-bright sea and the many galleys racing to and fro across the waves.

"Aye, lass," the cailleach said, her voice distant, almost as if she'd turned her attention inward or *backward* in time, "those who love so truly have each other for always—even beyond time and oceans. Such deep love burns ever bright and can ne'er be extinguished."

And as if they'd heard and agreed with her, two silent observers standing in shadow at the base of Reginald's tower smiled deeply into each other's eyes and nodded.

Then, in the pleasing knowledge that their blessing had finally been recognized and accepted, they joined hands and, turning, faded back into the tower's stones.

Warm stones, beautiful and shimmering.

Stones that would ne'er know cold again.

ABOUT THE AUTHOR

SUE-ELLEN WELFONDER is a dedicated medievalist of Scottish descent who spent fifteen years living abroad, and still makes annual research trips to Great Britain. She is an active member of the Romance Writers of America and her own clan, the MacFie Society of North America. Her first novel, *Devil in a Kilt,* was one of *Romantic Times*'s Top Picks. It won *RT*'s Reviewers' Choice Award for Best First Historical Romance of 2001. Sue-Ellen Welfonder is married and lives with her husband, Manfred, and their Jack Russell Terrier, Em, in Florida.

More
Sue-Ellen Welfonder!

✦

Please turn this page
for a special preview of
ONLY FOR A KNIGHT
available in
July 2005.

The Legacy
of the Black Stag

❦

*I*N THE MIST-SHROUDED FASTNESSES of Kintail, a rugged country of sea lochs, wild heather hills, and moorlands on the western coast of Scotland, one man has e'er held sway. Since time beyond mind some might say, Duncan MacKenzie, the famed Black Stag of Kintail, has called this hauntingly beautiful place his own.

His, and the great house of MacKenzie, the most powerful clan in the region.

Truth be told, those who visit Kintail cannot help but be awed by the grandeur and magic of the land, and the tall tales circulated about its legendary chieftain. A deceptive air of tranquility and timelessness clings to the dark peaks and shadowed glens, a peace made possible only by the puissant Black Stag's competent rule—and his formidable reputation.

Few are those who would cross him.

And most who have tried are no more.

Yet, of late, during long Highland nights beside the

fire, the more bold amongst the tongue-waggers declare that the Black Stag has grown complacent and would surrender his lairdship to his only son and heir, Robbie MacKenzie. A braw young man whose task would seem tame, inheriting a land so favored, its people already loyal and true.

But all is not as it seems in the soft Highland air and broad, cloud-hung hills of Kintail, its purple moors and empty glens.

For deep within the most remote corner of this wide expanse of hill and sea, change and disruption tremble and stir like an ancient benediction chanted just beneath the surface to echo and re-echo across the heather until even one so mighty as the Black Stag cannot deny its truth.

Or run from the burdens and memories of the past.

Robbie, too, must tread the path of fate.

A path indelibly inscribed on his destiny and unleashed by the whispered last wishes of a frail and dying woman.

Chapter One

✦

GLENELG IN THE SPRING, 1344

"*R*EPAY DUNCAN MACKENZIE?"

Juliana Mackay stared down at her mother, reaching to smooth the threadbare plaid tucked so lovingly about the older woman's thin body. She hoped she'd misheard the ill woman's unthinkable request.

After all, her mother had lost much strength in recent days, the words had been rasped in little more than a dry whisper.

Straightening, Juliana wiped her palms on the many-times-patched skirts of her kirtle and struggled against the urge to flee from the pathetic sight before her. She wanted to wrest open the rough-planked door and run from the mean little cot-house of sod, heather-thatch, and stone, until she'd put all her cares and woes behind her.

Instead, she drew a deep breath and fixed her gaze on the peat fire smoking beneath a heavy iron cooking pot. *Repay Duncan MacKenzie.* The very notion ignited her spleen and twisted her innards.

Aye, she'd surely misheard.

But in case she hadn't, she squared her shoulders and folded her arms. A stance meant as much to stave off any further such impossible appeal as to keep herself from yielding to her own panic and fears and raining a thousand well-peppered curses on the man whose family had brought such grief to bear upon her own.

Juliana clenched her hands. Duncan MacKenzie deserved a *hundred thousand* curses piled onto his head.

But she knew without asking that any such outburst would only plunge her mother into another coughing fit.

"The Black Stag is one of the most heavily pursed lairds in all the land," she said at last, trying not to see the feverish glint in her mother's eyes—the desperate plea hovering there.

But even by the feeble glow of a lone tallow candle, the ravages of impending death stood all o'er Marjory Mackay's once-beautiful face.

And the truth of it jellied Juliana's knees and brought out the worst in her.

Such as her seething resentment that her mother, longtime hearth-mate to the laird's unlamented late half-brother, Kenneth MacKenzie, had been forced to raise her children in a dirt-floored, one-room hovel, divided only by an ox-hide curtain. This, despite the scant monies and aid the MacKenzie laird had sent their way over the years.

"Duncan MacKenzie has trod heavy-footed over you for all your days," Juliana bit out, using her own booted foot to nudge a loose pebble from the hard-packed earthen floor. "He ne'er acknowledged your bond to his brother nor cared that my father sired two bairns on you—the Black Stag's own niece and nephew!"

Frowning, she paused to grind the pebble back into the dirt. "He holds gluttonous feasts in his stout-walled Eilean Creag Castle yet e'er left you, his own brother's leman, to scrape the barest living from these hard hills, soothing his conscience by having a milk cow or a jangling pouch of siller delivered to us whenever he recalled our existence."

"He had his reasons, child," Marjory Mackay wheezed from her pallet.

Juliana sniffed. "I mislike that you would even consider owing him restitution." Stepping closer to the pallet, she dabbed at her mother's brow with a damp cloth. "I have ne'er heard aught more . . . unnecessary."

Marjory closed her eyes, pulled in a ragged breath. "Times were worse than you ken, food scarce. Without the MacKenzie's largesse, you and your brother Kenneth would have had to endure an even harsher, more comfortless life. Think you I can . . . exit this world without repaying the man whose aid spared my bairns from hungering?"

"You are not going to die." Juliana wrung out the cloth, squeezing it tighter with each word before redipping it into a wooden bowl of cool springwater. "I will not allow it."

A delicately-veined hand, astonishingly strong, reached to circle Juliana's wrist. "The good Lord alone decides when a body is to join Him, lass, but I . . ." A bout of breathlessness stole Marjory's words and the flecks of pink-stained spittle she coughed up twisted Juliana's heart.

"If the good Lord or His great host of saints have any mercy in their wing-backed souls they shall work their wonders to see you well again," Juliana snapped, the words coming sharper than she would have wished.

"You must do as I ask and deliver the monies to the Black Stag for me. I have a missive for him as well, written when I first sensed my end was near." Marjory half-raised herself from the pallet, her glassy-eyed gaze sliding to the rolled parchment on the cottage's sole table. A crude and pitiful excuse for a table that wobbled on four uneven legs.

"I do not have much longer," she added, squeezing Juliana's wrist before letting her hand fall back onto the plaid coverlet, the last of her strength clearly leaving her. "I would know this done."

Following her mother's gaze, Juliana pressed her lips together and said nothing. She'd seen her mother laboriously scribbling away on the precious piece of parchment—the saints only knew where she'd obtained it or the inkhorn and quill now resting so innocently beside the curled missive. Such luxuries were scarce in this narrow glen where they lived, all but cut off from the outside world.

"Duncan MacKenzie has siller enough of his own—and to spare!" Juliana glanced at the rusted, iron-latched strongbox where she knew her mother kept what coin her brother Kenneth sent to them.

Hard-earned monies intended for their mother's use and not to be hoarded, unspent.

And of a certainty, the monies were not to be delivered into the hands of the notorious Black Stag for the singular purpose of adding to that one's already overflowing coffers.

Her gall nigh choking her, Juliana glared at her mother's pathetically battered money coffer, resentment flowing through her like a deep and sullen river. Truth was, if her mother had put the monies to good use, mayhap refurbishing the thatch of their cottage's leak-plagued roof or repairing the countless chinks in the stone-and-sod walls, perhaps then Marjory Mackay's ailing would not have taken such a ferocious turn for the worse.

As it was, Juliana could only pray to God for her mother's recovery—or a peaceful release from her travails.

That, and wish the Black Stag of Kintail to the lowest, most wretched of hells.

Bristling, she hoped her vexation did not stand writ upon her face. "The MacKenzie has not sent you aid since Kenneth and I have grown. Had the man e'er desired repayment, he would have surely demanded such by now," she said, amazed by the steady calm of her voice.

She jerked her head toward the strongbox. "Yon coin comes from Kenneth—your son, I'd beg you to recall. And I vow, were he here, he would be of like mind. Duncan MacKenzie is a hard and savage man. He has no need of restitution."

Biting her lip to tamp down the flood tide of heated epithets dancing hotfoot on her tongue, Juliana paused to press the cool cloth to her mother's feverish forehead. "On my soul, would you desire the truth of it, there are those who say Duncan MacKenzie has a devil in him and you ken he has e'er lived in fine style. I doubt he would even appreciate the gesture. So why deign him with such a boon?"

A long, shuddering sigh escaped Marjory's parched lips. "Are you so blind, lass? Can you not see the matter has scarce little to do with the coin—or even whether or no the Black Stag appreciates the message I would have you bring to him?"

"I see naught but sheerest folly and would wish you to desist with such a foolhardy notion," Juliana countered, her scuff-toed boot already worrying another pebble embedded in the well-swept earthen floor.

"Then I have not raised you to be as far-seeing as I would have wished." Marjory's thin fingers clutched at the plaid covering her. "Of more import than the good man's acceptance or refusal of my offering, is that the giving of it shall solace my mind. Whilst the breath of life is still in me, lass, I plead you to heed my wishes."

"Good man," Juliana couldn't help but scoff, her blood chilling with the implicated surrender in the words she was about to say. "Kenneth will be of sore wrath when he learns."

"That is as may be, but your brother is not here and we can ne'er ken when he shall choose to visit us. I would know this done now so that—" Marjory broke off to raise herself on an elbow. She fixed a determined stare on Juliana. "So that I may take my leave of this world in peace."

"And I cannot take myself off into the heather and leave you here alone . . . to . . . to die unattended." Juliana dropped to her knees beside the pallet, stroked a sweat-dampened strand of hair from her mother's brow. Fine, sunfire-colored hair, bright as Juliana's own. "I simply cannot do it."

"You can and you shall, for you are strong," Marjory argued, reaching to take one of Juliana's fiery red braids in her hand. "Let us say Godspeed now, my dear heart, and give me the closure of your word."

Juliana bit her lip, shook her head in staunch denial,

hot tears spilling free now, each damnable one nigh blinding her.

"I ask this of you only so I may know peace," her mother persisted, letting go of the braid to touch trembling, cold fingers to Juliana's cheek. "Promise me, lass. I beg you. Swear to me that you will do this—and be on your way by cockcrow on the morrow. So that I—"

"Pray God in all His glory, do not say it again," Juliana surrendered at last, pushing to her feet, amazed her watery knees could hold her upright. "If this means so much to you, aye, I shall go . . . I will see to this for you, I promise," she agreed, the words bitter ash on her tongue.

Swallowing hard, she squared her shoulders and pulled in a long, steadying breath. "Aye, I give you my word the deed is as good as done."

Later, just as darkness settled on the coast of Kintail and the quiet hush of evening began curling around the stout walls of Eilean Creag Castle, loch-girt stronghold of Clan MacKenzie, Lady Linnet, a comely woman of middle years and the same flame-bright tresses as Juliana, moved about the keep's well-appointed solar, ill ease niggling at her, dogging her every step.

An unpleasant and cloying chill it was, and persistent as the inky shadows laying gleeful claim to those corners of the solar not fully illuminated by the crackling fire blazing in the chamber's fine stone hearth.

Trying hard to ignore the frightfully familiar sensation, Linnet paused at one of the solar's tall, arch-topped windows and looked out at the pewter-gray surface of Loch Duich far below.

Most times, the view from this chamber soothed her. Indeed, she came here often, the lonely beauty of the empty shores and the great heather hills that stretched beyond in endless succession never failing to gentle any and all unwelcome thoughts.

Until now.

This night, far deeper cares than usual bore down upon her shoulders and occupied her increasingly troubled mind.

Truth be told, she scarce noticed the heart-rending lovely world whiling so still and tranquil beyond her windows. Nor did her ears catch much of the keening wind racing in from the not too distant sea to ruffle the loch's dark waters and whistle past Eilean Creag's night-bound ramparts and turrets.

For rather than the wind, the Lady Linnet heard the sound of bees.

A multitude of buzzing bees.

The most dread sound to e'er plague her—the sound that always heralded one of her spells.

Her visions.

Seventh daughter of a seventh daughter, 'twas a curse she'd been spared in recent years, but one that seemed determined to return with a vengeance this night. A night that should have been filled with naught but celebratory joy, for word had come at last that her stepson, Robbie MacKenzie, was finally returning home to Eilean Creag.

"Ten long years." She turned to her liege husband, Duncan MacKenzie, hoping her voice sounded level and firm. She could not tell for the din of the bees was nigh deafening now.

A nightmarish cacophony robbing her of her wits and making her weak.

Vulnerable.

Moistening her lips, she clasped her hands together,

lacing her fingers to stave off the trembling. "Do you think he is truly coming? At last?"

Her husband set down the wine cup he'd been drinking from, wiped the back of his hand across his mouth. "Think you he would dare not come? Knowing his betrothed is on her way here? Even now as we speak?"

A chill streaked down Linnet's spine at the word *betrothed*—a deep-reaching, breath-stealing cold that spread clear to her toes, enfolding her.

Still fighting it, ignoring the telltale signs, she shivered, drew her woolen arisaid closer about her shoulders. "Think you it is wise to wed him to Lady Euphemia?" she challenged her husband. "The daughter of a man you yourself have called a scourge upon the heather?"

Duncan waved a dismissive hand, shook his dark head. "She was chosen *because* she is that lout's daughter, as you well ken," he reminded her, coming forward to rest his hands upon her shoulders, kneading them. " 'Tis a necessary alliance if e'er we are to enjoy true peace in these hills."

"And if the lad finds her not to his liking?" That, from a tall, scar-faced man lounging in the shadows of a window embrasure. "Would it not be more prudent to let Robbie first return home and resettle himself before fetching the lass to his side?"

"Och, but there speaks the eternal voice of caution." Duncan aimed a dark look at his friend and good-brother, Sir Marmaduke Strongbow. "Euphemia MacLeod is already on her way here—as you well know. To send her back now would be an intolerable affront."

"Such insult might prove the lesser evil if Robbie finds the maid not to his liking," Sir Marmaduke gave back, ever undaunted by the Black Stag's scowling countenance.

Indeed, he leveled a penetrating glance of his own at his long-time friend and liege laird. "Perhaps you have acted in haste."

"In haste?" Duncan's dark brows snapped together. With a huff, most decidedly issued for Marmaduke's benefit, the redoubtable Black Stag strode back to the table, poured out a fresh measure of the blood-red wine, and downed it in one gulp.

"The lad has traipsed about the land these last years, doing as he pleases and garnering a reputation of valor nigh as untarnished as your own," he said, his hot gaze pinning Sir Marmaduke, daring him to declare otherwise. "Robbie gave his promise, his solemn vow, to wed the MacLeod lass *before he left.* Think you he would despoil his honor now . . . by refusing to accept her as his bride?"

E'er a paragon of level-headedness, Sir Marmaduke kept his unblinking stare locked on Duncan. "I warrant he will uphold his promise," he said, folding his arms—and doing so with enough practiced leisure to bedevil Duncan beyond endurance. "Aye, he will no doubt keep his word. And his honor. I only wish he would have had some time to . . . adjust."

"Sacrament," Duncan blurted, his dark blue eyes blazing. "He has had ten full years to adjust—or sample enough sweetness elsewhere, if you have forgotten. *Ten years,*" Duncan said, his tone—and the rapidly beating twitch in his jaw—giving his friend no quarter. "The MacLeod lass will suit him well enough, I say you. She is pleasing to the eye and of sound wits, unlike her oaf of a father."

Some might argue that Robbie suffers such a sire as well, Linnet thought she heard Sir Marmaduke comment.

And whether he'd spoken the words or no, Linnet's husband gave him a dark oath in response.

Or so she imagined.

Not that she could hear much of what either man had to say, for the droning buzz in her ears had reached a fever pitch.

Ignoring the men, for she was well-accustomed to their ceaseless ribbing, she turned her back on them lest they note her discomfiture, the perspiration beading her brow. Determined to remain calm, she stared into the hearth fire, peering intently at the red flames licking at the well-burning logs.

Red flames that soon became a tall and lithesome maid's unbound cascade of shimmering red-gold tresses. Beautifully waved tresses that spilled clear to the young woman's shapely hips, each shimmering strand shining bright as sunfire.

The lass stood tall and proud, untold happiness seeming to radiate from every glorious inch of her. And from someplace deep inside Linnet, a hidden corner far removed and safe from her hard-pounding heart and the sweat trickling cold between her breasts, Linnet knew she was staring at her stepson's bride.

A truth she would have recognized even if the lass weren't standing in front of the MacKenzies' famed Marriage Stone, a large blue-tinted stone incised with ancient Celtic runes, a near-perfect hole in its center. It was the main piece and pride of every MacKenzie wedding ceremony.

A clan tradition all down the centuries.

The MacKenzies' most sacred talisman.

Aye, the lovely maid with the flame-bright hair could be no other.

Trembling now, her knees nigh giving out on her, Linnet struggled to keep standing. She reached deep inside herself to maintain her composure even as she willed the lass to turn, to glance her way, so she could see the maid's face.

But such visions cannot be summoned nor steered, Linnet well knew, and even as she stared, the image began to waver and fade until the bright, shimmering tresses were once again nothing more than dancing flames, the beautiful young woman and the celebrated Marriage Stone gone as if they'd never been.

"Sir . . ." Linnet began when she could find her voice, forgetting herself in her flustered state and calling her husband by the title he loathed her to use. "Duncan," she corrected, careful to keep her back to him, feigning calm. "You say the MacLeod lass is fetching. I would know, is she . . . flame-haired? Perchance like me?"

"Nay, she is nothing like you." Duncan's answer came swift and, oddly, exactly as Linnet had feared. "Euphemia MacLeod is dark. A wee snippet of a lass with dark brown hair and eyes. She will make a meet bride."

"A meet bride," Linnet acknowledged, her heart sinking. *But not for our Robbie.*

That last she left unsaid.

Kintail.

Robbie MacKenzie reined in his sure-footed Highland garron on the crest of a windswept ridge and surveyed the wide heather wilderness spread out before him. He drew a deep breath, filling his eyes and half certain his heart would burst now that he'd finally crossed into his father's territory.

Wild, bright, and sunlit, the mountains, moors, and

glens of home stretched in all directions, rolling endlessly to a broad, cloud-churning horizon. Sweet, fair lands he'd ached to see every night of the ten long years he'd been away.

Necessary years, needed to earn his reputation and valor, but a trial all the same. And now he was a man of full age and abilities, well able if not entirely eager to step into his puissant father's footsteps.

And, too, to accept the daughter of a rival clan chieftain as his bride, thus assuring peace in this rugged and mountainous land.

"God's mercy," he breathed, staring out across Kintail at its springtime finest, taken unaware by the deep emotion coursing through him.

Saints, even the thought of Euphemia MacLeod, the lass he'd agreed to wed but had yet to meet, could not dampen his spirits. Indeed, with good fortune blessing him, the Lady Euphemia might prove none so ill a match. He might even surprise himself and find her to his liking: warm, voluptuous, large-bosomed, and . . . all woman.

And if not . . . then so be it.

He'd make do with his lot.

His honor demanded it of him.

But for this one blessed moment, the most perfect noontide he could have wished, naught would mar his pleasure or steal the sweetness of his homecoming. The heather ridge he'd chosen for his outlook bore clutches of silver birches and tall Caledonian pines, whilst the hills more distant wore deep blue shadows and sparkling white cornices of snow.

And, joy upon joy, beyond them waited Loch Duich and Eilean Creag Castle, as yet hidden from view, but there all the same.

Calling to him until he was nigh ready to fling himself from the saddle, drink in great, greedy gulps of the tangy gorse-and-juniper scented air. And, aye, even throw off his clothes, every last stitch, and roll full naked in the heather!

By the Rood, but it was good to be home.

Or so he thought until a short while later, when furious shouts, the near-crazed baaing of a sheep, and the sounds of wild, wet thrashing broke through the birch scrub and juniper tangle to his left, the panic in the shrill *female* cries shattering his jollity at once and dashing cold, stark dread onto the peace he'd let slide all over him.

A dread that clamped icy fingers around his heart when, as quickly as the fracas had arisen, the ear-splitting cries and loud splashings ceased.

From one lightning-quick blink of an eye to the next, naught marred the silence save the frantic baaing of the sheep, now joined by the equally distressed neighs of a horse, and the uncomfortable roaring in his ears of his own fast-thundering heart.

"Sweet holy Christ!" he yelled, spurring hard now as he sent his garron plunging through the prickly juniper bushes and gorse. *Saints have mercy,* he meant to cry when the beast burst free of the underbrush, but the words lodged in his throat, caught and held there by the horror of the scene before him.

Leaping out of the saddle, he looked about, but saw only the shaggy-maned garron whose neighing agitation had captured his ear. A sway-backed wretch of a beast, the aged creature watched his approach from near a jumble of boulders, wild-eyed, panting, and skittish-looking. A leather travel bag had been tossed aside, or mayhap slipped from its fastenings and now lay open atop a flattened clump of bell heather, a scatter of good Scots siller spilling from its depths to litter the peaty ground.

The baaing sheep, a drenching-wet ewe, stood beside a black-watered lochan, shaking water droplets from its oily fleece and looking more angry than frightened.

The lass, the one whose cries and thrashing had frozen Robbie's blood, stood in the lochan, submerged to her waist, the front of her gown ripped and gaping open to reveal a set of full, magnificent breasts, gleaming wet and with sparkling beads of water dripping from her tight-budded nipples.

But it was the crescent-shaped gash in her forehead that arrested Robbie's attention and had him tearing into the icy water, boots, plaid, sword, and all.

Bright red blood flowed copiously from the wound, discoloring to pinkish-red what surely had to be the fairest face he'd e'er laid eyes upon.

Swaying wildly in the peat-stained water, she stared at him from unseeing green eyes, her arms flailing, her mouth opened wide in a silent, ghastly scream.

"Hold, lass!" Robbie found his own voice as he plunged forward, the silty bottom of the lochan and his clothes sorely hampering him. "I will have you in a moment!"

But just as he closed the distance between them and reached for her, her oddly blank eyes rolled back into her head and she slipped beneath the surface, disappearing completely save the billowing skirts of her ruined gown, the top crown of her head, and two red-gold braids.

Nay, Robbie corrected himself as he gathered her in his arms and carried her, blessedly still breathing, out of the lochan.

Not mere red-gold, but a rare and shimmering flame-bright color.

Aye, that was it.

The lass had hair of flame.

And as he eased himself to his knees and gently lowered her to a grassy patch of delicate little flowers, yellow tormentil and buttercups, Robbie knew only one thing—he wanted her.

THE EDITOR'S DIARY

Dear Reader,

A dream is nothing more than your heart's fondest wish. But what happens when your heart gets everything it desires and it's not at all as you expected? Jump into our two Warner Forever titles this September and find out!

Romantic Times raves that **Sue-Ellen Welfonder**'s last book *Bride of the Beast* was a "powerful, emotional, highly romantic medieval that steals your heart and keeps you turning the pages." We promise all that and more from Sue-Ellen's newest title **WEDDING FOR A KNIGHT**. Lady Amicia MacLean has finally gotten what she's always wanted. She's married—even if it is by proxy—to Magnus MacKinnon, the roguish warrior who stole her heart when she was just a girl. But when Magnus returns from battle, his good looks marred by a grim scowl and his charm banished by cold aloofness, Amicia learns the truth: the union was made to fill the empty MacKinnon coffers with MacLean gold. Though he wants nothing to do with his comely new bride, Amicia refuses to give up. She wants more than a husband in name only. She wants his love and she won't rest until it's hers!

Journeying from the rolling hills of Scotland to the sultry heat of Florida, we present **Toni Blake**'s mainstream debut in **THE RED DIARY**. Lori Foster calls this "a sexy, compelling romance you'll want to savor. Heart-stopping sensuality!" and she couldn't be more right. So grab a cold drink—you're going to need it! Life hasn't turned out the way Nick Armstrong expected and he blames Henry Ash. Because of him, Nick's family has struggled for everything while Lauren, Henry's precious daughter, has the world at her feet. So when Nick is hired to paint Lauren's house, he can't help peeking into her life. But he never expected to peek into her innermost desires. After Nick finds her red diary, detailing her every delicious fantasy, he can't resist seducing her to break her heart. What begins as purely physical soon turns into something hotter than passion—love. But can Lauren ever forgive him for trespassing into her secret desires?

To find out more about Warner Forever, these September titles, and the author, visit us at www.warnerforever.com.

With warmest wishes,

Karen Kosztolnyik

Karen Kosztolnyik, Senior Editor

P.S. Halloween is right around the corner so grab some candy and relax with these two treats—no trick, I promise. **Karen Rose** pens a romantic suspense about a prosecutor and a homicide detective who find themselves trying to protect the criminals from a serial killer whose own brand of vigilante justice threatens them all in **I'M WATCHING YOU**; and **Kimberly Raye** delivers the funny, sexy story of a woman who must enlist the help of the man behind her worst sexual experience ever to test her latest invention: an aide that will guarantee mind-blowing pleasure in **SOMETIMES NAUGHTY, SOMETIMES NICE**.